THE
PIPER'S SONS

THE
PIPER'S SONS

BRUCE CHANDLER FERGUSSON

A DUTTON BOOK

DUTTON
Published by the Penguin Group
Penguin Putnam Inc., 375 Hudson Street, New York, New York 10014, U.S.A.
Penguin Books Ltd, 27 Wrights Lane, London W8 5TZ, England
Penguin Books Australia Ltd, Ringwood, Victoria, Australia
Penguin Books Canada Ltd, 10 Alcorn Avenue, Toronto, Ontario, Canada M4V 3B2
Penguin Books (N.Z.) Ltd, 182–190 Wairau Road, Auckland 10, New Zealand

Penguin Books Ltd, Registered Offices:
Harmondsworth, Middlesex, England

First published by Dutton, an imprint of Dutton NAL,
a member of Penguin Putman Inc.

First Printing, June, 1999
10   9   8   7   6   5   4   3   2   1

REGISTERED TRADEMARK—MARCA REGISTRADA

Library of Congress Cataloging-in-Publication Data

Fergusson, Bruce.
      The piper's sons / Bruce Chandler Fergusson.
         p.   cm.
      ISBN 0-525-94431-1
      I. Title.
   PS3556.E7215P56   1999
   813'.54—dc21   98-36192
                                             CIP

Printed in the United States of America
Set in Sabon
Designed by Leonard Telesca

PUBLISHER'S NOTE
This is a work of fiction. Names, characters, places, and incidents either are the products of the author's imagination or are used fictitiously, and any resemblance to actual persons, living or dead, events, or locales is entirely coincidental.

This book is printed on acid-free paper. (∞)

*To my mother, Doris C. Smith,
who let me write instead of mow the lawn that summer.*

ACKNOWLEDGMENTS

This book took wing during a tough time and without the support of family and friends the load might well have exceeded the lift. My deepest thanks to:

Jean C. Miller, Edward Smith, Jean Ferguson, Tony Mazzella, J.D. Ferguson, Scott Stolnack, Richard Clement, and the gang, past and present, at McCormick & Schmick's.

To Natasha Kern, agent, friend, navigator, whose perceptiveness, skill, and fortitude made it possible; and to Ed Stackler and Danielle Perez, editors who made it better.

And to my lefties, Brian and Patrick, who bring me home from third, and always will.

PART ONE

BEARS

Chapter 1

ABOVE SHILSHOLE

Would I have gone after the girl if my own daughter, Emma, were still alive?

I'd like to say yes, but the answer is probably no.

I had just delivered a bookcase in Ballard to some people named Langdalen, and was coiling rope by my pickup when I saw a stick arcing over the sidewalk. A young golden retriever scrambled after the stick, mouthed it, trotted back. Someone clapped.

"All riiiight, Zeke! Good dog!"

The stick flew again, landing this time near the end of the driveway. An oak tree blocked my view of the girl—it was a girl's voice. If I'd seen her, I would have stared, watching her play with the dog, and that might have made her uncomfortable. I catch myself doing that sometimes, when I drop my son, Michael, off at school: seeing Emma in a girl who is about the age my daughter would have been.

I listened to the high, playfully stern voice, the dog's barking, and folded the flannel sheet with which I'd covered the bookcase for the drive from my shop in Seattle's Fremont neighborhood. A beige Corolla passed slowly on the street, pacing Zeke as he returned another throw of the stick.

I got into the cab, started up the truck, turned on the radio, not wanting to hear the girl's voice anymore.

I didn't see the dog going after the stick, and the parent in me approved because it probably meant the girl had gone in for the evening. I glanced at my watch. Almost eight o'clock. Five minutes to get to the softball game under the lights at the Ballard playfield. My wife, Ellie, and I were half of the outfield for our co-rec team.

I pulled out to the street, ready to wave at the girl if she was still there. She wasn't on the sidewalk.

But the retriever was trotting down the middle of the street, away from me, the stick in his mouth. A block away, the beige Corolla was moving fast, too fast for this residential neighborhood.

The dog dropped the stick, confused, as if his play had been interrupted.

If the girl had gone inside, wouldn't she have taken the dog, too?

Who would have taken off like that? There was no reason for it, unless . . .

There should have been a scream, a shout. I would have heard that, even over the radio. . . .

Even over the roar of the falls and the river.

One minute she was there, and when I looked back, along the path, toward the falls, she was gone, my Emma, gone, forever.

It takes only seconds to get there. The seconds were ticking away.

The man in the Corolla had taken that girl.

I almost hit the dog, spinning out of the driveway, gunning the pickup down the street. I snapped off the radio.

The car took a left on Thirty-second Avenue. By the time I did the same, the Corolla was disppearing over a rise in the road. At the intersection of Eighty-fifth and Thirty-second, I lost the car. I looked down Eighty-fifth, easily a half-mile stretch, didn't see him. He had to have gone straight, taking the narrowing road that twisted around the Shilshole bluff. I pushed the needle to forty in a zone marked fifteen, careening around the curves.

I passed the entrance to the park. Trails in the thick woods sloped steeply down to the Burlington Northern railroad tracks and Golden Gardens beach. There, alone in the lot, next to the closed rest-room facilities, was the Corolla.

I braked—and was almost rear-ended by another car. There was no shoulder to use, to back up. I had to keep going and sped up, with getaway haste, only I had to get back—fast—before it was too late.

There was no reason why a father would take his little girl into the woods at this time of the day, leaving a game of fetch with the dog.

At the bottom of the hill, the road widened before switching back under the railroad tracks. Distantly a whistle sounded—Amtrak or a Burlington Northern freight bearing down from the north. I turned off so sharply I spun out, could feel the pickup want to keep going, to roll. I almost lost it then. The guy behind me shouted out, *"What the fuck're you doing?"* and flipped me off as he passed.

I crushed through the gears going back up the hill. The valves rattled in third. Down to second . . .

Too slow, Christ, too slow . . .

I swerved into the parking lot, right next to the Corolla, and grabbed the softball bat from the cab behind the seats.

If I was wrong about this . . .

The Corolla's license number was GGN-458.

I slammed the door loudly, so the man might hear, hear someone coming and stop what he was doing, or was about to do, but the train noise was getting louder, rushing through the woods.

To my left, concrete steps descended down the hill, flanked by troughs for the runoff. The main trail bordered a small meadow with braziers and picnic tables. Near the last one, the trail disappeared in the dense woods. At the edge of the meadow, a large stone sculpture seemed to be guarding that entrance. It was jarring to see my father's sculpture now, somehow made what I was doing inevitable, as if my own daughter had been taken.

I ran past it, hoping to find them a short way down the path, father and daughter walking hand in hand, looking for the something the girl needed for a craft project, a gift. Anything. Maybe there was a good reason why they'd left the dog behind, loose on the street, not taken him for a romp in the woods.

I felt the fear in my legs, gut, and hoped that I was wrong, that it was all a mistake. Would he snatch his daughter, shove her behind him, his eyes spilling fear at the sight of a six-foot-two, 190-pound guy barreling down the path with a thirty-two-inch aluminum bat in his hand? And here he was, all alone with this crazy, with nothing to protect his daughter but fists he'd never learned how to use. His anger would come as explosive relief, despite my apology. I'd want to tell him why I'd done this, but the man would just say, *Get the hell out of here . . . get the hell away . . .*

But I wasn't wrong.

Chapter 2

STEPS

He had the girl against a fallen log. He towered above her. He was taller than me but not so heavy. Short, well-trimmed, dark hair. Running shoes, blue polo shirt, khaki pants. I was running too hard to see more beyond the shock of his whiteness in the woods, his and the girl's.

His pants were down around his knees, underwear rolled to his thighs. He had his erection in his hand, the other hand full of the girl's brown hair, a fist by the back of her neck. The log was above the level of the path. He wasn't even going to have to kneel to rape her.

Twenty yards away. I closed on him, sprinting. But I was so consumed with getting to that guy, I didn't notice the roughness in the path. I tripped over a shelving rock and tumbled headfirst into the bushes to my left, slamming a shoulder into a tree. That stopped me from plunging headlong down the slope. I lost the bat, which slid down, poking out of the undergrowth, a silver snake far beyond my reach.

By the time I got to my feet, the guy had pulled his pants up and was fifteen yards up the winding path. Then gone.

I didn't chase; the girl was more important now. She was sitting up when I got to her. I kneeled beside her, still breathing hard from the run, the fall. She was shaking uncontrollably, so pale in the darkening woods. The guy had stuffed her panties in her mouth, wrapped tape around it, her head. Her jeans had been thrown hastily on a nearby yearling fir. She looked to be about nine or ten, younger than Emma would have been, but tall for her age.

I couldn't hear her crying with the train passing below, trembling the earth. She shook, and I was trembling, too. The whole world seemed to have come loose. Gently, I lifted her up and drew her close, to tell her it was okay, but she shrank away violently, and even though I wanted so much to hug her, and comfort her and stroke her hair and keep telling her she was safe, I couldn't She wasn't my daughter. I might have helped her, but I was a stranger, too.

"Hey," I said softly. "Hey, it's all right now, honey. You're safe now." I got her jeans from the tree, handed them to her. "I'll take you home now. Then we're going to call the police."

I didn't know how much she heard because she was still crying, not looking at me, and the tape was around her ears. She got the pants on, her shaking an awful thing.

"We have to get that tape off, okay?" I patted my head, then pointed at hers. If she didn't nod, at least she didn't back away, not much.

"It's going to hurt a little when I pull it off your hair." I began to unravel the tape around her head. Luckily it was only masking tape.

When finally this was done, she spit out her panties, and her crying was at last released. She didn't pick them up from the ground, and I didn't either. I thought of getting the bat, but it would have taken a lot of time to retrieve it from the steep hillside. The sooner I got the girl back home the better. The guy might be still in the woods, but he was unarmed; I hadn't seen a weapon on him.

We walked side by side along the path, heading back to the parking lot. She didn't look at me. Her left hand was over her mouth, as if she was going to vomit. Every now and then I looked behind me. I listened for the sound of the guy's car. I heard nothing except the scraping and screeching of the train below as it slowed down for the long approach to Seattle.

He wasn't far away. He was on one of the trails lacing the woods, hunkering somewhere, panting, an animal. I glanced at the trail below us. He was out there, perhaps near, watching us, seeing that I wasn't carrying the softball bat. I could sense his presence, feel his desperation, panic, hear the whisper: *He's seen me, he's got my license number. . . .*

We walked by the stone bear. *Rising Bear,* Dad called it.

Above the meadow, a few cars passed slowly down the grade. If they saw us, what would they see—a man coming out of the woods with a girl on a beautiful summer evening? Would they wonder why he didn't have his arm around her, her hand in his, as a father and daughter would?

The Corolla was still in the parking lot. I gave it a wide berth, for the girl's sake, so she could see he wasn't hiding behind the car.

He was still in the woods, had to be, waiting for us to leave. . . .

I opened the driver's side door of the truck and said gently to the girl, "Let's take you home now, honey. You'll be with your mom and dad and Zeke, too, real soon." For once I wished I had a cellular phone in my pickup, so I could make the call immediately. There wasn't a phone booth—or a house, for that matter—within a quarter mile.

She hung back, her lips trembling, obviously fearful to stay but also frightened to go in a truck as strange as the other car. Were they one and the same in her mind? And me? I'd helped her, maybe saved her life, but the other guy had probably come on as a nice man, too. He'd got her in there some way.

I had a very traumatized girl to get back home.

I kneeled down so we could talk eye to eye. "Would you tell me your name?"

She hesitated; she wouldn't—or couldn't—look at me. Her fingers trembled by her mouth. "It's Jess . . . Jessica."

"So which do you like better, Jess or Jessica?"

She shook her head.

"How about Jessica?"

"Uh-huh."

"Well, my name is Paul, and we're going to have to go in my truck, Jessica, to get you home to your mom and dad. Is—"

"My dad doesn't live with us anymore."

"Well, your mom then is going to be worried where you are. And to get back to her we've got to ride in the truck. Is that okay?"

She looked away, to the woods, but not back to me. She couldn't look at me. She stared at the logo on the door panel, the tartan weave of oak: SINCLAIR WOODWORKS.

"How about riding in the back, then? I'll drive slowly so you can even hop out anytime if you want. Just knock on the glass and I'll stop." I showed her, rapping on the cab window.

She wouldn't get in the truck. She began crying, shaking even more fiercely, upset because she wanted desperately to get back home and knew it would probably be okay with me, but she couldn't bring herself to do it.

I wanted so much to reach out, hug her tightly, be her father, but that might frighten her more. As I was thinking what to do, a loudspeaker echoed from far below, from the Golden Gardens beach house, a recorded message announcing the closure of the park, the nine o'clock curfew. It was reassuring and gave me an idea.

"Jessica, if you don't want to go in the truck, you don't have to. But we can't stay here, and it's a very long walk back up the hill and over to your house. So how about this? You and I walk down to the beach, where that big voice just came from. We'll find a telephone and call your mom and she can come and pick you up. Is that okay?"

Jessica nodded, wiped at her eyes.

"Good. It's a deal, then."

Jessica wanted to go first, even though she was apprehensive about the steepness of the steps. But it was clear she wanted me between her and the nightmare of the place we were leaving. She went slowly, using the handrail, and I kept two steps behind her.

Below, through the cut in the trees, I could see the road, and beyond, through the firs, the burnished water of the Sound, and some of the serrated Olympics far to the west. Sailboats angled home to the Shilshole marina. It had been the kind of August evening in Seattle that defied anyone to dream of other places.

The curfew announcement began again, and it seemed to help Jessica. People were down there. It would be safe down there. She began to walk more quickly down the steps, and I matched her pace. Her long, tangled hair bounced a little as she walked, and in this dim light, even with the bits of masking tape, I glimpsed Emma ahead of me.

The train had cleared the tracks below, but the song still came to me. I don't know why I thought of it, at this time, of all times, but it surfaced, the song from *Shining Time Station* that used to be one of Emma's favorite TV programs. It left me as quickly and strangely as it had come, replaced by such an anger and rage at what that man had done to this girl.

I stopped as she slowed to slip past the snag of a branch that partially blocked the steps. And it was then, as the curfew announcement began once more, that I had the feeling again.

For as long as I can remember, this habit has been with me: the feeling that someone is watching. Ellie used to call it my "condition" before Emma died, but we don't talk about it anymore.

There have been times when I was sure the unseen person was a friend, a powerful, benevolent presence. Other times I was equally sure it was someone dangerous, who meant me harm. It could happen anywhere: turnarounds on the street, in a park; glances, as uncontrollable as a facial tic, in the rearview mirror. The affliction has caused me insomnia; our family doctor, and one psychiatrist, have prescribed sleeping pills and tranquilizers, if not a name for the condition. It comes and goes but, like a psychological virus, never leaves. It's always with me, as Ellie's partial deafness is with her. It's something I'll always have, like the memory of my brother's disappearance so many years ago. It cost Ellie and me dearly, a life I would have exchanged for mine if I'd had the chance. But even that didn't end it. How can you stop a reflex? I've never seen anyone, but always, always I look back, wait at the window. Or turn around.

I did so now, a second before I heard him on the steps behind and above us.

Chapter 3

The Catch

He was three steps above me. He had the softball bat drawn back, and I thought, *He's going to use my own bat.*

Everything slowed down in that second before he swung. I saw him so clearly, so close now, a different person from the one on the path; the ripped shirt, the messed-up hair, the streak of dirt on his face, his lips thinned to a crack over the bloody scratch on his chin, the eyes wild and huge with whiteness.

He stepped lower, swung at my head, at a level, with a grunting shriek. I ducked. My feet went out from under me, my knee hit the edge of a step. The bat missed, but so closely I felt it scything the air above my head.

Behind me, the girl was hysterical, screaming. I forgot her name, shouted out the only one I could remember as I rolled away, into the deep culvert on the side of the steps. I felt my own piss or the trickling of the water in the culvert.

He loomed above, swung overhand. The bat smashed into the upturned edge of the culvert, the crack a rifle shot, spraying my face with bits of concrete, but I still caught most of the blow in my right upper arm. Through the needling, numbing pain I yelled for— Emma—Jessica to run.

She did, scrambling on all fours back up the steps, close enough for the guy to have grabbed her. He didn't. I was the one who could identify him. I was the one he had to kill.

I pushed away, skidded down the culvert, a log sliding down a chute. He kept swinging the bat, each time shouting something I couldn't understand, pacing me on the steps, a bear cuffing salmon in a river. I was stuck in the chute: he was on one side; the other rising from the culvert was too steep to climb.

My feet touched a horizontal iron grate that sucked water down into pipes below the tilting earth. He was still a step above me, swung the bat. I ducked to protect my head, turned, got it in the side. I tried to grab the bat. He slid it back. The gouges in the aluminum cut my right palm.

Run, get down the steps.

I thought of the girl and lunged at him instead, getting inside another striking arc, even though he retreated. The bat smashed into the backs of my thighs. My wet shoes slipped on a step, but I held on to a cuff of his pants and yanked as I fell hard to my belly.

His legs flew out from under him. He thudded to his back, dropping the bat, which clinked down the steps. I gripped both his ankles. He tried to kick out, free his legs. I kept pulling. He got up, but I kept going lower, pulling him. He shook one foot loose, smashed my shoulder so hard I lost his legs.

He got up but not far. I caught him with a short right hand, which snapped his head back to the concrete, stung my hand. I got up quickly, darted to a side. He twisted away. I grabbed his shirt, punched his kidney, not his head, or I might have broken my hand. I hit him again, harder.

He fooled me. Instead of trying to twist away and free of me, he spun a backhanded fist, a blind, desperate swing that caught me flush on the forehead as I leaned toward him. Stunned, I veered toward blackness. He grunted loudly; he must have hurt his hand, yet he kept on.

He was on me now. I was still dazed but managed to get a knee up. He went for my throat, but he didn't have the strength in his hands. I could smell his breath—*peppermint to rape a child?*—the stink of cheap cologne. He tried to pound my head on the steps, but couldn't get through my arms and slipped to my right. I kicked out, hard as I could, caught him just above the groin. He fell back, off balance, into the culvert.

I was sucking for air, couldn't get enough. Couldn't go on for much longer. I scrambled to my feet even as he recovered, came at me again. I stopped his lunge with a punch square in the face, bloody-ing his nose.

Then he was gone, arms windmilling behind him. He landed on his backside, flipped over, skidded. His head hit concrete steps, bouncing twice before he veered into the culvert and bunched up on his side.

I collapsed to the steps, panting. My arms and legs were shaking weights of lead. My right hand throbbed.

The trickle of culvert water was dammed behind his body. He still wasn't moving when finally I got up and retrieved the bat, to check him out.

He was still unconscious. Blood bubbled from his nose, dripping off his face. To make sure he wasn't going to be walking anywhere, I swung the bat hard into his knee. Cartilage popped. I flung the ru-ined bat into the woods and left him there. I took it slowly back up the steps, hurting every which way.

I didn't expect her to be at the truck and she wasn't. She was still out there with the last of the evening light, trying to find her way home, a long way for a kid scared out of her wits.

I had to find her quick, but I took half a minute to pop the Corolla's hood and do some damage.

There was something wrong with the license plates. There were two sets of plates, one screwed over the other. Both had current renewal-date stickers. So he'd sheared the extra set off another car.

I bent up the fake front plate and hurried back to the pickup, wincing with pain from my shoulder, my side, when I tried to close the door. I got it the second time. My hands were bruised and scraped from the fight, the abrasions of the concrete steps, and it took a while to get my keys from my pocket and longer still to get the right one in the ignition.

As I pulled out of the parking lot, I glanced in my rearview mir-ror, but there was no sign of the guy staggering up the steps. But there was a blue VW van I hadn't noticed before, in the far corner of the lot. Kids? Necking, drinking, defying the curfew, feeling safe behind the curtained windows? I didn't ask them if they'd seen the girl. If she was too frightened to have gone with me before, she wouldn't have gone to more strangers. The van startled me. Except for the color, the van looked just like the one Ellie and I had driven for five years before selling it. Same big dent in the side and lop-sided fender. But I was in too much of a rush to give the coincidence more thought.

I pulled out onto the road, Golden Gardens Way, and switched on my lights in the dusk. I took the bends of the road fast as I dared. Two cars passed and one honked when I didn't flick off the brights. By the time I reached the intersection of Golden Gardens Way, Eighty-fifth and Thirty-second, I still hadn't seen her. She could have gotten this far but not much more.

Where was she?

I kept going south along Thirty-second, in the direction of her home. I thought I saw her in front of a large pastel green bungalow. But it was another girl, calling for her cat or dog, while her father stood on the porch, backlit by the light from the doorway behind him.

I drove slowly. The man in the door kept looking warily at me as he called for his daughter to come in. I speeded up, away from the image of the rapist trolling for a victim.

By the time I reached Sixty-eighth, I knew Jessica must have been helped by someone or picked up by her frantic mother, searching the neighborhood. Had to have been. She couldn't have gotten this far by now without my seeing her. I decided to drive by her house, or at least the one I thought was hers, one or two away from the Langdalens', where I'd delivered the bookcase, ages ago it seemed. My lights shone on the stick the dog had dropped in the middle of the street.

A Seattle police cruiser was parked in the driveway, behind a late-model Pontiac. Another blue-and-white was in the street, and that's the one from which Jessica emerged. By the time I was abreast of the cruiser, the cop had walked around his car and Jessica was already in her mother's arms. Through my open window I could hear them crying as they stood on the porch, illuminated by the overhead light

I drove past, speeding up. My hands were sweaty on the wheel. I knew where the fear was coming from, and that fear was, at this moment, greater than that of failing to immediately report a crime. I just couldn't do it, go back and tell them what had happened. All I could manage was the promise to call the police first thing in the morning.

I told myself this time was different and it was. This time she came back home.

The softball fields were only a mile from where the girl had been abducted. Even if the glow of the lighted fields hadn't been directly on the way home, I would have gone to them. I would have driven an hour to get there. I had to see my wife and son.

Everything was as it should be for a few minutes after I arrived on the street that bordered the east end of the fields. I kept the truck idling. Michael was at the end of the dugout, the self-appointed batboy, leaning the bats against the chain-link fence. He left the dugout for a drink at the water fountain, turned his Mariners' compass rose cap around. Before bending down, he looked around, a deer at the lake.

Ellie was in left, where I would have been, wondering, no doubt, where the hell I was. The team was going with three outfielders.

She looked so fine out there.

Time and time again guys on the other teams made the mistake of underestimating her—as if only unattractive women could play—and deliberately hit to her or tried to get an extra base when she was fielding the ball. They rarely made those mistakes again.

I called her my Copper Bullet because even though she was only five-five, she was all legs and loved to run, loved to slide, and seeing her now, dusting off her jeans, was worth more to me than a half-million-dollar view anywhere in the city, because I'd been in the operating room when they'd lifted my son from the bloody slash in her belly.

She was only forty yards away and backed up even more when a burly guy stepped up to bat, to the exhortations and claps of his teammates. Runners on second and third. Ellie and others in the field shouted encouragement for the pitcher. Ellie must have known the batter's tendencies because she took a few steps to her right. The foul line was bordered by a sidewalk separating the field from a chain-link fence and the parking lot for the community center building.

That's when I saw the VW van. If it wasn't the same one I'd noticed before, it was exactly like it. The van had just pulled up, ten feet from the fence. The headlights blinked out. The glare of the playing lights made it impossible for me to see inside. I stared, waiting for someone to get out. My gut tightened. The van had been *there*. What was it doing *here*? Painted brown, it would have been our old beater.

Then Ellie bolted, and within a second her cap tipped off, her copper-colored hair flew out behind her. The ball was arcing into the lights, dying over the third baseman but not quickly enough for him to get it. He gave up on it. Ellie didn't. The batter rounded first.

She dove, almost horizontal, landed on her side, spun over. I couldn't see if she had caught it. Then she kneeled, raised her glove—with the ball in it—and our entire team began whooping and shouting.

"Way to go, honey," I whispered.

It was the third out. One runner kicked the dust in front of second; the others walked slowly off, still in disbelief that Ellie had gotten to that ball. The fielders trotted in, converging on Ellie, congratulating her. The center fielder plopped her cap back on her head, clapped her on the back. No rumps in co-rec. Michael was running, in the skipping way he does when he's excited, to greet her.

I glanced over to the parking lot.

The van was gone. One minute there, one minute gone. I immediately turned on the street and drove to the entrance of the parking lot. I didn't see the van, and maybe it was just as well, because there was nothing to gain from that. Follow the van and then what? Ask the driver what he was doing watching a softball game? Ask him if the van had had those dents in it when he bought it? If he had repainted it?

What's your problem? There a law against watching a fucking softball game?

I drove on to Sixty-fifth, and up to Greenwood, then home, unable to get the coincidence out of my mind.

Chapter 4

ELLIE

Darkness had fallen when I got back. Our house on North Forty-eighth Street was two blocks south of Woodland Park Zoo. The neighborhood was a kind of intertidal zone, between post-sixties Fremont—Freakmont as it was sometimes called—and upscale Phinney Ridge. The scruffiness of Aurora Avenue was far enough to the east to sometimes forget the corners where johns picked up hookers day and night, where the Green River killer—dormant, dead, or in prison—might have stopped.

The house was a rental, in need of paint and serious landscaping, but it had the character of homes built in the twenties, with nooks and hardwood floors inside. The high ceilings made it a good Christmas house, so we always went out into the country to cut the biggest tree we could find.

Normally at this hour Ellie would be up in her study, writing, in the upstairs room that faced the street, working on her novel till midnight and often beyond. I suggested once she take our bedroom, at the back of the house, as her writing room, but she liked the southern exposure, where she got the best of Seattle's reluctant sun and the view of the skyline and the Space Needle. We could see the Fourth of July Lake Union fireworks from her study. From the street, late at night, anyone could see her working

I felt protective, I suppose, because of her hearing loss in her left ear, the result of an infection she got from swimming in Lake Washington when she was very young, before Metro cleaned up the water.

If she'd been up there now, with Michael sleeping in his back room on the first floor, she wouldn't have heard me come in.

Not even if the door had been locked.

She was usually good about that. This time she'd forgotten. You can forget a lot of things, trying to get a six-year-old anywhere, on time. Locking the door can't be one of them.

I walked in, locked the door, feeling like an intruder in my own home.

I went straight for the downstairs bathroom, which had the shower. The Batman nightlight was on for some reason. I flicked it off, turned on the other, kept the door open and undressed, leaving my clothes in a pile, and looked at the damage.

It hurt to breathe deeply. I figured I might have bruised some ribs. The contusions on my stomach made the old scar even whiter in contrast. When Michael was three, the scar had frightened him because he thought I'd swallowed worms that were coming out of my belly. When we were at the Queen Anne pool for lessons or at the beach, he would stare at the scar for a moment before looking away. Someday I'd have to tell him how I got it. He'd know then, finally, that he had once had a sister.

My neck was stiffening. The bruise on my shoulder was raised and purpling. I rotated the shoulder. It'd be okay, but tomorrow it would hurt like hell. The trembling in my hands had almost subsided. They were toughened by my work, but even so, I was lucky I hadn't broken anything. Forget the head, Steven had once told me.

Here's the deal, Paul, this is what you do, some guy comes at you and won't go away: You make sure you hit him harder than he hits you, but not in the head. Even if you don't miss, you may hurt your hand. Deal? Promise me?

He had shown me a few lessons, in the caboose at Dad's house, the day after a fight with a playground bully.

I was ten minutes into the shower when they came in. Michael burst into the steamy bathroom so excitedly the door banged on the end of the tub.

"Daddy, you should have seen it! Mommy made a great catch, it was great and they won, too!"

"That's terrific, Michael."

"You should have seen it, I'm telling you!"

Ellie came in, patted the shower curtain. "Hey, we missed you tonight."

"Even the Yankees won without Babe Ruth every now and then," I said into the stream of warm, needling water.

Ellie smacked the shower curtain harder. "He usually showed up."

"Who's Babe Ruth?" Michael said.

"They named a candy bar after him," Ellie said, and shooed him out of the bathroom.

"It was a sweet catch, Ell."

"I got lucky."

"No, you got speed."

"Wait a minute. You were there?"

"For a little while. I just wasn't in any condition to play."

"Something happen at the shop?"

"No, nothing like that."

She peeked around the shower curtain. *"Oh, my Lord . . . Paul, what happened to you?"*

I turned and squeezed her hand. She still had a sweatband on her wrist. "The hell with the stupid game. You all right?"

"Better than the other guy."

"A fight?"

"Tell you later. The hot water's going and I want every bit of it."

"What else can I do after I put Michael to bed?"

"A shot of Macallan would be great. And, honey?"

"I'm here."

"Tell him who Babe Ruth was, will you?"

Ellie was upstairs in our room, on the bed, waiting. Even though she had a fan going and the largest window in the room open, it was sweltering. The tumbler of Macallan was on my side of the bed board, next to a windup toy, a sailor that did handsprings. The first week we were dating I bought it for her, at Archie McPhee's, a novelty store that was one of Emma's and now Michael's favorite places. Somehow the plastic sailor had survived the years since we'd met the summer my father began the sculptures for Seattle's Art-in-the-Parks program. I was twenty years old, home from college. Emma was six years away.

Ellie was wearing only a T-shirt and panties. She'd used the upstairs bathroom by her study to wash up. That one was hers; she had all her things there.

I took a sip of the whisky and sat down next to her on the bed I'd made for the home birth we had wanted to have for Michael. I finished it two months before the due date. She was having trouble getting to sleep in her last trimester. The only thing that helped was my reading to her. We got all the way through *Lonesome Dove* in that new bed. Michael was an early talker, and Ellie was convinced that was because he had been listening, too. The birth didn't turn out the way we had wanted. The midwives' optimism turned to worry and finally the decision to get Ellie to Interlake Hospital. We almost waited too long, but Ellie had desperately wanted to have Michael at home, maybe as a culmination of our healing. Her determination had almost killed her. She was in labor almost thirty hours before the cesarean.

"I was worried," she said. "I called the shop right before we started."

Her knees were roughened and red from the game, and I gently stroked them. "You love to slide, don't you?"

"Was it a fight?"

I nodded. And told her.

I finished off the whisky. The oscillating fan clicked off two passes before Ellie said anything after I had finished. "She's a lucky girl," Ellie whispered.

"It could have been a lot worse—for both of us. Steven and I used to get in a few Saturday night scrapes when we'd take the ferry into the city. But nothing like that, Ell."

"What did the cops say at—what was the girl's name?"

"Jessica."

"What did they say?"

"I didn't talk to them. The last thing the girl needed was a stranger butting in."

"You didn't butt in. You saved her life."

"And that's all that matters. I made sure that son of a bitch wasn't going anywhere—his car, too. Tomorrow I'll go to the police."

"They'll wonder why you didn't report it right away."

"Yes, they will."

"Why . . ."

"Why didn't I?"

"That's what I was going to ask."

"Ellie, I froze when I saw them. I got scared . . . for a moment."

"That she wouldn't get it . . . right?"

I nodded.

"But . . . don't you think that's all the more reason to have stopped?"

"Ellie, the bottom line is that girl is safe and they have the guy. He wasn't going anywhere fast."

She puffed her cheeks, blew out a breath. "The kids in that van may have seen you."

"I don't think so. It looked just like our old one."

"Honey, by this time, most old VW's look alike. So will we in forty years."

Neither her grin nor mine were quite enough of what we wanted then. I could tell she was still thinking, *Why the hell didn't he stop?*

She was quiet for a while. The fan ticked back and forth. "It's going to be rough for her for a long while," she said.

"Her mother, too."

"Father?"

"Not around."

We lay there on the bed as the fan bathed us in warm air.

"Think I'll check on Michael," she said.

"I'll go down."

"Sure?"

"The whisky was just what the doctor ordered."

She caught my hand and kneeled up on the bed and we held each other. I stroked her hair, which glinted copper from the stab of a neighbor's backyard light over the bed. Her breath was moist and cooler than the air on my belly scar where the robe had parted.

"How about the cabin this weekend?" she asked. "Michael was asking me today when we're going next."

"He can't get enough of the wreck, can he?"

"No, and for one weekend I can pretend to work on the book."

"We're there, then."

The routine was always the same when Ellie or I went downstairs to check on Michael, and the routine this night was something I had to have. She knew that, banged up as I was. I made sure the front and back doors were locked and all the lights turned off except for one in the living room.

Emma had slept like a log, but our son was a restless sleeper, hated covers, constriction of any kind. We'd given away so many turtleneck shirts and sweaters, gifts from friends and relatives, because he wouldn't wear them. I figured it went back to his birth, the emergency cesarean for Ellie. He wouldn't come down. The umbilical cord was wrapped around his neck. In the operating room I'd watched the doctor quickly unwind the cord as if it were a lariat. It had been close. A hundred years ago I'd have lost both my son and wife, the doctor said.

In two weeks he'd be seven years old.

I turned off the Mickey Mouse night light by Michael's bed but left the closet light on.

He was on his back, one arm up against the wall, almost touching the Ken Griffey Jr. poster, legs angling out to the other side, underneath a smaller poster of a space shuttle on the launching pad at night, brilliantly lit up. Half a dozen books were scattered around him including *Peter Pan*, but closest were X-Men comic books. Ellie and I didn't care what he read at this point, so long as he enjoyed it.

It was cool in the room, the coolest in the house because of the air conditioner. It hummed in the window. I didn't turn it off this time. I wondered if the hum of that white noise, like Ellie's partial deafness, helped him fall asleep more easily.

I kissed him on his forehead. He was a wonderfully spirited and bright kid, with an industrial-strength imagination, and we hadn't told him he had once had a sister and how she died on her sixth birthday. We didn't want him to think he was any sort of replacement. Maybe later he'd think that, when he knew, but not now. And I didn't want him to have any kind of fear when he was out somewhere alone, with his father.

I was grateful his sleep seemed to be peaceful, free of nightmares. I wondered if the girl was even asleep now, whether her mother was still holding her, warm from a shower much longer than mine had been, rocking her, the mother wondering when this day would finally be over and they could begin a new one tomorrow, wondering how bad the nightmares would be.

I went into the bathroom to turn on the night light and toss the pile of my dirty and torn clothing down the laundry chute. I got my keys and change from the pockets.

My wallet was missing.

I'd had it with me at the shop that afternoon because I remembered checking, before I left to drop off the bookcase, to see if I had enough money to buy a round of beers at the Sloop Tavern after the game.

If I'd had the wallet when I got in the truck at Shilshole, it wouldn't have fallen out of my pocket. But I went outside and checked the pickup anyway. It wasn't there. Bill Erickson's white poodle barked at me from across the street. Maybe the bathrobe fooled the dog.

Shilshole. The wallet was back at Shilshole, somewhere by the steps.

I wandered into the living room, toward the door, with half a mind to go back, in my bathrobe, and search for the wallet. I sat down on the couch in front of the window that faced the street, telling myself this didn't matter either. I watched Erickson fiddling with a lawn sprinkler.

The wallet would be there in the morning. The chances were remote that the guy would have seen it, been in any condition to spot it, get my address from the license and retaliate in some way, tonight, if he'd cleared out before the girl brought the cops back to Shilshole.

There was a chance, too, that the police might miss it in the dark. They probably had; otherwise they would already have been here.

So the wallet would be there in the morning.

So go find it in the morning, on the way to the police, on the way to tell them why you didn't immediately report the crime, though it wouldn't be a good idea to try to explain your fear that you weren't sure if the girl would get things straight. In her shock, maybe she would get things confused, merge the truck—which she wouldn't get into—with the other guy's car, then switch them. She would remember two men in the woods, then two men fighting, joined, a single writhing creature. "Jessica," they would have asked, "you said he had a baseball bat. Which one, which one had the bat?"

"They both did."

How could I explain why I went after her? They'd want to know that. If I actually saw her abducted, why didn't I stop it then? And if I didn't see the abduction, what made me think that had occurred?

How to explain the sense of danger, the adrenaline surge, the certainty that I had only seconds to act before it was too late. The instinct to go after her had flared, like a seizure of guilt, though not with the immediate understanding that here was a second chance—to be close enough this time, to be where I should have been nine years ago, when I was looking behind me, and not ahead, when I wasn't where I should have been and so my daughter died.

That day nine years ago was Emma's sixth birthday. I'd taken the day off work. She and I were going to bake her birthday cake together. But first she wanted to see where the Indians used to be.

The night before I was brushing Emma's long black hair. I don't remember how Sunday evenings came to be Dad's night for that, before reading bedtime books. Ellie came into the room, her arms loaded with folded laundry. Her smile was mostly for me: *not bad for an old-boy rugby player. . . .*

She said something about Emma's hair being long as an Indian maiden's from a story. As she put away Emma's clothes, we all talked about how Seattle was named after a Suquamish chief, Sealth, about the others who had their own name for the Puget Sound area, before their world was taken from them. Later as I kissed Emma good night, she asked me to take her where the Indians used to be.

There were times, after, when I wanted to say to Ellie, *If you hadn't come in, if you hadn't said that about her hair, we never would have talked about the special place in the mountains, and I never would have taken Emma and I never would have looked back on the trail for someone I thought was there and Emma would never have died.*

Ellie and I said many things to each other, after, as we staggered through our grief to the precipice of divorce, but those words I somehow withheld.

Erickson and the yapping poodle went inside. A streetlight caught the glistening arc of the water sprinkler. I had the urge to go over and turn off the water. We hadn't had rain in a week and none was predicted soon. What a waste of water, just so you could have the greenest lawn on the block.

There hadn't been a drought back then, that day at Snoqualmie Falls. It had been raining solid for a week before the skies cleared, an invitation to go, it seemed. That rain had made the falls glorious, thundering. The mist was thick, thick as a cloud descended to earth, mysterious and shifting, and you could easily imagine the hunters moving on the trail in the thick woods on the other side of the surging river.

Daddy, I want to see where the Indians were.

The trail winding past the turbines of the Puget Power station wasn't in good condition after the heavy rains. And Emma, my bold Emma, who was frightened of little, not even the freighter wreck on the beach below the cabin; Emma, who always hated to have her hand held when she sensed excitement, who was eager to get as close as she could to the roaring falls—let go of my hand.

She wouldn't have done that if we'd kept going. She let go because I stopped, then turned around, utterly convinced someone was behind us on the path. No one was there, of course. But that didn't satisfy me. The path veered so all I could see was ten yards back. That wasn't enough. So I walked back. Here in this misty, thundering place where a sacred past still seemed alive despite the turbines and fences and power lines, it seemed possible that my brother had appeared on the trail. We had been here before, twice. The last anyone had seen of him was at a trailhead only a few miles away.

For a few moments it seemed possible, until I looked back up the trail to see my daughter slipping underneath the fence where there had been a slide in the trail, where the earth had given way.

It happened in silence, because of the noise of the falls, her sudden and silent descent to the river torrent. I didn't hear her scream, but I heard my own as I ran back and went after her through the same rip in the earth.

The fence raked a ten-inch gash on my stomach, but the pain then, and later, was absolutely nothing compared to the rabid emptiness of the days and months that followed, the recurring nightmares that always ended with Emma's hand above the white, frothing water—the last I saw of her before I plunged into the shocking cold water where nothing was possible for a girl of six except death.

It was a green King County police car that I saw in front of my house. A report had to be taken before the autopsy. The police officers—I can still remember their names, Madsden and Cole—didn't think it had been anything but an accident. I'd almost drowned and had broken my leg when the river smashed me into rocks, not far from where Emma's body had been recovered.

Or did they? The very presence of the police car seemed to insinuate something else. But that was me. I told them that Emma had run ahead of me; not that I'd turned back and why. Not even Ellie knew that.

Yes, it was an accident, but it was more than that. No one—the police, my father, Ellie's parents—ever said what I felt, not even Ellie, not even when our marriage was heading over the falls; no one ever said, *You killed her.*

That was the reason why I didn't pull in behind the Seattle police cars and tell them what had happened. There was the fear that finally someone was going to say those words.

There is such a thing as so much noise it is silence: the roaring of the falls and the river, or a train below dense woods where the only person ever to be *there*, when I turned around, had wanted to kill me.

I suppose I was waiting, but no one called that night or knocked at the door. The last thing I remembered before falling asleep on the couch was the sound of the morning newspaper thumping on the front porch, the sound so much like that of a man's head hitting concrete steps.

THE CAGE: 1

The overhead light flicks out, plunging the room into a closet of darkness. I can hear him sliding back the two dead bolts. When the door is closed, that snick-snick *is the only sound I can hear, evidence of his thoroughness in soundproofing the room, and the futility of screaming.*

The time between his opening and closing of the door is only a few seconds. But it's like a drug to me, better than anything I have had before. There is a current of fresher air, and sometimes the sound of music from downstairs—usually classical stuff, not the country music I like. Still, music is music. The only light comes from the downstairs, but it's enough for me to have once seen part of the stairwell and to know I'm on the second floor. The light is not enough for me to see his face. I've never seen his face, not even in the parking lot outside the restaurant at Fisherman's Terminal. All I saw then was the stocking mask with cutouts for the eyes and the baseball cap.

That's where it happened, just before midnight. I was tired and pissed off because my boss was on the rag about the dinner counts. His bonus, more than mine as an assistant manager, depended on them. He'd been complaining about the memorial service earlier in the evening outside on the dock, by the bronze statue, bitching about the seventy people who had come to pay respects to four halibut fishermen whose boat had capsized two days out of Ketchikan.

"You'd think that would've meant some business, for crying out loud," my boss said as I left an hour after closing.

A two-minute walk to my car in the employees' area where the light isn't so good and it happened. I was looking at the damage to my Blazer. He'd rammed it earlier, stove in the driver's-side door panel, to set me up. Teed off on my head with a kid's baseball bat wrapped in half an inch of high density foam and duct tape. He showed it to me once. Said he used chloroform to make sure I stayed out like a light. I never smelled it.

I could be anywhere—three miles away or three hundred.

It's mealtime now. Dinner, lunch, breakfast. The meal always varies. I can never tell what time of day it is by the food. That used to bother me, but no more, just his changing the times he brings the stuff. It's another game of his, a precaution, to catch me trying to claw my way out of this room like a rat, which I've tried to do, until my fingers are bloodied.

He slides the cardboard meal tray along the low tunnel inside the cage surrounding the door. Calls it his shark cage, as if I'm the shark, as if I'm the one who's dangerous. Shoves the tray just far enough for me to reach it from my side. I can't get at him through the four-by-fours of the cage, which go all the way up and are bolted to the ceiling. I've tried, but the studs are so close together. I can only get my hand through. Even if I could force my arm through, the cage is too big for me to reach him in his safety zone by the door.

He's somewhere in the cage. Kneeling or sitting or standing, left or right, somewhere near the humming Sears air purifier. I can't tell exactly. Even if there were something in this room that I could use as a weapon, I wouldn't know where to strike. He had to have spent a lot of time working this all out. He's not a short-term guy. He stinks of patience, so he's probably not a businessman. But that's useless speculation. Everything now is useless. He's like a disease that takes its time killing you.

"You're eating the apples," he says. He talks slowly. As if English isn't his native tongue. But I've never been able to detect an accent. If he once had a speech problem that's made him talk slow, he doesn't now. I get the impression he's older than me. Maybe it's the big words he uses sometimes.

"Did you hear what I said?" he says.

I stare up into the darkness.

"You haven't done that up to now. That's good."

"Why is that good? Are you putting something in them?"

He laughs. "Like Snow White's bad witch? Now, why would I do that?"

"You did it before so you could come in here and shave off my beard."

"The tranquilizer wasn't in the apples, though. You're due for another shave, too, by the way. You don't look right in a beard. Anyway I'm glad you're eating the apples. We live in apple country. Apples are good for you. An apple a day keeps the doctor away. Didn't Mom ever tell you that?"

He answers for me. "No? Mine neither. Even when you were throwing them at the cage, they were good for you, to get some of that anger out."

"Go to hell."

"Now, now, watch your manners. Attitude is everything, like they say. Our only true choice in life."

Every day he brings an apple and I used to count the days with them, but I've given up doing that, just as I did throwing them in the dark. They got rotten and shriveled, shrunken heads around the room. The room still smells like apples, that and my shit and piss in the plastic painter's tray that I slide out for removal every day.

"Would you like to hear the news?" he says. "It's been a while. I took the trouble to go back to your restaurant."

I want to hear but I won't tell him that.

"No? Well, I'll give you some anyway. There's a new assistant manager, of course. She doesn't seem to be as much of a bean counter as you were, so the employees seem happier, not that I asked many questions. No one's wearing any black armbands."

"Fuck you."

"Oh, now, Robert. I thought we'd progressed beyond the locker room. You've had time to get used to your new life here."

"Leave me alone."

"It's mealtime. It's customary to talk at mealtime. So we'll talk. You're also not in the newspapers anymore, not that you were ever front-page news. You know what they say: Solve it quick or forget it. While I was in the area, I also swung by your house again. It's up for sale. It'll go. Your old neighborhood certainly sustains body

and soul, no question there. I once counted, on a whim, two taverns, a pizza place, and four churches within a three-block radius; five, actually, if you want to include the Rosicrucian Lodge on Twenty-second, which you really can't because it looks like a bunker without the apex of a steeple. Your brother will sell the house, I'm sure. You mentioned you had one, that he wouldn't forget you, even if he is in Minnesota. I imagine he'll keep your golf clubs, but not the Blazer. I kissed it a little too hard, but I had to distract you, understand. He'll probably keep your porno videos, too."

"I don't have any of those."

"Oh, Robert, really. When I was tracking you, getting your habits and routes and times down, I used to follow you to Blue Video on Aurora. You went there almost every Saturday night, the end of your week. You always were in a hurry to get there before the place closed at midnight. During the two months after I first saw you and began tracking you, you missed exactly two Saturday videos."

"I had dates."

"Liar. You lived alone, had no steady girlfriend, no one who might keep after the matter of your disappearance. You're a lonely guy."

"You're not? You call putting up this, doing all . . . this . . . a social life?"

"I've crafted my life. You took the path of least resistance. You've probably been at one restaurant or another for your entire working life, slowly burying yourself, because you know you couldn't make it anywhere else. You trapped yourself. You counted the beans, bullied your employees, kept a decent enough bottom line for your bosses as you rose to the highest level of your incompetence, to keep your—what?—thirty grand a year intact?"

"It's called making a living. At least I'm not some . . ."

"Some what? Some faggot? Some queer? Is that what you think this is?"

"Why don't you just leave me alone until you do whatever it is you're going to do."

"Maybe I'm lonely." He laughs. "I think you'd feel a lot worse if I did just leave you alone. At least someone now is paying attention to you, making a fuss over you, literally caring for you."

"Think again."

"You think I'm kicking a dead horse? Well, you're actually more like a bait horse. You know what that is?"

"No, and I don't care."

"Of course you don't care. You only bought the Blazer for a little personality, not to actually take to back-country trailheads." He pauses. *"It's a trapper's term. I do know something about that."*

"So you're going to kill me. Tell me something new."

"Oh, my! Tough, aren't we?"

"You're going to kill me, so why won't you tell me who you are?"

"Can't do that, my friend."

"What does it matter?"

"I will soon. It's almost time now. I've waited so long and we're almost there. Ground zero. Michael is almost seven and almost ready for his new life as an orphan. No sooner, no later. I had to wait because first it was going to be his sister who was going to be Little Orphan Emma—but she died. Stupidly, incredibly. You can't be orphaned if you're dead, can you? So I had to wait. I'm not complaining, mind. Expectation is always the greater part of happiness."

"Not if it's death, asshole."

"That's what we're talking about, Robert."

"I was talking about me.*"*

"You're included, my friend."

"I don't know what the fuck you're talking about."

"I'm talking about the old seesaw: You always hurt the ones you love. Michael and his dear parents are just like family, what I should have had, instead of having it taken from me. I've teased and played with them as family, after my fashion, watched them go through their trials and passages, as my own parents would have— should have done. We'll play until it's time to go. Which is very soon."

"Who are you?"

"Not yet."

"No, you tell me now."

"Let's not badger, please. We've talked before about how I don't like that. I'm not one of your waiters or busboys."

"You're doing it to me."

"I'm your priest, Robert. I'm slowly mummifying you alive. I'm

*giving the rest of your life meaning and purpose. You had none be-
fore. Oh, excuse me, you had a cat. I saw you carrying out a bag of
kitty litter from a Safeway once, where all the food-stamp junkies
and midnight zombies go. Your life was so pitiful it infuriated me,
even as I was tracking you. That's why I sent you that anonymous
postcard, a month before the parking lot. You probably thought
one of your employees did that, didn't you?"*

I don't answer. Yes, I thought it had been Kerrie Caldwell who
sent the Felix the Cat postcard, who had typed on the back: GET
A LIFE.

I scramble to my feet, rush the cage, scream at him. "Tell me,
you son of a bitch!"

His voice doesn't retreat, he's so sure of the cage, his damn cre-
ation. "Not yet, Robert, not yet."

I slink back in the darkness, saying no more. Neither does he.
But it has been different this time. He's gone on and on. Something's accelerated. I listen to the hum of the air purifier that sits,
out of my reach, within the shark cage.

He flicks on the flashlight. He does that every time, to check on
things. He shines it in my face, causing me to avert my eyes, then
around the room. "You're due for a shave, all right." He clicks it
off. "I'd like the books picked up, please. They've been there too
long."

"So have I."

"Oh, by the way. I'm leaving something else for you on the
tray."

"What?"

"Paper and crayons. You're obviously bored, so I thought you
could help me out with a little art project. I know you haven't used
crayons since you were a child, but do your best. It's for a good
cause."

"Crayons?"

"Of course. You might find some other use for a pen or pencil."

"And this 'good cause'?"

"Just draw some nice apples for Michael and I'll take care of the
rest. Do a good still life for me and there'll be a reward for you. See
you next time, Robert." He leaves. A few seconds later the outside
dead bolts slide home. Snick-snick. The light goes on. A minute
passes before my eyes adjust to the light again.

The walls of the room are covered with floor-to-ceiling book-cases. I've long since checked behind to discover the padding, nailed into the wall. The single window is sealed with plywood and padding, probably two sheets of plywood, knowing him. The books are everywhere, piles of them that I swept from the shelves in a rage. I can't move without stepping on one. I flung so many of them at the ceiling, until I was exhausted.

Fuck him. Let him pick them up himself, after he's killed me. I pick one up and hurl it against the cage, then another. Then it occurs to me that the books might reveal something to me about him, something I could use, something to pass the time, besides staring at the scarred ceiling, before he comes in again. Besides, it is a mess. I don't like messes, either. I like things neat and in order. If that makes me a bean counter, so be it. I'll bet his house is immaculate, too. Careful men are not slobs.

He has enough books in here to be a college professor. They know a lot, and what they don't know, they get from books. Maybe I can, too. Stuff about him, his preferences and thus his weaknesses. Stuff about trapping? Bait horses? Whatever that was all about.

Weaknesses? He has one, all right. I'm not so stupid as he thinks I am. And he's not so smart. If he was so smart, he wouldn't have shown how much my life bothered him. If that isn't a weakness, I don't know what is.

I leave the meal where it is. I don't care whether it gets cold or not. I'm not hungry. Certainly not for the apple. He likes the things so much, he can eat this one himself. I stare at the paper and crayons, taking a little satisfaction because he's wrong about that, too. My parents never bought me any crayons when I was a kid, so how am I supposed to draw these fucking apples for his nephew, or whoever the hell this Michael is?

Chapter 5

THE EAGLE

The Siamang monkeys woke me early.

Our house was close enough to the Woodland Park Zoo to hear them trilling, whooping. Sometimes they did it in the morning but mostly in the afternoon. The first time Ellie and I heard them, after we'd moved in, we were making love and their whooping seemed so curiously loud, so close, our randy mood dissolved with laughter about audience participation. We took Michael over later and saw them climbing the trees within their cages, watched their bulging throats pulsing like bullfrogs'. Since then I've preferred to imagine them as a formally dressed chorus, ecstatic over the prospect of breakfast or teatime.

Michael was still asleep when I went up to get dressed and kiss Ellie good-bye. The monkeys had woken her, too.

"I missed you," she said, still sleepy.

"It was cooler downstairs. I'll see you tonight, after dinner."

"Oh, that's right. You're going to your dad's."

I kissed her. She was up now, on her elbow, remembering the other thing I had to do.

"Paul?"

"Uh-huh?"

"It'll be okay. Just tell them what happened. It'll be okay."

Heading west, I slowed down for a cop turning from Fiftieth onto one of the roads that meander through the wooded area of the park, between the zoo to the west and the playing fields to the east.

I didn't expect to get much work done today, after I retrieved the wallet and went to the precinct station, near North Seattle Community College.

Dad would be getting an earful this evening, and so would Ellie, after I got back.

I sped up Greenwood Avenue, heading north. Not having a license was the least of my concerns now.

The area along Eighty-fifth Street, the old northern boundary of Seattle, from Greenwood to Fifteenth Avenue, is littered with all the usual crap of our Jiffy Lube culture. But one of the things about Seattle is that no matter where you live, there are always views of the mountains and the water.

The Olympics were hazy in the sun, and there wasn't a cloud in the sky. The temperature would probably hit ninety by the afternoon. This run of heat wasn't usual, at least on this side of the Cascades. If it continued, there would be fires in the Olympic Peninsula forests and the Cascades.

People in Seattle reveled when it was like this. So I wasn't too surprised when I ran into traffic at the end of the line, where Eighty-fifth met the woods and fancy, secluded homes on Shilshole bluff. I joined the cars going down Golden Gardens Way at a funereal pace, figuring that every other person in north Seattle was heading down to the beach on this gorgeous day.

But it wasn't the weekend. And it was too early still.

An accident?

Right here? Right here where it happened?

My view was blocked by a Metro bus a couple of cars ahead of me. It wasn't until I had almost reached the parking lot that I saw the reason. I knew what it had to be, felt it like the shock of running aground.

The small parking lot was jammed with cars, three from the television stations and four blue-and-whites closer in to the woods. One TV reporter was doing a take—against the backdrop of my father's sculpture—in the meadow where the light was better. Near the entrance, a disgusted-looking cop was waving at the traffic, trying to speed up the rubberneckers, while another was dispersing joggers and bicyclists who had paused to look.

Something began squirming, feeding in my belly. My arms felt heavy enough to fall from the wheel

They'd found him dead.

But the son of a bitch hadn't been dead when I left him.

There was no other reason for all this, for the yellow police tape that stretched from a tree near the closed rest rooms, across the steps down the hill, to another tree where two plainclothes cops were talking, one looking below, the other at the mess in the parking lot, and beyond at the cars crawling by. He was smoking a cigarette.

He seemed to be looking at me, I was sure of it. Or looking for me, looking for the blue pickup the girl had described, if she got it right in the twilight, if she remembered. The guy who helped her but killed the other guy.

Or was it the other way around? Did Jessica get it right, get it the way it happened?

I was sure that any second now, he'd suddenly flick away the cigarette and begin walking quickly toward the road, yelling at one of the other cops to come, because sometimes you get lucky, sometimes they return to the scene.

There was no place to go. I was stuck in the line of cars. Somewhere beyond that yellow crime-scene tape was my wallet. They must have found it by now.

Were they at the house now, waiting for me to return? Ellie didn't have to go to work at the University Book Store till nine.

My husband? Paul Sinclair . . . I don't understand. He was going to talk to you fellows this morning. He saved that girl's life. He said the one who tried to rape her, the one who tried to kill him, was unconscious after the fight. . . . If he isn't at a precinct station . . . No, he wouldn't be at work. I told you, he said he was going to report what happened.

The entrance to the lot was just ahead, close enough to see where the cop had spilled some of his morning coffee on his uniform. As the cars and bus moved ahead slowly, I told myself I was going to turn in, tell that cop from my window why, see the annoyance change to serious business.

Turn in.

Turn in. Get it over with. Better now than later, when the first thing they'll ask is why it took me so long.

My hands were slick and shaking on the wheel.

I didn't kill him.

Then tell them, turn in and tell them what happened.

One of the TV mannequins laughed, walking back from the meadow take with the reporter. The cop looked away, frowning, shaking his head just as I approached the entrance. He looked back, one hand on the barrier in front of him, another waving the cars on. His eyes flicked to my truck. The moon could have eclipsed the sun in the time it took me to pass by that cop. He was only ten feet away. Was it my imagination or did his gaze stay with my truck longer than with the other passing vehicles? I was ready for the shout, the jabbing arm: *Get out and put your hands on the roof of the truck.*

I glanced in the rearview. The driver slowed to ask the cop what was going on. The cop ignored him and just kept swinging his arm, rhythmic as a harvester. Another car honked.

They should have found that wallet by now. Either they'd missed it or someone had come along, taken the twenty bucks from the wallet and tossed it where no one would ever find it. Otherwise I'd still be at home, talking to them in my bathrobe.

So they still didn't know who had killed the molester of that girl. I drove past the entrance. I had to get the hell away.

I was almost at the ferry terminal when I realized I hadn't called my father on Bainbridge Island to let him know I was coming over early.

I didn't go back, but I did slow down to watch an eagle circling over the double E of the sign for the Edgewater Hotel.

Was it the same eagle Ellie, Michael, and I had seen two years ago from the little park at the top of Shilshole bluff? The sight of the bald eagle, soaring to the height of the downtown buildings, slumming the city thermals, was such an unexpected treasure that I forgot about calling my father at home.

The eagle wasn't supposed to be there. As it turned out, neither was I, on Bainbridge.

Chapter 6

The Letter

You can always tell who the island residents are on the ferry: They stay in their cars for the half-hour passage across Elliot Bay and the Sound, reading, catnapping. I usually stayed in mine, too, but this time the congestion of cars, packed bumper to bumper, made me feel penned in, and I spent the time on the upper passenger deck with the wind in my face, next to a group of Japanese tourists. They asked me to take their picture and positioned themselves like soccer players for a penalty kick, to make sure the Space Needle would be in the background.

The bay was crowded with daysailers and harbor tour boats. A Foss tug suckled a Hanjin freighter stacked high with containers. A Maersk freighter steamed north, outward bound for the Strait of Juan de Fuca and the Pacific beyond.

I didn't expect this slight geographical displacement would make a difference. Still, there was something about going over the water that helped. It wasn't so much the expectation of landfall, the promise of what lay ahead, but of what had gone before.

It was after one when I disembarked the *Spokane* and drove through the main street of Winslow, which still had no stoplight.

The route to my father's house on the southern edge of the island seemed new, though I had been back only a few days before, just after he'd come back from Harborview hospital after his accident.

The house on South Beach Road was the only one I ever remembered; we had come to it from Seattle in 1961 when I was four and

Steven six. Dad always said he chose the place because of the light. The house faces south, looking out over Rich Passage, where the Bremerton ferry turns to the north around Beans Point. The explanation always made sense, since Dad is a sculptor, but I've since thought it was more than that. The last house we left near the University of Washington was dead in the construction path of interstate 5, which bisects Seattle. Dad always said it was just as well, since he wouldn't have to look at the Space Needle, the legacy of the World's Fair in 1962, which always reminded me of the Martian machines in George Pal's *War of the Worlds*. Dad could have taken the government compensation and gone anywhere. But he chose an island, a place safe from so-called progress. Our house was a farther outpost because it held fast to the southern shore where, on the good days, we could see Mt. Rainier materialize like a guardian spirit.

The feeling of being on an outpost had decreased as the years went by, as more houses were built around older ones like ours along the road. But the feeling was always there, in part because of the proximity of Fort Ward, where Steven and I spent countless hours playing in the abandoned, turn-of-the-century batteries built to protect the approach to Bremerton and its naval shipyard. The five-inch guns and mounts were gone by the end of World War I, the underground magazines with their thick, rusting iron doors empty save for graffiti and the smell of piss. Steven and I garrisoned the ruins nonetheless, pretending we were the only ones left after the battle. It was just as easy to imagine our house as an extension of the fort, to see the Bremerton ferry idling out in the passage, waiting for the submarine net to part, and to wonder where the mines were in the deep water.

The house was set back from the beachfront road, on a slope just steep enough to protect us from storm surges but not too steep to discourage activities like playing catch with Dad. He was always game, though not very good. Even so, it always surprised me how quickly Steven and then I surpassed his skill.

He put one of his bears in the front yard, a "second" that didn't make the final cut of ten for Seattle's parks. There were still smears of faded paint on its half-raised body, one paw poised to cuff a salmon from a river—evidence of decoration from long-past Halloweens and boyhood whim. He let us do anything to that bear, short of taking a hammer and chisel to it.

The aged tawdriness of that broken-eared bear, and the general messiness of the house and property, probably were the reasons why our closest neighbors, the Snyders, put up six-foot fences, not caring a fig that Charles Sinclair was once the Northwest's best-known sculptor, his bears featured prominently in a *Newsweek* article on the arts renaissance in American cities.

It probably pissed them off as well to have to look at the old Great Northern caboose parked at the rear of the backyard, where the trees on the hill leaned over the property. Dad had bought it at auction, after the Wenatchee depot was torn down following the consolidation of the railroads that became the Burlington Northern. He got it, I think, because of Mom, when her MS was getting bad and she had two boys with enough energy to fuel a rocket. Dad needed time alone for his work, so it was easy to bribe us: *Okay, you hooligans, take it outside, the caboose.*

On an island where home landscaping tends toward anchors and driftwood, the old caboose, with its mountain-goat-on-a-rock logo, was guerrilla sculpture. It made you look twice, turn around after you passed, to make sure you were seeing right, like Dad's stone bears in Seattle's parks. The caboose gave our place the air of a gypsy caravan, of traveling people who happened upon money, but weren't quite comfortable with the idea of permanence.

I parked between the caboose and Dad's large skylit studio adjacent to the house, taking the spot where his old Econoline—currently getting an engine rebuilt—usually was. I didn't bother to see if he was in his studio. He wouldn't be there, not with the cast on his leg.

As soon as I entered the kitchen, I heard him snoring in the living room. The back of his head and the pads of his crutches were just visible over the top of the brown leather easy chair. He was facing the front of the house. Through the picture window a ferry was veering northwest to Rich Passage and Bremerton.

The front door was open, knocking gently on the stop as a cool breeze came in off the Sound, bringing with it the distant thrum of the ferry and the calls of seagulls.

Dad didn't usually nap in the daytime. He was sixty-seven, an early-up, early-to-bed kind of guy, and lived alone. His napping, the crutches, his long, graying hair still thick in back, gave me a sudden sense of his mortality. I had the urge to wake him, to interrupt the descent.

I didn't. He wouldn't be napping if he didn't need the rest.

He'd been sketching. A short pencil was lodged behind his ear, an artist's pad propped against the chair. Crumpled sheets of paper lay scattered about the footstool upon which his broken ankle rested. A dozen names were scrawled on the cast that was revealed, like white bone, in the long split of his jeans leg: mine, Ellie's, Michael's with the *e* reversed.

He'd also been reading letters when he fell asleep. An oak box full of them was on the floor between the stool and the chair, the lid opened, the brass chain taut. I recognized the box. I'd made it for him as a Christmas present years ago, when he said he wanted to organize the family photos.

His small hands, much smaller than mine, but scarred and toughened as a laborer's, were folded in his lap. A letter stuck out, almost vertically, as if he were offering it to someone, to take, to read.

And I did, despite the stab of guilt. It was none of my business, prying into the private remembrances of my father's courtship with my mother, the letters she had sent him when he was in Korea, or later when she was still in Connecticut, finishing up the last two years of college and he was discovering the country in his '49 Ford in lieu of the diploma he never got from Pratt Institute in New York.

I expected him to wake up the moment I lifted the letter from his callused thumb and finger, as if the letter was somehow connected to his dreams. But that gentlest of friction didn't rouse him.

The letter wasn't from my mother.

It was addressed to him, at a post office box. I never knew he had one. The return address was a post office box number. Bellingham, Washington. I also didn't remember us having any relatives there.

The letter was a long one, but that wasn't the reason I had to sit down in the chair opposite Dad's to read it. The letter was dated May 6, 1980—almost two weeks before my wedding to Ellie, on the Sunday Mt. St. Helens blew. The letter was signed: *Sara.*

Dearest Charles,
I finally picked out the dress to wear to Paul's wedding. Bellingham may not have much to choose from in the way of stores, but then again, as a small-town girl from Wenatchee, I'd

probably have been uncomfortable at some fancy Seattle store. Frederick and Nelson's always made me nervous when I went there. I hope you like it, because it's for you, too, Charles. Ever since you suggested it when we had dinner at that wonderful place overlooking Chuckanut Bay, I've thought of little else besides our "shadow wedding, and shadow wedding night." By now your 45-year-old "bride" holds few surprises for you, which is just as well!

Excited as I am, I know the 18th will be Paul and Ellie's. From your last few letters, it's plain that Paul has chosen well. I got a kick out of what you wrote about Ellie's family—the San Francisco madam taking her savings to Seattle for a new start, marrying a man who made a bundle on the foolishness of Klondike dreamers! Things come full circle, don't they?

Now Ellie's the black sheep, the dreamer who wants to be a writer and never mind what her family wants her to do. I guess I feel a kinship with Ellie since I always had this silly hankering to write, too, ever since Mr. Cranston in high school said I had a way with words. Most I've done, though, is do a journal, but I always tear up what I do after a while, maybe because I'm scared someone will find it and think I'm nuts or a lousy writer, whichever is worse.

I bet Paul will help her stick to her guns. Her family will come around about him, too, you know, about marrying into a family that doesn't get paychecks twice a month. If they don't, it's dollars to doughnuts he'll tell them to go fly a kite. Lots worse things than doing that with people who get on your case.

Ellie's chosen well, too. If Paul can't decide, as you say, whether to put his degree to use or follow in your shoes, he will. At least he has talent to choose from. That goes for Steven, too. I wouldn't worry about him, so much. That anger stuff you mentioned. He might have a knack for closing the door to the world, but there's plenty others to open. Maybe he'll be a writer, too. He's got the goods. That was plain as day from that story of his you sent.

I know they're young to be getting married (for these days anyway!). I hope to God Lisa waits a while after college. I look back on my 17th year, look at my beautiful daughter who has T.J.'s eyes—and shudder. Kids will do what they will do, I guess. I should know. If Paul's water and Steven's fire, I think my Lisa's somewhere in between.

Oh, I'm going on! I always do, don't I! Tell me if I butt in too much. We've always been able to talk about things. We've had to, especially during the times when the nightmares came back, even worse than ever, after T.J. was killed. Then Hannah. Oh, Charles, I just wish she were able to be at Paul's wedding. He and Steven were so lucky to have her around for as long as they did. But still . . . That we've found each other doesn't lessen the wish. Maybe because I know you feel that, too, I can say this.

All is well here. The restaurant is doing good enough so that I'm considering hiring a manager. Lisa has been doing "boss" work for the past year, but she's going to college soon. Sam says he's going to help with that. Pretty sweet of a brother we don't see much, though we all understand why.

Been thinking about selling the place, but making whoever buys it keep Pickles as the name! I've gotten an offer that's 10X what I paid for it with the money T.J. left me. The guy was a developer, so he just wanted to buy the property so he can tear it down for parking for the shopping mall. Sound familiar, Charles? It can be mind-boggling, thinking about the causes of things and the results. You've said yourself the island has been a good place for Paul and Steven, but if you hadn't been rousted by I-5, that might not have happened. And if the interstate hadn't been built, with the exit for Fairhaven, there'd be a lot less business for the restaurant that's kept me and Lisa going and maybe the cabooses here wouldn't have been brought in!

It overheats my mind and I'm better off with practical matters. Lisa is the same way, I think. She says she wants to become an engineer. Can you imagine, 17 years old, her head spinning with boys and proms, and school spirit? Now where did that come from? Maybe she made a promise to herself, one afternoon when she was refilling coffee cups and taking yet another order for ham-on-rye, that she wasn't going to wind up like her mother. Maybe it was all those times she watched me changing the oil on the Mustang or tuning it. I sometimes think it was easier for us to talk, with me under the hood, and she sitting nearby. It's scary to think what kids pick up. I don't have to tell you it's not just the big things, either.

I'm going to keep that car until my fingers are so stiff with arthritis that I can't hold a wrench any longer to change the oil. It's going to be the only car I ever own. The engine's good as new and I must have put 150,000 miles on the car (most of it down to Seattle and back!) ever since T.J. bought it before he went to Vietnam. T.J. showed me how to change the oil, and sometimes I think I became obsessive about it because of him. Changing the oil as regularly as, ahem, Saturday night sex. I guess I'm just as obsessive about getting the dirt out of my hands, my fingernails. Once, when I was doing that after working on the car, Lisa muttered that I was like Macbeth's wife. This was a year ago, and she was doing Shakespeare in English class. I had no idea what she was talking about. So I went to the library and read the damn play to find out what she meant. I may never have paid much attention in high school, but I've always made a point to know where the library is wherever I've been. But after I read that Shakespeare play, I thought that maybe there's another reason why I'll spend half an hour getting my hands clean after working on T.J.'s Mustang.

I know one thing, Charles. That car will be washed and waxed and purring like a kitten when I drive down for the wedding. My hands will be clean as a whistle before I put on the new dress and before I take it off for you, Charles, after Paul and Ellie get married.

All My Love,
Sara

P.S. Lisa says to say hi, and thanks for the art supplies. The kids in her Drafting II class are envious!

I got up, slowly, and put the letter, gently, on his thigh, where it would have fallen from his grasp.

Dad had never mentioned a "Sara" that I remembered, never mentioned this woman, with whom he was in love.

I kneeled. The box wasn't big, but there had to be over a hundred letters in it. I pulled out a dozen, at random, and each one had the same return address. The postmark dates were from the seventies. I was going to check more, to see how far back . . . to see if they went past 1968, when my mother committed suicide.

The phone rang in the kitchen, startling me so much my elbow knocked the chair. I put the letters back, rising quickly even as Dad stirred.

My father had no answering machine, so the ringing went on. Receiver in my hand, I hesitated, sure it was the police. Seattle or Bainbridge. I took a deep breath, saw Dad looking around the side of the chair, clearly surprised.

It was Ellie.

"Paul, thank God you're there!"

The relief at hearing her and not the police instantly dissipated with the urgency in her voice.

"Ellie, you okay? What's the matter?"

"He's dead. You . . . what happened last night. The guy was killed."

I lowered the phone. Ellie's voice was distant, chiming my name over and over.

My father was bending down. I couldn't see him, but I knew he was there, rustling the crutches, and I thought for one wild second he was bringing them in for me. I stretched the telephone cord taut, tight enough to play it, or yank it out. I pulled over one of the kitchen chairs. And sat.

And brought Ellie back, to find out who the dead man was.

Chapter 7

VIGILANTE

His name was Thomas T. Van Horn, and he was a registered sexual offender recently released to the Ballard neighborhood after serving a five-year sentence, including rehabilitation.

His death wasn't front-page news in the *Seattle Times*, but it was close. Ellie read most of the article, her voice over the phone scarcely louder than the background noise of the busy bookstore. He'd been beaten to death, castrated, and mutilated on the face and hands. That had left the police puzzled, even considering the quote "brutality" of the homicide.

There was a long silence, and I covered the phone so she wouldn't hear my breathing and what I was saying to myself again and again. I was tingling all over, and my hand on the phone was trembling.

When she finally said my name, she sounded as if she was on the verge of tears.

Somehow, I found my voice. "Ellie . . . I didn't leave him that way. It was a fight."

"Yes, that's what you said. You said it was a fight."

"I wasn't even carrying a knife or whatever was used. I didn't hit the guy that hard. On the knee, yes. My God. The guy was alive when he went down those steps and his head took some shots, but I've taken worse on rugby fields."

"Then something isn't right."

"That van . . . whoever was in that van, they must have gone back and done that to him. Someone did. I sure as hell didn't."

I heard an odd scraping sound. It wasn't background noise over the phone, from the bookstore. I turned and saw Dad pushing the box of letters, with a crutch, along the bare floors of the hallway. I missed some of what Ellie was saying because it was such a bizarre thing for Dad to be doing, pushing that box, scraping it along, as if it were a tiny coffin.

"Paul?"

"I'm here."

"What're we going to do, where does this leave us?"

"Not going to the police. Not now. If they haven't found the wallet by now, they won't."

"The wallet? What wallet?"

"Mine. I didn't tell you I lost my wallet there. It must have fallen out during the fight."

"Oh, shit, no . . ."

"I was going to get it, before I went to the police. But they were all over the place."

"Okay . . . okay. Will they . . . how hard will they look for a rapist's murderer?"

"They'll look. He's a vigilante. Or they are. How hard, I don't know."

"If they find that wallet, you'll never be able to convince them you didn't . . . do that."

"The fucker deserved what he got when I left him, but what happened later . . . that makes them little better than he was."

Dad was back in the living room, clicking his crutches together and taking a last hop to the chair.

"I've got to go now," Ellie said. "I can't talk about this any-more, not here at the store. We'll talk about it tonight, when you get back."

We said good-bye. And after the line was dead, I wanted to tell my wife again that Thomas Van Horn hadn't been dead when I left him.

Chapter 8

The Sculpture

By the time my mother was thirty-eight, she couldn't tend her rose-bushes because of the multiple sclerosis. Steven and I helped my father build gravel walkways between the rose beds so her wheelchair wouldn't get stuck in rain-softened earth, but then her hands went. One day in the summer of 1968, a period of remission, Dad took her to the Bloedel Reserve, a former estate with gardens and nature trails in the northern end of the island. He was going to go back and pick her up after a couple of hours. In that time she somehow managed to get to the Agate Pass Bridge. The police found her cane before they found her.

Steven took the cane to Alaska with him and claimed it saved his life in a bar fight in Anchorage, when he shattered some guy's cheek with it.

In 1980, twelve years after our mother committed suicide, Steven disappeared the day of my wedding. We've never seen him again.

After Emma, when Ellie and I were going through the separation, Dad's place was where I would go. He knew about a Laney Andrews, a woman with whom I had a brief affair during the time Ellie and I lived apart, but I didn't know then about this . . . Sara, in Bellingham. When I wasn't with Laney, I worked in his shop, distracting myself by making things, anything; anything to get my mind off what had happened.

During those times, I remember entire days when Dad and I would say only a few words to each other in our routines and meals.

Everything was so familiar, the signals clear, like that of a catcher to a pitcher, that often gestures would suffice. Every now and then there would be a trip to the mound.

Today was one of those.

That's how it began again, sitting with him in the living room. Tobacco smoke swirled around him from the bent-stem Peterson pipe I'd brought him from Ireland years ago. It wasn't a big pipe, but it seemed large in his hands. He'd been using the same Scottish tobacco—Rattray's—for years. That and single-malt whisky were his only extravagances, and his only friends, really. I don't think I ever saw him go out with the boys, or have friends over. It was always just him in his studio or with family—Mom and Steven and me. With them gone for so many years, it was just me.

The smoke matched the color of his still thick hair.

"I heard some," he said finally. "How bad is it?"

"It's in the paper."

"That," he said, "would qualify, all right."

"It's why I'm early, Dad."

"You caught me napping."

"It looked like you were doing a little work, too."

He shrugged. "Sketches."

I almost asked him about the letters, why they were so important he felt he had to take them away to his bedroom while I was on the phone. I hesitated too long. Perhaps I wanted to.

"So what happened?"

After I told him, he said, "What you came early for is a drink. Pour one for me, too."

I took down the bottle of Macallan from the cabinet over the fridge, poured two fingers into tumblers. Like father, like son.

Handing him the glass of Macallan broke his stare out the window. A sailboat was crossing the path of an eastbound ferry. Probably not as narrow a miss at it seemed from our vantage but close nonetheless. "Moth to flame," he muttered, shaking his head. "If you can't handle a boat, stay out of the water."

I downed half the Macallan, tilted the glass at his ankle. "How is it?" He'd broken the ankle helping out on the *Constellation*, a 127-foot schooner.

"Itches like hell. I keep tapping the damn cast, like I'm trying to find a stud behind the wall. Doesn't do any good."

We finished off the Macallan. He didn't bat an eye, say a thing when I flung the empty glass across the living room. I missed the maw of the hearth by a foot. The glass exploded against the brick, and one shard tinked off the corner cabinet; others skewed in front of the bookcases flanking the fireplace.

"You want the other one?" He held up his.

"No, it's all right."

"Okay."

He relit his pipe, looking away to the water again, as if he were waiting for someone, remembering someone, something. This Sara, the letter he'd been reading?

"I don't suppose Michael knows," he said.

"No. There's no reason to tell him anything, not right now."

"You may never have to. You'll know within a few days whether you're in trouble with the police. You'll never be in trouble with yourself because you did what any man would do—defend yourself and that little girl."

The sun was slanting across his legs, the cast, and I noticed then the name scrawled on the cast, at the top, within his easy reach, the irregular block letters facing away from me, toward him, like a code that only he could read. Their small size made them seem secretive.

Seeing Steven's name shocked me almost as much as the letters. Dad saw me staring.

"What the hell," he said. "I couldn't leave him out."

"Dad . . ." I said softly.

"Go ahead, tell me I've got to let it go—but only if you've done the same."

"It's not like he's going to walk through the door, like some Foreign Legionnaire, with eighteen years of stories to tell."

"But if he did, he'd have a few, wouldn't he?"

He had me there.

Steven was like a comet, with all its flare and brilliance. An A student, and maybe even a better athlete. If I had a dollar for every time a teacher said in September, "Oh, you're Steve Sinclair's brother," I could have bought a new car at eighteen. I was the fullback for the Bainbridge Spartans—three yards and a cloud of dust. I did okay, though I was probably a better baseball player. Steven was the wide receiver. The routes he ran were beautiful in their precision. He made the catches—and everything else—seem so easy. He could have gone to any college in the country but chose Williams. I stopped in Minnesota, at Macalester. Steven left Williamstown after three years, saying he had been bored, but there were hints of some kind of trouble. He never told me what it was, which bothered me because we'd always talked before, especially in the caboose. He drove a used Harley across the country, then up to Alaska. That was the same summer he and I were at a reading at Elliot Bay Books, and he was the one to notice the striking, copper-haired young woman sitting in the café after. We all got talking and he never did get her phone number, maybe because he was leaving for Ketchikan in two days. But I saw Ellie McKenna at another reading two weeks later, and this time she gave me her phone number.

Steven worked construction up there for a few years, and on fire crews in eastern Washington, and by 1980 he said he was writing a novel. If he had been, I never found it.

Now, like a comet, he'd come back, in this bizarre little memorial, on this day, of all days. If he'd been here, truly here, we'd go into the caboose and I knew exactly what he'd say: The guy got what he deserved. He'd tell me I was dumb not to tell the police, and then he'd say to forget it. If they hadn't paid a visit by now, they wouldn't.

I suppose it wasn't a good sign that Dad had scribbled Steven's name on the cast. But I wasn't so good with the past either, and it was none of my business, like the letters, if my father maintained his love in this way for his elder, lost son, even though the two of them had been at odds much more than Dad and me. I'd loved Steven as much as I'd envied his brilliance, his unassailable self-possession, and I had never let go of either. He was taken from my life, and I—none of us—ever said good-bye.

"Paul?"

I'd been staring out the window, too. I shook it off, covered up. "You were sketching . . ."

Before you leave tonight, you ask him, you tell him you read one of the letters.

He paused. "A few things."

"That's good to hear."

"They're nothing to sell."

"You were in the paper a while ago. Did you see?"

"I missed it."

"The *P.I.* art critic wondered why the Seattle Art Museum didn't choose a Northwest sculptor for their signature sculpture outside the entrance. I think the quote was: "*Hammering Man* is two-dimensional—literally and artistically. Where's Charles Sinclair when we need him.""

"He's too old, doesn't work in metal or in that scale."

"Bullshit, Dad. The thing's sterile."

"You want something to pat?"

"Hey, these days it couldn't hurt."

"Do you really want to see what what I'm doing?"

" 'Course I do."

"I was going to wait to show you. It's not finished, now."

"Don't worry. I won't chase away the bears."

That was Dad's name for inspiration, the creative muse, whatever you want to call it. Sometimes they're hibernating and you have the devil of a time rousing them. Sometimes you run into them at the most unexpected moment. They can be dangerous or tame. Sometimes you feel you know them enough so they'll feed from your hand, then they might turn on you. But sleeping or active, they're always out there in the wilderness.

He made a bear, a small one, for Ellie's birthday once. She keeps it in her study. She never threw it away, even during our tough times.

I knew what had chased away Dad's bears for too long, and they were never coming back, for me or for him, no matter how many times we scrawled their names on a cast.

Dad and I never talked much about his artistic doldrums, but when we did, it was always in terms of the arthritis that bothered him, or the Reiter's syndrome that flared up occasionally. Christopher Columbus was thought to have suffered from the same thing. It was the brightest part of a terrible day for me to know that the bears had come back for my father.

With Dad on his crutches it took us a while to get out back to his studio, time enough for me to tell him I'd read one of those letters and apologize. I felt bad about doing that. He'd been here for me and just being with him had helped so much. Reading the letter seemed like a betrayal, maybe minor, but devious. In the end I didn't bring it up.

He took the keys from his pocket and unlocked the studio. It had once been a two-car garage, to which he'd run power, adding dormers on either side of the roof for better light and ventilation.

I hadn't been inside in years. His hand tools and supplies were shelved on opposite walls. One long bench ran the length of the work area, filled with power equipment for sharpening his tools and saws, for cutting and polishing stone. Safety glasses, masks, and respirators hung from hooks. Dust covered everything, even the vac. Toward the rear he'd shrouded pieces that had never sold or hadn't worked for him. Closer, on a sturdy table of four-by-fours, two drop cloths covered the prize I had no idea existed until now.

"It needs some setup," he said. He leaned his crutches against the worktable. "This needs to go in front." I helped him slide a large wooden frame in front of the covered work. The tops of the cloths were easily six feet off the floor.

"Come around here and look across the table."

After I did, he took off one of the cloths.

The frame enclosed three figures. I recognized all of them: my mother, Steven . . . and Emma.

I looked away, for the photos Dad had been working from. I didn't see any lying about. He'd done it from memory.

Emma was in the middle, just high enough for her head to show over the sill of the frame, her left hand raised, flat against the invisible plane of the frame, pressing against it. Dad had remembered that she was a lefty, or at least we'd been pretty sure she was going that way after she'd walloped a tormenter named Billy Binns, who'd shoved her down on the asphalt school playground. Dad had captured her mischievous smile, the single brow she would raise because she knew it always made Ellie and me laugh. She looked as if she'd just found hidden candy, had it in her other hand, and no one knew it yet.

Steven had an arm around her, pressing her long hair close to her head. His grin was typical Steven: ear to ear, nothing held back, early Steven, before Mom died. Dad had gotten him perfectly: the wild hair, and slightly fleshy nose, the large but deep-set eyes with heavy brows, the slight cleft in his strong chin. Dad hadn't given him the later drooping mustache, which Ellie once said made him look like *The Dying Gaul*. Another sculpture.

He was closest to my mother, the protectiveness apparent in the way his arm was draped around her shoulder. Not casually, but fiercely, so that his long fingers were pressing into her skin, supporting her, his smile big, as if he wanted to make up for the thinness of hers.

She was trying, but the pain and resignation came through in the tightness, the almost sleepiness of her widely set eyes. I used to call them Kool-Aid eyes, because they were the color of my favorite drink.

I hadn't remembered my brother being so tall, and then I realized that Dad had exaggerated his height, if only to contrast with our mother next to him, to suggest her physical deterioration.

He'd brought them together from different times. Steven had never known Emma, nor had my mother. She had died when Steven was thirteen and I eleven. The surfaces of their skin were still rough, fractured in a thousand planes.

I went close enough to touch the gray-white stone. To smooth it out, I don't know. I wasn't even aware I'd brushed Dad's crutches until they clattered to the floor. I picked them up, in a daze still at the beauty of my father's work, handed them to him. His smile seemed not unlike what he'd given my mother.

"How long have you been working on them?"

He fitted the crutches under his arms. "Off and on, about two years."

"You never told me."

"Think I should have?"

I shrugged. "We're not in there."

"They have to be saying good-bye to someone."

"There's a name in that. Have you titled it?"

"You're close. Unless I think of something better, it's going to be *Leavetaking.*"

I pressed my hand against Emma's. Hers was so tiny and I felt the urge to squeeze it, give my warmth to her fingers, make them curl around mine. The feeling was so powerful I withdrew my hand, fearful I'd snap her tiny fingers.

"I haven't decided either if I should put glass in the front. That was the original idea."

"Don't."

"No, perhaps not."

"The window will be up high, won't it?"

"Yes, the sill about eye level, with a blank front, so you can't see them standing. But you can walk around."

I did.

Emma was holding something in her hand; Dad had left that to the imagination. Garden shears stuck out of Steven's back pocket. Mom had four roses in one hand, her cane in the other. Stephen had cut them for her. We all took turns doing that for her in the last years, but Dad had given Steven the last ones in stone.

"She had the garden, remember," Dad said to me when I came back around. "Next to the caboose."

"I remember." Steven and I would knock on the window when we were inside and shout to her to get out of the way—we were coming through. For a while, before she got worse, she'd go along with it and pretend to be so relieved when the train stopped just in time. Steven always stopped it since he was the engineer. I was the guy who fed the coal into the fire.

"I used to listen to you two in that caboose," Dad said, then smiled. "At least when you were younger. When you got older, I made a point of not listening."

"I'll be doing the same thing with Michael with his friends. Sooner than you think. He wants to have his birthday party in the caboose."

"It's all yours. Always has been."

"It sure beat a tree house, hands down." I pointed to the shrouded sculpture just beyond *Leavetaking*. "Take a look?"

"You can, but it's just a blank."

"For what?"

"One at a time, boyo, one at a time."

The shrouded stone made me think of two people, but I only asked him about one.

Dad and I had talked about Steven's disappearance so many times, but not recently, years it seemed. But the fact that Dad had written his name on his cast, that the woman in the letter had mentioned Steven's name, made me wonder, too, if Dad had shared everything he knew about my brother.

"What do you think happened?"

"To who?"

"Steven."

"Steven . . ."

"You wrote his name on the cast."

He leaned on his crutches, kicked a bench leg gently. "Think your old man's going Looney Toons?"

"Hey, tell me now if it runs in the family."

"So what good would that do? Oh, sometimes I'll go for months without thinking of him. Sometimes there'll be weeks when I can't think of anything else. I think about him more than your mother because it isn't . . . finished. Sometimes I just can't help but wonder if he's out there, still. You read about a body found somewhere . . . you just want to know, that's all. After a while you only want it confirmed, so you can go on, so you can take out the splinter.

"What happened that day?" I said.

"You know as much as me."

"And I was in Dublin. Ellie was sleeping off the jet lag in the Hibernian Hotel and I was buying her roses from a Grafton Street vendor and tea from Bewley's."

"We lost Steven, but it was still a crappy way for you and Ellie to begin your married life. I mean, getting upstaged by Mt. St. Helens, for God's sakes, coming back to find out your brother had been missing for two weeks."

"At least we had a chance to come back."

Dad could say it, I suppose, but I'd always felt ashamed to admit there were times when I resented, even hated, Steven for what had happened to him. The first years of our marriage were overshadowed by his disappearance, the wondering, the waiting for him to return. If our first child had been a boy, Ellie wanted to name him after Steven. I didn't, and we had our first big fight over that. I even wondered what would have happened if Steven had returned from Alaska at the end of the summer. Would he have put in a claim on Ellie? Maybe it was more than Dr. Carey, who looked like James Joyce with his slight build and dark, round glasses, thought: *You were looking for your brother on that trail, Paul; you turned around to see him, to find him again, to recover your loss.*

"Well," Dad was saying, "at least you had your honeymoon. That's why I didn't call you, even after I got worried, so at least you and Ellie would have that. If you had known and stayed in Ireland, it would have ruined the two weeks. If you had flown back right away, you would just have waited here like me and everyone else."

The state police had found his car parked at a trailhead just off

I-90, on the way to North Bend, in the foothills of the Cascades. It had always seemed strange to me that he would have wanted to go hiking the day after my wedding.

"He drank an awful lot at the reception."

"He picked that up in Alaska, the drinking," Dad said. "He wasn't like that before."

"No, he wasn't." I remember asking Ellie's sister if she'd drive him home. There were jokes about that because they both were single and Becky had caught the garter. He should have been sleeping it off the next morning.

But one of the neighbors said he saw him getting on the ferry around ten a.m. I always thought maybe he felt the fresh air was just what he needed. Maybe he wanted some time alone, to think about things. Your brother just gets married, you're the best man, your thoughts tend to come back to your own life, after the champagne's all gone.

They never found him. They searched for a week—King County Police, Search and Rescue, even Explorer Scouts. It was so strange and so sad. One of the first things I did when we came back was go to his apartment and confirm that he'd taken his hiking stuff— boots, even that walking stick he'd made. He'd wrapped the grip with sticky string, did it the year before, while we drank Henry's and watched the Pirates beat the Orioles in the seventh game of the World Series. Took him two and a half hours.

"They should have found him," Dad said.

"They haven't found most of the victims of the Green River killer either. It was rough country around there, then. Even now. I read somewhere that in the Rockies every year, a few hunters always disappear and are never found. Some people think they're guys who do it deliberately, to get away from a lousy marriage, or creditors or the law—for whatever reason, a new start."

"He wasn't running away from anything like that."

"That we knew about. And the other explanation doesn't seem any more likely. I used to spot for him in the weight room his senior year. He could bench-press his own weight ten times, and that from a guy who had a 10.6 hundred and finished off college in Alaskan bars. It's hard to imagine someone taking him down, one-on-one, unless there's a gun."

"He should have been found, by now," Dad said, and there was nothing else to do but let that go, let him keep on writing Steven's name wherever he had to.

He shuffled over to the table, and the last thing I saw before he covered the sculptures of my mother and brother and daughter was Emma's hand, raised flat against the invisible pane of glass, saying good-bye.

I couldn't help but think how that had been done, sometime today in the early morning, to a corpse that had been found on the concrete steps in the woods above Shilshole. And I thought of how Dad had covered the tracks of his own past, even today, sliding the box of letters from a woman I hadn't known existed, sliding it away with his crutch while I was on the phone.

"Let's go back," I said.

He nodded. "I should put this damn foot up."

I didn't lock the door, and Dad didn't ask me to. He seemed lost in his thoughts. On our way back to the house, I still was thinking about Steven and so was Dad: "What you said, Paul—your brother wasn't like that. He wouldn't have done that. He hadn't lived long enough to be running away from something—"

That we know about.

"—and keep on running for eighteen years." He said it as if he were trying to convince himself. Or me.

In the distance a ferry's horn sounded twice, then twice more— someone getting in the way again.

THE CAGE: 2

He brings in a cat this time. I can't see, but I assume he's holding, stroking, the cat. I can't hear the purring over the hum of the air purifier, but he has it, all right. It's meowed six times for food already. He knows I will ask if it's my cat. I hold out for minutes, because I know that's what he wants. But I can't help myself, can't contain the anger: "It's mine, isn't it? You took my cat."

His calmness infuriates me. He knows that, too. "Now, what makes you say that, Robert?"

"Why else would you bring it in here?"

"Maybe it's mine. If I'd taken not only the risk but the time to go all the way back to your house to pick up your cat, why would I wait this long to let you know I had it?"

"Because it's a game, like everything else you do here."

"All cats sound alike in the dark. What was your cat's name, not that that will make her purr? This one doesn't seem to want to purr."

"She's scared out of her wits."

"Just tell me, what's her name?"

"It doesn't matter."

"You say that a lot." He pauses. "You don't want to tell me. Are you embarrassed by your cat's name? How odd."

How odd . . . I wish I could smash his face. "No, I'm not embarrassed, you son of a bitch."

"Good. You shouldn't be. After all, you named it."

"*Her name is Suzy, all right? You've got her goddamn name. All* right?"

"*See, that wasn't so hard now, was it? Nothing wrong with that name, I might have chosen it myself. You named it after a woman?*"

"*No, I didn't name the cat after a woman.*"

"*Why Suzy then?*"

"*The kitten seemed lazy to me, so I named it after the lazy Susan I have on my kitchen table.*"

"*Had, Robert, had.*"

"*No, I* have *it. It's still there and I still* have *it, no matter what you say.*"

"*And you'd spin her on the thing?*"

"*Yes.*"

He chuckles. "*Then you'd put a match to her tail.*"

"*That's something you would do, not me.*"

"*You said you had dates. What did the woman you were dating think of your cat's name?*"

"*She thought it was . . . well, never mind what she thought. It doesn't matter.*"

"*But it does.*"

"*What am I doing even talking to you about this? Christ.*"

"*We're talking, is all. Relax.*"

"*You sound like my doctor. Relax yourself. You're not the one in this cage.*"

"*We all have our cages. I made yours; someone else made mine. Well?*"

"*Who made yours?*"

"*We're talking about your girlfriend, Robert. Go on.*"

"*Go on, he says, go on.*"

"*She thought it was kind of odd for a guy to name his cat Suzy, didn't she?*"

"*Look, I make thirty-two grand a year and that wasn't good enough for her, okay? She'd rather have some cowboy who makes half what I do, rides a motorcycle. I overheard her laughing with one of the waitresses once, telling her she likes guys who 'ride 'em hard and bring 'em home wet.' She's from Montana so it figures.*"

"*Her name?*"

"*What do you care?*"

"*Telling me her name can't hurt.*"

"*Kerrie Caldwell. Her middle initial is D, so we also called her K.D. Katy. She used to be a cocktail hostess for me before she went to work at Anthony's at Shilshole. She's doing the same there.*"

"*Hmmm. She does sound like a Suzy, you have to admit.*"

"*Is that so?*"

"*You know, most men who are successful—sexually, that is— with women either truly like them or work very hard at giving that impression. The most successful men know how to earn that trust quickly, whether it's feigned or real.*" He laughs. "*Of course, having a lot of money doesn't hurt either.*"

"*Listen to the big expert. I don't see a lot of women hanging around here. But, hey, next time I see Kerrie, I'll work on what you said.*"

"*Your cat's purring now,*" is all he says, as if I can't hear the cat now. I couldn't before but I can now. The only thing that's gotten better is my hearing.

I can't believe I'm talking to him, talking about Kerrie Caldwell, who had the most perfect ass I've ever seen. And it still pisses me off he has my cat, that she's motoring so contentedly in the hands of a stranger, someone who'd going to kill me after he's done with these games. If he puts Suzy into the tunnel right now where he's put today's food, I have half a mind to strangle my own cat.

He continues, in the dark, always in the dark. God, I wish I had a cigarette, if only for the glow in the dark. I'd ask him, but he doesn't smoke. I know he doesn't smoke. If he did, I could hear it in his breathing.

"*Once, when I was a boy,*" he says, "*before the bad accident happened to my older brother and we moved, I woke to a sound I thought was that of a baby squalling. My brother woke, too, heard it and I said it sounded like a crying baby out there somewhere, abandoned in the night. He said it did, that they used to do that way back when. Or maybe something terrible had happened to the parents.*

"*We heard it again the next night, and my brother said he wouldn't tell if I went out and saved the baby. I didn't want to go, but he spent the next hour daring me, so I did, but not for long.*

"*The next night the crying baby sound came again, and maybe because it stopped I was out for a longer time, looking for it. I didn't find it, and I told my brother that someone must have taken the baby or maybe it died.*

"That's when my brother began laughing and telling me what a baby I was because the sound we'd been hearing wasn't a baby but the squalling of mating cats, what they do when they make kittens the way people make babies.

"I didn't believe him, told him he was lying. Even at that age I was nothing if not stubborn and persistent. I remember thinking, for a moment, at least, that wouldn't it be something if I actually came back with what I thought it was? Could I do that? Bring something to life that didn't exist?

"I went out again the next night, and the next, and each time my brother laughed a little less because the joke was wearing out. I knew by then, of course, there was no baby, but it didn't matter anymore because I was beginning to like going out into the night after everyone was asleep. When my parents finally caught me, my brother could only say, when they asked him why he didn't stop me, 'It's what he does.'

"Just like my sister asked me why I didn't run for help or throw my brother something when he was drowning in the swimming hole. Unlike my parents, she didn't buy it that I was too young to do anything. I didn't tell her about the dead branch I could have tossed toward him. I was strong for my age. I could have. I was going to, but I stopped, suddenly more fascinated with what was happening than with trying to do something to stop it."

It seems like he's taken a half hour to tell me this. *"You let your brother die?"*

"Watch them die?" He laughs. *"It's what I do. I just didn't know it then."*

"I'm supposed to believe this?"

"It's true."

"And this is supposed to make me feel better?"

"In a way, perhaps. You're the first person I've ever told."

"So that's what this place is, a confessional. I'm so honored."

"Tell me, did you have any pets when you were a boy?"

"No."

"Cats, perhaps, that squalled when they mated at night?"

"I said no."

"Why not?"

"We were always on the move."

"Military?"

"My father was a migratory beekeeper—go ahead, I've heard all the jokes about the 'Flight of the Bumblebees.' "

"How about 'Honeycombs of Wrath'?" He laughs. "I'm sorry. It's just that I've never met someone who did that."

"Most people don't even know they exist."

"Tell me about it."

"You're not interested."

"I am."

"Like hell."

"I'd like to know more. Please."

"It's no secret. There aren't enough wild bees to do all the work, so bees have to be brought in to pollinate the crops. About a quarter of the food we eat depends on the bees, including the apples you keep giving me to eat."

"No wonder you don't like them. It doesn't sound like you're brimming with fond memories."

"Fond memories? We lived in two glorified mobile homes, one in Eagle Bend, Minnesota, the other in Dos Palos, California. Two different schools each year, different teachers, friends. When I was twelve, I got to spray the hives with water to keep them cool when we trucked them in hot weather. We had almost a thousand hives my father would rent out to farmers to pollinate their almonds and cherries and alfalfa. You come home with your clothes dusted with bee venom, bee shit all over everything, the cars, everything. Which I had to wash off. Even with all the men-from-Mars suits we wore, you got stung a lot. To this day I can't stand honey."

"I'll remember to keep that off the menu, too."

"Well, it wasn't all bad, I suppose. There was one time when our semi blew a tire, went off the highway in the desert, near Sparks, Nevada, and half the hives slid off the trailer. Busted open. All over the place. A serious mess. A glorious mess. Even now, I want to laugh, all I have to do is think of my father and uncle stomping around, foaming at the mouth, swearing words I didn't even know existed, and all those bees swarming, all dressed up and no place to go. Served them right. I got stung a lot but it was worth it."

He laughs, tells me he liked the story.

"If I'd known you'd like the story, I might not have told it."

He goes quiet again and I can hear Suzy purring, the air purifier humming.

"You do realize that you've come full circle?"

"What's that supposed to mean?"

"I was thinking about what you said earlier, about people not knowing migratory beekeepers exist."

"Why am I talking to you?"

"Because you want to. Because your fear is now your hope. Is that a mark of going crazy or is it a survival instinct?"

"Hey, I'm not the crazy one here. I'm not the problem here, Houston."

"Oh, we're all crazy to a degree. Sanity is merely deception. Some of us are better than others at that. You used to be scared when the light went off, scared you would never see it go on again, that I'd come in, to do to you whatever you thought I was going to do."

"You're a butt-pirate, plain as day. That's what this is all about."

"Very colorful. Believe it if you want," he says. "You see, so long as I keep coming in, you think there is a chance, however small, of getting out. Maybe I'll take pity on you. After all, you haven't seen my face or know where you are. A better dose of barbituate injected into your food or water could knock you out for longer than before, when I had to give you the shave. I could drop you off somewhere, and when you wake up, this would seem like a nightmare, nothing more. But we can't do that, because whether you like it or not, your life has a purpose now. Your fear, however, remains abandonment. That something might happen to me."

"Bullshit."

"I had the same fear once," he says.

"I hope you have an accident, some car piles into you. Anything that would bring someone to the house, to find this room."

"You're wrong. If I was hit crossing the street, if my car blew a tire and I lost control and it overturned, for instance, you'd be done for. My hospital stay would kill you. You'd starve to death. You're right, I live alone. And like you, I haven't any close friends or family in the area. It's why you're perfect for me, Robert, why you're here. We're so different, worlds apart. Yet we're so very much alike in certain, crucial ways."

He flicks on the flashlight, the signal he's ready to leave.

All along I've been sitting in front of the window, but I get up, to block the gouge in the thick plywood. I found a metal bookmark in one of the books and a penny on one of the shelves. I folded the thin metal of the bookmark to make it work more effectively, but the penny's better. I've managed to put an edge on it. Still, the tools are pitiful. The hole is only a half inch deep, but it's a start. I'm sure there is padding behind it and probably another sheet of plywood, so it will take a lot more time to get through everything, break the glass, stuff a message through. Use the crayons he gave me: HELP ME. THIS HOUSE. Something like that. I'll glue the words on a piece of paper with my blood or maybe the yolk from the eggs he sometimes gives me. Maybe a neighbor will hear the outside glass break, see the message float to the ground.

"You're usually in the corner," he says. There's a long pause, then he says, "It makes so much difference that we can talk. I didn't expect that."

My cat is still purring in his other arm, though I can't see her. "How big is the hole, my friend? Big enough for the bee to escape from the hive?"

"Why don't you come in and see for yourself?"

"That won't be necessary. Whatever you've done, you won't have time to finish it. Things are proceeding well on the outside—for me. Now Paul—he's Michael's father—Paul isn't having a good week, and I'm afraid it won't be getting any better the closer we all get to Michael's birthday.

"But the hole—keep trying, my friend. I'd be doing the same thing if I were in your shoes. By the way, the room looks better now that you've put most of the books back on the shelves and cleaned up the mess from the dummy. Perhaps I'll consider a reward for next time."

"How about my cat now? I could use company that doesn't make me sick to my stomach."

"You have company when I'm not here, Robert. You have the dummy."

"That thing. Why don't you just go now?"

"I spent a lot of time making that thing, sewing on the button eyes, stitching a nice, insipid smile, making sure the canvas seams were tight enough to keep in all the sand. I must have put in ten hours practicing with it, dragging it into the van, carrying it out, *into the garage, into the house, up the stairs. Two hundred pounds is a lot of sand to drag around. You're probably less than that now, but it was a close enough estimate before."*

"I was one ninety-two."

"Don't be a bean counter. That annoys me. You're not in the restaurant anymore, going over your price-control printouts. I suppose you want the cat."

"I said I did, didn't I?"

The flashlight flicks off. Then a tap on the floor. He's put the flashlight down.

It takes me a moment to realize what he's doing. There should be more sound, but I hear only a brief squalling. It's pitiful, it's over so quickly.

I rush the cage—"Noooo!"—pounding on the four-by-fours, shaking them, trying to rip them loose. "You fucker . . . you fucker . . ."

I bruise my wrist trying to ram my hand through the cage to get at him. I can't. He's so near, close enough for me to smell his cleanliness, the soap. He—he—gets his showers, I get nothing but wet washcloths and towels.

"You motherfucker!" I scream at him, over and over, even as he's sliding my cat into the tunnel, jostling the plastic cups and containers on the cardboard tray. I have no shoes on. The water spills, pooling around my toes.

"Call her Kerrie," he says, laughing. "You probably wanted to do that to her anyway."

"Why are you doing this to me?"

"While we're on names, I've thought of a new one for you, Robert. Bobby. Bob-Bee. Bzzzzzzzzz. I couldn't resist."

"It's not my name!"

"You have no sense of humor. Enjoy the cat. I thought it sounded like a baby's cry. What did you think?"

He leaves, closes the door. The bolts slide home. Snick-snick. The light goes on.

I'm whirling away, and if my eyes hadn't seized on the dummy, sitting in one of the corners nearest the cage, I would have hurled myself at the wall, again and again. I grab the dummy. The lolling, grinning head snaps the other way, brought to idiot life. BobBee the dummy.

The weight is heavy and it's nothing. I whirl the thing, swinging it by the arms almost off the floor, smashing against a bookcase, shearing books off the shelves. I pick it up and whirl again, screaming, grunting, smashing it against the cage, then letting it drop. Dance with the dummy. I can't stop. I get it by the legs this time and crash the head against the flat wooden bars again. Sand sprays out of the arms, where he'd sewn up the amputated hands. I hear it sizzle against the far wall, the bookcase.

The arms are soon empty of sand, and I keep smashing the head till it bursts, too, and I'm finally exhausted and let the thing drop at the front of the cage. On my hands and knees, chest heaving, I stare at the dummy.

He was done with it. He had to put it somewhere. He knew I'd do it. Maybe he wanted me to. Save him the trouble of dismembering it.

That's what he's going to do to me.

I can't very well put out a two-hundred-pound dummy for garbage pickup, now, can I, BobBee?

The head is almost torn off the shoulders. Sand leaks out at the end of the tunnel. If only it were blood.

My cat, Suzy, is still in the tunnel.

Of course she is, where else would she be. He killed her.

I crawl closer.

The cat isn't mine. It isn't Suzy. Suzy was a tabby. This one is black and white. The neck looks like a squeezed white rag. The tongue is so pink and tiny.

A stray, a neighbor's? No, he wouldn't risk that, just as he wouldn't have risked going back to my house and taking mine. I should have known that.

It's his own.

He killed his own cat, purring in his arms, trusting him. For some reason that's worse. I wish it had been mine, so I could hate him a little more, and fear him a little less.

Chapter 9

THE JEWELRY BOX

I fixed us dinner, from groceries I brought over on my last visit. It was too hot to cook so we made do with fruit, cheese, and cold cuts. I turned on the radio for the news: forest fires on the eastern slopes of the Cascades.

I turned off the radio and wheeled in Dad's small TV and stand from the living room, opened a couple of bottles of Moss Bay Extra for us, and found Dave "Fly Away" Niehaus—the best announcer in baseball—calling the Mariners game against the Red Sox from Fenway.

The game reminded me of the present I wanted to give Michael for his birthday: a rack to hang up a mitt, bat, and ball. Over the summer he was constantly hunting for each whenever he wanted to go out with me and play. The rack used to be mine, and when I asked Dad where it was, he said it was out in the caboose, along with all the stuff of mine and Steven's.

Dad and I stuck it out until the last inning, as was our habit, TV or Kingdome, it didn't matter. I cleaned things up in the kitchen, and we went our separate ways, after; another habit. He settled himself in the living room with a book written by a guy also named Sinclair, who claimed to have proof that the St. Clairs of Scotland gave refuge to the Knights Templar—the defenders of Jerusalem— who were busted by European kings jealous of the wealth they'd accumulated since the Crusades.

He used to fill our heads with that kind of stuff—castles and knights, ill-fated and sometimes glorious quests. It took with me more than with Steven. One reason I had wanted to go back to Ireland for my honeymoon was to visit all the castles there and in Scotland that I'd missed the first time around, the summer before I met Ellie.

I went out to the caboose for more recent history: to find the present I wanted to give to Michael for his birthday.

Getting the old Great Northern caboose to our backyard from Seattle's King Street Station probably cost Dad three times as much as he paid for it at auction in Wenatchee: flatbed truck to ferry and a boom truck at both ends to lift it on and off. Two newspapers did feature stories on it. Whatever the cost and trouble and later doses of notoriety, Dad never once betrayed any regret about the caboose. Mom wasn't getting better, he needed time alone to work, he had two young boys. And it was rough going after Mom died. As much as anything could help after that, the caboose did.

Later, Steven and I lost our virginity in the caboose. We had a language of our own, based on that caboose and, more often than not, the raging hormones of those years: getting *caboosed* or *boosted*, *railed*, *sittin' high*.

The caboose was now a storehouse that still didn't leak, unlike Dad's damp cellar. Boxes were stacked two or three high on the bunks, piled in front of the woodstove in the far right-hand corner, on top of the old conductor's desk near the A door, in front of the compartment that used to be the head. The only place in the caboose not full of clutter was the cupola, to which one climbed via a straight ladder through the hole in the ceiling. The two chairs that came with the caboose were still up there. Even before the high school parties and the girls, the cupola was my favorite place in the world. I've cleaned few things as well in my life as I did the windows, inside and out, of the cupola. I still do it, every couple of months, a habit really, though as the years have passed that habit has taken on the dimensions of a promise—to myself, to Steven, I don't know.

When I was alone, it was a high tower, a refuge within a refuge where, utterly secure, you could keep watch, look out between our house and the neighbors', to glimpse the water. Just being up there made you feel good.

Doing okay, Paul?

Sittin' high.
How'd it go today, Steven?
Sittin' high.
That's how we signed off our letters to each other, the first few years anyway after we left home: *Sittin' high.*

Being up in the cupola was like having another person around, whom you could trust but couldn't see, like a confessional without the bullshit. Being up there somehow made it easier to say things you might have trouble with otherwise. I first told Ellie I loved her in the cupola. When she was very young, Emma had had trouble sleeping in Dad's house when we'd all visit, but I'd take her up into the cupola and rock her and that always did the trick. Maybe that's why Ellie hasn't been in the cupola for a long time.

I climbed up and sat awhile in the chair with the leather so old it cracked when I settled in. Yet the cupola seemed different somehow. I thought about it for a while, trying to figure out what it was, until I realized it was the letter of Dad's. I'd known every person who was familiar with the caboose, except this woman, this . . . Sara, Dad's lover, who'd written to him on the eve of my marriage and Steven's disappearance.

I had to ask him, before I left tonight. Ask him why, using his crutch, he'd slid the box of letters down the hall.

Is it because you two were lovers before Mom died? Did she know, Dad?

You always take a lot longer than you expect going through the old things. The memories have to be sized and fitted again with the unsettling knowledge that you've forgotten more than you remembered.

In a large packing box on one of the bunks, I found the baseball-bat rack. It had my name painted on it, but I could replace mine with Michael's after some sanding. And I found something else.

I wouldn't have picked it up except everything else in the box had been put in helter-skelter, but this was carefully wrapped in thick cloth and tied off. I didn't remember doing that, though I must have.

It was the jewelry box I was making for Emma, for the sixth birthday she never had.

The light wasn't the best in the caboose, so I left for Dad's studio with both the jewelry box and the baseball rack.

Michael's gift needed a little more work than I'd thought.

Emma's?

I'd been a day away from finishing it. The lid was on, hinged, but there was no chain to keep it in place. It needed a lot of sanding, and stain, something not too light because the box was made of birch and maple. I chose birch because the tree's suppleness reminded me of youth, how I once "swung birches," shinnying up a young one, then letting my weight, and the tree, bend me back to earth: something I'd thought Emma was sure to love to do, too, given her spirit. The maple I chose for its grain, the sugar of the tree, a kid's sweet tooth.

I'd finished the more difficult steps, the delicate dovetails—six to a corner to mark her years—the marquetry in darker woods on the lid, the parade of Winnie-the-Pooh and friends from the cover of *When We Are Six.*

The box was still waiting for the trinkets of my little girl's life, and later, the first jewelry, all the precious things she might keep forever.

There was a gash on the side and a discoloration, the evidence of when, a day after we lost her, I threw the box into the garbage. Ellie took it out, but I didn't know it until weeks later, when it just reappeared in my workshop, when we had begun to imagine the world without our daughter. I still couldn't bear to look at it, so it wound up here. But I was glad that Ellie had saved the box, saved whatever of Emma's that we had. She'd even saved that strange condolence note that had arrived anonymously, with no return address, only the words *Can the ripest apple be plucked too soon? Sadly, yes. My heart grieves in ways you cannot imagine.*

I found sandpaper in the workshop and began working to remove the gash and stain from the wood. I don't know how long I was at it, but gradually the evidence of that day after began to disappear.

I heard the clatter of crutches at the door.

"I thought something happened to you," Dad said. "You've been out here a long time."

I glanced at my watch. It was nine-fifteen. "Looks like the ten-thirty back to Seattle."

He shuffled in, saw what I was working on.

"I remember that," he said, tipping a crutch at the box.
"Never did finish it."

"Stay as long as you want then."

He brushed a hand over the lid. He'd had another whisky and his evening pipe. I could smell both on him. "It's well done, Paul." Then, after a few moments: "You were always making things for your mother and me and Steven. Are you going to take that with you tonight?"

"No, it's getting late. I'll have to leave it here, if that's okay."

"Sure, means I'll get you back here to finish it. This weekend?"

"We're getting out of Dodge this weekend. The cabin."

"Don't blame you."

"How's Monday night?"

He nodded. "Pop in before you go tonight, okay?"

"Will do."

At the door he turned, twisting around on his crutches. "It's for the girl, isn't it?"

He'd caught me by surprise. "I hadn't thought of that."

"The box just needs finishing is all, someone to give to. It's a beautiful thing. It's a shame to keep it hidden away."

He left. I listened to him moving slowly to the house.

It's a shame to keep it hidden away.

I still think about those words, the last I ever heard my father say.

Chapter 10

UNDERNEATH

I worked on the jewelry box longer than I had intended. I wanted to finish it now. Give it to the girl? It was meant for someone younger than her. The last thing her mother might want is a gift from a stranger who'd returned from that night, even if the gift came with the hope that her daughter would find other dreams besides nightmares.

I lost track of the time. When I glanced at my watch, it was ten-fifteen. I'd have to hurry to catch the ten-thirty ferry.

Dad'd fallen asleep, snoring in his chair, his hands loose on the book on his lap, the crutches angled off an arm of the chair.

I decided not to wake him up. I was relieved, in a way, that the time was short. Monday would be soon enough to ask Dad about the letters. It wasn't just the apology for prying into his private life. Why did he want to hide those letters from me? So he had a lover he kept secret. Was there something else in the letters he didn't want me to know about him?

I spun gravel leaving the driveway. A neighbor two houses down looked up casually from leashing his dog on the porch. Hasty departures were standard fare on an island where ferry schedules rule.

The roads were pretty much deserted now. Bainbridge is still a bedroom community, and most people turn in early for early morning commutes to Seattle.

I slowed way down going through Winslow. As I turned onto the holding area for the ferry docks, I saw I was too late. The last few cars had just gone on, their brake lights winking in the fluorescent glare of the ferry's holding lanes. Workers were chaining off the end.

I stopped the car short of the ticket booth. I didn't have to ask the attendant when the next ferry was. Steven and I used to call it the Midnight Express, the next to last run to and from Bainbridge.

I could either go ahead, first in line for an hour's wait in the dark, or go back to Dad's. Or go have a couple of beers somewhere. The Stem n' Stern was the only possibility nearby in town. I'd worked there briefly as a bartender before I got shitcanned for tossing the owner's son, a University of Washington frat boy, from the bar. He said he hadn't been drunk. I said he was. He managed the place now.

I turned around and headed back to Dad's. The least I could do with time on my hands was to clean up the glass littering half the living room.

The lights were still on when I pulled in, so I figured he was still ripping away where I'd left him a half hour before. I went to his studio to get the baseball rack. Michael's birthday wasn't for two weeks, but I decided to take it with me anyway. I dropped it in the truck on my way to the house.

One of the neighborhood cats darted in anticipation toward the back door. They come begging and mewling periodically for a handout, usually two or three of them. I don't know why Dad fed them because he didn't much care for cats.

I gently shooed the tabby away and got out my keys to unlock the back door, then remembered I hadn't locked it, in my hurry to get to the ferry.

He'd been up after I left because the radio in the kitchen was on, turned to a station playing blues. Pops Staples: something I would have chosen, not Dad. He wasn't in the living room. He'd obviously gone to bed, even though he hadn't turned off the lights or the radio.

I got the broom and dustpan to clean up the glass by the fireplace, but stopped in the hallway. His bedroom door was closed, and I saw no light in the crack by the door. So he'd turned in. So what was bothering me?

Something wasn't right.

The air was different. A scent of apples? I noticed the core of an apple on the side table, next to his pipe. And a burnt, acrid smell.

As if he'd been burning something. I checked the stove. The burners were cold. The fireplace?

Had he burned the letters?

The fireplace was cold, clean, except for the litter of glass.

I felt the pressure of this feeling that something was wrong. I forgot about cleaning up the glass, dropped the broom and dustpan with a clatter, headed for his room.

The smell was stronger in the hallway. For a moment before I knocked on the door, I was sure he'd been smoking in bed and had fallen asleep, and the ashes of his pipe were smoldering on the rug. Except that his pipe was in the ashtray next to his chair.

It was dark in the bedroom he had once shared with my mother, in another, separate life. The smells in the room should have been enough: acrid, sulfurous, overpowering the other fetid release.

As soon as the light seared my eyes in that room, I knew my father was dead.

His face was puffy; the blackened, staring, crimson-rimmed eyes remained vacant and fixed on the doorway when I rushed to him anyway.

He had no heartbeat. The pillow behind his head was soaked with blood. I stared at my father as one looks out the window of a train passing a station.

Blood seeped from his mouth, the rivulets merging on his neck. And the gun. He still held the gun, the barrel pointing to the corner of the room, the dresser where photographs lined the borders of the mirror.

I shut down. I couldn't move. I stared at my father but I wasn't seeing anything. We had played on that bed, he and Steven and I. Wrestling, pillow fights. Games where he was the Lava Man—*you can run but you can't hide!* Or Net-Head—*gonna fix me up some boy sam-witchees, yessireebob!*—with a butterfly net over his head. We'd sneak up on him, from the floor, and he'd rise, a kraken from the deep, and grab us as we squealed with delight and his beard would scratch our skin and he'd tell Steven how quick and strong he was already, how I . . .

should have locked the door . . .

never knew he had a gun, never knew . . .

I bolted from the room, seized with a wild certainty that he couldn't have done this to himself, put the gun barrel in his mouth . . .

Someone had been here.

It had been only minutes.

I ran from room to room, hunting for the killer. He had to be hiding somewhere in the house, couldn't have just . . . disappeared. I hadn't been gone long, seen a car speeding away.

Plunging from room to room, banging doors, ripping through clothes in closets.

Ran outside. Flung open the door to the studio, checked the caboose, the cupola, expecting any second for the killer to step in front of me or call softly to me from behind . . .

Here I am . . . still here . . .

and fire.

I didn't care. I had to find him, know he was there and hope for a few more seconds, to get him before he got me, like he got my father, who couldn't run . . . couldn't get away.

There was no one.

It had to stop. I stumbled from the caboose to the side of my truck and stopped, jarring my arms with the impact. I leaned against the truck, my arms and legs shaking, sweat dripping into my eyes, stinging my eyes. My chest heaved, heaved.

A dog barked somewhere. More distantly came the fading burr of a powerboat. Kids. Joyriding on a summer night. I did it once with Steven driving. Playing chicken with the ferry. Getting in the way.

I went back to the room to be with my father because I don't think I could have spoken then, and once I made the call, they would come and I'd never see him again. A note? I could have looked for one but didn't, couldn't through the squeezing, watery blur that soon burst into a torrent, and I wanted to drown in that one, too.

Dad, oh, God, Dad, Dad. What happened . . . why . . . WHY?

I don't remember going into the kitchen to make the call. I just remember being there and turning off the radio, and thinking that I shouldn't have because maybe Dad didn't turn it on.

I walked through the house, left the front door wide open and went outside, down the porch steps, and across the lawn that needed mowing, to the bear, to wait for everyone to arrive.

The air was moist and heavy off the water. The sound of the powerboat was faint now, then gone, as if it had never been there.

Like a gun that had never been there, but it was. All along.

You never told me you had one. You never told me . . .

I leaned against the bear.

You want something to pat?

I turned into it, pressing against the stone, then began pushing hard, grunting wildly, screaming into the stone, and kept on pushing, driving, tackling the thing until it toppled to the ground and I stood over it, exhausted. The answer to why he'd done it wasn't underneath.

I collapsed by the fallen bear, put my head down on its rough coolness, listening for the heartbeat within the stone, but there was nothing, nothing anymore, only the tremor of my hands, and that wasn't enough.

Chapter 11

FORT WARD

I remember only a few things from the hour after they had all arrived: how the flashing lights played on the screen separating the backseat of the patrol car, where they'd put me, from the front; the pauses before and after the detective asked me the questions, before he went inside and I went back to the patrol car with one of the officers.

They talked to me later on the steps of the front porch. The detective stood with his back to the stone bear. All I remember about the questions is one he never asked: if I knew how the bear had toppled over.

They gave me a trace-metal test, sprayed my shaking hands with something from an aerosol can and then looked at them under an ultraviolet light.

When we finally left for the station, there must have been four of them inside the house: the detective, whose name I can't remember, the crime-scene investigator, the Kitsap County coroner, and a patrol officer. The other two policemen were down by the street, making sure the onlookers and neighbors kept their distance. There were a dozen, even at that late hour.

Bill Drawdy, the chief of police, drove me. "We'll get your truck to the station later." Meaning, they wanted to take a look at the pickup.

The air was cool through the open window. Drawdy looked at the two officers talking by the fallen bear. "You do that?" he asked, nodding at the sculpture.

"Do what?" I knew what he meant, though.

"The bear."

"Yes."

"Paul, here's how it's going to go. We'll be at the station for a while. We have to get a statement from you. You can call a lawyer, have one there if you want."

"I just have to call my wife. I don't need a lawyer."

"Okay, it's up to you."

"I didn't kill my father. You must know that."

He looked at me as if I'd cut myself and he wanted to see how the blood was flowing. He said nothing, started up the car, and we left.

They knew, all right.

Bill Drawdy had been a captain in the Seattle Police Department when my mother committed suicide.

But when you come to live on an island, you get to know a lot of things that otherwise might escape. On an island the past has a way of turning back at the shore and drifting through the air, like woodsmoke on a winter's night, for all to breathe.

He knew about my mother's suicide years ago.

Tell me now if it runs in the family . . .

We didn't talk for the rest of the ride to the police station.

At 5:30 A.M. there's more traffic than you'd think going to Seattle. I was second in line for the ferry. I'd been waiting for two hours, and hadn't slept a minute of it.

I wanted to go home—and I didn't. The cost was so high, bringing this home, after what had happened at Shilshole, bringing this home to Michael, who had been so close to his grandpa.

If there's anything else you want to add to your statement . . .

Yes. You're wrong.

What makes you say that, Paul?

He was working again. He hadn't finished what he was working on. He was going to see me Monday and he was going to give his grandson a birthday present. He didn't kill himself.

I'm afraid he did. You're going home now because we know you didn't. The neighbor saw your truck leave the house ten minutes before he heard what sounded like a firecracker.

In the car, waiting for the ferry, I could still hear it, in my mind, how Steven had screamed at the two officers who came to our house to tell us our mother was dead.

From a ferry someone had seen her body floating in Rich Passage.

Steven kept screaming, "*I don't believe you,*" until Dad took him away to the kitchen, to help him, hold him tightly. Steven bolted away, out the back door. I went after him. I saw him in the caboose, the back of his head visible high in the cupola. Dad said to let him be. I did. But after a while I went out to see him and he wasn't there anymore. I checked a few of our haunts and wound up at the old battery emplacements at Fort Ward, down by the water.

It was getting dark and the fortifications were darker still, even more menacing than the woods, but I wasn't scared. I was eleven. Steven was thirteen.

I called out for him. No answer. Yet I knew he had to be here, the closest place he could be to the water where our mother had been found. I looked in all the underground magazines, where they'd kept the ammunition, looked in all of them except the last one. It was the most ruined, overgrown, and neither of us had even been inside, unlike the others we'd explored, daring each other to be the first to go in. This one we'd left unexplored because we'd once seen a rat scuttle out.

The rusting iron door open halfway. He was inside.

"Steven?"

I heard him sobbing.

I went inside and kneeled next to him. We shared each other's warmth in that cold, damp place. I didn't understand why he'd gone in there, except maybe because he'd never done it before, and no one but me would think of looking for him there, would dare to go in and see him crying.

I'd never seen him cry before, and I didn't now, either, because it was so dark. I felt his shuddering. That was one of the things about Steven: he never cried. I was always so envious of that. It seemed like a powerful ability: mind over matter, over skinned shins, things you want and can't have. But he was crying now. I cried, too. Because if Steven was crying, then it must be true. My mother was dead.

I never went back to that place. I had the idea now, as I watched the ferry sliding into the bundled creosote arms of its berth, to go back there. The idea was so strong in my mind that I'd find Steven there, and we'd stay together, as we had before, until it was time to go. Out of all the places everyone had looked for him after he disappeared, no one had looked there. I wondered why I hadn't.

If the ferry had not come, I believe I would have gone back, so strong was the feeling Steven would be there, after all these years.

Steven would be crying, as I was now, so hard my hands were dancing on the steering wheel, and the last part of me would realize that it was true. I'd never see my father again.

THE CAGE: 3

The darkness wakes me up. He is rummaging around, moving something. My back is to him, and even after he calls to me, I take my time turning around. Let him wait for company.

"Take a look at what I've brought you," he says.

He's been jogging or working out. I can smell the sweat, the stink. Nothing compared to me, but it's there. I know it because he usually comes clean into the shark cage. Isn't that a joke. As if I'm the one with the big teeth who goes into a frenzy when someone spills blood in the water.

He shines the flashlight on the floor. Next to the cardboard tray of my food something glints golden.

"Go ahead. You can't stay in the corner forever. Pick it up." He laughs. "The gold at the end of the rainbow."

He keeps the light on it for me.

A bracelet? No, the chain is too big for that. A pendant. Round like the world, the finely etched longitudinal lines interrupted by the initials KDC.

I'd never seen it this close before.

He moves the flashlight. The beam crawls up my leg, stops at my hands, as if he's offering me the light, too. Then it keeps going up. He's letting it feed, graze, finally on my face. I turn from the light as he drops it to my hands again.

"Where did you get this?"

"No whispering, BobBee. It's Christmas morning and I've given *you something you've always wanted but never dared to put on your list—you should see your face!"*

"Where?"

"Where do you think I got it?"

"She gave this . . . to you?"

"Oh, *gave is* perhaps too generous a word."

"I don't believe you. You had this made up. It's another one of your games, like the cat."

"No, it's the real McCoy. I have pictures of her, too—with someone else. They rigged up a bedside camera. Not bad shots, really. She certainly does have a nice ass. Her face is turned in two of them but not in the last three. You have good taste—in women, anyway. Would you like to see them?"

Why should I answer him? The air purifier hums.

"No? Yes? No fence-sitting now. The pictures are yours to keep, to masturbate with if you want. I'll slip them in the tunnel when I leave. I'll need the ankle bracelet back, though. I hate to be an Indian giver but this is one toy you'll have to share with someone else."

"You raped her, didn't you? You fucked her."

"They're not the same thing, BobBee. One or the other. Which would please you more?"

"Neither. I'm asking you."

"I'll leave to your imagination what I did. It would be disloyal of me to admit to either. After all, she's your woman."

He laughs again. He laughs quick, but he's a slow talker.

"You killed her."

"Would you be sorry if I had?"

"She wasn't my woman."

"Now, what kind of answer is that? Don't be afraid to say you wouldn't be sorry. Why should you be sorry for her?"

"Seeing as how I'm going to die, too?"

"Carpe diem, my friend. You have the anklet for a few days and the smutty pictures. We'll leave it at that for now. By the way, you're hung better than the guy she was screwing in the pictures. I don't know if that's any consolation to you."

"Why did you do this?"

"Because she was there?" *he says lightly.*

"It has nothing to do with all this. It could hurt that. It was a risk. That's pretty stupid of you."

"So thoughtful of you to see things from my perspective. That's progress, BobBee. Yes, it was a risk, but I'm careful. Taking risks is like any skill: the more you practice the better you get. Besides, remember the Golden Rule we talk about all the time. I told you if you cleaned up the dummy and the books, there would be a gift."

"Bullshit. That's not the reason. It's insurance."

"Insurance?"

"If I ever get out of here, I'd be the first one the police would come looking for. Everyone knew I liked her a lot. They probably thought the reason why she left the restaurant was because I was bothering her."

"The boring term for that these days is sexual harassment."

"That's a joke, coming from you. I don't want to talk about her anymore."

"Oh, come on. A little guy talk won't hurt. Think of this as a hunting lodge. You have a beer in your hand, the dogs are snoozing by the crackling fire . . ."

"You're forgetting the most important part. We can't get out. We're snowed in. We'll never get out."

"All the more reason to talk," he says. "Well?"

"I got as far as sending flowers to her once, with a note that said thanks for the time we had. I thought it was a date. She thought it was only a drink after work and a ride home. She probably had a good laugh about that and so did all her friends. Now everyone will think I killed her because she didn't want to have anything to do with me, then disappeared."

"I didn't say I killed her. Your theory is amusing, BobBee, but you forget I erased you from the world before I took this little gift for you."

"Of course you killed her. How else did you get the ankle thing?"

"Perhaps I paid her for it."

"She wouldn't have done that."

"Perhaps I paid her a lot," he says.

"And the pictures?"

"Stole them while she was gone at night, serving margaritas to the yachty set at Shilshole."

"No, you killed her and took everything. You killed that cat."

"So one follows the other, is that it?"

"It's what you want me to think."

"One can still drown unwanted kittens and not go to jail."

"What're you talking about? I wanted the cat."

"It wasn't yours, nor was it wanted."

"You're going to kill me. You've said so."

"I haven't yet. Really, I'm no more a murderer than a judge handing out a final sentence."

"She wouldn't take it off."

"Take what off?"

"The ankle thing."

"Oh, so you did do more than send her unwanted flowers. Bob, you dog!"

"I'm talking business, restaurant rules."

"I don't understand. You asked her and she wouldn't do it?"

"The ankle thing was a violation of our dress code. I told her she had to remove it, but she refused. I let her keep wearing it, hoping she would appreciate my lenience, make her realize I wasn't . . ."

"Such a stuffed shirt, a bean counter? That you might be a panty moistener after all?"

"She was mad at me so I decided to give her a break. A few weeks before I'd told her to get rid of the balloons a friend had sent to the restaurant for her birthday."

"Oh, BobBee. No wonder she thought you were a drip."

"Look, it was policy. I told her that. Just like with the ankle thing."

"What harm could it have done to let her wear that?"

"I let her. Didn't you hear what I said? You're the one talking about harm? I'm not the one who fucked her or raped her, whatever, who took the ankle thing off her for crying out loud."

"Do you like it? It's a totem."

"What's to like? I'm supposed to wear it or something?"

"It's hers. I could have taken anything of hers for you, but that seemed the most personal. When you talked about it with her, did she say why she wore it?"

"She said it was a personal thing, an expression. To remind herself there was a big, wide world out there, and that she could have part of it if she wanted. Something better than a cheap apartment building facing the Lake City Safeway Dumpster, and cocktailing, and the Chevette that kept breaking down. She was late a lot but it couldn't always have been the car."

"You knew where she lived, you followed her, prowled around."

"Whatever. Just go, I'm sick of you."

"I understand; you want to look at the pictures." He pauses. "By the way, I'll have something else for you next time."

"You're a regular Santa Claus."

"Santa's sack is getting full. It's time you were enlightened a bit. Enjoy the pictures. By the way, nice job on the apples. You can keep the crayons."

By now his leaving almost has a rhythm, it's so precise and measured. The door closes; the dead bolts sound: snick-snick. One beat, two. The light goes on.

I expect the pictures to be of someone else, or else not there. Another game, like the cat.

But there they are, in a manila folder, tilted up by the large apple on the tray. I reach into the mesh tunnel and snag the folder—and stop.

No. It's what he wants me to do. Look at pictures of a woman he killed. What I should do is rip them up in protest over what he must have done to her to get the pictures. But maybe they aren't of Kerrie Caldwell. Maybe he didn't kill her. Maybe the game is to make me think he did. What else is there to do here?

I also can't deny the obvious fact that I'm excited by the prospect of seeing them. If they are of Kerrie Caldwell.

I take the pictures out. And it's too late then because they're hers.

I take them to my corner of the room, feeling shitty and exhilarated, like some beast that's dragged a kill back to its lair.

Five pictures, three different positions. I recognize the guy who's fucking her. A bartender at the restaurant. Phil Quigley. I fired him for scamming free drinks for his buddies three weeks before Kerrie left.

No wonder she was mad.

In two pictures Kerrie's on top, her back arched, her head turned enough for a profile. The length of her dark hair surprises me. At work the rules are that the female servers have to put their hair up, keep it out of the way. Health codes. Quigley is digging his fingers into her ass. God, she does have a nice ass, just like I remember, when I'd walk through the bar and see her bending over a table, serving or clearing drinks. It's raised above him, far enough for me to see his cock. He was right. It's not that impressive. The relief is foolish, but I can't deny it, or a smugness. I suppose I have him to thank for that; I'd never have known otherwise.

Two other pictures have him on top, but they must have moved the camera, so it isn't just a picture of Quigley's backside. No, his eyes are closed, as if he's concentrating on not coming. Hers are open. She's smiling, self-conscious about the camera, her arms over her head. Her breasts have a sheen of sweat. They've been at it for a while. When? It's been hot in here lately but . . . when before? You don't sweat when you fuck in the winter. Her nipples are smaller, lighter colored than I'd imagined. The brief disappointment fades quickly. Beggars can't be choosers. But I don't feel like a beggar with this . . . treasure trove.

The last picture is shot from the same angle though Kerrie and Quigley are on their sides, him in back. He holds her top leg up. Kerrie the nutcracker. Her eyes are closed in this one. She's getting serious.

In two of the pictures, I can see the ankle thing. KDC. Dragging the world around, Katy?

I spread the pictures out, feel myself getting hard.

Something's going on here and it's not just the pictures. Or is it?

I feel frightened and excited at the same time, like I imagine a love affair would be if I were married. I can't get it out of my mind—why he did this, why he brought this . . . totem, he calls it.

He's done it for his own reasons, to show how ruthless and powerful he is. Right? But there's something else. He wants to share, to show off, too, doesn't he? Look what I've brought home. At once powerful but also the opposite. Like a boy, a kid, who wants approval, wants to please, wants someone to acknowledge his cleverness, his daring. I'm the only game in town. He's like me. He has no one else to share this triumph with. And it is a triumph, you betcha. He got to her, got into her apartment, got closer to her than I ever did, until now.

I'm rock hard now. As if I had gone out and gotten these things from her. It's crazy, because I'm the prisoner here, right? I don't believe how confident I feel, in control. Why would he want that?

I might have to squat over the painter's tray to shit. But who has to take it out? Who has to feed me?

He's my orderly, is what he is. I mention something, about a woman I liked, he acts on it, like one of my waiters.

There's hope, too. That maybe he was less careful than he boasted. Maybe the cops will figure it out, who did . . . this to Kerrie Caldwell. They'll come here and find me—with the best alibi a man could ever have.

So . . . so part of him did this for me. He said it was a gift. He can't help getting close. He talks to no one else but me. It's inevitable, what's happening. He has to get close to me, to do what he's going to do. If we get closer, like brothers, maybe he'll have second thoughts. That's the key: get closer.

Have an apple.

But he killed the cat.

Well, maybe it wasn't his cat. Maybe it was a stray. And it was only a cat. I'm a man, after all, right?

I glance at the pictures and smile, feeling warm and . . . safe. Abso-blooming-lutely safe. As if it were me who had gone to Kerrie Caldwell's apartment, done all that, and gotten away with it, careful to leave nothing behind, nothing that could lead the police here.

I unzip my pants and pull myself out—with some difficulty because I have a bigger hard-on than I've ever had before. Looking at the pictures, I stroke it, going from one picture to the other, my eyes landing lightly, silently as flies on a dinner table.

This is the best day I've had since I came here, the best day for a long while, even before I came here. Maybe the best is yet to come. He said he will have something else for me.

I stroke it harder.

Easy now, easy. Don't want to make Uncle Dickie sneeze too soon. It's been a while. Don't want to disappoint Kerrie, or myself. After all, it's taken a long time to get this close to her.

So I turn to get more comfortable for the business at hand—and then I see it.

I see her.

Kerrie Caldwell.

He's propped her up, naked, against the far wall in the shark cage, next to the door. She's facing me, her mouth open, her neck and jaw slack, the skin greenish red, one eye open and cloudy, the other hidden by a tangled wave of her hair. She looks as if she's taking a turn on a toboggan.

I scream but I don't hear it. Something must have come out because the light goes out. The door opens just enough to let a stab of light and laughter in.

"Take your pick, BobBee. But if I were you, I'd stick to the pictures."

Chapter 12

CONSTELLATION

We buried Dad at sea, in the Sound, with the Port Townsend bluff in the distance off the bow. We left Lake Union at eight a.m. and he was gone by mid-afternoon; it took us that long to get the sails up. I had to have that for my father.

A week had passed since he died, and the shock of that eclipsed everything, including what had happened at Shilshole. Those days were terribly weighted. But part of that, I know, was the expectation of seeing a police car pull up in front of the house. None came. And if Ellie and I wondered why, we didn't talk about it.

Twenty-two volunteers worked the *Constellation* that Sunday. Don Hollner, a friend of Dad's, was at the helm; the rest of us raised the four-thousand-square-foot mainsail.

I could have given my father's ashes to the garden at the house, as he did those of my mother. But I wanted to be away from that house, wanted to give Dad over to some other place. Anyway, there was part of Mom on the schooner.

On the way to the ship, we'd talked about Grandpa's death, how we were going to say good-bye to him on the boat, that he'd had a bad accident. We said Grandpa had chosen to have his body turned into ashes, but that his spirit was elsewhere, in heaven. We talked about constellations and Dad's bears.

"Grandpa can be another one in heaven if he wants, can't he?" Michael said.

A person's ashes have the texture of granulated sugar, and when

I leaned over the rail and slowly poured them out, the wind swirled them away, funneling them aft. I looked on the water, saw nothing but a blurry wake. Ellie's hand moved gently across my back. Michael was next to me, arms draped over the rail, his mother's hand hooking his belt to make sure he wouldn't fall.

No one said anything; the sails were benediction enough.

"What are we going to do with it?" Michael said, pointing at the urn I was holding like a football.

"We'll think of something," Ellie said.

"Can I steer the boat now, Dad?"

"Ask Don. He's over there at the wheel."

We watched him go tentatively up to Don at the great tilting wheel. I put the urn back in the box atop the lazaret housing. Ellie and I watched our son a while longer. He stood to one side of Don, one hand on a spoke of the wheel. He was only half as tall as the wheel and the binnacle. But I saw him for a moment anyway, as a young man, taller than Don, who was only a few years younger than my father.

We made our way to the bow. One of the crew had the watch there, but he left after we said we'd keep an eye out.

Ellie wanted to take a look at the figurehead Dad had made. She leaned over, one arm draped around the bowsprit. I snagged her belt, as she had Michael's, just in case. She had her look, straightened back up from the rail.

"Dad put a lock of Mom's hair inside the figurehead," I said.

"I never knew that."

"I never told you."

"What did your mother say about the lock of hair in the figurehead?"

"I'm not sure she ever knew."

"He told you, though."

"I walked in on him in his studio. There was literally a sheaf of hair tied up in a red bow, lying next to his mallets and chisels and drills, and I asked him about it, and he told me what she hadn't the day before, when she'd cut her hair so short, that she'd been diagnosed with MS. After we talked about what that meant, he told me what he was going to do with the locks of Mom's hair. He never said not to tell her, but at that age it seemed to me a weird thing for my father to be doing and I never told Mom, though I blabbed to Steven and he may have told her."

"Does it look like her . . . the figurehead?"

Sometimes I forgot that Ellie had never seen my mother. "Dad came pretty close, except for the hair. I just remember Mom's hair as always short. It's tough for me to see it as her, since Dad carved the hair long, windswept."

"Seems to be the thing for figureheads."

"He also painted it black, to contrast with the white hull, he said. Mom's hair was blond, like Steven's, before his turned brown."

We leaned together, Ellie and I, sharing the schooner's liveliness and each other's warmth. Despite the sun, it was cool out here on the Sound. The wind seemed to be kicking up. Ellie's long, coppery hair was wild and turbulent, the brightest thing on the *Constellation*.

"I wish I'd seen them together," Ellie said. "He always seemed so alone when we'd visit."

"That's the thing. He wasn't. I mean not really. He gave up so much. Ah, Jesus, Ellie, I loved him. We all did. Michael loved going there. Dad was talking about Michael's birthday. Why did it come to him so suddenly to give it up?"

"I wish I had the answer."

"He didn't even leave a note, Ell."

"Maybe that's the thing we'll never understand, how for some what seems like enough, what should be enough, just isn't for another."

"But that's just it. That day . . . we were as close as we've ever been. I don't mean what happened at Shilshole. He was working again. We were celebrating that. I just don't understand."

She let it go. And I did. I tried. We were holding hands but she was facing toward the deck now, watching Michael at the wheel, and I was looking out, at the *Constellation*'s wake, thinking of the other woman in my father's life.

Had he given up the Sara of the letters, too? Or was that part of the reason why he killed himself? I hadn't been to the house in a week, couldn't do it. But I was going to. I was going to read all the letters in that box Dad didn't want me to see.

Because facts can be lousy answers. The Kitsap County coroner ruled Dad's death a suicide.

My father had held that gun. I hadn't told Ellie that I had believed otherwise that night, leaving the police station. That belief was not fading as quickly as I'd hoped it would.

At the stern, Don bellowed out the command: we were going back.

Halfway home Michael fell asleep in the backseat.

"I think we have a sailor on our hands," Ellie said.

"Don thought so, too. He didn't get seasick. I was sure he would after he wouldn't take the Dramamine."

"He asked me again why Grandpa died, when you were below. If he was sick."

"What did you say?"

Ellie shrugged. "What we decided on before. That Grandpa had a bad accident and died.

To each generation its secrets.

"But I still think Michael somehow connected the sea-sickness and your dad." Ellie looked back at him. "No way were you going to get sick, were you, big guy."

"I can't think of what else it could be," I said. "He used to get so carsick when he was younger. I mean, it's not like we're a family immune to motion sickness. Steven wouldn't get near anything that floated. He would get woozy just standing on a dock and watching boats toss and shift. But get him in the woods, hiking, and he'd set a pace you couldn't match."

"How about your dad?"

"We were never out together in rough weather on the *Constellation* or any other boat for that matter. But I doubt he was prone to getting green in the gills."

"So how do you know then?"

"Well, once, before Mom got MS, we went to the Puyallup Fair and they couldn't get me to go on any of the rides, not after Steven spent five minutes on something called the Jolly Wobbler—"

"Now there's a name that'll empty your belly."

"It emptied Steven's all right. Mom and Dad took turns watching us while the other had some fun. They both came off as fresh as when they went on. I remember asking Dad if I'd be able to go on the rides when I was a grown-up. They both laughed at that, though at the time I didn't quite know why. Then Dad suddenly got serious and said, 'Sure you will, Paul, both of you, any goddamn ride you want, a rocketship to the moon, if that's where you set your sights.' It was the first time I'd ever heard him swear when he wasn't angry."

When we got home, I went ahead, telling Ellie I had to run to the head—a white lie that left her gathering up our day gear and son. But I couldn't find the words to tell her the real reason, one that had occurred to me minutes before we pulled into the driveway of our darkened home. I wanted to check the house first before I brought my family inside. I suppose I could have mentioned that, how I wanted to turn the lights on first. A normal enough concern. But it was more than that. There was that half hour on Bainbridge.

How could you decide to take your life in half an hour?

That house had been a haven and it was no longer. We'd been away from ours for a long day. I didn't trust the darkened house, or the time away.

I quickly checked all the rooms, even the ones upstairs, turned a few lights on, then went back outside.

"That was a long one," she said, coming up the front steps with Michael in her arms, our bags draped by their straps over a shoulder.

"Let me take him," I said, and hefted him into my arms. Ellie was strong for her size, but Michael was too heavy for Ellie to carry far. In another year he'd be too big even for me to give him "carry-yous"—what he'd always called them since he could talk.

I carried him into his bedroom, took only his shoes off, and turned on his bedside light. He stirred only a little, even when I gave him a kiss on his forehead, about the only time he'd let either Ellie or me do that. His hair was wild from the wind, stiff with salt. He smelled like the sea.

When I came out of his room, Ellie was by the living room table, mail in one hand and something else in her other.

"This was in the mailbox," she said, and held up the wallet I'd lost a week ago in the woods above Shilshole.

Chapter 13

▲

MISSING

The next morning, after taking Michael to his summer day camp, I called the only real estate agency on Bainbridge Island that had not already contacted me about the house and set up an appointment with a Meg Sorensen for three p.m.

I got to the house on Bainbridge just before noon. I hadn't been there since the night. The heat had built up inside; the day was pushing ninety, way over Seattle's usual summer day. I kept the front door open to cool things down as I walked around to all the rooms, including the bedroom where it had happened. They'd stripped the bed down to the mattress. The bloodstain was shaped roughly like an hourglass.

I poured a double shot of Oban, sat down in Dad's chair in the living room and sipped the whisky, and stared at the broken glass from a week before. I didn't feel like cleaning that up before the real estate agent arrived. Or covering the mattress. What did it matter? She knew. There would only be the delicate matter of what to say to people who might know that Charles Sinclair had killed himself in the master bedroom. And for those who didn't know, the house would be like any other, safe, waiting to be filled with new history.

Just one shot.

The Bainbridge police couldn't get a trace on the gun. Wherever Dad got it, he probably did so after Steven disappeared. But whatever he was scared of, it certainly wasn't the crime rate on Bainbridge Island.

And if you had to lose a wallet, Seattle was the best place in the country. A magazine did an article about that once.

Whoever returned mine left the twenty bucks there, too.

And took the cracked plastic sleeves with the photos of Ellie and Michael.

Who would take pictures of people they didn't know? Ellie had shrugged it off. What did it matter, so long as the wallet was returned? Maybe the sleeves fell out.

Why couldn't I accept that?

This afternoon Meg Sorensen would tell me, softly, that the house would sell, though most likely to someone not from Bainbridge or Seattle. Every house had ghosts, its tragedies, and if you didn't know about them, they didn't exist.

But if you knew about them?

There was another possibility. Maybe the person who returned the wallet knew.

Knew what?

Ellie and Michael.

Oh, Jesus, Paul, you're looking behind again. Steven again. You're thinking, who else would take the pictures? So he could see how the little guy's turning out? And an up-to-date photo of Ellie?

Nothing else fell out of the wallet, so why just the photos? Who the hell else would leave the cash and take photos of strangers?

Sittin' high, Paul, sittin' high.

I wandered aimlessly through this house of ghosts. The place had gone to hell since Steven disappeared and even before that, when Mom's body decided to do what it wanted to do. The room where she had had her indoor garden needed a lot of work. She called it the Eden room, and Steven and I would bring in our toy soldiers to play with among all those plants, pots, the waterfall and lily pool.

I thought again about what happened to Mom. How she got to the Agate Pass bridge from the Bloedel Reserve. Sure, she was in remission, and it isn't all that far, but still, for a woman in her condition? What was Dad doing after he left her with her crutches by the pond? He should have stayed, but Mom was such an independent woman, she wanted to be alone in a place she loved, to both savor the reprieve and wonder how long it would last.

That was it, wasn't it?

Time was running out before the real estate agent was due to arrive. She would tell me the house would sell, easy: waterfront property and the good Bainbridge schools to lure some young family from California or New York, trying to escape the millennium blues. That's why Dad moved us all there, too, the escape factor. There wasn't much time left to find that box of letters. Maybe one of those letters had pushed Dad over the edge. Maybe all of us were a lot closer to the edge than we thought, always that half hour away.

I got up to go to Dad's bedroom.

The letters had to be there. He'd scuffled the box in that direction down the hall while I was on the phone to Ellie. Then a little clean-up for the real estate agent. Tonight, Ellie and I would read those letters, and we'd find out that "Bellingham Sara" had been the love of his life—before or after Mom, or both?—and maybe the latest letter had been a Dear John or one from a friend, telling Dad she'd died.

Something so personal and private *had* to be in this room. I searched everywhere. I went to the other rooms. Nothing.

Where were the letters?

I'd been out back awhile. Long enough for him to have destroyed the letters. If he'd decided he was going to do it, he might have destroyed the letters, to keep forever from me and Steven the secret he had kept for years.

But what would it matter after he was gone? What was in those letters that he didn't want me to see even after his death?

Could Dad have ripped them up and flushed them?

If he had, he did a perfect job. I found not even the smallest shred of envelope in the bathroom, nothing sticking to the insides of the toilet.

The fireplace?

There was no residue of ash or soot. Just dirt, black smudges. Not enough proof of burning. If Dad had done that, swept the hearth clean, wiped it with a rag, why wouldn't he have also cleaned up the nearby glass? He would have had the broom and dustpan right in his hand.

There was only one other possibility.

Someone had taken the box of letters. A keepsake?

The same one who . . . who what? Forced Dad to shove the gun in his mouth and pull the trigger? Who could possibly have made Dad do that? But that had to be the case. If this someone had done it himself—wearing gloves, of course—there would have been *some* evidence of a struggle. The killer then wraps Dad's hand around the gun? That wouldn't work. The prints wouldn't be clean, proof that Dad didn't fire the gun. The recoil of the gun smudges prints, and the prints *were* smudged. Then there was the positive trace-metal test on Dad. He fired the gun. So . . .

So it was crazy. The letters had to be here.

Why would a . . . killer take those letters? Who could want someone else's old love letters? Was there something in those letters that could make someone want to kill my father? What had he done that he wanted to keep secret from me? And Steven. Or did Steven know? Was that the reason he disappeared?

I went into Dad's room again, to look again. You keep secrets like that close to you. Nothing. Not a damn thing. I shouted at the walls.

That's when the real estate agent saw me, facing the far wall, yelling and swearing.

"Excuse me . . . Mr. Sinclair? "

I took my time getting up. The damage was done. She was probably already thinking how she was going to tell this one at the office. *He was slapping the floor with his bare hand, the one with some blood on it, bellowing out, "Where are they? Where are they?"*

"I see you're . . . busy here," she said. "Am I early? "

"No, you're on time. I was . . . I lost track."

"Well, pardon me for barging in. But I saw the truck and called out. I guess you didn't hear me."

She was short, plump with yellow hair cut short in a fashionable way. That and the red in her business suit made me want to squint. Maybe brightness sells houses. I'm sure she had a nice big smile to go along with her professional sunniness, but I didn't get much of it. I couldn't blame her. She stayed where she was in the doorway, watching me tuck in my shirttail. She saw my filthy hands. The room was a mess.

I suppose I could have played it for a laugh: Dennis the Menace getting caught by Mrs. Wilson this time. But Meg Sorensen obviously wanted to get the hell out, and hesitated only because that might mean walking away from a waterfront property sale. She was nervous. Maybe it was the streaks of blood on my right hand. Was she wondering if this was the room where Charles Sinclair killed himself a week ago?

"I shouldn't have called you this morning," I said. "I'll get back to you at a better time."

She nodded quickly. "Please do that. I'll, uh, leave a card on the kitchen table on my way out. I'm sorry, Mr. Sinclair."

I left shortly after she did. I didn't look any more for the box of letters. They weren't there. Or if they were, it was someplace I would never find.

Chapter 14

GOING AWAY

I tried to get some work done at the shop after coming back from Bainbridge, but it was no good. I just couldn't concentrate. Later that evening, while Ellie was off playing softball, Michael and I went to the car wash on Leary Avenue to do the pickup.

I could have done the job more thoroughly in half the time and expense, but that wasn't the point. Someday, before I knew it, Michael would be going off to wash his own car before a Saturday night date.

We'd just finished the waxing and pulled the dripping truck ahead to an empty stall in the vacuuming area.

At first I didn't see the dog. They were on the other side of the glossy black Land Rover parked next to my truck. Michael had just closed the truck's passenger-side door. The dog bolted around the front of the vehicle, stopped at the last second by the lazy command of the dog's owner nearby—a guy with a forty-dollar haircut, tan slacks, and a green polo shirt.

But the dog still snarled viciously a few yards away from Michael, who was pressed up against the truck, terrified.

I rushed around, stepping in front of him. The owner of the Land Rover merely glanced at me, said something I couldn't hear over the noise of the vacuum hose. He snaked the hose, smacking the dog back a little, but it wasn't enough, not nearly.

His girlfriend, or wife, came around the car, cuffed the dog. It slunk back to the fence with her. She leaned against it and began doing her nails even as the dog began barking again, coming closer once more. She smiled at me, in a surreptitious, flirting way, as if my interest were in her long, tanned legs and filled-out Wimbledon T-shirt. She was oblivious to the dog's behavior.

I like dogs, but an unchained rottweiler, snapping bared teeth and dripping spittle is something else. Forty-dollar Haircut was bringing the vacuum hose to the rear seats of his car.

"Michael," I said, "go on and hop in the truck."

"Are we going now?"

"Nope."

I went over to Haircut, had to shout so he could hear me over the vac and the barking rott. "Could you please keep the dog inside the car? He's scaring my boy."

If anything, the guy was more tanned than the woman. He glanced at the snarling dog as if it were sleeping peacefully. "How am I supposed to clean the car with him inside?" he shouted back, shaking his head as if I were an idiot.

I took a deep breath. "He's not supposed to be loose."

"I'll be done in a few minutes," Haircut said.

"No, that's not the point."

"Look, she's over there, keeping an eye on him. He won't do anything. What's your problem?" He took off his sunglasses. His right eye pointed off toward the Red Hook brewery down Leary. His pants matched the car mats, but that wasn't the least of this guy's problems.

"I told you what the problem is," I said. "Your dog isn't under control. So it seems to me you have three choices." I stared at his crazy eye, not the other. "You can put your dog in the car, you can leash him like you're supposed to do. Or I can go over to the attendant and have him tell you to do that."

By now others in the car wash were looking on.

Haircut glanced at his dog, and for a moment it seemed a close thing; possibly he would give another command and I'd have a face full of rottweiler.

"Fuck it," he said, and threw down the vac hose, yelled out two names—Laurie and Josie. The dog scrambled into the Land Rover first, then the woman. I resisted the urge to ask him which one was the dog.

As I walked back to the truck, the rott was at the back window, still snarling, scrabbling at the glass with claws and teeth, smearing it with slobber. As Haircut got into the Land Rover, he screamed out, "You were right about one thing. He thinks you're shit."

He gave me the finger as he sped out the exit. Brave fellow, Haircut.

Michael and I cleaned the truck. We didn't talk about it then, the vac was too loud, but as we were leaving, he said, "That dog was mean."

"He probably wasn't born that way."

"Is it because that man had funny eyes?"

"No, it's because he's probably been mean to the dog."

"You looked like you were going to fight him, Dad."

"Well, I was upset, sure. But fighting him wouldn't have solved anything."

"Your hands were shaking. Were you scared?"

"I suppose I was." I tried a smile. "That was a scary dog."

"Mom says it's better to walk away."

"She's right. People get into fights mostly over stupid things, and if you walk away, it just means you're smarter than the other guy."

Except if the guy's trying to kill you and just harmed a little girl.

"So . . . I mean, what if you can't walk away?"

"If you can't walk away?" I repeated.

"Yeah."

"If you've tried to use your words and smarts about it?"

"Uh-huh."

"Then, Michael, you make sure you hit the other guy harder than he hits you."

Ellie had a great softball game and I had the car wash, so that night we talked more about her game than the bozo with the rott.

She sat in the chair under the N. C. Wyeth print of *Robinson Crusoe*. I was on the opposite couch by the front window. Across the street, in the last of the light, Erickson was putting away garden tools in the shed by his garage. The front door was open to help cool off the house, so we could hear his poodle yapping about something.

Ellie asked me about the real estate agent on Bainbridge. "You were quiet on that at dinner."

"She left quick."

"Bainbridge waterfront property isn't supposed to do that."

"I didn't have much chance to clean up. And then there's the fact that she knew what happened at the house."

"Whoever buys it doesn't have to."

"We set up another time."

"You look for that box of your dad's letters?"

"Didn't find them. Either he destroyed them or some kid ten years from now will be looking for a Lego piece and find them in a place I never thought to look. I'll never know if there was something in those letters that pushed him over."

Ellie looked away, drinking her iced tea. It occurred to me that maybe she wasn't even sure if there *were* any letters. She'd never seen them. They only existed because I'd told her about them. Just as . . .

Just as what? Just as you told her you were right next to Emma when she slipped through the fence, and not twenty yards away, with your back turned to her?

Ellie asked me if I really wanted to sell the house. "We'd be giving up the Bainbridge schools for Michael."

"I can't live in the house, Ell."

"No. No, I don't suppose it would be the best for you . . . for any of us, really. You want to stay here?"

"Not especially. We'll get some other place, Ell. But how about Ireland for a year first? We've talked about that before."

"Not when we were very sober."

"How does this sound? We rent a cottage for six months, a year. You could research that novel you talked about years ago, about Grania O'Malley, who ran that pirate fleet out of Clare Island. Wasn't she some sort of Gaelic sorority sister to Queen Elizabeth?"

"It's been done."

"Not by someone as good as you."

"You're sweet and I'm still unpublished."

"Think about it."

She finished her tea, put the glass aside. "So what would Michael be doing all this time?"

"The Irish schools are better than ours. Don't worry, we'd leave before we had to emigrate."

"You're not serious."

"I am. We should shuffle the cards."

"Speaking of cards, did Michael show you the one he got in the mail today?"

"No, he didn't."

"I'm not surprised. Nice handmade card, though, with a picture of apples. No name. Michael said no one *he* knew *still* used crayons. Poor guy. A secret admirer in the first grade."

"Secret admirer?"

"One of those grade-school phenomenons—the mash note."

"It was anonymous?"

"Anonymous."

"What did it say?"

"Jesus, you sound like it was a subpoena."

"Ell, I just asked what it said."

"It said, 'You're the apple of my eye! Happy 7th, Michael!' So I figure her father must have written it for her."

"It said that, 'You're the apple of my eye'?"

"That's what it said—hey, what's the problem here, honey? It's a common expression."

"A little early for his birthday, isn't it?"

"What, a week?" Ellie tried to lighten me up. "Hey, she's hot to trot, all right?"

"Okay, hot to trot takes it. We were talking about Ireland and Grania O'Malley."

"She went though two husbands, you know," Ellie said with an arch to her brow. "Or was it three?"

"Think about it, okay?"

"I already am. I'm thinking about what we did in the middle of Doon Fort, in the middle of that black lake, in the middle of that afternoon rain."

"Hot to trot?"

"Takes one to know one," Ellie said, grinning.

I got up first and took her hand and with the other turned down the lamp to its lowest illumination. As we left the living room, we paused by Michael's door, to listen for his breathing, as we always do before going up, even though Ellie couldn't hear it unless she was in the room. Her hand tightened over mine, tugging gently but insistently.

Sometimes we're playful, closing the door to the stairs and going up. A little race with her scampering upstairs first and maybe I'll smack her bottom to get her to squeal. Sometimes it's deliberate. Or one of us is pissed off at the other for some reason and there's no way, not tonight. Sometimes it's just going up the stairs to go to sleep.

Tonight we went up and didn't even light the Aladdin lamp—a wedding gift from her sister, who still preferred to be married only to the sixties. I had to slow her down, because I'd decided on the ferry from Bainbridge to do something she didn't know about yet and I didn't want to hurry now. She throttled down and we took our time undressing each other and she leaned back, at the edge of the bed. I took her there, sliding into her silk.

Ellie has skin of an Asian smoothness and, after so much of the summer, a color and sheen of koa, and I almost stopped to light the lamp so I could see her, but she wouldn't have forgiven me that pause.

Her hips rose and she pulled me down, all the way, pressing my head to her breasts, her nipples, as gently as she'd claimed my hand before. She loved me to coax them softly, then hard, and I did. She flung her arms back to the rails. Sometimes she liked me to tie her hands to the bed, behind her, but it was too late for that, too. She was lovely, just so beautiful, and I told her so before I kissed her for the longest time as our tongues danced. A light came on in a neighbor's yard, and she laughed and murmured something about "the eye" turning it on for us. I could see not only the whiteness of her smile but also the sheen of her flesh now, broken only by the cesarean scar.

I tasted the salt of her, the slickness of her, all over, as we moved together, until she shuddered. I kissed more of her and we shifted to our sides and she tucked her leg in and over, and I stayed with her as her buttocks rose, a leavening that accelerated our lovemaking into fucking.

We were the engine of the world right then, just us, running hard, sweating, and noisy. My hands gripped her flesh. Hers had found the arching bed rail. Her head was half buried in a pillow, muffling her cries and her urgings. One hand flew back and I caught it, a quick bird in flight, and it stayed in mine until it twisted free.

I lifted the wet strands of hair from the nape of her neck and blew, feeling her shiver. She took one of my hands and held it tightly, and with my other I caressed her contours as far as I could reach, again and again, kissing her neck, nuzzling her shoulders, licking the sweat and heat from her, even as a breeze came through the window, to cool us a little. We hadn't even turned on the fan.

The light from outside flicked off, taking the copper of her hair with it, and we had a laugh about the timing of that, as if the neighbors knew, and maybe they did. We weren't much for quiet, never had been.

"Remember the box you gave me after our first date?" she said. "Nothing in it but the wind-up plastic sailor and the note that said, 'I can't fill this with jewelry, so handsprings will have to do.' "

"A shameless knockoff. I figured if it worked for Charles MacArthur on Helen Hayes, it'd work for me, even if you knew about the peanuts and emeralds."

"Well, I did and it did."

We nestled together on our sides for a long time, slick and fetid, until the heat trapped between us and the whispers—what we always said to each other afterward—had finally escaped. I didn't, couldn't, move from her because this was the furthest I could ever get from keeping a secret, from what I hadn't shared with her, what I hadn't told her. She didn't know I'd found Emma's unfinished jewelry box, that I had been working on it again when my father came in.

It's beautiful. It's a shame to keep it hidden. . . .

You're always making boxes, Stephen once told me. *You'd have the soul of a coffin-maker if you weren't such a flake.*

"I'm going away for a few days tomorrow," I said.

"I thought so. Ireland was a stalking horse."

"I meant that."

"Where?"

"I don't know." The lie came out softly. "I'm just going to get in the truck and drive."

"You should." I could feel her breath on my shoulder. "You should," she said again, almost as if she knew. "Ireland, too. All of us. In the spring."

"It'll have to be a place where I can do some work. Michael and I can't traipse around ruins and castles all the time."

"Sure you can. How else am I going to get any writing done in a tiny Irish cottage?"

I turned and kissed her. "In the spring, then."

I fell asleep thinking of some place in Donegal or Kerry, where no one would know where we lived, where the country lanes and hillside tracks were so empty you knew no one was behind you, so you wouldn't have to turn around, but even if you did, no one would be there.

If Ellie fell asleep too with thoughts of Ireland and finding another Doon Fort, at least she was safe from these other, secret ones, including the coincidences of apples in two anonymous notes to our children, one to Emma, who was almost as old as our son was now. And my wife might not have fallen asleep either if I'd told her the last words of my father's life, the reason why I was going away.

THE CAGE: 4

"Smells like a whorehouse in here," he says this time. "Or maybe a doghouse." He laughs.

"It's about time you replaced the filter in the machine."

"Wouldn't be worth it now, BobBee."

"Is that why you're in a good mood?"

"It was a good day at the office, or should I say car wash. God, I hate mean dogs who scare little kids."

"You wouldn't know what a whorehouse smells like. What did you do with Kerrie?"

"Grumpy, are we?" he says, not answering me. "Scabs on your dick?"

The air purifier hums. He shifts in the cage. I lean back against the wall, hands behind my neck, waiting for him to shine the flashlight, so he can see me, not as a crouching animal waiting for scraps.

"I've been practicing."

"Practicing what?"

"Not having anything left to lose."

"I hear the violins."

Practicing being your equal, I want to tell him. Go ahead, tell him: I don't even know your name, but you bring me my food, you bring me gifts. You have no one else to talk to. You have no one else but me.

Instead I say, "You left the door open a crack. Usually you keep it shut after you come in. You've changed the music; no more of

*that soporific classical crap. You're speaking faster, like you're ex-
cited about something."*

"Soporific? BobBee, I'm impressed."

"You left a Webster's Third *in here.*"

"Ah, the budding jailhouse lawyer."

*"That's an oversight on your part. I could probably crack a hole
in the wall with the dictionary, or fracture your skull if I got the
chance."*

"Too bad you won't have nearly enough time to get your degree."

"You'll be an inspiration to me up to the very end."

"And you're eating the apples, too!" *he says.* "What a week I'm
having!"

*I hear him drink something, only a sip, barely registering over
the thrumming air purifier.* "What's that?" *I ask him. It's another
change. He's never done that before. Or maybe I just didn't hear
him before. There was a time when I wouldn't have heard the sip.*

He slides the cup—glass?—in the tunnel, next to the tray of food.
"Try some." *He shines the light.*

*As I cross the room, one of the glossy pictures of Kerrie Cald-
well sticks to my foot and I have to shake it off, as if it were a dangling turd.*

*I pick up the glass, back away, but he follows me with the light,
which moves up and down, twitching, betraying his eagerness for
me to drink the booze.*

"Go ahead," *he urges, but I keep on sniffing at the rim.*

"What's the matter," *he says,* "you don't like single-malts?"

"There's probably poison in it."

"Don't be ridiculous. Think, for God's sakes! What would be
the purpose now to act like some crazy old woman and poison
you."

*"You haven't told me anything, so don't talk ridiculous to me—
for God's sakes."*

"I thought you were practicing not having anything left to lose."

*"For all I know still, you're just some guy who likes to keep
people in cages like hamsters and then poison them slowly and
watch them die slowly. Why else would you want to share this
Scotch with me; and eagerly, too, I might add."*

"I'm not eager, not at all." *His defensiveness keys another vic-*

*tory for me. "Here, give the damn cup back to me. I should have
known you wouldn't enjoy the Laphroaig."*

*"What a little boy you are." It feels good to laugh and so does
the fiery Laphroaig, but neither is as good as getting to him.*

*I toss the cup at the cage. The cup rattles off the wood some-
where in the dark, loudly enough so that he knows I drank it all.*

*Of course he's right, but even so, as the seconds pass, I wait for
my stomach to seize up, my dummy's heart to race toward the
dummy crash wall. Strangely, there's no fear. Maybe I just don't
care anymore. Now or later, what's the difference? There's something else, though: the aftertaste of victory. I feel I've stepped up to
a threshold—and gone beyond. Or am I just imagining the impor-
tance of his wanting to share something with me? It's only another
of his gifts.*

*I thank him. As soon as I say it, I wish I hadn't, but it's too late.
Is there a name for that? Thanking someone one minute and wanting to kill him the next?*

"You're welcome," he says. "From one little boy to another."

*We're both silent for a long time. There's only the hum of the
Sears machine, and the livelier music from downstairs. It isn't angry or frustrated silence. It seems more like the kind I always
hoped for, the kind where there's no need for words. Our quiet has
a foxhole weight to it, not that I'd know anything about that either.
I'm not queer and I don't think he is either, but . . . something has
passed between us, two people who only have each other, and it isn't
just a shared cup of expensive whisky.*

"You're not the first this has happened to," he says.

"You've brought others in here before me?"

"Two others."

"You killed them?"

There is a silence, as if he's weighing a confession.

*"You know I did, yet you persist with hope; it's in your voice.
An admirable thing."*

"Oh, and that makes my week, that you find me so satisfactory."

*"I do. I didn't kill either of the others in the way you will die,
however. I had to get rid of Chris because of Paul's inexcusable
carelessness. Emma died, so I had to start all over. Paul never paid
any consequences for that death, either, but he will soon, along
with Ellie-belle."*

"How dare a little girl waste your time like that."

He ignores my sarcasm again. *"You haven't asked about the second one I brought here."*

"Because it's just words. You say anything you want. All I have is what you tell me."

"It's more than you ever had before in your life. But words? Was Kerrie-the-Ass just words?"

"All right, tell me then. You want to."

He pauses, annoyed at my casualness. He'd like to tell me to go to hell if I don't want to know, but he wants to tell me.

My round.

"It was Steven, Paul's brother. A remarkable man, whose presence here still lingers."

"I see. I'm some sort of junior varsity victim, is that it? Not fit to shine Steven's shoes, huh?"

"My, sensitive, aren't we?"

"So where are his scratchings on the wall?"

"You are his heir, in a way."

"Sure, a cozy family, all of us. Is that what you're getting at? You're wasting your time."

"Nothing is ever wasted, BobBee, not even this."

"Not for you it isn't. This is your show."

"I was talking about you, but I've been where you are now."

"What do you mean?"

"That I was in a closet once," he says. *"When people say they can smell fear, what they mostly mean is they can smell someone who's pissed in his pants. And after I pissed in mine, I took the first thing my hand grabbed in the dark, to stuff into my mouth, so I couldn't cry out, so my cries wouldn't be heard. It was a dirty sock. My father's. I kept my hands over my ears. The radio in the kitchen was on. I heard that. Someone had turned it on. Maybe my mother, so I wouldn't hear the other things. She was the one who screamed at me to get in the closet and be quiet."*

"What was it? What are you talking about?"

He goes on, and he doesn't hear me, or pretends not to.

"Everyone else was outside. If I hadn't been in the closet, I wouldn't be here. You wouldn't be here, either. I waited a long time before going out. During that time I found things in the closet, things a boy's mother and father wouldn't want him to see. And I

remember thinking it must be bad out there *because there are things* in here *they wouldn't want me to see. Maybe those things saved my life, too, keeping me in the closet until it was safe to come out. It wasn't, though. But you can't stay in a closet forever."* He laughs, so suddenly I start, as if someone's just pricked me with a pin. *"You have to leave the closet sometime, don't you, BobBee?"*

"I want to."

"Don't you?" he says as if he didn't hear me. How can he not hear me?

"Yes," I say louder.

"Even if you're dead."

"I don't know why it has to be that way. You haven't told me."

"Why you have to die?"

"Yes."

"I wasn't going to tell you. It didn't seem necessary, but it does now. It's strange how you have become the least predictable part of the plan when I thought you'd be the most."

"I want to know."

"You still have to die."

I say nothing to that. There's nothing to say.

"I'll tell you after I get back. I'm going away for a few days."

He leaves, quickly it seems, closes the door, and I squint my eyes, ready for him to turn on the light as he always does. But he doesn't bolt the door. The light doesn't come on.

What's he doing? The routine has never varied up to now.

He returns in a few minutes.

"More Kerrie?" I ask.

He laughs. *"How much more of her do you want?"* Then, slowly, seriously: *"Take care of what I'm going to give you. I'm trusting you. Can I trust you, BobBee?"*

The question so astounds me all I can do is repeat what he just asked me.

"That's what I said," he says. *"They're very important to me."*

Trust me? After all he's done? If I were free now, I'd kill him or die trying. But there's only one answer I can give him. Because he knows my hope: the closer we get, the better my chance he won't kill me. I've been reading all right, more than I ever have before. I feel that things are going out of control, but how can that happen when you're stuck in one place?

I know it's easier to kill if you demonize the intended. A killer needs striking distance. But the question remains, just how far or near is that distance? The price of that hope? Bringing me closer, dissolving who I am. That's his kick, getting the answer he wants from a man who's been kept like an animal, in a cage. A closet.

But who's playing the more dangerous game?

"BobBee?"

"If whatever you want to give me is so important, how come you're doing it?"

"Because it's part of what you want to know. Your answer, please."

"All right. I'll take care of it."

"See that you do, otherwise I will kill you very, very slowly."

"Sooner or later—what does it matter?"

"Oh, it would matter."

"I said I'd do it."

"And I believe you will, if only because you think I'm softening, that you still have a chance." He laughs. "Maybe you do."

I hear him sliding something into the tunnel.

"So what is it?"

"Another gift. The first look at these. I'm a busy boy so your eyes will have to be mine until I can savor them at my leisure. I'll be back in a few days."

He leaves. The door closes, the bolts ram shut. Snick-snick. *The lights go on.*

I kneel down at the tunnel. On the tray is a wooden box, which I pull out.

It's full of letters.

As if I can live on letters while he's gone.

PART TWO

FIRES

Chapter 15

FAIRHAVEN

I got to Bellingham, a city of fifty-five thousand, ninety miles north of Seattle, about eleven a.m. Our run of hot and sunny weather continued. Southern California was getting more than enough rain to make the news. El Niño on steroids again?

Bellingham's timbering past hadn't quite been replaced by the business of Canadian shoppers. Clear-cuts scabbed the hills to the east. Logging trucks still rumbled through the town along North State Street to the Georgia-Pacific mill on the waterfront.

As always, the fashionable neighborhoods held the heights. The city had its share of turn-of-the-century mansions—old by Northwest standards—where smug Victorian barons once had their choice of views: the gritty source of their wealth below, or the beauty of the San Juan Islands beyond the bay. Some of the mansions were bed-and-breakfasts now.

I'd been to Bellingham a lot—mostly to play rugby on soggy, narrow fields against the local teams—but also because of the *Constellation*, which ran its San Juan charters out of Fairhaven, the city's historic district, its sixties Brigadoon.

That's where she was . . . Sara. In Fairhaven. That's where she still ran her café, Pickles. It was still around. Before leaving Seattle I'd made the call. But I didn't talk to her. This wasn't something that could be done long-distance.

I parked the truck half a block away, killed the engine.

It was hot in the truck and I was sweating and nervous. I had no idea what to say to my father's lover. There was only one way to find out.

The lunch rush had not begun yet, just a couple in one of the six booths and an older guy nursing a cup of coffee and a thick, tattered Tom Clancy paperback he obviously hadn't bought in the adjacent bookstore. He glanced at me as he stuffed a couple of muffins into his jacket pocket. Behind the ten-stool counter a waitress was stacking coffee cups. I asked her if I could see Sara.

"Sara?" she said.

Ten minutes later I was back in my truck. There was no "Sara" at Pickles. I'd only read the letter once, and quickly. But she was here. She had to be. The cabooses were here. A young man was checking his wallet before entering a jewelry shop housed in a caboose across the street. Fairhaven had two of them, and three old passenger cars, brought in to add color to the district. They bordered an entire block.

Was that where Dad got the idea for the caboose for Steven and me?

It wasn't a bust. After all, I couldn't really expect to go back all the years and walk into the place and find . . . Sara pouring coffee refills for the customers. A lot could have changed since 1980.

She was going to come to the wedding. She'd bought that dress. It would have been a suitable time for my father to introduce her, bring her into the family. He hadn't, and there was a reason why he hadn't.

I decided to check Whatcom County records, to find out whom the present owner of Pickles had bought the place from, and keep going until I saw the name Sara and an address for starters.

A thumping on my side window startled me. The guy doing the knocking was not quite skid row but close enough. He looked like the Tom Clancy reader who'd been stuffing the café rolls in his pocket. But he was tapping the window with the stump of a forearm.

Under an old Mariners cap, the one with the upside-down trident, his thin hair was streaked with gray, shiny with grease. Crumbs speckled his stringy beard.

He waved the stump in a circle, then stopped. The skin at the end of his arm was puckered, like the casing of a sausage.

I rolled down the window. "Yes?"

"It's Bowers."

He said it so softly it was hard to hear him, even though I was close enough to smell the coffee, the best thing about his breath.

"You're looking for Sara. Her last name is Bowers. I heard you in there."

As I got out of the truck, he backed away, swiping at the fine red scratching on his flattened nose.

"Sara Bowers, the woman who used to own that place?"

He sniffed, in then out. "That's what I'm telling you." He stuffed his right stump into a pocket of his jeans, not wanting anything to do with a left-handed shake.

"Name's Jimmy Trinket. Used to be longer."

"I'm Paul Sinclair."

"How come you don't know the last name of someone you're looking for?"

"It's a long story."

"Never heard of one that isn't. Look, I just followed you out to save you some trouble."

"She's . . . dead?"

"Couldn't say one way or the other, but she disappeared long ago enough so she probably is."

I leaned back against the truck. *What now? What the hell now?*

Jimmy Trinket scratched his beard. The greater surprise at that moment seemed not the fate of Sara Bowers after so many years, but Trinket's single, immaculate hand, so clean it seemed like a lighter shading of his skin. The nails were trimmed. He wore rings on all four fingers.

"How do you know about her?"

He shrugged. "I been going to that place for a long time."

"When did she disappear?"

" 'Bout maybe fifteen years ago. Police came around and asked me a few questions, but not many. Not many women couldn't get away from a one-armed man they want to. Well, maybe, guy's got a gun. But he wants to do anything else, drive a car, take her some- place, and you know, do what the creeps all do, he's gotta put the damn thing down sometime."

I nodded toward the café. "Look, can I buy you some lunch? I'd . . ."

He shook his head. "I had my charity for the day. They let me come in just so long as I'm out before the lunch crowd. It isn't so bad, even if some of the prettiest girls there wear those shit-kickers. Then again I suppose if the owner didn't let them do that, most likely he wouldn't be the type to pass out free coffee and day-old Danish."

"Do you know where she used to live?"

Trinket pointed, flourishing the immaculate hand, rings bright in the midday glare. His stump was still buried in his pocket. "Way up the hill on Mill Street. Smallest house on the block and the biggest yard. Kiddie-cornered from the school up there. The place is blue now. Sara kept it white. People live there now never take off the damn Christmas lights."

"What did she look like?"

"She was a beauty, all right. Long black hair, green eyes. She once told me someone wanted her to do some catalogue work for Sears, but she never did, which surprised me because it seemed easy money and she had her little girl to take care of."

He looked up the hill. "That's not why I remember her, not because she was pretty. Whenever I stuffed my other hand in my pocket, she'd look at me such a way that damned if I didn't always pull it out."

I thanked him as he left. "Nah," he said. "You did me the favor. I hadn't thought of Sara in years." He waved his stump and was gone.

Sara Bowers's old house looked like a late-forties veteran's starter. The lot seemed bigger than it really was because the house was so small and sandwiched in between larger ones. The corner house blocked the view of the water. But Sara Bowers would have had all the view she wanted, walking to and from her restaurant.

The owners weren't home. I wouldn't have gotten much from them anyway. Signs by the doorbell read BEWARE OF DOG and COME TO SELL? DON'T RING THE BELL! A sticker below them warned trespassers like me that the house was protected by Northwest Security Services. Christmas lights were everywhere, thick as ivy.

I walked around to the back. The addition on the side looked as if it might have been the garage where Sara Bowers worked on her Mustang.

On my way to the truck I saw the curtain drop in a window of the corner house.

Maybe this peekaboo neighbor could have known Sara Bowers or knew where her daughter now lived, so I could go to her, tell her that Charles Sinclair had committed suicide. And maybe she could tell me more: why the woman in those letters had to be a secret.

Because Dad had something to do with her disappearance?

I walked over.

The woman who came to the door may have been elderly and diminutive, but certainly not timid. She took over the doorsill, moving so close I caught the smell of apples on her hands.

"Can I help you, young man?"

Before I could answer, another voice bellowed from within, over the noise of a television: "Is it that guy you were spying on, Mary? Whaddus he want?"

"I was just about to find that out, dear."

I cleared my throat, told her my name. "I'm the son of an old friend of Sara Bowers. I'm looking for her daughter, but the only address I had was the old one, next door."

The woman nodded. "I believe Lisa is back East somewhere. One of those college towns. They have a lot of them back there."

"So I hear. If—"

"Don't buy it, Mary, if he's selling anything," came the rasping voice of an old man.

"He's not selling anything, Henry."

"Did you know them pretty well?" I asked.

"Sara and Lisa? Oh, I expect so. We were here when they moved in, and when the place was sold, after—well, you know what happened to her?"

"Just that she disappeared."

The woman shook her head. "Terrible thing. Lisa had to finish out school with a friend's family. When she went off to college, she drove her mother's car across the country. Sent me a few postcards before they stopped."

"Do you still have the postcards, Mrs. . . . ?"

"Clarke—with an *e*. Not anymore, no. But here, I'm forgetting my manners. Why don't you come in and we'll chat more? Henry won't mind."

"I promise I won't sell you anything. Thanks."

"You're welcome. You have a generous smile. That's important these days. I'll finish up my apples for Henry's pie while we talk."

As she led me inside, she whispered over her shoulder, "I wasn't spying, you know."

"Well, you caught me, all right."

"Aren't you the Honest Abe! Don't mind Henry. He just says things. His mouth is about all that hasn't quit on him. I really was just doing my apples in the kitchen."

"I'm sure you were, Mrs. Clarke."

The living room was cool and smelled like eucalyptus and apples. An air conditioner—always a rarity for the Northwest—hummed in a window.

"This is my husband," she said, waving a paring knife between us, as if she couldn't decide which of us she was going to pare next. She must have kept the knife hidden at the door; I hadn't seen her pick it up. "Henry, this young man here was inquiring about Sara Bowers."

Mr. Clarke grunted. He sat at a TV tray table ten feet away from a soap opera that was showing three other people talking in another room with the television going. I felt as if I were inside one of those Russian nesting dolls. Mr. Clarke's lumpy, arthritic hands curled over a scattering of playing cards on the table.

"I'll bring my bowls out here, so we can talk," his wife said, and left for the kitchen.

"Whaddayou think of all these owls," the old man said without taking his eyes off the television.

Shelves on two walls were filled with owls of all shapes and sizes. Wooden owls, ceramic owls, plastic owls, cuckoo clocks with owls, owls in tiny houses, owls on fake branches.

"I think you have a lot of them, Mr. Clarke."

"They're not mine. Not a damn one."

Mrs. Clarke came back a minute later with aluminum bowls, one big, one small, with a knife in each. She adjusted the shawl that had slipped from her husband's shoulders, gave him a little pat, and sat down at the dining table and flicked the channel changer until she found a game show.

"She likes owls because they're always watching," Mr. Clarke said.

"I've always liked them. We had one in our barn when I was a girl."

"Once people know you like something, that's all you get," Mr.
Clarke said. Staring at the television, he moved a few cards with
the back of his hand. Evidently he still liked the idea of cards, even
if he couldn't pick any up.

"Henry's right as rain, Mr. Sinclair. Sara gave me four, including
that large one over there"—Mrs. Clarke pointed with her knife—
"and that momma owl and her little ones, next to it. She was always so thoughtful. Never forgot me Christmases or birthdays. Of
course we *were* neighbors—here, have an apple; there's more than
enough for the pie."

"I don't like apple pie," Mr. Clarke said.

"You always say that, Henry, and you always eat it," Mrs. Clarke
said, paring another apple.

"I think I'll save it for later," I said. "Thanks."

Mrs. Clarke winked at me. "I'll bet you were a Boy Scout."

"Excuse me?"

"Boy Scouts save things for later, when they're more hungry
down the trail."

"Well, I never was a Boy Scout, but that sounds like a good
idea, Mrs. Clarke. I'll bet Sara liked your apple pie."

"Not as much as Lisa, but she did, she surely did. She was from
apple country, you know."

"They're having those fires there now," Mr. Clarke said. "Two
men killed so far and a lot of roasted apples and owls. Saw it on
the news last night."

"Henry, I watched the same news and there was nothing about
owls, and anyway, the fires haven't gotten to Wenatchee yet. That's
where she was from, Mr. Sinclair. I never did hear her complain
about the weather on this side of the mountains, like most people
do if they're from where it's sunny, like Wenatchee."

"Weather-shmeather," Mr. Clarke grumped. "If those horse asses
in the government took care of things like Sara did that Mustang of
hers, there wouldn't be these problems today, right, Sinclair?"

"Oh, we've always had problems, Mr. Clarke, even before the
chrome left the bumpers."

"You in the car business, fella?" he said.

"Actually, the wood business."

"No wonder you like her owls."

Mrs. Clarke leaned over her bowl to whisper. "Between you and me, Mr. Sinclair, I think Henry was always a little jealous of that car, not that he was around much." The knife pointed briefly at him as she straightened up. "But I've done the best I could. Always have. Took care of Lisa, too, baby-sat, you know, and with our three, that made a full house, believe you me. I always knew Lisa would up and leave."

"Why's that, Mrs. Clarke?"

"Well, I think Sara raised her to make damn sure she'd move on to bigger and better things. Always kept her busy. Not that Sara was ashamed about cooking and serving up food to truckers and mill workers and the like. She'd say her place might be a greasy spoon, but it was a silver one."

"Did she talk about her friends with you?"

Mrs. Clarke paused, smiling, her knife halfway through an apple. "You mean did she have any beaus?"

"That's bozos you mean," Mr. Clarke said.

Mrs. Clarke halved an apple. "It's French for boyfriend, Henry. Isn't that right, Mr. Sinclair?"

"That would be French, yes."

"Tell him what those Frenchies next door do on Saturday night when they leave the shade up," Mr. Clarke said.

"I most certainly will not. It's disgusting."

"Mary, people been doing that since before there were bumpers to put chrome on, right, Sinclair?"

I shrugged out of that one, but if I'd had a referee's whistle, I'd have blown it. "Was Sara seeing anyone else, Mrs. Clarke?"

"Not that I recall. I mean we were neighbors, but we didn't talk all that much. Not like hours and hours over coffee in the kitchen, you understand. She never mentioned anything about Lisa's father, anything like that. We did have some things in common, both of us being from the same side of the mountains. I believe her brother still lives somewhere back there. But she was younger than me, and busy. Her days off, she'd leave for two days and then come back."

"She ever tell you where she would go?" I asked.

"No, but I always assumed it was Seattle. Where else would you go for a weekend, and not take any camping equipment, that sort of thing. That's where she was going the day she disappeared. A terrible thing. Nobody knows what happened to her. They found the car in a restaurant parking lot, Marysville or someplace like that south of here. I always thought there was some connection, she having the restaurant here, you know. I told the police as much when they came to talk to Lisa after, but they didn't pay much attention to my theory."

"Did she say for a fact that she was going to Seattle?"

"No, I just always assumed, because of where the car was found. She didn't say much, just that she was going to give me a birthday present when she got back, and I was hoping it might be Seattle because the stores are better there."

"When was that, Mrs. Clarke?"

"My birthday? I turned fifty-six that year. On a Monday. Nineteen eighty. May nineteenth. The police found her car the day before. She disappeared the day Mt. St. Helens blew up, if that doesn't take the cake."

"Boom," Mr. Clarke said, cackling.

Everything seemed to recede in the room. The room became silent. I couldn't hear the television or Mrs. Clarke paring apples. She said something; I didn't hear her.

May 18, 1980. My wedding day. That morning, Mt. St. Helens blew out to the northeast, sending a cloud of ash so thick the streetlights turned on at noon in Yakima.

The letter Dad had been reading on the day he died, the one I took from his fingers while he napped . . . that letter had been the last one Sara Bowers had written.

Mrs. Clarke was handing me an apple and I couldn't understand why she was doing that; I hadn't asked for one. I heard her now. "Go ahead. The one you knocked off the table will have a bruise on it. It's okay. I've got plenty."

The apple had rolled under Mr. Clarke's table. He was staring at the TV. A contestant had just won and was jumping up and down, clapping her hands.

"Are you all right, Mr. Sinclair? You look like you just remembered something you shouldn't have forgotten."

"I should be going now, Mrs. . . . ." I couldn't remember her name.

"It's Mrs. Clarke, dear. Are you sure you're all right?"

"Vapor lock," her husband said. "People get it, too."

"I just remembered I'm supposed to be somewhere else now."

"Well, we won't keep you."

"You said she . . . you said Sara had a brother in eastern Washington?"

"Well, I think it was either Wenatchee or Chelan. Try Chelan first. It's closer. That's apple country, too, you know."

"Do you recall his name?"

"Oh, dear. It was a while ago. Was it Sam? You know, I believe it was, yes. Sam. Sam . . ."

"Jameson," Mr. Clarke said. "Like the whisky. Only time I ever saw him, he came over to borrow tools to fix his truck and the son of a bitch never returned them. His breath stunk like whisky. That's how come I remember."

"Sam Jameson, that's it, Henry. Good for you. That's what Sara called him."

"Thank you both," I said. "No, don't get up, Mrs. Clarke. I'll see myself out."

"Don't forget your apple now."

"Take one of those damn owls, too, why don't you," Mr. Clarke said. "I'm sick of them looking at me."

"Henry, honestly, you're a broken record sometimes. Say good-bye to that nice young man now."

"I hate people who borrow and don't return," Henry said.

Near the door, when I looked back at them, Mrs. Clarke was still doing her apples. She easily had enough for three or four pies. The bowl was mounded over. Henry Clarke was going to have to eat a lot of pies.

Back in the truck, I put the apple on the dash. I hadn't had any lunch, but I wasn't hungry. Be a Scout and save it, for the long haul over the mountains, to Chelan? Looking at it made me queasy, and it wasn't the realization that what Mrs. Clarke most liked doing was slicing the apples with her knife, that if her husband wasn't careful, he might wind up on a shelf, along with the other owls.

The apple was going to sit on the dash, uneaten for a long time, so I rolled it into the gutter, feeling that Mrs. Clarke was watching me dump the coal that would never get to Newcastle. This time I didn't look to see if she was.

Chapter 16

CHELAN

The North Cascades Highway hugs the course of the Skagit as the river flows down to the sea from its stranglehold high in the mountains—Puget Power's Diablo and Ross Dams. Until you get to the wilderness of the National Park, there's a lot to keep you going: mangy clear-cuts, small towns along the way that are sores upon the pelvic regions of the mountains, places that do not grow so much as they heal.

I stopped in mid-afternoon at an overlook high above the dams. The glacial water of Diablo and Ross Lakes was a creamy blue-green. "Like that Mr. Yuk stuff you put in the toilet," Michael said once, when we stopped here two summers ago, doing a loop of the Cascades.

You never know what prompts dreams. Maybe it was Michael's observation, or the dams' seeming vulnerability from the height of the overlook, but that night in the Apple Barrel motel near Wenatchee, I dreamed of a time in the future when everything had all gone to hell. We had taken refuge in the ruins of one of the dams, were trying to make a home in a nest of the twisted metal of fallen towers and high-tension wires that had once carried power to far-away cities. I woke up when we saw people coming, people who clearly wanted our home for theirs. Unlike us, they had rifles.

I never told Ellie about the nightmare. We used to tell each other about our dreams but stopped because she could no longer remember in the morning what she dreamed about at night. She joked about it, as some sort of creeping Alzheimer's, a deficiency, like her hearing loss, as if writers should be the ones who never forgot their dreams. I suggested to her that she dreamed her dreams at the typewriter, that at night her mind wanted to rest. That didn't make her feel much better. She said she used to remember but no longer. I never asked her when the change happened because I knew.

Fifteen miles north of Chelan, heading south from Pateros, I turned the truck's headlights on, even though there were five hours of daylight left. The smoke from the forest fires was so thick I couldn't even see the far bank of the Columbia River to the east. I kept the radio on. A thousand marines from Camp Pendleton in California were being brought in to help the three thousand firefighters, from all over the west, who were already battling the fires.

Route 97 was still open, so I'd be able to get to Chelan, but parts of Alt. 97 on the west side of the river were closed, as were other roads around Lake Chelan.

The "Tyee" fire had already devoured forty-five thousand acres between Chelan and Entiat, to the south. The newest worry was another blaze that had started at the north end of the lake. Two other big ones, around Leavenworth, were threatening that Bavarian-theme village southwest of Chelan, forcing a large stretch of Route 2 to be closed. I wouldn't have wanted to be one of the firefighters, risking my life to save ersatz chalets and service stations with names like Der Gas Haus.

The streetlights were on in Chelan when I arrived at five-thirty. Normally this time of year the resort town of four thousand would be jammed with vacationers, but now it had the feel of a war zone. The Chelan Rodeo Grounds, on Union Valley Road, was a command center, stockpiled with supplies and equipment for the firefighters. There had to be an acre of the flatbed trailers—a vast, undulating grid of a stage—that had carried the bulldozers. Scores of firetrucks—yellow, white, red, light green—had come from as far away as Seattle and Spokane. Yellow-jacketed firefighters filed into yellow school buses. The marines hadn't arrived yet, but the Washington National Guard had.

I stopped at a convenience store to buy a local map and look up Sam Jameson's address in a phone book. He lived across the Chelan River, at 23 Webster Street.

His two-story house—dark blue, with red and white trim—was one of the best-cared-for in a neighborhood of modest frame homes a few blocks away from the high school. Shielded by neatly clipped lilacs, the porch formed an L around the front and driveway sides of the house. Twin beds of carefully pruned roses flanked the walk. The grass looked as if it had not been cut in a while and, like everything else, was dusted with gray ash from the fires. An old Ford pickup was parked halfway down the driveway. He obviously didn't drive it because the license tab had expired seven years ago.

Sighting along a picket fence bordering the driveway, I glimpsed the faint outlines of the river and the P.U.D. dam.

In the yard next door an older boy of eleven or so was pitching underhanded to another who looked about six. He missed, and as he dropped the bat to go after the ball, the older boy said, "You can do it, Casey, but you gotta keep your eye on the ball."

I made the only tracks in the fine coating of ash on the porch steps. The porch was bare except for an Adirondack chair and a larger woodbin, stuffed with evenly cut logs stacked on end. The mailbox was empty.

I wondered what Sam Jameson had inside his house that was so valuable he had to bolt a thick wrought-iron grille across the porch window. The door, too, had been strengthened, with a brass plate screwed in around the knob and lock. You weren't supposed to have to do that in a place like Chelan.

I didn't bother to knock because of the note, neatly written in black permanent marker, taped to the door at eye level:

If I'm not here, I'm in Stehekin

There was no phone number where he might be contacted because there wasn't any telephone service to Stehekin, or roads, for that matter. Only float planes and the day boats could get you there.

Lake Chelan was fifty-five miles long. Stehekin was at the wilderness end of it. So was Sam Jameson.

Stehekin, then. I walked back to the truck.

As I was about to leave, I heard a thunk, saw a baseball carom off the porch steps and roll into one of the rose beds.

The younger boy—Casey—had hit the ball, and his brother

seemed annoyed. Because his kid brother had walloped the ball a ton? Because he'd have to go around the picket fence to get it? Casey whooped with joy at his unexpected prowess and started to run off to get the ball. But his brother grabbed him by the arm, stopping him. He didn't protest. He just gave his home run fence one last look and left. The older boy lingered, looking, too, and he seemed on the verge of going after the ball. He didn't. He just picked up the bat his brother had dropped, whacked it against a tree in disgust, and followed his brother inside the house.

I assumed they'd gone in to get a parent to retrieve the ball, but then the mother came around the side of the house, pulling on a hose, and wearing a white mask over her mouth and nose because of the smokiness in the air. She lifted the hose, shouted, "We're ready, you guys!" A moment later she squeezed the nozzle and began spraying the house, the stream of water arcing up to the shingle roof.

I got out of the truck, and by the time I'd walked over to pick up the baseball, both boys had scampered out and were watching their masked mother hose down the already dripping house.

When I was at the hedge, she noticed me and let the water stop. I tossed the ball over and gave them a wave, but the mother, her mask pulsating with her breathing, just stared at me, as if I'd flung over poison meat for the dog. Neither boy went to pick up the ball, which had rolled to the plywood scrap of home plate. Even after I'd gotten back to my idling truck, they still hadn't gotten the ball.

I checked the rearview. The mother was still staring after, and it certainly wasn't because of any curiosity at the modest gesture of a stranger who might want to buy next door to hers.

Sam Jameson couldn't have known I was going to be journeying up the lake to see him, but as I left, I had the feeling that note was written for me.

I checked in at Campbell House, a place that had been around since Chelan's prospecting and trapping days. The old lodge, located downtown near the confluence of the lake and the river, used to be a boardinghouse back in 1901 and served now as the restaurant. The main resort now had 150 rooms facing the lake, and half of them were empty.

From my fourth-floor room I could see the long stretch of beach, empty except for two die-hard tourists who were enjoying the warmth of the evening if not the sun. The smoke was thick enough still to obscure the far side of the lake and Chelan Butte, where fire crews were working to stop the wildfire from cresting and burning right down to the water. Not a single boat was out on the lake. Three school buses pulled into the shore-side city park. Firefighters trooped wearily out, heading toward the curving beach, to cool off in a lake that was chilly even when the sun was shining.

I went over to the lodge for dinner, picking up a schedule for the Lake Chelan Boat Company on the way, as well as material about Stehekin.

Only about one hundred people lived there, and only recently had the one-room schoolhouse been forsaken for a larger one. In the days of the lake steamers, the trip up the lake to Stehekin used to take two days and twelve cords of wood. Now, the trip took four hours via *The Lady of the Lake II*, which left the Chelan dock at 8:30 A.M. and got back at 6:00 P.M. with a ninety-minute lay-over. But there was also an express boat that left Chelan at the same time. I decided to take the *Lady Express* up the lake and the slow boat back, which would give me more time for Sam Jameson.

Something told me I would need it.

I had a Guinness and trout. Next to my table on the upstairs veranda, four people were comparing disaster notes, talking about the fickleness and ferocity of the fires. Evidently their homes along the Navarre Coulee Road had been spared, and one of them said the only damage had been a cigarette-sized burn in their back porch from a cinder. But most of their neighbors who hadn't cleared the trees away from their homes hadn't been so lucky.

"I talked to one of the firefighters when Peg and I went back to help Benny Matheson and some of the others," one of the men said. He wore a Colorado Rockies cap. "Benny lost everything. All that's left is his chimney. And his house isn't thirty yards from ours."

"The tree stumps were still sizzling like bacon," a blond woman said.

Before I paid up, I had the waiter put a round of drinks for them on my bill. Later that night, around eleven, I walked down to the beach and watched the bright crest of fire on the ridge above the south side of the lake, an orange ribbon that extended all the way from Chelan Butte to Lake Chelan State Park a few miles north.

To the people who once lived in the area, Stehekin meant "the way through." Tomorrow it would be the way through fires that probably would not, even given the stiff lake winds, roar down to the lake's edge. The hillsides facing the lake had few trees.

It was different up around Stehekin, deep in the Cascades. Why was Sam Jameson there now, during this time of wildfires, when he should be at home, hosing it down like his neighbor?

Why Stehekin? I had the feeling the answer to that question would, like the fires, consume all the others I had—about his sister, Sara Bowers, who had disappeared on the way to my wedding, and maybe even why a couple of boys wouldn't take ten seconds to dart into his yard to retrieve a baseball and keep on with their play.

Chapter 17

LADY OF THE LAKE

At its deepest point, over fifteen hundred feet, Lake Chelan is four hundred feet below sea level. In some places the lake is two miles wide; at the Narrows it constricts to a quarter mile. It's in that class of lake capable of fueling the imagination, of believing some things may exist when they do not. Chelan, like Loch Ness and Lake Okanagan in British Columbia, once had its own resident legend: a white dragon supposedly responsible for local Indians' fear of the lake, and the disappearance of various prospectors last seen swimming in the water.

The day I left for Stehekin did nothing to dispel the perseverance of imagination. The smoke was still so thick that nothing could be seen of the homes and rectangles of apple orchards that color the tan, sparsely wooded hillsides of the semi-arid Chelan Valley.

The lake seemed to have no finite dimension. Given the invisible shoreline, it could have been a hundred miles across. Even the water, normally so clean and azure, was tinged with fallout from the gray-brown sky.

The *Lady Express*, a sixty-five-foot, all-aluminum boat, left the Chelan Boat Company dock at eight-thirty. Only thirty were making the journey, none firefighters. There were quicker ways to get personnel to the newest fires at the end of the lake.

At the Narrows, we passed a flotilla of barges to starboard, giving it a wide berth to minimize our wake. The barges were hauling five fire engines to Stehekin.

We kept on in the smoke. Then the thunder began, explosions that reverberated in the gradually constricting chasm of the lake.

A man, dressed in camo pants and slouch hat, sidled along the stern rail, closer to me. "It's like a goddamn war zone," he said, shouting, though he was only a few feet from me. He had a cigarette laugh. "If the water was a lot warmer and the mountains a lot smaller, I'd think I was back in 'Nam."

Firefighters must have been dynamiting breaks into the mountainsides beyond the summits to starve the wildfires. Handworked lines were effective against ground fires consuming grass and brush, but not against crown fires so fierce they created their own winds and tornadoes, yanking mature trees from their roots and spinning them into the air. The flames from crown fires could reach up a hundred feet or more.

There were vicious fires beyond the pall over the shore, and beyond. For these you needed dynamite, to deprive a wildfire of fuel. We were paying the price for coddling the land, instead of letting nature periodically do its lesser burning and so prevent the greater.

Had my father been trying to starve a wildfire by keeping a secret?

We heard the helicopters before we saw them. They appeared within the smoky cauldron, to hover over the water and lower thousand-gallon buckets, then rise again, the buckets swinging and streaming with excess.

Two Jet Skis—from vacation homes along the lake—were more than a nuisance to the helicopters which arrived and departed every five minutes or so. The drivers played a dangerous and foolish game, buzzing in and around the hovering helicopters, waving, hotdogging, completely oblivious to any concerns except their own entertainment.

"They oughta be shot," War Zone said, and picked them off with two flicks of a forefinger. I was thinking more in terms of the white dragon.

We kept on. The sound of helicopters and the dynamiting diminished. The lake was narrowing with the enfilade of six-thousand-foot mountains. You could sense, even if you couldn't see, their steepness because they blocked the light, making the day seem darker, though the smoke wasn't any thicker.

We passed another stop for the slower *Lady*: Lucerne, a tiny village visible only because of a red fire engine stationed there. A rough, seven-mile road led from Lucerne to Holden, from whose mine $69 million in gold, zinc, and copper had once been taken before the wealth ran out in the fifties.

Stehekin wasn't far now, perhaps eight miles away. The down-lake wind had picked up and the smoke lessened here and there to reveal the thick forests of the converging mountainsides. The steep terrain was blotchy with outcroppings of rock where only mountain goats could wander with ease. Each mountain had a story. Deeper into the Cascades, there was McGregor Mountain, named after a trapper who didn't return from a hunting trip in the fall. In the spring his body was discovered. He had broken his leg. His snowshoes were still tied to his hands.

I should have expected that the first things to be seen of Stehekin Landing were school buses, one yellow, one blue, used to take quick layover tours to the lower valley, to the old log schoolhouse, the old homesteads, and Rainbow Falls. They weren't going to be getting much business from this run. At the opposite end, a lone fire truck kept vigil.

The *Lady Express* cut back her engines, then again as we angled in, slowing for the starboard docking, and I heard, distantly, the *thwap-thwapping* of more helicopters working the mountainsides beyond the landing.

Smoke wreathed the dozen or so buildings in Stehekin. At the tiny marina just beyond the docking area along the landing embankment, a young woman was hosing the ash off perhaps twenty boats, mostly runabouts. One sailboat rocked in her slip, halyards clinking. The woman paused to watch us disembark, then went back to her work.

Beyond the white gravel and dirt strip where the trucks, the cars, and the buses were parked, twin stairways rose up to a promenade atop the ten-foot-high seawall. There weren't too many tourists, but plenty of off-duty firemen were on the promenade and in the North Cascade Lodge Restaurant.

Below the WELCOME TO STEHEKIN sign at the apex of the central stairway, and at those at either end of the promenade, visitor information was posted. There were maps of Stehekin and the valley and also visitor advisories. Because of helicopter operations, several campgrounds were closed, as well as the Purple, War Creek, Rainbow Loop, and Boulder Creek hiking trails.

At the post office adjacent to the ranger station I found out where Sam Jameson lived—along the Lake Shore trail that begins at the visitor center and continues seven miles to Moore Point.

The postmistress was a formidably large woman, with crossed pins in the bun of her graying hair, a prominent gold tooth set among the off-white. She told me the path up to Sam Jameson's cabin was marked by a rusting leg-set trap hanging from a tree.

"He calls it his wind chimes, but I never did hear it go in the wind and I did that trail often enough when Sybil Mapes was sick and couldn't come for her *Reader's Digests*."

She leaned on the varnished pine board between us. Her arms were as big as mine, her fingertips darkened with ink from sorting. It didn't take much to get her talking about Sam Jameson.

"He built the cabin himself after Sybil died seven years ago and left him with both the land and the house in Chelan. She got both from her husband, of course, when he died before. Sam worked construction for him around Chelan. That itty-bit of land here has been passed on more than the plate at church. They were close, those two, like mother and son. Sybil and Sam. Kind of rhymes, doesn't it. I suppose he was the child she never had."

I offered to take his mail up to him, since I was going anyway.

"That's neighborly of you, but he's already come for his papers. He never gets real mail, only the newspapers and a day late at that. Most folks here, it's the other way around. I kid him about that. I tell him, why bother reading about all the crap you've moved away from? Habits die hard, he says, like he's got a few more." She winked. "When you see him, tell him Cynthia says hi."

"I'll do that. Thanks for your help."

"Don't mention it, honey. Hereabouts, I'm close as there is to the Welcome Wagon."

The rusty leg trap was there, almost a mile from the visitor center, nailed to a ponderosa pine where the trail curls away from the lake. Through the smoke, the far shore of the lake was dimly visible as a darker shading of the smoky pall.

The hillside was too steep for me to see the cabin, but he was up there, all right, splitting wood. The *chunk-chunk* of the ax dispelled the quiet of the surrounding forest.

There had been a railing once, to match the half-log steps up the hill, but it had fallen away, skeletal and rotting in the brush and rocks. The steps went on for twenty yards where it was steepest, then ended where the hillside smoothed out into a basin, shielded on one side by a shear of rock.

The cabin's thick chimney made Sam Jameson's place seem even smaller than it was. A storm porch hung over the slope of the land with a neat woodpile underneath. Even with the smoke in the air, the light was good in the little clearing, because Sam Jameson had cleared the pines around his cabin. Five or six of them lay on the ground, all felled in the same direction, already chainsawed into precise sections. A Stihl rested on one stump. The smell of gasoline hung in the acrid air.

You can tell a lot about a man by the way he works. At the rim of the clearing, by the closest tree Sam Jameson had left standing, I watched the man.

He swung the splitting maul expertly and easily for a man of his age—early sixties, I guessed. He didn't take one or two swings, then stop to rest or swipe away his sweat. He kept going. He didn't attack the work furiously, then take five. He went at it with a steady persistence: *chunk . . . chunk . . . chunk.*

His red bandanna draped low around his forehead. He wore braces, jeans, and an olive-drab T-shirt, army surplus, stained with sweat, which didn't bulge in the middle, though the short sleeves were tight around his ropy biceps. He had a long scar on one thick forearm. Gray hair curled over the top of the T-shirt. A trimmed beard compensated for the thinning hair. But the man was in shape and, at six foot three or so, big enough to account for the hefty postmistress's wink.

Just as I was about to announce myself, he noticed me and lowered the head of the maul to the ground. He stared at me for a long time, as if assessing my worthiness to help him do the wood. He blinked away sweat that had dripped into his eyes and kept on staring. Then he went back to work.

I walked ahead, skirting the fallen logs, so I had to come up around and behind him. For some reason he didn't like that and moved around so his work—and the ax—was still between us. He finished the log section, not stopping, and hefted another log section onto the stump.

His eyes were the azure of the lake on a better day. A scar, whitened by the reddened face, ran an inch from his right eye down to his chin, faintly visible through the beard, not quite hidden.

The last of the log sections fell away and toppled from the stump. He one-handed the maul, burying the blade in the stump.

"That should do for now," he said, and took off his bandanna and wrung it out. The sweat trickled in a stream. He stuffed the bandanna in his back pocket. "Give me a hand with these." He said it as if I'd already been helping him since sunup. I gave him the help.

It took us five minutes to stack what he'd split under the storm porch. He topped the pile with the Stihl.

"They say you'll have to leave if the fire gets closer," I said.

"They can say what they want. I've cleared around. I won't be going anywhere."

"Maybe you should."

He glared at me. I shrugged and said, "The fire seems close."

"It isn't as bad as people are making out. So far it's been useful, burning away what should be burned away, and revealing what should be revealed."

"Which part of the Old Testament is that from, Mr. Jameson?"

"My part." I didn't expect his grin.

"So how is it useful if people are getting burned out and getting killed?"

"Maybe people won't be so inclined in the future to bring lawn mowers and satellite dishes close to wilderness."

The sound of the helicopters rose with a gusting wind that spiraled away ash.

"My name's Paul Sinclair."

He took my handshake. It was the grip of a powerful man who'd been doing physical work all his life. "I know who you are."

"How did you know?"

"Let's get a drink and talk inside. We have three hours until the next boat comes, and that may not even be enough time for what I have to tell you."

He turned for the steps leading up to the door of the storm porch. I hesitated only because it suddenly seemed likely the world would not be the same when I got back on the boat for the down-lake passage.

On the steps he said, "There's not much time."

"Why would Sara tell you about me?"

"We all go back a long time."

"How long, Mr. Jameson?"

"It's Sam." He paused. "What do you know?"

"I know she was my father's lover, that she disappeared on the way to my wedding."

"I expected you'd know more."

"It was enough to know she loved my father."

"I'd have to say that's true. She was your mother, Paul."

He took the rest of the steps slowly and went inside, the screen door banging loudly after him. I was too numbed to flinch.

The helicopter sounds were close now, and I looked up, following Sam Jameson up the steps, in time to see a helicopter releasing a crimson fire-retardant that blossomed and sheeted, as if the sky had suddenly been wounded and ripped apart.

Chapter 18

THE CABIN

He'd stacked more wood inside the storm porch, along the outer wall. The door to the other half of the porch was ajar, revealing a washbasin and a crude toilet, no more than a slop bucket. The door to the cabin's living area was open.

Partially obscured by the ladder leading up to the loft, Sam Jameson sat waiting on one of two pine-frame/mattress couches that formed an L in a corner. A large Coleman lamp and a scattering of books, trail guides, and folded maps filled a small table sandwiched by the couches. A small trestle table ran the length of one of the couches, with a chair in front. He took a swig from a liter of bottled water, then cupped his hands around a smaller glass. He was a pipe smoker like my father. The tobacco stink permeated the cabin.

Every inch of wall space was filled: a rifle set on pegs, a cougar hide, topographical maps littered with his own markings in three different colors, and a framed board for newspaper clippings yellowed with age.

The loft, crammed with supplies and boxes, extended over this sleeping area at a height that allowed him standing room but not much more. The kitchen shelf was clean, the wall above lined with pots, pans, two wide shelves of supplies. The hearth had a cooking grate and swinging iron strap holders set in the stone. Flanking the hearth were shelves of books and thinner notebooks stacked tightly as his firewood. There was one black-and-white picture on the mantel: a smiling young woman, turning around on a ladder set close to an apple tree, her shoulder sling bulging with apples.

Something else bulged in a side pocket of the JanSport pack leaning within an arm's reach of where Sam Jameson sat. The pocket zipper didn't quite cover the butt of a gun.

He saw me glance at it. "I go out in the woods. I'm out there a lot. A side arm is useful in the wilderness."

I sat down at the table. He leaned forward—the couch frame creaking—and pushed a glass, two fingers full, toward me, past the tobacco pouch and matches. He didn't tell me what it was; I didn't ask. I downed half right off—bourbon—and stared at the photo of the young woman picking apples.

"Is that her?"

"Yes, that's your mother. Charles and Hannah adopted you both, when you were one year old and Steven three."

"Did he know?"

"Steven? Not that I'm aware of—careful, you're going to break the glass, Paul."

"Why now? Why not keep it going?"

"Because you're here. You have to know now."

"It's reassuring to know that someone is deciding what's important in my life."

"There were reasons. Good reasons."

I could have said any number of things at that, but I'd come for answers, and Sam Jameson had them. "Then maybe we'd better get started," I said. "Three hours for thirty years is cutting it close."

"It was back then, too, in 1957. Different boats, same lake, a lot less people. Sara asked me what I thought she should do. She was twenty-two, three years younger than me. I told her what I thought she should do, probably what she'd already made up her mind to do anyway, but she wanted someone else to say it. So, yes, I had a hand in it."

I finished the whisky, squeezed the glass, and slid it, slowly, to the edge of the table, together with the wild idea that he was lying, that the gun in the pack was insurance, in case I'd decided to do more than listen to another version of my life. He didn't know me.

I listened. I didn't say a word. I couldn't. It wasn't my story, though Steven and I were near the center of it. All the questions had disappeared, backfires consumed by the wild.

"That day," Sam Jameson began, "wasn't anything like this one. It was in early September, not a cloud in the sky, the kind of day that makes you want to do the right thing and lots of it. A beautiful day and it seemed like such a joke, for Sara to be talking about giving up her two boys. All the while we talked, she held you, never put you down. Steven had a truck I'd given him, and he played with it until he dropped it and it rolled off the boat as we passed Lucerne.

"I remember that because it set you off crying and that seemed funny because you'd have thought Steven would be the one doing the crying, but he didn't."

He brought the bottle up from the floor by his chair. Maker's Mark and almost empty. I shook my head when he offered more to me. He poured another two inches for himself and drank half right off.

The couch creaked as he settled back.

"What I'm telling you is that your mother didn't want to give you two up. She was losing you forever, but she had to, because she didn't want you to know she had ever existed. She didn't want you to know who your father was.

"But that's not all there was to it, Paul. She was frightened he'd come after her, do something to you two. She felt she had to protect her sons, and the only way to do that was to give you up. He might find her, but he'd never find you and Steven. She said she would die before she would tell him, and knowing Sara, there was no doubt about that. She wouldn't even tell me who had adopted you, not their last names anyway.

"Your father's name was Russel Mark Strickland. Who the hell knows why his mother only gave him one *l* in his first name. You probably haven't heard the name before. You won't read what Russel Strickland did in those pretty regional magazines that tell all the yuppie readers where they can piss away their weekend money.

"About ten years ago a reporter for the *Wenatchee World*, name of Bayles, was going to do a book about Strickland. I never returned his call. I found out later he'd left the paper for the *Chicago Sun-Times*. He never did the book. Maybe he had his hands full in Chicago.

"Whatever the reason, he screwed up, could have been another Ann Rule or Jack Olsen, not that I was going to tell Bayles anything. His story was here. The first thing he should have done was go to Grand Coulee. He could have gotten that far at least from the newspaper's morgue. That's where it started, Grand Coulee. That's where Strickland's mother and father met, if that's the word. At the dam project.

"Strickland probably told Sara their names, but for all she told me later—what I'm telling you now—she never mentioned their names. Nobody knows where they came from. It was 1935. Strickland's father probably hired on as a laborer with Mason-Walsh, Atkinson and Kier, the consortium doing the dam. Probably got about thirty dollars a week, which wasn't too bad considering you could get a loaf of bread for nine cents in those days, a glass of beer and a dance for a dime with what they called taxi dancers. You could get a whore for two bucks and pretty much anything else you wanted on B Street in Mason City. It was like an army base, with all the dust, then mud, then dust again and few of the rules. Newspapers back East called it the cesspool of the New Deal. There were upwards of fifteen thousand people living around there in everything from fine houses on the hills to cardboard shanties.

"Strickland's father was one of the seven thousand guys doing the work at the height of the construction. His mother worked in one of the dance halls.

"She probably wasn't a prostitute at first. At least she wasn't living in any of the so-called rooming houses like the Red Rooster or the Swanee Rooms. But she got pregnant.

"The only thing that seems certain about Strickland's father is that he wasn't much liked. Wouldn't take any crap, is what Strickland told Sara. Got him killed. That or a grudge or an unpaid gambling debt.

"Strickland said his mother told him his father and some guys he had problems with were working the night shift a couple of weeks before FDR's first visit. They were pouring cement and someone pushed Strickland's father in. The foreman didn't like him either, so instead of getting him out quick, they kept him under, murdered him, to become part of the dam.

"I don't know how many times Strickland told that story. The boosters always said at the time that the project rivaled the Pyramids, changed the face of the Northwest forever. Strickland was proud of it: his father buried in a tomb bigger than the pharaohs'.

"But that's not what happened. You see, they poured cement in four-yard buckets; it wasn't a continuous pour. They lowered the buckets down to a foot or so from the previous pour. For a man to get swallowed up by the concrete he'd have to lie flat, unless it was one of the bigger forms they were pouring into.

"Oh, I suppose a man could have been held down, but there were always a lot of guys around, and not all of them could have hated Strickland's father. Seventy-seven men were killed during construction of the dam, mostly from falls, blasting, and vehicle accidents, but no one was ever reported to have been actually buried in the concrete.

"So it *might* have been possible but not likely, not with so many men around, like I said. What probably happened is what usually does: Strickland's father just took off one day, leaving a woman he never married, pregnant with Russel, leaving no more of a trace than when he arrived.

"About the only reason I can think of to back up the story Russel got from his mother was that his father left behind a concertina he used to play. Sara said she saw Russel almost kill a man in a bar when the guy pooh-poohed the story. It took four men to pull Strickland off him, as Strickland was screaming, 'He would have taken it with him.' Over and over.

"Well, Strickland's mother—your grandmother—may have just been a taxi dancer before, but with a kid to support, she couldn't live on ten cents a dance. But they survived. Strickland used to tell Sara that his earliest memory was of his mother giving him the squeeze box to play with while she 'entertained.' Maybe it was his only toy, I don't know. He said he learned to play quick, or at least pound on the keys, to drown out the other noise in the other room.

"Strickland's father may not have taken the thing, but his son did, when he and his mother left Mason City at the dam site as the war was starting and drifted first east to Spokane, then west to Wenatchee.

"Then, when he was fourteen, she left. Disappeared. Again, Strickland claimed that she'd been murdered, and that no one gave a shit because of what she was.

"Sara said he thought that because of the music lessons. Said that any woman who would always spare enough for his music lessons, no matter how poor they were, wasn't the type who would abandon him.

"Maybe the music lessons were as much of a story as his father being entombed in the Grand Coulee Dam. A story to explain away his killing her, if that's what he did. No one came forward later to say what an excellent student Russel Strickland was on the piano or clarinet or guitar. Of course, there isn't a teacher alive who would have wanted to do that, after what he did.

"But the thing is, Strickland was a prodigy. I heard him play. We all did. He got the talent from *somewhere*, and maybe if his mother hadn't been murdered in some migrant camp or run off with some guy, he would have done something with it. For a while I made the mistake, too, of feeling sorry for him, a guy on his own at fourteen. We all did for a while. Sara did, for longer, too much longer.

"Strickland never finished school, left an orphanage in Wenatchee, drifted into the mountains, probably lying about his age to set chokes as a lumberjack. He must have gotten his size early. He was a trapper later, so he had to have done some of that, learned that somewhere. He drifted out of the mountains again, working the Cascade foothills orchards in the season, finally to the orchard of my father. That's where he met Sara. They were both twenty years old, but he was so much . . . *older*.

"Strickland was one of those men who easily impress the first or second time around. You think, 'Here's a guy who has it all.' He had this confidence of bearing that comes with people who've been on their own early, learned to take care of themselves right off.

"He was this big, handsome guy, well-proportioned. Not clean-cut, frat-boy handsome. Had a few missing teeth, a nose a little flat and bent from fights in the camps or two-bit prize matches, and that's what made his hands so unusual. A guy's a brawler, done what Strickland did in the woods, his hands are marked, nicked, hurt some, scarred. It shows. But his didn't. His fingers weren't delicate, but they weren't coarse either. Somehow he'd protected them. He could span a dinner plate, pick it up flat.

"And the man was strong. Watching him work the orchards, you could see that right off, stacking the apple boxes. They use forklifts now for that work. Here was a guy who'd been around a lot for someone so young, at least he had the stories about the timber camps, setting traplines. You believed him when he said he had killed bears and cougars in the mountains."

Sam Jameson pointed the pipe stem at his face. "I killed one, too. But it also hurt me. I still think something was wrong with the cat; usually they steer clear. But I took thirty-two stitches in my face and a couple of shots in the ass in Chelan. It was lucky I'd just started carrying a side arm when I started leaving the trails, a .22 Woodsman."

I watched Sam Jameson's rough hands as he began slowly, carefully, packing his large pipe from a tin, picking up curls of tobacco that strayed to the table and tapping them into the pipe.

"So Strickland had his stories and he had his music, and when you heard the music, you just had to wonder where the hell it came from. We didn't hear it at our place. Our parents were Adventists, strict, and everything but church music was off limits. The first time we heard it we were over at a neighbor's helping out with the picking because Mrs. Causland's husband had died over the summer. Dad gave her Strickland and me to help out, and Sara went, too, leaving two other guys Dad had hired a week before along with Strickland.

"We'd been at it for a while, long enough for me to wonder where Strickland was. Then I heard this piano music coming from somewhere. At first I thought it was the radio, coming from Mrs. Causland's house. I kept on working, called out to Sara and Strickland, but they didn't reply. I went to the house, figuring maybe they'd gone in for a drink. It was a hot day in early September. There in the parlor was Strickland, Sara, and Mrs. Causland. She was smiling ear to ear, which I thought foolish considering that no work was getting done. And there was Strickland at the upright, playing ragtime, and Gershwin, which he got bored with after a while and then picked up the guitar of Mrs. Causland's daughter, who'd left it on a weekend home from college. And Strickland finger-picked through some Weavers, and Elvis, and finished off with "Roll on Columbia," in a voice a lot better than Woody Guthrie ever had. But I didn't hear all of it in the parlor. I still heard it an hour later from the orchard. Somebody had to pick the apples. It might have been Mrs. Causland's business if she preferred to listen to Strickland's music on her dead husband's piano rather than getting the crop in. And the rapture I saw on my sister's face in that parlor was certainly none of my business. Sure I was jealous of Russel Strickland. Any fool could pack an apple crate, but few had the talent I heard in that house. But what bothered me was the look Strickland gave me, that I don't think anyone else saw. It was quick, but came hard, enough to bring heat to my face. I felt like I'd been blindsided, because Strickland and I had gotten on well in the week he'd been working for us. It was a look of triumph, and for all the music there was nothing behind it, except a hostility deep and cold as that lake. It said, 'Fuck you.'

"I knew something had entered our lives that wasn't going to go away without a lot of trouble. I didn't know how right I was.

"The trouble, of course, had everything to do with Sara. To a twenty-year-old girl, coming from a family like ours where jam on your toast was limited to one day a week, yearning to bust out, a guy like Strickland seemed worldly, independent, self-assured. He may have dropped out of school at fourteen, but I heard him quote Jack London's story 'To Build a Fire,' word for word, and I know that because the night after he did it I read the story to make sure. I never saw him with books, but what the man read, he . . . *owned*. Show him once and he had it stone-cold. He was like that with music, with everything . . . including my sister.

"If she'd seen the look he'd given me, she'd probably have felt it mirrored her own disdain for the world she'd known. Later, when she'd found out more about Strickland, she made the mistake of taking pity on him, even as she marveled at how he'd survived, giving the finger to the world. 'He needs me,' she would say to me when others—and I was among them—when we tried to talk to her about the guy. We were part of the problem, not him. You see what you want to see. There was a lot to see in Strickland, sure, but it was only on the surface, thin as piano keys. What Sara saw over the next few weeks made the guy exciting, without a doubt: 'Here's someone who can take care of himself—and others if he had to.'

"Sara was a beauty, too, but she wasn't aware of it so much as other girls might be. Our parents saw to that. They wouldn't even allow a damn mirror in the bathroom where you could look too long at yourself. She had some trouble with guys because of that innocence, an innocence which was fine if you were going to spend the rest of your life in a small town outside of Wenatchee. Our parents kept close tabs on her, and if I hadn't covered for her every now and then before Strickland came along, she wouldn't have stepped out any *sort* of way. I did what I could to help her; she was my little sister. I figured the more she knew of the world, the safer she'd be in the long run, but nobody was prepared for Russel Strickland.

"Even after she met him, she had problems with guys. I saw what he did to one who gave her some trouble one weekend. She must have told Strickland. This other guy was a linebacker at Washington State. He never went back, not after Strickland got through with him. It was never proven that Strickland did it. The guy was hit from behind, he said, and never saw a face. But I knew, because Sara would always mention what happened, in general terms, about people who are in love, taking care of each other, doing whatever they have to do.

"It took Sara too long to see, really see, what lay beneath that man. She found out, but by then it was too late. By that time Strickland had another name the newspapers had given him. The name they gave him didn't exactly describe what he did, but it was close enough to sell a lot of papers.

"They called him the Pied Piper."

THE CAGE: 5

He comes in this time with food and water, apologizing for leaving me without any, saying he went all the way across the mountains before he realized what he'd done.

"I drove right back. I'm sorry, BobBee."

In the dark I reach into the tunnel for what he's brought. I spill half of the carton just to get it right in my mouth. Orange juice.

"You planned it," I tell him. "Just to show me how much I need you."

"Think what you want—but think it through. I haven't done all this with you, waited so long, come so close to Mr. Mike's birthday only to have you die of my neglect before I need you. That's Paul's province. You are as important a part of my plans as anything, or anyone. I need you, please believe me. Things can't work out without you."

He says it so emphatically I can almost believe him. But I say nothing. I'm still angry. I reach into the tunnel for the food and come up with apples—but I take it anyway I'm so hungry.

"Did you read the letters?" he asks.

"I was too hungry and thirsty to do that. I can't live on letters."

"All right, but please read them."

"I'm sick of talking to you."

"Then maybe you'd like to talk to someone else. We can do that."

"Oh, sure we can. 'Hello, hello, 911?'"

"Well, there have to be some rules. I dial the number and hand you the receiver through the cage. I'll also have a pair of scissors to cut the line, should you say anything . . . provocative. Fair enough? Who's it going to be?"

" 'Fair enough,' he says."

"BobBee, stop whining. I'm giving you the chance to call anyone you want. Come on, who are you going to call?"

"Ghostbusters. Quit rushing me. I'm thinking."

"While you're thinking, I'll go get the phone."

The five minutes he's gone isn't long enough. "Okay," he says. "Let's hear the number."

"You've killed the only person I can think of I'd want to call."

"I'm trying to be constructive here. Keep thinking. There must be someone. I'll even spring for long distance. Your family."

"If I'd wanted to talk to them, why do you think I moved to get away from them?"

"No other friends?"

"You remember the telephone numbers of friends. I can't remember any."

"I have a suggestion, then. How about Ellie? Paul isn't home. Give her a jingle, make her feel better. She's a writer, prettier I think than Kerrie Caldwell. But I'll let you decide."

I hear him move, hear a crinkle, feel something flutter against my arm. He shines the flashlight on an eight-by-ten picture of a woman in a softball uniform, throwing the ball. She has red hair. She is prettier than Kerrie Caldwell.

"Well?"

"I don't know her. She's just a name you mention."

He sniffs. "You would have known a bit about her if you'd read the letters. Come on, BobBee, yes or no? Do you want to hear someone else's voice—a woman's voice at that—besides mine?"

"Give me the receiver."

He does. I grip it like a weapon. Is it one?

"You can have as long as you like," he says, "though I rather doubt Ellie will stay on the line for long. That's your problem, to capture her interest for a decent chat. I shouldn't be letting you do this, but I want to show you how I understand how you feel being alone. That's who I am, too. Remember, though, you say something you shouldn't, I cut the line. Ready? Here goes."

My heart is already pounding when she answers. It's as if I'm using this thing for the first time.

"Hello," I say. "Is . . . Steven there?"

I hear faint clapping and it's him. He hasn't cut the cord. It's obvious to him I'm doing something good, and in spite of myself, I feel the pleasure of solving the problem of keeping Ellie Sinclair on the line.

"Hello?" she says.

"Yes, I'm sorry. May I please speak to Steven?"

"Steven?"

"Steven Sinclair."

"I'm afraid . . . Steven Sinclair is . . . well, he's deceased. He . . . who's calling, please?"

"Oh, no. He's dead? My God. I'm an old friend. I was told he could be reached at this number."

"You must want Paul Sinclair, his brother."

"Well, this is strange. Steven is—was—my friend, not your husband, and I was specifically given—"

"How did you know Paul Sinclair is my husband?"

"I'm sorry, I just assumed . . ."

"Who is this?"

I hesitate. For a moment I forget my name: BobBee. "My name is Bobby."

"Bobby . . . ?"

Bobby what? "Bobby . . ." *I look frantically around in the dark.* "Cage."

"Mr. Cage, Steven Sinclair has been dead for quite a long time."

"I've been away."

"For eighteen years?"

"I didn't have much choice. If you know what I mean."

"I'm not sure I do at all. Look, Mr. Cage, my husband might want to talk to you about his brother. If you'll—"

"Is Paul there now?"

Hesitation. "He'll be back any minute now." *Smart woman.*

"If you'll—"

"No, it's better if I call him back. I don't want to inconvenience you any more than I have already. I'll get back to Paul. I'm sorry about Steven."

"Well, thank you, but it's been a long time."

"Maybe not so long for me. Good-bye—"

He snips the cord. As if he knows, as if he knows I was going to say "Ellie" at the end and he knows that might arouse her suspicion, maybe enough to get a trace, if that's possible.

He's clapping and this time it's an ovation, a sold-out audience of one.

"You were brilliant, BobBee! Brilliant! I couldn't have done better myself. Do you feel better now?"

I say nothing to him because I do and don't want to.

"Okay, I'll take that as a yes. She does have a sweet voice, doesn't she? You keep the receiver as a memento of your triumph. The picture, too."

He tells me he has to go away again but he'll be back soon, with another present. He leaves and the light goes on before the snick-snick of the bolts.

I stare at the severed phone cord, the useless receiver, as if it's some magic thing. It almost seems that way. I haven't seen a telephone in a while. I can almost believe Ellie's voice still resides somewhere in that phone, waiting only to be coaxed out again if I listen hard enough.

I had won her over, hadn't I? She thanked me at the end. I have part of her now. I wish I had had someone else to call. But there's only Ellie, isn't there?

I suddenly want more of her, more words. An audience of no one? Who cares? It's just me and her, this time. All alone here, with no one to laugh at me for what I'm doing. I can say anything I want. I did say I'd call back, didn't I?

I stare at her picture and pick up the phone.

Besides, there's not much time to talk to her, since she'll be dead in a few days.

Chapter 19

Bait Horse

"See for yourself," Sam said, nodding at the wall where he'd tacked the newspaper clippings into the chinked logs. "Those are just reminders, about the killings. I've got a lot more in a box in the loft, along with all the journals I've written and kept for the book I'll probably never write. You can always come back and go through them if you want."

"My father kept a box of letters from Sara," I said. "They're gone."

"Gone? What do you mean *gone*?"

It was my turn to talk and I told Sam about my father's death and the single letter I'd read.

"I was wondering how you found me," he said. "Have you told Steven about Sara and the letters?"

"Steven disappeared at the same time Sara did."

"What?"

"We've never found him."

"Ah, hell. Goddamn him to hell."

Sam put down his pipe, propped his elbows on the table and covered his face with his hands, pulling his hands down slowly with the sound of sandpaper to wood. He sighed, shook his head. "He took the letters, too, Paul."

"He?"

"Strickland."

"You think he's . . . *alive*?"

"Of course he is."

"You really think that's possible after all this time?"

"Do you have a better explanation? Someone killed Charles Sinclair, Sara, and your brother, too, probably."

"Dad committed suicide. The police ruled it a suicide. He held the gun."

"You don't believe that, no matter what the cops say. The same person who took the letters killed Charles and Sara, at least. Russel Strickland killed the man who took his sons and the woman—his lover—who gave them to him. Who else would want to do that?"

I got up then, walked to the porch, kept the outside door open. I needed the air, smoky as it was. The smell of the cut logs made it better.

The boat was still two hours away. There was no place to go to escape. I felt trapped, imprisoned. The trails in the woods were closed by the encroaching fire. Stehekin was an island in a wilderness choking with air that carried the hint of suffocation.

Did it really happen, was Strickland's father . . . *my grandfather* . . . drowned in cement, held down by a few, while others crowded around to hide his thrashing?

That didn't happen. That was a lie, the belief of a boy who had to salvage something, but it wasn't anywhere close to being enough.

Just as my life—and Steven's—had been a lie, which they excused as necessary to salvage our lives.

Can you really kill something in order to save it?

And now the lie was over. Or was it?

From within the cabin I heard a faint rasping, as if someone inside, trapped as well, was slowly, patiently working the sounds of escape.

I went back inside.

Sam was sharpening a hunting knife on an oilstone. He tested the edge as I sat down. "I didn't think you were coming back."

"The boat's not here."

"It will be in about an hour and a half."

"Tell me the rest of it."

He stroked the knife on the stone, keeping the angle perfect, steady, again and again, despite the booze.

He's used to it. He's a boozer. Comes up here to the woods and drinks and summons old demons long since passed.

"There was no more work for him—for Strickland—by late September," Sam said, "and he left. Sara didn't know she was pregnant then. He said he was going back into the mountains, to set up a trapping business with someone he'd met before in the woods, a mountain man named Harold Hasselbach, who was getting on in years and wanted someone to take over.

"He came back in April, and by then Sara was getting close. It had been hell for her in the household, maybe more so because she wouldn't say who the father was, as if no one knew. What did it matter? she told me then. 'He's gone and he won't be coming back.'

"But he did come back, and all hell broke loose. My father wanted no part of Strickland in the family, and he chased him off with his .30/06. This was two weeks before Sara had the baby. Steven.

"From Sara's point of view our father couldn't have done anything worse: keeping Strickland away, the father of her child, driving him away at the point of a rifle, just because he was different and didn't want to box up apples for the rest of his life.

"She knew Strickland's prospects weren't much, but at that age you think anything's possible if you work hard enough at it, together. She was in love with him. And it wasn't like he'd run off on her. He didn't know she was pregnant, of course, but he'd come back, hadn't he? That was all the proof she needed that he loved her, too. Her resentment festered for two years, and then she moved out, got a room in Wenatchee, a job waitressing.

"Strickland came back again. He found out where she was living, through one of her high school friends. And they took off together, with little Steven. Strickland had money, he had a car. Sara didn't know he had stolen it, but even if she had, it might not have mattered to her. They were two against the world, a hostile world that didn't want them together. She told me later that, at the time, taking off like that was the most exciting thing she'd ever done, playing out some New World encore of Romeo and Juliet.

"They weren't married, of course, but they were planning to go down to Chelan later in the summer to do it—after everyone calmed down and quit looking for them."

"Had you?"

Sam nodded. "There comes a point when all you can do is step back and let the mistake be made, and be there to help clean up the mess after. There was always the chance it wasn't a mistake. It wasn't as if Strickland had done anything to my sister . . . yet.

"He took her to a cabin, about six miles above Rainbow Falls, and two more off the trail.

"Romeo and Juliet lasted two months up there. Steven watched him skin a cougar he killed. Strickland liked that. Sara said he wrapped the skin around the boy, but took it off, laughing, when Sara screamed at him to get it the hell off her son.

"Two months. It wasn't just cabin fever with a toddler. Strickland wouldn't let Sara and Steven out when he wasn't around. They had to stay in the cabin. He said it was because of the bears, and cougars, that he was afraid they would get mauled by the animals that smelled all the trapping bait he had in the shed. He said he had to protect her. By now, she was pregnant again.

"It seemed reasonable enough at first to Sara but not after a while. Strickland came back once, found them outside playing, and flew into a rage, hit her, and kept on hitting her. Steven started crying and Strickland hit him, too, to shut him up, and only stopped when Sara came after him with a hatchet.

"She knew it was over then. She wanted him to take her and Steven back. She asked him only once because that one time he got so angry she thought he was going to kill her and Steven. He kept them locked in the cabin during the days. She thought of escaping at night, but didn't think she could make it back to the trailhead at night. She knew she had one chance and only one chance.

"She saw a pattern in his day activities. Twice he'd been gone for a three-day period, checking the traplines, along Salleks Creek, farthest from the cabin. He was after marten mostly, and bobcat and beaver, but he also would take the occasional ermine and mink. And always cougars, too, because of the bounty on them then.

"She had to time her escape for one of those times, but the weather had to be good, too.

"Strickland had a concertina, harmonica, and a guitar up there, and Sara encouraged him to play. She felt he could turn on her and Steven at any time; anything could set him off. As long as he was playing music, she figured they were safe. But it was bizarre, a nightmare rendition of the happy-cabin-in-the-woods fantasy, sing-alongs by the hearth. She said listening to him at times made her almost physically sick, but she had to. She thought it was the music, but it wasn't just that. She was pregnant again. She had to make her move before she was physically unable to escape down the trail with a toddler.

"Finally the day came. The weather was decent, and she saw Strickland making preparations for a longer than usual outing. After he'd left, it took her a frantic three hours to bust out of the cabin, and she prayed he wasn't watching somewhere close by in the forest. He'd done that twice before, to test her, pretending to leave for the day, then coming back, saying he'd left this or that.

"Strickland was a very intelligent man and sensitive, in the way that those who have gotten the short end of the stick are always on the lookout for more of the same. Sara wondered if he'd picked up anything, if she'd masked her feelings and intent well enough. If she hadn't, if Strickland had seen behind, she knew he'd kill them.

"The rain came in the afternoon and turned the trail to mud. She had to carry Steven most of the way and she fell again and again, looking back, terrified, and not looking where she was going. It was a miracle she didn't miscarry. By nightfall she'd made it to the gravel road that goes from Stehekin, past Rainbow Falls, into the valley a ways. Someone picked her up near the Buckner Homestead, took her into Stehekin. She spent the night in the ranger station, told them she'd gotten lost."

"That's all?"

"They were different times back then. She was scared and ashamed and guilty and angry, but mostly scared. She said she just wanted it to end there, wash her hands of the son of a bitch, and felt that if she said more, the connection with Russel Strickland would go on. She knew he would come after her. She just didn't want to make matters worse when he did, by bringing the law into it. She made a mistake. But then, so did I later."

Sam paused to repack his pipe and I saw her then, my . . . mother . . . *looking behind her*

Coming out of the woods, carrying my brother. She had long since ceased to look back along the trail because night was falling and it was no use and she was too tired anymore to make the effort. She could sense him back there, hear his rage at being abandoned yet again, hoping it wasn't this day but the next, so she'd have time, time. All she needed was a little more time. . .

"She took the boat the next day," Sam was saying. "Called me from Chelan and I drove from Wenatchee to pick her up. We drove back. I put her and Steven up at a friend's house in East Wenatchee, then waited for Strickland to show. I didn't have any room anyway where I was staying, in a boardinghouse.

"A week passed, long enough for me to think that maybe he had stayed in the woods after all. Then one evening—it was a Friday and my roommates had gone down to the Liberty to see *Bridge on the River Kwai*. I had gone to the window because some kids playing ball in the street had whacked one against the house. Somewhere down the street someone kept playing 'Hound Dog' over and over.

"I saw Strickland go right through their game in the street, and I had just enough time to go to my room and get my gun. It was the .22 Woodsman I'd bought the year before. I'd kept it loaded for a week.

"I opened the door just as Strickland was coming up the front porch steps. I had the gun in my right hand, in back of the door. He stopped four feet away from me, close enough to smell the clean on him. He didn't look like he'd come from the woods. His hair was combed, he had on better clothes than I'd ever remembered him wearing. Those big hands were at his sides, the fingernails clean. He'd come courting, if you can believe that. A harmonica was sticking out of his shirt pocket, like he was ready to charm the family.

" 'I'd like to talk to her,' he said.

"I told him it was over.

"He said, 'I'd like to hear that from her, not you. She inside?'

" 'I'm telling you what she told me. She's not here and she doesn't want to see you again.'

" 'I want to see my son.'

" 'You should have thought of that up in the woods, when you were beating up on them both.'

" 'He's mine, too.'

" 'Not anymore he isn't.'

"I thought that he would come at me, then. I wanted him to come at me. I could see his body tense. His eyes blinked like he had something in them. He wouldn't have made it. The gun was right on him. Through the door. The first shot wouldn't have stopped him, not a .22. Nor the second. But I would have brought the gun around for a head shot. He was close enough for that.

"I should have killed him then. It might have been sticky for a while, but after what Sara had to say, it would have been all right. She still had bruises to show. It would have been my word against his, that he had attacked me, that I was simply defending myself, my home. It would have been okay, I know it would have.

"I wished to hell I'd done it then. If he'd taken one step toward me, I would have. I swear it."

"What did he do?"

"Oh, he knew I had a gun in my other hand, all right, because of what he said later. He knew. He knew. But even though I had the weapon, he was the one utterly in control of the situation. It was unnatural how calm he was. How could a man be so calm with a gun pointed at him, and then fly into a rage like he had up at the cabin. But that was just it. He could turn himself off and on like a basement switch. I didn't need Sara's bruises for proof that she and Steven were lucky to be alive. I felt it in my gut. I could have pissed my pants. Maybe I did.

"He smiled and said, 'You'll regret it.' You don't know how many times since then I've wondered whether he meant keeping him away from Sara, or . . . not shooting him when I had the chance. He took out the harmonica, a silver and black Hohner, slid it across his mouth, then shook it at me, like he was a priest flicking holy water. Then he backed down the steps.

"The kids were still there, and he walked through them as he had before. One of them hit the ball, and Strickland reached out and caught it with one hand—he still had the harmonica in the other. He caught it and whirled in one motion, and I thought he was going to throw the ball at the house, break a window. But he threw it dead-on to a kid standing thirty feet away.

"And for the next ten minutes he played with the boys while I watched. He told the kid doing the pitching, 'Keep it up and you'll be like Warren Spahn one of these days.' I wouldn't leave. I wanted to see him walk out of sight, be sure of that. But I didn't want to watch him. It was obscene, playing with those kids, talking to them, after what he'd done to Steven. Maybe he knew that, I don't know. Maybe that's what he was doing. He played one-handed, impressing them. Catch the ball, scoop it up, throw here, get the runner. He was smooth, effortless. He was enjoying himself. Keep it up and you'll be like me someday—that's what he could have said. That's what I was seeing.

"Every now and then he'd look back at me and just smile, as if to say, 'See, that's how it's done. That's what a father does. Play ball with the kids. Who's the one with the problem here? Me? Or you, standing at the door, hiding a fucking gun?' He was taunting me: 'Your last chance. I'm still here. Go ahead. Do it. Do what you want to do. If you don't, you'll regret it.'

"He knew I wouldn't do it, not with the kids there. But he was still taunting me, knowing that if I shot him there, surrounded by all those kids, it would be my ass in the sling.

"I almost did it. In spite of all that, I almost killed him. I remember even bringing the gun down to my side, from behind the door. Because I suddenly knew what he was capable of. It was almost like a seizure, it came so quick. A premonition, like the time my father was on a ladder, shuffling stuff in the crawl space above the garage and I was by the door at the back and I suddenly had the thought: 'What if he fell?' And ten seconds later he did slip, fell to the garage floor and got a concussion.

"It was like I knew what Russel Strickland was going to do, once he left. I remember telling myself, 'Shoot him, *Shoot him*! Do it *now*!' I couldn't. Not with the kids. They were laughing, talking to him. He was, for those minutes, part of them. So I didn't. I couldn't. That was my mistake."

"There were kids—"

"No, I should have done it.

"He went around to three or four of them then, whispering something. They stopped playing, looking confused. Then he talked to a couple more, and soon they had all left, some faster than others, looking back, looking at my house.

"When the kids were all gone, he turned to me, shrugged, his arms raised, waiting for me to do it. 'They're all gone now, Jameson,' he said, taunting me with a grin. 'It's the last chance I'm going to give you.'

"Maybe he wanted me to do it, I don't know. Sometimes I've thought that not shooting him then was the difference between us, but that doesn't help much when I think later about what he did.

"He walked slowly down the street; he cupped the harmonica with both hands and began playing 'She'll Be Coming Round the Mountain' real slow, twisting the notes all around, a funeral march, the son of a bitch, instead of how it's supposed to be played. My own hands were shaking, and he, *he* could play his goddamn harmonica like it was going out of style. I never saw him again.

"Neither did those kids, who never played ball on the street again while I lived in that boardinghouse. Those kids are now ten, eleven years older than you, Paul, and they still don't know that the Harmonica Man who played ball with them one-handed, and told them the guy in the house over there had a gun behind the door, murdered seven people in the space of eighteen hours, two days later."

Sam stopped sharpening the knife, reached for his wallet, took out a folded newspaper article, handed it to me. The paper was warm, the edges curved and frayed. "It's all in there, the last article I've kept. Don't read it now. It'll make more sense after we're done."

I put it away in my shirt pocket and waited for him to continue.

He flipped over the whetstone and began honing the knife again. *Rasp . . . rasp . . . rasp . . .*

"The first ones were an elderly couple with their granddaughter. They'd stopped at a turnout overlooking Rocky Reach dam north of Wenatchee. He needed a car and he was probably sick of hitchhiking. They had a Rambler. They were probably standing there, the car idling, looking at the dam, and he must have come up from behind. Slit the man's throat first and then the woman. A Mr. and Mrs. Corcoran, visiting from Iowa. Maybe the girl tried to run. Who knows? He slit her throat, too. She was only eleven years old. Just dumped the bodies over the bluff. They weren't found for two days, but someone later reported that they had passed a man walking along the highway and had driven slowly by the overlook, closely enough to hear the radio going in the Rambler, and saw the man kneeling beside the little girl and pointing at the dam. Minutes later they were dead.

"We don't know why he stopped at the Stivers farm, just off Route 97, north of Entiat. He left the highway and went down to the river where the farm was. It was isolated; the next closest farm was a mile away. It was a hot day. Maybe he was thirsty. The Stivers had some acres of apple trees, some peach, asparagus.

"Evidently he caught John Stivers on a ladder, working the orchard. Once he killed him, the rest were easy. He raped Rebecca Stivers, then killed her and their two children, six-year-old Karl and ten-year-old Rina. When the police got there, they found the bodies decapitated. The heads were never found. Maybe Strickland dumped them in the river; no one knows.

"He took their truck, left the other, went north, abandoned the truck at Field's Point, took the boat to Stehekin. He wasn't done yet.

"On a trail less than a quarter of a mile from the lodge, he ran into Trudy and Carla Martell. Trudy was fifteen, and being from Chelan, knew the woods pretty well. That's why her parents, who stayed at the picnic area near the ranger station, had allowed her to go off on the trail with her six-year-old sister. The parents told them to be back in an hour. You could do that back then.

"They never saw Trudy Martell again. The search party found Carla two miles up the trail, in shock, with a sprained ankle. I don't know why Strickland didn't kill her, too. Maybe because to do that he would have had to risk Trudy getting away, so Carla got lucky. But that's where it began, in the papers, with the Pied Piper. That and a few other details."

"What details?"

He put aside the knife and stone, swiped at his glistening forehead, took a long drink of water, offered me some. I shook my head.

"The harmonica, for one," he said. "It was actually found somewhere else than Mrs. Stivers's mouth, but that's what the newspapers said."

"What tied Strickland to the Stivers killings?"

"Their truck. It wasn't just that he liked the Stiverses' Ford more than the Rambler. He couldn't know how quickly the Corcorans would be discovered, and the police looking for their car. He bought himself some time, left the Rambler at the Stivers farm, and took the Ford to Chelan.

"He shouldn't have been able to get away, but he did. It was more than just being smart and lucky. To disappear into the woods, taking a fifteen-year-old girl, with only an hour's lead time . . . it was like the mountains just opened up and closed behind him and that girl—you can see why they called him the Pied Piper."

"What did you do then?"

"I was just starting up a construction business at the time, but I dropped everything, left a house half-finished in Wenatchee to join the search. I came in at the request of Bill Burke, who was about to retire as Chelan County sheriff, the day after they found the Corcorans. What we found at Strickland's cabin never made it to the newspapers. Bill put a lid on that quick."

Sam poured the rest of the whisky into his glass, took a swig. Even after all he'd had, he still wasn't slurring his words.

"You know what a 'bait horse' is?"

"No."

"Well, I'll tell you. Time was, trappers would buy horses down-country—nags, any animal long past its prime that they could get cheaply—then take them into the woods, kill and butcher them, use the meat to bait their traps.

"Strickland hadn't bothered with that. He got bait, all right. That was another reason he didn't want Sara out of the cabin. We found the remains of five men in that shed, so far gone there was no way to recognize them. We figured one of them was the old man Strickland got the cabin from. Two of them were probably men reported missing from hunting trips in the area. Every year that happens and some of them are never found. The others were trappers, guys who only come out once or twice a year and wouldn't be missed. There were still some of those in the woods then.

"There may have been more. We'll never know what Strickland's total was. Bad as it was, we got hung up at that cabin. Dogs were flown in to track him, but that still took time. We needed more men, so Burke had to get guys from the Okanogan and Kittitas county sheriffs. Things had to be organized. They didn't call them task forces then, like they would now, but that's what it was. The feds and the state had to be involved. Meanwhile, Strickland's trail was getting colder by the hour.

"We searched for three solid weeks, and at the end we had one hundred and fifty guys from four counties, state troopers, Fish and Game, guys from the Department of the Interior, the FBI—and about as many ideas where Russel Strickland had taken that girl.

"Some thought he was still within a twenty-mile radius of Stehekin, holed up in an abandoned mine. The mountains used to be as full of prospectors as trappers. There weren't many who thought that he could have gotten as far north as Ross Lake, which runs into Canada, but I did, because of the dams. The longer it went on, the more it seemed possible he could have gotten into Canada, so we alerted the RCMP.

"If it had happened today, he would have been caught. No question there. More people to spot him, more roads, better technical support. Back then it was tougher. Hell, the North Cascades Highway wasn't even opened yet.

"We kept looking, but after a while things began to wind down. You couldn't keep that many people in the field for too long. The task force shrank to twenty-five men, then ten, and I was one of them. But the longer it went on, the more things got political. Strickland wasn't caught yet, and the papers began to run editorials about why. One compared the failure of the manhunt, the jurisdictional squabbles, to the way the Pied Piper in the goddamn fairy tale immobilized the townspeople, so they couldn't go after the kids. The *Wenatchee World* ran a piece, written by their big stick, Hu Blonk, called 'The Music of Incompetence.'

"So there was a lot of egg on a lot of faces and the ass covering began. If you can't solve the problem, you minimize it. That's one thing that hasn't changed. You sweep the dirt out the door—in this case, over the Cascades to Seattle. Even back then, people out here loved to shit on Seattle. Since Strickland wasn't found east of the mountains, he must have gone west.

"The problem with that was that Seattle was preparing for the World's Fair, and the city fathers didn't much like the idea of people thinking a mass murderer was walking the streets. So over a year before the World's Fair was going full blast in the summer of 1962, the word came out that the remains of Strickland had been found at a cabin near Curlew Lake, north of Republic in Ferry County, east of Okanogan.

"It was a politically convenient location: far from Seattle and outside the jurisdiction of all those most closely involved in the search. I don't know whose remains were found, but I don't think it was Russel Strickland."

"Why not?"

"The girl, Trudy Martell, was never found."

"He may have killed her, buried her someplace else."

Sam shook his head. "The idea was to take her, keep her. She . . ."

"She was Sara's replacement."

"Yes. And that's why if it was Strickland they found, she would have been with him, or dead next to him."

"She could have gotten away."

"Sure, but I don't think she did. Russel Strickland wasn't going to let another one get away. They also said they found a ring, identified as his. I didn't remember if Strickland ever wore one, but Sara said he didn't, on account of his playing."

"Where was Sara all this time?"

"She had her baby, and we had our talk on the boat, and she left for Seattle and gave you and Steven up for adoption. I also think she was punishing herself, because there was a point when she knew what Strickland was like but she kept on with him, not wanting to admit she'd made a mistake. She was stubborn. Maybe she found what was in that shed, though she didn't tell me that. And the shock of that—and the other murders—sent her into a spin of guilt, made her feel like she wasn't fit to be a mother. But most of all she wanted to protect you two. Do you see that now? Do you understand now?"

"Yes. And I also would give anything to have had one ride in that Mustang with her, an hour's ride, anywhere, just talking to her, and listening to her voice. I . . . well, I just wish that could have happened."

"She wanted the same thing, Paul. But it couldn't work like that. She'd have had to do it again, take her boys out and . . . it doesn't work like that. She made her decision, and to do anything else when you were growing up wouldn't have been fair to the ones who took you."

"No, it wouldn't have. She thought Strickland was still alive, too, didn't she?"

"She did. She could never be sure that Russel Strickland wasn't there, watching her take her boys for a ride in that Mustang. She married the man who gave her that car. He was in the army, stationed at Fort Lewis. I always felt she married an army guy to feel more secure somehow. She had Lisa, in 1964."

"What happened to him?"

"Killed in Vietnam. Nineteen sixty-seven. That was a damn shame all around. That one would have worked. He was a good man. It busted up Sara pretty good at the time."

"Did they . . . did Sara and my father get together before or after my mother committed suicide?"

"Paul, that was after. Hannah died a year after Sara's husband was killed if I remember."

"What was Sara doing all this time?"

"She got a job at Boeing after T.J.'s death and worked there until the bust in the early seventies, then moved north of Seattle. Part of the reason was to get out of the picture, not that she didn't have her hands full, being a single mother.

"She would go down to see you boys on playgrounds and playing fields, graduations, watching you make your passages. She'd given you up, she knew the rules, but she could still see you from a distance. Once I called her a ghost, and she didn't like that, because it reminded her of two others: one she wanted to remember and the other who gave her all her nightmares.

"But what happened with Charley, that didn't begin until after Hannah died. Sara wasn't waiting in the wings. The three of them—Hannah, Charley, and Sara—they knew each other well. They wrote to each other. Sara picked well when she chose the parents for her sons. What happened later with Charley and her, that was another chapter, and one that never ceased to amaze my sister, and Charley, for that matter. She thought the danger period was over. You both were grown-up now. It was one of those things you read about. But it wasn't really so surprising, looking back. It may have begun with the shared secret . . . but it became more than that."

"Did they also share an opinion about the body in that cabin?"

"Sara never really believed it was Strickland. She wouldn't even tell me where you boys were, in case Strickland surfaced, tried to get it out of me. He wouldn't have killed them, but he'd have taken them away, like he did the girl.

"If Strickland found Sara, she would have died before telling him, but someone else? No. Not even her brother. I wouldn't have; I told her so. But that was how she wanted to keep it."

"So where were you all this time?"

Sam shrugged. "My business went tits-up. Went to Spokane for ten years, back to Wenatchee and then to Chelan before taking off to the East Coast after Strickland killed Sara. Lisa was in Connecticut at a college and I went to keep an eye on her."

"What about my father?"

"Well, at first he believed Strickland was dead, but that changed—for both of us. James Martell, Carla's father, changed his mind, too. I talked to him several times, the last time in Grand Coulee, where he'd moved after his divorce.

"Charley didn't commit suicide. I don't care what the cops told you."

"What happened, then?"

"What happened was that Russel Strickland forced your father to pull that trigger, but he probably wouldn't even have had to do that. He could just have told Charley he had just killed you. You weren't there when it happened. Two sons dead, Sara dead, every-one dead. He would have said, 'Do you really want to live out the last few years with everyone gone—except for me? I can leave, but do you want to live knowing I'll be back?' "

If I'd doubted the suicide, I didn't now and never mind the miss-ing letters. Sam Jameson had just convinced me.

"You really think he's still out there?"

"Yes, yes, he's out there. Scot-free for what he's done."

"But why would Strickland wait to kill my father? The lapses in time don't make any sense."

"Perhaps it just took him a long time to locate your father. If Sara was half as careful contacting him as she was with me, it'd take a while. Maybe he was in prison.

"But all that aside, what have I been telling you, Paul? Patience is a function of intelligence, and Strickland is one smart son of a bitch. How do you think he's remained free all these years? He waits until we think he's finally gone from the face of the earth, then he strikes again, then returns to his refuge. He's drawing it out. This is his purpose, his life work. He's been playing with our lives, drawing out the notes. We're his music, *don't you see?* That always was his *genius.* Can't you *see* that, after all I've told you?"

What I saw was a man haunted by that day when he believed he could have prevented all those people from getting murdered—and didn't.

"You said you didn't think he'd kill his sons. But if he killed Steven, why wait to kill me?"

"First of all there's the possibility that Steven met his fate with someone other than Strickland, though the coincidence of timing with Sara would indicate otherwise. There could be any number of reasons, but we won't get an answer until we find him. I'll be sure to ask him—before I kill him. Or maybe you can ask him yourself, if you get to him before I do."

"I'm not looking for him."

"You are. You didn't know it before, but you should now."

"You're so sure he's alive, but you haven't even seen him."

"No, but less than a year before Sara disappeared, my house in Wenatchee burned to the ground. I was on vacation. I'll never know what he took to lead him to Sara, but he must have found something before he torched the place.

"So you can bet the bastard just wanted me to know he was still around. It's his game. Not so long ago, before I came here for good, I'd sit out on my porch in Chelan, with the .22 in my lap waiting for him—and don't tell me it's any more waste of time than watching crap on the boob tube. The neighbor had some prime hissy fits about that, called the cops, but I told them a man can still clean his weapon on his own front porch, thank you."

I glanced around the cabin of a man—my uncle—who sat on his front porch with a gun, waiting for a second chance, and frightening the neighbor's kids so much they were scared to retrieve a baseball from his yard.

Something about the old newspapers he'd tacked up bothered me. I got up for a closer look and realized it wasn't what was shown on the yellowing newsprint, but what wasn't.

"There's no photo of him," I said.

"No. There's no existing picture of Russel Strickland."

"But there must be, somewhere."

"Maybe somewhere there might be a school photo of him, when he was a kid, before he left for good, but after that, nothing. If there was, the police would have gotten it. That was a big problem with catching him. He'd committed crimes, but the police didn't nail him, so he had no record, no photo to circulate."

"Sara must have had photographs."

Sam shook his head. "They weren't married so there were none of those. He was a drifter, a loner. He spent a lot of time in the woods, and when he was with Sara, there just weren't the opportunities, the jolly family outings and picnics where you bring along the camera. You take pictures of things that please you. No one was much pleased with Sara's infatuation with Russel Strickland."

"You saw him enough."

"Yes, and I'd recognize him in an instant. Other people saw him, too, but people see things differently. Ask two people what a third looks like and you'll get two different answers.

"He's *out there*, Paul, and no one but me knows what he's all about. He's not a creature of the city. I think he sees the city as a cage. He will go there. He has gone there and you know why . . . but he returns to what he thinks of as his range, his freedom. He knows, he's known for a long time what they called him. It's been a part of him for a long time, his identity. Those woods were the scene of his greatest triumph—his escape. So always he returns. But it's different this time. The fire will flush him out, force him from hiding, or it will draw him to me."

"They don't usually stop until they're caught," I said. "Isn't that how it goes? If Strickland were still alive, he would have killed again, and sooner or later he would have made that one mistake."

Sam shrugged. "That may be the pattern for most of them. But I've been telling you that Strickland wasn't like the rest of them. He was smarter, more clever, with the discipline that comes from self-reliance.

"Anyway, Paul, who knows what happened afterward? Maybe he met someone who turned his life in another direction. Perhaps even Trudy Martell. Maybe he just got older and the fires were banked. Or maybe he was careful with killing, spreading it out between city and wilderness, because he had his unfinished business to take care of.

"One thing's for sure. I'll ask him when I find him."

A horn blared distantly: the *Lady of the Lake* had arrived at the landing and I was suddenly eager to get the hell out of this place, away from the torments of my uncle's fantasy, the faceless killer, *my father*, who wrapped a bloody cougar skin around my brother and laughed, who had to remain alive in Sam Jameson's imagination so he could dream of killing him and finishing the business of revenge.

"It's time," he said, and stuck his pipe, still unlit, into his mouth.

I stood by the door, listening to the helicopters still working beyond the valley, watching him preparing to leave. He sheathed his knife at his belt, shouldered the well-worn JanSport, then looked around his cabin, carefully, taking his time, like a man who didn't want to leave any evidence behind.

We took the trail at his pace. Despite the pack he walked fast, impatiently, as if the boat had not just arrived but was departing immediately.

He was ahead of me when we reached the Golden West Visitor Center, where the lakeshore trail ends and another begins, for the wilderness beyond Stehekin. He stopped and said, "I want to show you something."

I asked him what it was and he shook his head. "You have to be there." And he took off. I waited for a moment, as a young couple passed, talking in German, heading up toward the Visitor Center, dutifully perusing a map. Below, the *Lady of the Lake* rocked gently at her mooring, and I realized then what it was that Sam Jameson wanted to show me.

There was no one else on the trail, which wound past a few cabins, a water tank. After ten minutes we met a team of firefighters coming down the trail, single file. Their yellow Nomex fire-retardant jackets and pants were smudged with soot and dirt. Most carried Pulaskis—a combination ax and hoe—over their shoulders, wearily, exhausted soldiers returning from the front. But one of them wasn't too tired to mutter as he passed Sam, who still had his pipe in his mouth, "Hey, pops, I hope you're not going to light that thing up out here."

Another told us the trails were closed a mile farther up because of the helicopter operations.

"Not for us it isn't," Sam said, but the firefighter passed and didn't hear him.

Us? Did he mean me or the ghost he was going to hunt in this smoke-shrouded wilderness?

We continued on for another five minutes until we came to a place where the trail leveled out from its steep grade, widened, and continued on over a creek big enough for a log bridge with rails. Beyond, the trail disappeared around an outcropping of rock big as a house.

He sat down on a split-log bench facing the bridge, even though he wasn't breathing as hard as I was and didn't need the rest. My uncle was in superb shape for a man his age.

"It happened here then, didn't it?"

He nodded. "They said a float plane landed and took off again during sometime after the girls left for their walk. That maybe was the reason why no one heard shouts or screams. If there were any. I wanted you to see how easily he could have done it, just kept on going into the mountains with her, not leaving a trace."

It seemed I had been here before. Then I realized what it was. Someplace else where I'd glimpsed from a height, where the slope through the woods is steep down to the water, too. The girl, Carla Martell, who Strickland left behind, had been about the same age as the other one. Jessica. Jessie.

"Where does she live?" I asked.

"What?"

"The girl Strickland took. Carla Martell."

"I don't know."

"What about Lisa—Sara's daughter—where is she?"

"Connecticut someplace. One of the colleges there."

"Does she know?"

"She knows I'm a crazy old coot who believes the man who killed her mother is still alive and kicking. I was back East for a while myself, looking after her, making sure she was okay. She's a good kid and she put up with me, but she was probably glad I came back here."

He got up, shrugged the pack on. He was all set. He had the hunting knife, a two-quart canteen, he had the gun in his pack. He had a smile of a man who was exactly where he wanted to be. I'm sure there were some men who smiled as they dropped into Vietcong tunnels. He lifted his walking stick so it almost touched my belly. "You want to go with me?"

"Was that the other reason for this detour?"

"No detour, no problem. I have enough food and pills to pure the water, an extra jacket. It's the least I can do for you, after all these years. He's close. I thought you might want to be with me when I find him."

"You're serious."

"I'm serious. But you go ahead, think I'm out of my mind. It's all right. There've been plenty others."

"Sam . . ."

"Yes or no?"

I shook my head. "This is your territory, not mine."

He's mine, too.

Not anymore he isn't.

He shrugged. "Maybe you do have your own territory, like you say. It's okay. But there's something for you in the glove compartment of my truck. There's an extra set of keys in a metal box behind the woodpile on the porch."

He lit his pipe, drew on it, tossed the match on the trail. "They were right, the firefighters. But smoking saved my life once when I was out here snowshoeing in early spring, near Bowan Mountain. I stopped to light up, and just as I did, the snow gave way not more than two feet in front of me. If I hadn't stopped for the pipe, the avalanche would have gotten me, no ifs ands or butts." He grinned at his joke.

The pipe had gone out and he struck another match, flicked it away. "I feel bad for those guys fighting the fire, but it was necessary. One way or another, I'll get the son of a bitch who killed Sara if you don't get him first. He's both our territory now, Paul."

He gripped my arm hard. "Never mind about Strickland, it's been . . . hell, it's been good seeing you, seeing how Sara's boy turned out. I just wish Steven were here with you."

He turned away quickly, then he headed up the trail.

One way or the other . . .

My God, he did it, he really did it.

He briskly crossed the bridge.

"Sam!"

He waved, but didn't stop. He wasn't going to tell me anything more, but he didn't have to. I called out again but he only raised the walking stick in the other hand. As much as I'd believed anything about what he'd told me, I knew he was going into the woods, toward a fire of his own making.

It's been useful, burning away what should be burned away, revealing what should be revealed.

He stopped, unshouldered his pack, stepped in front so I couldn't see. What was he doing? What had he forgotten? After a minute he put the pack back on and kept going.

The sound of the radio was muffled, incongruous here in the woods. A radio for a lonely man in the woods. He'd kept it hidden in his pack, switched it on now. Instant companion.

He disappeared around the huge, shelving rock where Carla Martell had last seen her sister and the man who'd taken her, and when Sam Jameson was gone, too, it seemed as if he'd never existed at all. And with that, all he'd told me.

I headed back down the trail, as eager to get out of these woods as Sam Jameson was to venture into them, into his obsession that could only consume him—and others—in the end.

Because only a crazy man—an arsonist—would put a match to a forest, coax the flames to life, a fire to bring back the dead and a second chance.

Chapter 20

LEAVING THE TERRITORY

When at last Stehekin had faded in the distance, obscured by the smoke that still hung over the lake, I took out the article Sam Jameson had given me. It was from the *Wenatchee Daily World*— "published in the Apple Capital of the World and the Buckle of the Power Belt of the Great Northwest." The date was September 12, 1960, when you could drive a new station wagon off the lot for $2,000.

The picture over the headline showed a grinning, rail-thin sheriff and deputies standing by a ramshackle, leaning cabin with a lake and mountains in the background.

NOTORIOUS KILLER FOUND
DEAD IN FERRY COUNTY
Search for "Pied Piper"
Ends at Remote Cabin
by
George Richardson

REPUBLIC—Two Wenatchee men have done what the largest manhunt in Washington history failed to do.

Ferry County's sheriff's department announced late Saturday that the body the men found Wednesday afternoon in an abandoned cabin on Curlew Lake was that of Russel Strickland, the so-called Pied Piper killer, who went on a murder and kidnapping spree three years ago in Chelan County. . . .

During the trip back to Chelan I read the article four times and refolded it carefully one last time. The creases were mostly slits. Sam had carried it around for a long time, underlined the part where Sheriff Roy Gebbert commented on the possibility that Strickland might have staged his "death" with the body of someone else he'd killed. After all, he'd been clever enough to elude authorities for three years.

"We thought of that," Sheriff Gebbert said, "and we don't think it's a possibility. I saw plenty in Korea, but nothing like this. This one was chewed at, scavenged."

Gebbert's reasoning? If Strickland was trying to fool the authorities, he couldn't know the body would be savaged by predators. He couldn't assume that would happen, certainly not that badly. He could plant all the evidence he wanted—and Gebbert said they had found "a substantial amount"—some of the kidnapped girl's things, a harmonica. But if the body in that cabin could still be recognized as someone besides Strickland, all that evidence wouldn't do any good.

They found the upper arm, part of his left shoulder, where he had the lumberjack's tattoo he was thought to wear. There was the ring with his initials on it. Only one person remembered him wearing a ring: the sister of the girl he kidnapped.

"Plain as day we got him, any reasonable person can see that," Gebbert concluded, "and in the backyard, so to speak."

In the margin, by an arrow pointing to the quote, Sam had written "No!"—the ink from his pen long faded.

He hadn't mentioned Strickland's wearing a tattoo; then again he just might have never seen it. Sara would have seen it, of course. So why had she mentioned it to the police when they talked to her, but not to him?

Even so, any reasonable person, as the sheriff said, would have to conclude that the body in that cabin was Russel Strickland. Trudy Martell's body was never found in or around the cabin. But that wasn't a factor. Strickland could have disposed of her anywhere, at any time since her abduction. Or she could still be alive.

A reasonable person . . .

Did that go for the ruling of Dad's death, too? And the letters. What would a sane person conclude about them? Not what Sam did. If anyone died in the fire he started, Sam Jameson would be a murderer as well as an arsonist and all because he had to believe Russel Strickland was alive.

Russel Strickland alive?

Even assuming he had fooled everyone at Curlew Lake, was it likely after so long a time that Strickland, a man who easily found trouble, could still be alive? Surely at some point he had run into someone who, on one particular day, proved to be quicker, more powerful, or more vicious.

The price of believing otherwise was the madness and delusion of Sam Jameson's going back into the woods, again and again, eighteen years later, with a gun and a radio in his backpack, looking for the man he was convinced finally tracked down his sister and murdered her, murdered her lover, and possibly her eldest son.

You think your old man's going crazy?

Tell me now if it runs in the family.

Everything that had happened could have another explanation besides Strickland's presence, starting with Sara.

The only ghosts that existed for me were my brother and Sara Bowers, who had always been present on the periphery of my life, and somehow I'd sensed her presence, her closeness in the stands, the audience, wherever the passages were, as she watched us, the sons she'd given up.

I couldn't follow Sam into those woods. One day he would die out there—a heart attack, a fall—and like Strickland might never be found until years later. He'd given up everything to pursue a specter, and the obsession was going to kill him surely as Russel Strickland claimed his victims so many years ago.

There are stands of larch trees in the higher elevations of the mountains that rise from the Chelan water. In the summer it's hard to see where they are, but in the fall you know, because the stands turn a brilliant yellow, like the jackets of the men and women fighting the fire my uncle ignited in the wilderness above Stehekin. The larch is one of the few conifers that drops its needles in the fall. So when the winter storms arrive, the snow does not weigh down the skimmed branches of the larch to the breaking point.

It was time to shed the needles.

*   *   *

The *Lady of the Lake* arrived in Chelan at six, and by six-thirty I was back at Sam's house. Neither the boys nor their mother were in the yard next door. I didn't see the baseball anywhere.

The keys to the truck were just where Sam had said they'd be, in a tin cookie box behind the woodpile. When I opened the glove compartment in his pickup, I found two things besides the usual detritus. And for a moment I wondered which Sam had meant for me to take.

One was a revolver, carefully wrapped in an oilcloth, bound by rubber bands: another Colt .38. Same as my father had used to kill himself. I flipped out the six-shot cylinder, rotating it clockwise.

He'd loaded it for me. There was also a box of ammunition.

And the second thing?

A photograph.

She looked to be in her late thirties, leaning against the sparkling, cherry red Mustang. I recognized the Bellingham house in the background. Her hair was pulled back, in a practical fashion. She'd probably just been working on her car. She looked tired, but the pride was unmistakable on her weary face. Maybe it was the work she'd just been doing, taking care of the car. Or perhaps it was her daughter next to her, old and tall enough now to rest her head, in a mugging sort of way, on her mother's shoulder.

Sara's arms were folded, but not in a stern way. Maybe just to hide the dirt and grime on her hands from the camera. I knew that much from the letter—she'd always been self-conscious about her hands.

I saw an attractive, confident woman. She had her own business by then. She was in love with the widowed man to whom she'd given her sons, and if her sons did not know she existed, at least they were doing fine. She had let them go, but she had saved them. She'd come through it all, too. Her daughter was close to her; I could feel through the picture I held the love between them. Sara's head was tilted down a little, as if she had just whispered something to her daughter, or was about to. My half sister looked as if she was just about to giggle. She had braces, a pretty girl with long, dark hair like her mother's, wearing a Crosby, Stills, and Nash T-shirt.

Who had taken the picture? Sam? My father? Mrs. Clarke?

Something about the picture made me think that even then Sara Bowers had not forgotten and never would. It took me a minute to realize what it was, and even then, it could only have been my imagination.

I kept the picture and put the gun and keys back where I'd found them.

Before I left Chelan I called Ellie from a gas station after filling up the tank.

"Hi. It's me."

"I was hoping it would be you."

"Holding down the fort?"

"The natives are restless."

"One in particular?"

"Oh, Michael's fine. We bought a game today, where you have to remember where the hidden pairs of symbols are. Your son is mopping me up. We ought to check his memory. I think it's photographic."

"Maybe it's just your diminishing short term—"

"Paul, when are you getting back?"

"Hey, just how restless *are* the natives, honey?"

"Where are you?"

"I'm in Chelan. I'm heading home now."

"Chelan? What're you doing where the fires are?"

"I don't know . . . moth to flame?"

"That's an odd thing to say."

"It's . . . well, there are some things we have to talk about when I get back."

"Yes, there are."

"What is it, Ell?"

"There's no point in talking about it over the phone. Nothing you can do about now, or even when you get back."

"Ellie, hold on . . ."

"I have to go."

"Are you and Michael all right?"

"We're fine. . . . Paul, do you know a guy named Bobby Cage?"

"No."

"I got a call from Bobby Cage, asking for Steven."

"*Steven?*"

"Steven. Said he was an old friend and implied that he'd been in prison, so he didn't know about what happened."

"That's bizarre. I mean, Steven must have met some hard-core guys when he was in Alaska, but I don't remember him mentioning a Bobby Cage. Did you get his number?"

"No, he said he'd call back."

"Is this what you wanted to talk about?"

"No, it's something else. I better go. The teakettle's shrieking. I love you, Paul."

"Well, I love you, too," I said. But she'd already hung up. I hadn't heard the teakettle shrieking.

I headed toward Pateros, on Route 97. I was going to take the same way back over the mountains, since parts of Route 2, the more direct road to Seattle, were closed because of the fires. At the juncture of 97 and 153 I pulled off onto the shoulder, pulled over by the phone call to my wife. I gave myself five minutes to decide: east or west?

I was worried and, yes, fearful. *There's no point in talking about it over the phone. . . .* That's what you say when you're thinking about leaving someone. But the bottom line was that they were okay—Ellie said they were. She was just upset about something else, besides being puzzled by the odd phone call about Steven.

They're safe so admit what you want to do, that you're in the grip of what Sam Jameson has told you, what he has become, what you're becoming.

I turned east, putting apple country and the mountains behind me and home.

You see, I had the picture of Sara Bowers on the seat beside me, and by the time I reached Pateros, I just couldn't ignore any longer what the picture was telling me about the woman who had bought a new dress for the wedding anyway.

She was looking away, even as she seemed about to say something to her daughter. Her eyes were lifted, as if to the distance, and there was a watchfulness in them, despite her obvious fatigue, a protectiveness, an alertness to something that might intrude upon the scene. Maybe it was only a car speeding down the street, a neighbor's pesky dog.

Maybe. But I had to find out, and only one other person in the world would be able to tell me. I couldn't go home before I'd gotten rid of the last bit of doubt that maybe Sam Jameson wasn't as crazy as I thought he was.

Chapter 21

GRAND COULEE

Columbia River basin land has been roughed up, worked over. Alternately scoured, then iced by the ages, then flooded—at one time to a depth of eight hundred feet—the results for the time being are dry, bare scablands that bake in the summer sun. Impermanent-looking towns huddle in the lee of shallow valleys, where the green has been laboriously grafted on the scrubby brown, gray, and white landscape. There's little to burn.

Grand Coulee Dam is the mother of all the dams that have turned the Columbia River into a succession of reservoirs that nurture the scaly, reptilian land. The barrenness of the surrounding country plays tricks with scale, so the size of the dam didn't impress me at first, as I swung down from the plateau in the fading daylight, through the town of Grand Coulee.

Far above the buildings and offices of the project a huge set of discharge pipes disappeared into the earth, to pump water into a canal that fed Banks Lake to the southwest. To my right, the backed-up water of Lake Roosevelt was tinged with twilight reds and oranges. A few cars traveled slowly on the top of the dam, dwarfed by the towers of the power plants, the mantis-like cranes.

The immensity of the dam was still hidden, until I drove down, past the visitors center perched at the end of a parking lot and overlook. I kept driving down, then through a tree-lined neighborhood and across a narrow bridge spanning the river, to the other side of town, a junction of motels and stores and houses. The road veered north, into the Colville Indian Reservation, where Chief Joseph was buried at Nespelem. I parked the truck near a phone booth. Stretching high over the road, a banner touted the nightly laser show at the dam.

There was only one Martell—William—in the slim telephone book. Not a good start. The one I wanted was James. I waited for an answer, staring into the distance at the dam, high above, feeling vulnerable, despite the twelve million cubic yards of concrete between me and Lake Roosevelt.

"Yeah?" The answering voice was sleepy. I glanced at my watch: eight-thirty was an early bedtime even for this place. Maybe he was going fishing early in the morning.

"My name is Paul Sinclair and I'm looking for James Martell?"

"What?"

"Do you know where I could get in touch with James Martell?"

"What's this about? You woke me up, for chrissakes."

The people on the dam were pencil points from this distance.

"I'm sorry about waking you up, Mr. Martell, but I didn't think the time was too late to call. I'm a writer researching a book about what happened at Stehekin, in 1957."

"You're late. My brother's been dead since 1984."

I heaved a sigh, stared at the racist graffiti and phone numbers scrawled on the POW-WOW POWER bumper sticker slanting across the phone-booth glass at eye level.

"I see. Well, could you tell me where I might find his wife?"

"Carol the bitch? Why the hell should I do that?"

"No reason if you don't want to. I'd just appreciate it, that's all."

He said nothing. I listened to his tidal breathing, as if this were an obscene phone call. Maybe it was for him. I didn't much care.

"Perhaps you might tell me where I could find her daughter, then. Carla."

More silence.

"Mr. Martell, I understand your reticence—"

"My what?"

"Look, if you want, I'll give you some references and phone numbers. After you check them, call me collect at home. I'll reim—"

"She's in Seattle."

"Mrs. Martell?"

"Carla. She went there after she dumped Hank. Most of them do. Go to Seattle, I mean."

"Is she—"

"She kept her own name. She was way out of his league."

"In what way?"

He snorted, exasperated at my ignorance over this obvious fact. "You don't know shit. They never did."

It was my turn to pause. "About what?"

"Such as where Carol is."

"Okay, Mr. Martell you've got me. Where is she then?"

"Phoenix. Living with her third husband. She dumped the guy she was fucking while her daughters were in those woods alone. Jimmy wasn't even there."

"I see."

"You keep saying that but you don't."

"I heard differently about that day."

"I ought to know. I was with him. We were helping pour the foundation of a cold-storage warehouse in Bridgeport. It wasn't the first time Carol was screwing around. She could have been hidey about it since Jimmy was away a lot, but she didn't even bother with that. She just loved to twitch her ass. She even tried to hit on me once at a Fourth of July picnic, but I told her to go fuck herself."

"Trudy knew what her mother was doing?"

" 'Course she knew, and she might even have been angry enough to tell her sister, if Carla didn't know already. I mean she had eyes. But we had to get a different story to the papers. How hard you gonna search for a girl kidnapped in the woods while her mom had set up to fuck someone beside her husband?"

"You'd look hard anyway, Mr. Martell."

"You're probably from Seattle so you'd say it wouldn't matter. But it did back then, and maybe it still would, in this part of the world. I've had enough of this shit. Good luck with the book. If you're really writing one, that is."

I heard the click, then hung up, too. Carol Martell might have been a real gem, but the only thing bigger than the chip on William Martell's shoulder was the dam, all 12 million cubic yards of it, darkening now with the last light of day.

* * *

I drove back up to the visitors center and spent a half hour looking around the exhibits, one of which even had the wheelchair FDR had sat in for the opening ceremonies.

Including the enlargement, completed in 1975, the dam was almost a mile long, as high as the Washington Monument. Enough concrete was poured to build a sidewalk around the equator. The spillway alone had thirteen acres of surface area. Grand Coulee Dam was the largest producer of electricity in the country.

When I went outside again, the dam was jeweled with lights in the darkness. The parking lot was crammed full of tourists and families with vans, campers, Winnebagos—all the vacation Conestogas. The locusts had descended, and I was one of them. Give us a screen big enough and we will come. I heard British accents, German, Japanese, French, Spanish.

From where I'd parked the truck, I could see the entire length of the dam. The noise, the commotion from hundreds of gathering spectators, never rivaled the humming of Grand Coulee's generators. The air was chilly enough for a jacket. A voice boomed over a loudspeaker introducing the program, a voice that came from everywhere and nowhere, disembodied: the spokesman for Oz.

The spillway blossomed in the darkness, opening just enough to let a hushing sheet of white water descend, unfurling to become the biggest drive-in theater screen in the world.

The lasers came to life, four of them, prismed by hundreds of mirrors. The flickering needles of color exploded on the white, thirteen-acre flag like silent fireworks—moving, forming, expanding, shrinking, beginning the story of the Northwest, its history, and geology.

I leaned against the hood of the truck, arms folded, dazzled by the video acupuncture. Still, I was glad when this high-tech public relations event was over, somehow relieved that Michael was not here to see it. He would have loved it, of course, but that's all he would probably have remembered, how the dam was used as a giant television screen.

Without it, seeing the dam in the dark, one could easily imagine its lights as torches on an immense ark, or go back eons and see it as a wall of glacial ice, or as a fortress guarding a strategic pass in a desolate land where brigands still roamed in the night.

The Great and Powerful Oz thanked us all, reminding us that

there was no overnight camping: "Please clear the lot." It was a reasonable enough request, considering the danger of kids horsing around and falling off the terraced promontory. But given Grand Coulee Dam's pharaonic stature, the announcement had the hint of a warning to vandals and grave robbers among the spectators after a royal burial.

Despite the announcer's request, I lingered on this bluff that matched the height of the dam, where Sam Jameson had said it began, where Russel Strickland's father—my grandfather—had worked until he abandoned the woman he got pregnant. Or had he, as Strickland insisted, been buried alive, entombed, merged with the huge mass of concrete and steel behind the white screen that disappeared as quickly as it had appeared?

Within twenty minutes the lot was empty, except for one other vehicle, a blue VW van, parked across and down from me, closer to the visitors center.

I was suddenly back at the Ballard playfield.

Now you see it, now you don't.

Was it the same one?

Don't be crazy.

There were probably twenty thousand old, banged-up blue VW vans in the state.

I was staring so intently at this one, making up my mind to walk over, that I didn't notice the park service ranger until she was a few yards away.

"You'll have to leave now," she said.

"Okay. Sure. I was waiting for everyone else to go."

"Well, sir, they're all gone now."

Except for the blue van.

As I drove slowly for the exit, I looked back to see her rousting the van. I turned right out of the lot, wanting to go down, for a last look at the dam, before hunting for a campground. The motels were probably all full.

I checked the rearview. The van was behind me. It turned again as I did, to cross the narrow bridge over the river, following closely enough for me to see the Washington plates, the VW insignia on the front.

I went straight, then pulled off into an access road that wound its way down to a security checkpoint in front of the entry to the dam's third power plant. I didn't go far. I turned around in the truck to see the van going west on Route 155, feeling foolish for thinking the van might have been following me.

I backed up and went back the way I'd come. There had to be campgrounds along Banks Lake. It was the way to Route 2, and home. When I was on the bridge, I had the feeling again, looked into my mirror.

And saw the van.

Was the driver wandering around, too, looking for a place to spend the night? But he hadn't had time to check for vacancies at a motel. And he'd passed the one at the intersection, near where I'd called Martell.

It was as if he'd waited just long enough to see where I was going and turned around. He knew I wasn't going down to the base of the dam.

Was he just playing games? Or lost? How could he be lost? There were only two ways in and out of the area around the dam.

He kept on my tail, and when I passed the Bureau of Reclamation Plant Protection Office, above the visitors center, I almost turned in, to tell them someone was following me.

I didn't. He wasn't harassing me, playing a teenager's road games. He was just there, close enough for his headlights to glaze the inside of the truck.

I drove past the project offices, heading for the town of Grand Coulee, and Electric City beyond.

He stayed with me.

He could have turned off at any of the gas stations, shopping areas, road junctions. At one stoplight he slowed, so he wouldn't get too close, staying back farther than another vehicle normally would. I thought of getting out, confronting him, but then the light turned green and I went on. My hands sweated on the wheel.

I saw a sign for a camping area. Banks Lake. I decided to give it one last chance, before stopping, getting out, putting this bullshit to rest, once and for all, asking the guy what the fuck he was doing, who the fuck he was.

I swerved abruptly into the entrance without signaling.

The van went on, kept on Route 174, heading west, toward the scablands and the far mountains, as if he were done escorting me from Grand Coulee Dam.

I stayed there by the entrance for a minute before going after. I hit some lights that slowed me down. I thought I'd made up the time, but I never caught up with him. I didn't see the van anywhere. It was as if the van had never existed.

I went back to the campground slowly, so he'd see me if he'd pulled over, was hiding somewhere. I waited for him, sure he'd come back. He had before. Fifteen minutes became an hour. I talked to myself the entire time.

To Sam.

He's out there, Paul. I know he's out there. Now you know it, too. Maybe you have your own territory.

This isn't it. It's some guy who thought he was going the way he wanted, to the west, then realized it wasn't.

If it hadn't been for Sam, and his obsession, there wouldn't even have been a question. It was Sam. Sam Jameson's problem, not mine.

That's not true. He was there long before you. Who was? The one you went back to look for at Snoqualmie Falls when you should have had your eye on Emma? Who? The person who returned the wallet that fell out during the fight there, took the pictures of Ellie and Michael and nothing else?

The one who took the letters? Killed Sara? Killed Charley Sinclair? Who? Are you listening? Turn the radio down so you can hear the questions.

So here's the question that can make you our all-time champion. Quiet, please, audience. Noooooo helping! Good. Now, Paul, are you ready? Okay, then, here it is, for the whole kit and caboodle: Which one is crazier—the one who believes or the one who doesn't?

The campground was almost full, and after I unrolled the sleeping bag in the bed of the truck, I found out why the only site not taken was the one I found near the washrooms and toilets. The light glared from the open door of the little building, the men's side. Campers came and went with flashlights and dogs. I heard toilets flush, and belches and radios too loud for the hour, and after a half hour I wasn't any closer to sleep than before. Late arrivals cruised the campground, looking for space, headlights sweeping over my head. Twice I rose, screwing up the sleeping bag, to see . . .

. . . if the van had returned? To see Russel Strickland, his hair graying now, get out?

He's my son. I want to see him.

And ask him why he beat Thomas Van Horn to death.

I bundled up my sleeping bag, left the truck, found a spot by the edge of Banks Lake, down below the campers, where the headlights and sounds wouldn't bother me.

Another answer came then.

If you are about to die, and you know it, the last thing you will see is your killer over you, astride you, and that distance, that height, is as great as the difference between life and death, between killer and victim. Which is the better way to grasp that immense height, from below or above?

At that moment when someone takes the life of another, he is as powerful—for that one moment—as anything that spans a chasm, holding back waters that have risen to obliterate entire towns, the evidence, the ochre and ash depictions of long-ago hunts, the remains of what has come before. He feels that if he could harness that moment of release, sharp and defined as a ray of laser light, he could light—*ignite?*—a hundred cities.

There on the shore, close enough to hear the water lapping, I searched and couldn't remember feeling any of that on the heights above Shilshole. It didn't matter that I hadn't killed that man. I'd left him alive. I could have killed him. I wanted to for what he'd done to the girl.

I found no residue of triumph or pleasure in what I had done, only relief that I'd been in time to help the girl, that my will or luck had been greater than his. I remembered my fear and panic to get the hell out of there and the hope that something like that would never again happen to me—or that child.

There was no way I could become what Sam Jameson had. No way I'd ever do something like set a forest afire in some bizarre attempt to catch a killer.

This was enough to let me slip into the pool of sleep, thankful the water wasn't as cold as that of Chelan. Nor could there be a white dragon, ready to break the surface of a lake that hadn't existed seventy years ago.

THE CAGE: 6

I think I'm going to suffocate before he returns.

The heat is killing me. The room has become an oven with the windows sealed, the door locked. It's hard to breathe. I feel like I'm slowly being roasted. I've gone through the water too fast. I know he'll tell me, when he comes back, that I was weak about the water, that I should have been more disciplined. But he wasn't here, he doesn't know I couldn't help myself, and if he had been here, he would have done the same.

The heat began after he left. Cause and effect? Like I'm being punished? At least the heat tells me it's still summer, and an unusually hot one for Seattle. If that's where I am.

I wake and fall asleep to the smell of my own stink, the pan of toilet water, dreaming of corpses bloating in the sun, and loosed swarms of bees who discover that freedom is a desert where nothing blooms.

The air purifier doesn't do any good. It plays along impotently, humming the single note, the filter rancid and clogged.

He's left me like a summer's dog in a car with the windows shut tight. I wish I could sustain either my hatred for him or my . . . what? My need? One hour I'll pray to a God that's never listened to me before, that he'll come back in time, that nothing has happened to him. The next hour I'll feel such disgust and loathing for myself, for clinging to hope for the very one who's done this to me, that I'll swing back to skin-crawling rage, convinced he's left me here as another of his games, to prove to me I need him as surely as you need air to breathe.

How much more of that is there in here?

I'm lying on my back, next to the box of letters, staring at a fly on the ceiling. It's the first time I've noticed it. Where did it come from? How can a fly get in here, come and go, and I can't? The room is sealed too tightly for even a fly, except when he opens the door. He must have gotten in then.

I get up to kill the thing. I'm not quick enough. It goes higher on the wall, out of my reach. Everything is out of my reach. Can't even kill a fly. I throw half a dozen of his books at it. I try to hammer it with the telephone receiver, but miss with everything, sink back into the swamp of the floor, a tongueless fucking frog.

Maybe the fly didn't get in. Maybe it was born here, hatched here, whatever the hell flies do to come into being. That's better. That's got to be it. The egg he came from was always here. He just needed a little coaxing to come out. He has all he needs to survive, and thrive.

Survive and thrive.

The thought makes me smile, and in this heat that's something. All he needs. The right stuff: my shit in the pan, old food, and crumbs.

It needs a name. Why not? Froggy? What kind of name is that for a fly? Frank Fly? Better. Franklin Fly? That's it. A fly should have a more formal and longer name to make up for such a short, pointless existence.

I'm glad that I couldn't kill him after all. He's got a name now.

Light vanishes.

He's back.

He's been gone long enough I feel a thrill of newness in the sound of the sliding bolts, the opening of the door. I hear the music coming from below. Not classical this time. Old folk. Peter, Paul and Mary. My anger and resentment surface but they're no match for the current of fresh air that wafts into the room, and everything else is meaningless, even what I feel, compared to getting what I need. I reach for that air greedily, sucking on it in great gulps, the music along with it.

Breathe music. Can you do such a thing?

"It's hot in here," he says.

I don't know where it comes from, the sudden will to keep my mouth shut, not to scream out the torture of the past days, not to give him the satisfaction. The scrap of pride appears from nowhere, like Franklin. I seize it and hold on.

"I'll leave the door open while we talk." *He crosses the shaft of light from the hallway. A big man. But I knew that before.*

"How are you, BobBee?"

I'm thinking of Franklin, wondering if he will go to the light and escape. "I've been climbing the walls." *My laugh comes out like a bark. I see myself in a car, barking.*

"Did you think I wouldn't come back?"

"I knew you would." *I flip him a finger in the dark.*

"Did you read the letters?"

"No."

"Why not? No excuses this time."

"They looked like love letters. Other people's love letters are boring. I don't care, why should I? I don't know these people."

He kicks the door shut and the room is totally dark now. I can feel him burning. He can't see me grinning. He says nothing for a long time. I know he's forcing a calm on himself.

"You jack off to pictures I brought you of other people screwing, you used to buy videos and do the same thing in your other life. But you find other people's lives . . . boring? You're an example of what's made this country great." *He lets the sarcasm steep for a few moments.* "I should kill you now. One less American with the attention span of a . . ."

"Fly?" *I can't help the giggle.* Oh where, oh where has the little fly gone . . .

"You think it's funny?"

"Sure it's funny. You killed them, you're going to kill me. Sooner or later. Time flies when you're having fun." *I giggle again, just to anger him more.*

"You should read the letters, BobBee."

"What's this, homework? Keep me alive and I will. It's payback. You're the one who gets the fresh air."

"The very best, too. Mountain air. Not like your golf courses. That's the kind of air mourners breathe at funerals, coming from a highly manured and manicured landscape. Why do you say I killed them?"

"The letters are important to you. You did, didn't you? Just like you're going to kill me."

"You get to live longer than the others. One more week, give or take a day or so. After all this time, a day here or there won't matter."

"What did they do to you that you killed them?"

"Everything and nothing."

"Don't give me that."

"About which part, the nothing or the everything? You don't always have to have a reason to kill someone. It helps, of course. You certainly have a reason for wanting to kill me."

"The other part?"

"They escaped."

"Escaped what?"

"Consequences. It's what's wrong with the world these days. There are no more consequences anymore. We're born with them, we incur them with the very fact of our existence. But now it's as if those consequences were some sort of virus that we have to eradicate."

"That goes for you, too."

"I've paid mine, and yours will allow Paul and Ellie to pay theirs."

"What about the consequences of killing them?"

"That's a balancing of the scales. I said I've already paid mine. Any more are those for the others to suffer."

"You've told me nothing."

"I've just told you everything."

"What more do I have to say? They have to suffer as I did. They have to pay, do you understand? I have crafted my adult life with the sole purpose of making sure they do. There is only one price on the sticker, there has always been just one price, and I've told you what it is. Nothing less will do, do you hear me, nothing less. Do you hear me?"

"It's hard not to."

"It's important you do because you are a part of it now, part of who I am now."

He shines the flashlight, flicks it around the room, his rant on simmer now. *"What a mess. All those books on the floor. I thought we were beyond that."*

"I thought you'd be back sooner. Consequences."

"Touché." He laughs. *"Did you know one of them is mine, one I wrote?"*

"*I don't care.*"

"*No, I suppose you wouldn't. Still, I thought we were coming closer, you and I. You read the letters. You take your jabs at me, and they're getting better, I must admit. I didn't like that at first but now I find it's amusing. You're curious about my purpose—which is really yours, too.*

"*I mean, really, you can't be upset about what I told you, that you have a week to live. You knew the first day it wasn't going to end well for you here. I thought you'd accepted that fact.*"

"*Think what you want.*"

He flicks off the flashlight and says, "*If you had the chance to kill me, would you?*"

"*It's not like you to ask stupid questions.*"

"*Exactly. It isn't a stupid question. Think about it while I slide the gun over to you. I promised you a present.*"

I don't believe him, even when I hear the hard, scraping sound in the tray tunnel.

"*You haven't moved. Go on, get it. I thought of offering you a .22 pistol, but that's not much stopping power. You'd have to be pretty lucky to kill me with it, in this dark. So what you have there is a five-shot, Smith and Wesson Model 36 Chief's Special.*"

I crawl over, feel around. When my fingers touch the metal, they recoil, not from something burning hot, but cool. The heat hasn't gotten to it yet.

I pick it up and scurry back to the corner of the room, as far away from the shark cage as I can get with this unbelievable prize. The revolver is solid, weighty, heavy in my hand.

"*I can't think of anything more perfectly made for a hand to grasp than a gun,*" he says, and not for the first time it occurs to me he can read my mind.

The gun can't be loaded, of course. This is one of his games. He's chuckling in the dark. Again, he seems to know.

"*Go on, swing out the cylinder. You don't need to see, you'll be able to feel.*"

There's one bullet.

"*You get one shot, BobBee. Not enough to blast out of here, but enough to kill me. Or yourself. You won't do that, though. You're not the type.*"

I'm so astonished, dumbfounded that he would do this, I have trouble finding words. Like the bullet, I find only one, a whisper.
"Why?"

"You sound sad, almost disappointed. Why? Maybe I'm thinking you won't try to kill me because you know if you do, that means you die, too, of starvation or dehydration. There's no one to take care of you but me."

"You're going to kill me anyway."

"But that's a week from now. Today is today. Anything can happen in a week, and isn't that the first order of survival—do what you can now to keep alive, and hope for a later reprieve? Maybe I'm lying about the date, and this will go on and on, until I put on your hood and jesses and let you go free. I've done that before with certain people I could easily have killed, wanted to kill, but didn't."

I point the gun at the sound of his voice. My finger feathers the trigger. "Do you know how good this feels, to be so close to just . . . blowing your head off and fuck everything else."

"Yes, I do know. That's the point. Now you know. But you won't do it. Most people choose survival over revenge, if they have any time at all to think about it. I have no doubt, however, that I'd be dead if I'd put rounds in all the chambers or even just two perhaps. But one bullet is a precious thing, not to be wasted. One bullet makes you careful with a decision."

"When the time comes, you won't be able to get me. I'll kill you first."

"Oh, I will. That would require only a minor adjustment."

I still have the gun on his voice. I use two hands now. I wish I could keep the gun on his voice forever, but my wrists, my arms, aren't used to the weight. Already I feel the strength flagging. I tell myself it's the heat in here. I want him to keep talking, so I'll always have a target.

"You still haven't told me why."

"Our time together will soon be over. We can't get close enough to cut our wrists and mingle our blood. Giving you an empty gun would be a worthless thing. I'm grooming you."

"That's the worthless thing. I'll be dead in a week."

"Yes, you will."

"So why?"

"Why did ancient priests celebrate and fete the chosen before they were sacrificed, why did servants tend to their dead king, knowing they would soon join him?"

"Tell me your name, then. Those others, they know."

He doesn't answer. The door opens and the light illuminates the gun I hold with both my hands. All I can see of him is the big hand and muscular arm that grips the edge of the door, that and the fact he isn't wearing any shoes. It's enough for me to adjust my aim. If I shoot now, I could kill him. Maybe.

When he steps sideways into the light, his back to me, the brief silhouette is an even better target. He moves slowly, as if he wants to offer that target, and I wonder if part of him wants me to do it. If he wants to die, maybe it still isn't crazy for me to hope—for reprieve.

That isn't the only reason why I don't do it. For a moment I see myself going out that door, the briefest of visions of myself leaving him inside the cage.

"Tell me your name," I ask, but he's already closed the door, his only response the slamming home of the bolts. The light goes on, as it always does, and I squint until my eyes adjust, as I always do.

But it's different now.

It always will be, even if I wake up to find the cage, the door, unlocked. I will never walk out to what I had been before. That's already dead, a stinking, bloated corpse, bees dropping in the furnace of the desert.

I swing out the Smith & Wesson's cylinder, to make sure of the alignment of the lethal chamber, the single bullet that he, like the priest who alone hoards knowledge, has greased with a sort of magic. I snap the cylinder back, point the gun at Franklin, who's crawling on the wall, and fire twice. Two clicks. Snick-snick. The next shot is business.

I put the gun down on top of the letters in the box. Treasure.

Franklin is still on the wall, this time where I can reach him. I smash my hand on him, wipe the mess off my palm.

"You should have escaped when you had the chance, Franklin. The door was open, you stupid shit. Besides, I need your name—for him. If he won't tell me his name, I have to give him one."

I pick up the books on the floor, put them away on the shelves with all the others, wondering which is the one that he wrote,

Franklin that is, and what kind of book I'll write when I get the chance. It's a pleasant thought, something to pass the time, something I'd never thought of before, a fantasy of killing people whose names I didn't know before but do now.

Chapter 22

BEAR HUNTER

The zoo was supposed to be an attempt at normalcy. Just walk the two blocks from our house. A family outing. Then, at night, with Michael asleep, we'd talk. Big time. That was the plan. And it was Ellie who actually suggested the zoo, at breakfast the morning after I got back very late from eastern Washington.

It happened at the brown bear exhibit, after an hour of stops at the elephant house, the tigers, and the reptile house—all favorites of Michael's.

I was thirsty but I didn't go with Ellie and Michael, who wanted to find a vendor and get some ice cream or a drink to cool off. The bear kept me at the railing.

Don't worry, Dad, I won't chase away the bears.

The bear wasn't caged. Between the chest-high railing there was only a ledge below, then a pit, deep and wide enough to keep the bears in. Their run was a rocky slope, not too steep, with various paths and levels on which to lumber around or sleep. Beyond, the den, a sanctuary from humans, had two entrances.

The bear had just emerged, dripping, from its pool at the right of the enclosure. That was when Ellie and Michael left.

"I'll catch up with you two," I said, and watched them go and felt a stab of fear, that this would be how it ends, with them going away.

Someone next to me said, "So how much do you think that big ole thing weighs?"

The guy was at the railing, so close I instinctively moved away a few steps. I don't know where he'd come from. It was as if he'd just appeared. He repeated his question. I shrugged.

"I'll bet that one goes twelve hundred pounds."

"He's big, all right," I said.

"It's a she, not a he. You can tell by the way it's squatting to piss. See?"

"Uh-huh."

A few kids farther down were giggling about that, until they drifted off with their parents. I was about to go off, too. The guy, the kind who talks loudly all through a movie, was bugging me.

"I oughta know," he said. "I seen enough of 'em in the woods."

I could believe that. He hadn't shaved in a few days at least, or washed for that matter. The bear probably smelled better than he did. His thinning hair was slick with grease and tied in the back in a ponytail. He was as tall as I was, but thinner, with a scrawny neck and bulging Adam's apple. The thickest part of him seemed to be his brand-new motorcycle boots. Gumby gone to seed. Give him Jet Skis in the summer and snowmobiles in the winter and he'd be one happy fella.

The bear climbed higher. Her long claws, so useless in the cage, clicked on the stone. She turned away from us.

The guy chuckled. "Can't get away from me, honey."

"What?"

"I'm going to get me one. Maybe more. Next week. I know where to find 'em."

He lifted out a necklace of claws—yellow as his teeth, from underneath his Jack Daniel's T-shirt. Ten claws on cheap string. "See? Like a fucking Indian, that's what I am." He slid a thumbnail over the claws, playing them like a xylophone.

It happened quickly, a reflex, too quickly for anger. Before he could put the claws back, I grabbed the necklace, yanked hard, snapping the string, and backhanded the claws over the railing. They flew out, spinning in the air, a few splashing in the pool, more by the bear, who leaned over to sniff them.

"*What the fuck* . . ." He backed away, his hand going to his throat, ludicrously, like a matron robbed of her pearls. "*Asshole . . . you fucking asshole!*" Then he came at me, throwing a screwy right-hand punch I was waiting for.

I ducked. His fist grazed my neck and back as I moved into him, grabbing him at his knees. He tried to knee me, pound on my back, but I had him now. I wasn't going to let him go.

I heaved him up, over the railing. Screaming, he held on with one hand, but it was too sweaty and he let go and I heard him tumble to the ledge six feet below.

I was breathing hard, but the words still came out explosively: *"You . . . want them, go . . . get them."*

The bear crouched by the edge of her run, tiny, weak eyes squinting in the sun, her nose bobbing to catch this new scent of fear. She lifted a paw, growled, swiped the air over the ditch, unable to get any closer to the man on the ledge.

They were all staring at me, couples, knots of families—including Ellie and Michael, coming back with ice cream bars. Michael held two—and dropped mine to the path at the same time Ellie shouted my name.

The others who'd seen were now pushing along kids, looking back as they walked hurriedly away, afraid of what this guy might do next, the one who wasn't in the cage screaming.

Ellie took a few steps toward me, her arm around Michael, then she spun around and began walking away.

I could have gone after her. Explained.

Explained what?

Told her what? This guy deserved it, too? There was no time for any of it now.

I walked away, too. I wasn't going to be around when the police arrived at the south gate, where we'd come in. Soon enough someone would give my description to an employee and the police would be called. Or before. What do they do if the lookers get out of hand? Throw a net over them?

Goin' to the zoo, zoo, zoo; how about you you you? You can come too too too, we're going to the zoo zoo zoo . . .

He played Woody Guthrie, too too too. Guy was a prodigy. Music? No. They never could find him. He's still out there.

Sometimes it's better to walk away . . .

What if you can't?

I walked. I didn't run. I wasn't going to run.

Why're you taking off? You didn't do anything.

Yes, you did, and they saw you lose it bad. You going to tell the zoo police you dumped the skinny loser because he had a string of claws around his neck? Because your real father was a mass murderer who finally found the guy who took his place with his sons and killed him?

Near the raptor exhibit I took off my T-shirt, the Rainier cap.

Maybe it's the heat.

Forget it. The guy deserved it.

A little girl of five or so saw me dump both into a trash can, but her parents didn't. They stared at the row of posts on a small lawn where hawks, eagles, and a condor were chained by a leg.

The exits were out. Another way, then.

Over the mountain and through the woods . . .

One of my early morning jogging routes is around the perimeter of the zoo. I run past the Rose Garden, then the huge steaming piles of ZooDoo—bulldozed animal shit mixed with straw and leaves—then along Aurora Avenue, which bisects the zoo and Woodland Park, where sex poachers sometimes roam the woods at night between the playing fields below and the bowling green above, then west to Phinney and around back home.

So I knew that at the extreme northeast corner, where a lot of construction was going on, there was a gate in the barbed-wire perimeter fence, to allow access for working vehicles, supplies, and equipment. It was a woodsy, still isolated area, though it wouldn't be for long.

I walked fast but it was still a fuck-you walk. Five minutes got me to the east fence. Below, the traffic on Aurora whizzed past and underneath bridges leading to the park. I headed north along the fence. A siren in the distance seemed to be coming closer. It could have been for anything. Or it could have been for me. How had the report finally gotten out?

Some crazy guy at the zoo going around dumping people for the lions and tigers and bears to get, oh, my . . .

The gate was open, partially blocked by a dump truck with SDL Construction stenciled on the side. The worker was sleeping in the cab and I startled him awake. If he was surprised to see a bare-chested man hurrying along far from where the animals were, he also was plainly relieved I wasn't the foreman.

I went on through, jogged across the street, then kept on to the next block. I slowed down because of the hill up to Phinney. But I didn't have to. I wasn't tired at all.

He couldn't have been either. You don't get away if you're not in shape. You get caught.

Only then, as I trudged up the hill, feeling the sun drying off the sweat on my back, did I realize I still had a bear's claw in my hand, that I must have kept that hand clenched all the way. I don't know how I could have taken off my shirt without dropping the claw.

Then again, Ellie and I had always wondered how Michael, at four years, could carry around in his hand one of his favorite Matchbox trucks, while climbing proudly to the top of the play castle I'd built him in the backyard.

Steven had a truck I'd given him and he played with it until he dropped it and it rolled off the boat as we passed Lucerne.

I kept the claw. It might help later on, to explain.

Think that's going to help?

I got to Phinney, the 7-Eleven at the corner. Across the side street I'd come up, the north entrance to the zoo seemed as normal as ever, just the way it was supposed to look, with families coming and going and not knowing yet about the guy who was, by now, free of the cage I had put him in.

Chapter 23

EIRE

I walked down Phinney, past the western entrance to the zoo, and the Norse Home where we once sang Christmas carols, across the park with the cannons and statue of the Spanish-American War soldier. Familiar territory. The stained bear's claw was smooth in my hand.

When I got home, Ellie's car was gone.

This was how it came to be, too, after Emma: Ellie and I taking turns not being home, avoiding each other, afraid because of words that might hurt and only make things worse.

They still hadn't come back after I'd showered and dressed. I turned on the radio, which was set for an oldie station, KBSG. I kept the back door open so I could listen, went out to the backyard, had a Navigator ale.

I drank the beer and tapped the bear claw, the totem, on the Adirondack chair and drank some more.

A few houses away, kids were splashing in the pool, one of the plastic ones that gets so brittle after a year, you can snap off pieces like shrapnel. Real pools are rare in Seattle, even in the wealthiest neighborhoods, because heat like this is uncommon, even at the height of summer. I finished the beer and listened to the children for a few minutes before taking the claw and going inside.

I found the address quickly enough in the phone book and walked to my pickup.

The cab was so hot I had to roll down the windows all the way and wait for the heat to dissipate before leaving.

I spent the afternoon at the house on Bainbridge, drinking more whisky than I should have. I never found the box of letters, though I went over every part of the yard, every square foot of flooring, looking for a hiding place. I pulled the attic apart. There was no place—where a man with a broken ankle could have hid that box—I didn't look.

The letters were still gone.

The last of Dad's whisky was gone, too, when I left for the six-fifteen ferry back to Seattle. For once the wait was good for something; I sobered up a little.

She lived in a small, wood-framed house, three in from the corner of Thirty-second Avenue and Sixty-ninth, painted a light blue with green shutters, sandwiched in between a brick Tudor and a larger, dark gray house with flaking paint and a small, unkempt lawn. An old man trimming the rosebushes on the side of the Tudor paused to wipe the sweat from his red face. A younger man, with a pony-tail and bare feet, was playing catch with his son in front of the other. Whatever the shabbiness of his house, at least he had his priorities right.

No car was parked in front of Carla Martell's house, nor was there one in the short driveway that led to a garage underneath the house. A gold, green, and blue wind sock hung listlessly from a cherry tree in the closely cropped lawn, with nary a dandelion in sight. The drapes were pulled, and her mail was still stuffed in the box on the front porch.

She wasn't home yet.

The street faced a parking lot and a two-story brick school that was now the home of the Nordic Heritage Museum, where Norway's royal couple had once come for a celebration honoring Ballard's Scandinavian immigrants. The parking lot was obscured from the street by a row of oak trees and a rusted chain-link fence.

I drove past her house again, more quickly this time, and around the old school to the entrance to the lot and parked the pickup close enough to the fence to be able to watch the house. The few other cars in the lot would be leaving by nightfall, but the fence, the darkness, would make me less conspicuous.

I waited for her to return, never considered the possibility she might not, that she was on vacation or a business trip. I just assumed she would, that the day would finally come around for this.

I'm sure I was noticed, after the first hour, by someone, unseen perhaps. I thought of going off, to kill time elsewhere, before returning.

Drive by the girl's house, Jessica's? She was only a few streets away to the west, close enough for her, in another time, to have walked to this school. She wouldn't be playing out in front of her house, not yet, perhaps not ever again. Even if she was, what would I do, stop and tell her who I was, and not to be afraid, and ask her if her nightmares were subsiding, tell her how much she had reminded me of Emma? Tell her that I had been going to give her a gift to help her, because I make things, you see, and sometimes hands can help heal the heart, but that I never finished it, twice now, because something had happened and wouldn't stop?

I waited until darkness had closed in around me, leaving only the streetlights shrouded by the oak trees. People walked by on the sidewalk, glancing at me through the fence as if I were caged.

Her porch light was on, too. Either she had forgotten to turn it off in the morning, when she left for work, or she had made sure it was on because she knew she would be back after dark.

It was too late for me to talk to her now. To approach her in the darkness would ruin any second chance. I waited. I had to see her. She was the only other survivor.

It was close to eleven when the two cars slowed before her house; one pulled into the driveway, the headlights rising, then falling, with the grade. The other car parked on the street. Doors slammed shut; the drivers converged at the front walk. Together they walked to the steps and up. Carla Martell laughed as she got out her jingling keys, unlocked the door. The man, his suit coat draped over an arm, whispered something into the blond curls around her ear. She turned into the light, toward him, and before they kissed I caught her fine, strong profile. She looked to be in her mid-forties.

In the doorway they took off their shoes, carried them inside. In her bare feet, Carla Martell was a foot shorter than her friend. The door closed, and a few seconds later the porch light flicked out.

I started the truck, flicked on my own lights, just for the hell of it. Insects darted crazily through the links of the fence. The low beams illuminated the putting-green lawn. The highs caught the porch, the glistening porch railing, the mailbox that had *Post* scripted pretentiously.

She liked things tidy. Shoes on the porch—no dirt in her house. Ellie and I had tried the shoes-at-the-door habit but, with a young boy, gave it up after a week.

The guy? Some lawyer or businessman boyfriend. They weren't married. They would have taken the mail in if they were; they wouldn't have kissed on the porch.

The pickup idled. I watched various lights go on in the house, not wanting to leave, not yet. Maybe it was the prospect of sharing the secret with someone else who knew, finding something that might prove things one way or the other. I couldn't find the letters, so Carla Martell would have to do. The heat of the day had gone with her arrival, but the voices of the past days and weeks remained, transmissions from . . . out there.

He's out there. I know it, now you do, too.

Carla Martell was reentry and she had something for me. She had to. She was there when it happened; she could tell me things even Sam couldn't, such as . . .

Such as what, Paul? What he was like? Your father, the Pied Piper? Why hers changed his mind? What else? You know what they say: be careful what you wish for because you might get it. You're not sittin' high with her, this last chance. There's a name for what you're doing now and a law, which isn't the worst of it. You're doing what that guy was doing in the van, not five minutes from here. Was he watching you, or Ellie, or both of you?

An upstairs light, the bedroom light, flicked out, and the house was now dark. I flicked off mine, too, until I left the parking lot and headed home, thinking that it was likely Carla Martell would not want to get the only thing I had to give her. It certainly wasn't the bear's claw I'd had in my hand the entire time I'd been waiting for her, and watching.

Ellie wasn't working; the front window of her study was dark. She hadn't been getting much work done lately and I certainly hadn't. I put the claw on the cutting board in the kitchen.

I checked in on Michael. Near his bed was the book Ellie had been reading to him: *The Indian in the Cupboard,* about an English boy who can make toy plastic figures come alive with a magic key and a magic cupboard.

I went upstairs. She was reading in bed. The heat of the day was still trapped upstairs, but the oscillating fan was going, clicking at the end of each slow, humming turn. She put aside the book she'd been reading: Russo's *The Risk Pool.* I sat down on the bed.

"I went over to Dad's."

"I can smell the whisky."

"I looked for the letters again."

"Don't you think it's time to let that go?" She said it carefully, slowly.

"I can't, Ellie."

"What happened . . . with that guy, Paul? We have to talk about that. You said . . . before that you wanted to talk."

"So did you."

"What did he say to you?"

I told her about it. "I lost it, no question. It's going to be tough to explain to Michael why I'm glad I didn't just walk away from that skinny asshole wearing shit-kicker boots and a bear-claw necklace. I just hope that's the worst of me he ever sees."

But neither of you have seen the worst. You weren't at Shilshole.

"Michael kept asking me tonight at bedtime why Daddy did that."

"What did you tell him?"

"A bad day. People have them. I didn't tell him about the dog."

"The dog? What dog?" I realized my wife was sitting on the bed farther away from me than when I first came into the room.

"The dog that was found dead and mutilated in the dumpster behind your workshop."

"*What?*"

"The guy who runs the frame shop next to you called up while you were gone, said it looked like it'd been there for a few days."

"Oh, Jesus. What did you tell him?"

"What did I tell him? I'm not sure that's the question to be asked right now. What did I tell him? You tell me."

"What kind of dog was it?"

"The kind that scared Michael at the car wash. A rottweiler. I don't like dogs either that threaten my son, but my God, Paul . . ."

"Ellie, listen to me. I didn't kill any dog. I don't know what the hell happened, but I didn't do this. The guy left before me and Michael and I came home. How would I know where the guy lives? It's a coincidence."

"A coincidence? The same kind of dog found in the dumpster behind your workshop?"

"It *has* to be something like that, Ellie, because I *didn't kill* the damn *dog*. You think if I *did* do it I'd bring the evidence to where—"

"Paul, Michael's going to hear. He's heard and seen enough today."

"*Fuck it, Ellie. You're accusing me of butchering a dog and I'm telling you I didn't do it!*"

"What am I supposed to think? Put yourself in my place."

"Someone else must have done it. Someone there who saw what happened, who has a huge chip on his shoulder because his kid once got bitten bad by a rott or something."

"Or something. It's—"

She bit it off: *It's always someone else, something else, a coincidence . . . an accident . . . Emma. Full circle to a nightmare. The old territory. Ellie and I sure as hell share that territory.*

We didn't speak for minutes. We knew where it was heading. We stared at the oscillating fan, its current passing us in turn. A siren grew, then faded, heading north.

I tried to bring us back.

"We need Ireland. We have to forget this and talk about Ireland."

"I can't. I don't want to." She was crying softly now. "Things are . . . closing in, closing shut. I have to—we have to come up for air."

I went downstairs.

Closing in? I should have said then, *There's a woman in Ballard named Carla Martell who got as close as you can get and not be dead. That's where I was tonight, after the whisky, getting closer, and wanting to, because I have to get closer to find out. And there's my uncle you haven't met, who goes into the mountains because he still believes the mass murderer who took her sister is close and always has been. I don't believe him, but I have to be sure. That's why I spent the evening waiting for Carla Martell to come home, and feeling good about it, like it was the only place in the world for me to be. For those few hours, the only place that mattered was the secret I keep holding back from you, Ellie, because you'll think I'm nuts, crazy as Sam Jameson, even if it wouldn't bother you that my real father was that mass murderer they called the Pied Piper.*

Ireland was now a busted dream, when so recently it had seemed the only possible place to isolate and exile the heartache and ghosts, those I alone knew about, and those we shared.

There were a hundred places there to tell her everything, places in the West, strands and lanes emptied of tourists in the autumn, castles like Aughnanure where Michael could prowl the parapets and watchtowers while I told her everything. Or on the ferry to Inishmore, where the stone walls of Dun Aengus curve out from the cliffs, ready to receive the desperate for another last stand and maybe this one would be remembered.

Not here, not yet, not now. Because I still hoped that what Carla Martell would tell me, tomorrow, would somehow wipe the slate clean, make the past the past, and bring Ireland back, leaving only one man still crazy enough to keep pursuing the ghost.

Later that night I opened the back door and flung the bear claw into the night, a totem for someone else to hold and wonder how it got here in the city. The claw clicked on something hard in the distance, a clicking sound that Sam Jameson had undoubtedly heard before, the sound of a bear moving through the stony, mountain wilderness.

Chapter 24

THE PENDANT

The next day I insisted on dropping Michael off at day camp in Montlake, even though Ellie usually does it. I wanted to tell him myself about what had happened, to own up to it. A kid should know his father can make mistakes, but there's just so much you can say in a fifteen-minute ride, and thankfully we ran out of time before I could betray the complications of feeling good about something you're not especially proud of doing. In this case, dumping that shitheel over the railing.

"I don't think I want to go back to the zoo for a while," he said.

"Neither do I," I said.

I arrived at the shop around ten. Chris Arkills, who'd called Ellie about the dog, wasn't in his shop, and the dog was no longer in the dumpster I share with three other businesses, a fact I neglected to mention to Ellie. Animal Control had undoubtedly taken it away.

I talked to others—Ken Persson, Leo DeNatale, and Scott Clement—who ran businesses in the area, to see if they had seen anyone dumping the dog. No one had.

I decided to work through the day, to get my mind off everything. I hadn't put in any time at the shop. I had a backlog of orders for children's wagons, up to ten now, almost a month's worth of work.

A stack of white oak needed to be cut to size for the wagon sides, before the work on the hand-cut dovetails. I hoped I never got so busy that I had to use a jig for joinery work. The older I get, the more I value the route and not the destination. Cutting dovetails by hand may be inefficient, but it's the way I like to work. I'm never going to make much money pushing oak and cherry this way in a fiberboard world. I should have been born in the age of frigates.

I measured the oak. The Delta table saw hummed to life.

I should have been nowhere near the thing on a day like today.

I was thinking about Ellie mostly. But I was also thinking about the end of the day, and what Carla Martell and I might say to each other, if anything. I was thinking how foolish it was to even hope the woman would choose to see the Pied Piper's son, and that sometimes the unlikely is the only option.

I assumed I was concentrating on the ripping. I wasn't.

The very first board kicked back viciously, snapping my hand back, so close to the whirring blade I felt the cutting breath. I missed losing my thumb, in a pinwheeling spray of blood, by a quarter inch.

I turned off the saw, leaned against the workbench as the motor whined down. That had never happened before, not that closely, not that badly.

Five minutes after the near miss I revved up the Delta again and did the damn boards, putting money where my mouth had been with Michael so often. Fall from your bike, get back on. Hit by the pitch? Get back in the box. It's okay to make a mistake, just try to learn from it.

Like Emma?

Like with Sam, making the mistake of not blowing away Russel Strickland when he had the chance?

Was going to Carla Martell a mistake?

And how many more would Ellie give me, before she took Michael and left?

I did the boards, but not without the feeling that there was a grinning guy behind me wearing a dog collar of blackened thumbs, ready to shove me into the whirring blade.

I pieced together the rest of the day with finish work, business calls, cleanup, and read forty pages of O'Brian's *Desolation Island* at the canal instead of taking lunch. I didn't feel like eating. At four o'clock I called Ellie. We had what was, at best, a long-distance conversation. I told her I would be late, had to go see a customer in the evening. It was the closest to the truth I could get to, and it still hung on me like a week in the woods.

*   *   *

I waited in the Nordic Heritage Museum parking lot again, farther away from the fence this time, but close enough to see her arrive.

At five-thirty her Celica pulled into the driveway. I left the parking lot, drove around the block, and parked on the street in front of her house.

I knocked on the door, knocked away the voice. She answered almost immediately.

"Yes?" she said, one hand on the knob, the other fiddling with a pendant around her neck.

She had her shoes off. I'd caught her before she had a chance to change. Black skirt and a light red blouse, not summer colors but the kind of colors you wear to offset paleness, and she was pale even for Seattle. Veins surfaced blue—delicate tributaries on her neck and forehead that glistened with the heat of the day. She kept her blond hair up, but wisps and tendrils had escaped here and there.

It wasn't her natural color; her dark eyes betrayed that. They weren't dark brown, or gray, but black, the perfect match for the skirt, the kind of eyes that made me think of the sun eclipsed behind a passing moon.

I told her who I was, and was ready for her to close the door, to shake her head, for those dark eyes to grow wide with disbelief. But she looked past me, as if trying to see if someone else was with me, or assuring herself others were around. Maybe the guy working on his bike in the yard next door was enough for her, or the teenagers skateboarding in the parking lot beyond the fence.

She stepped back to let me in.

It was as if she were expecting me. It was so easy. Too easy. Seeing this woman was all I'd thought about for a day, and something was pulling me back, telling me not to go in. She should have been the one backing away.

"You'll have to take those off," she said.

"All right. It's your house."

I paired my shoes next to hers on the low rack. "A friend of mine suggested the idea," she said. "I've kept with it."

I went in first, she followed, leaving the door open. I was about to sit down in one overstuffed chair by the bay window but she motioned me to another. "That one. Please. Would you like something to drink? I was just going to get one when you knocked."

"No, thanks."

I looked around while she was in the kitchen. The room was a paean to consumerism. A large-screen TV in one corner with a VCR next to it. In another corner a Sony stereo system that probably cost two months' worth of my rent. There was nothing of wood in the room. You could have eaten off the brick of the fireplace. The lamps, chairs, coffee table, were all metal; even the small dining table and chairs off the kitchen were metal. The mantelpiece above the hearth was bare save for a vase with fresh daffodils and lilies. No photos. Not a book in sight, nothing in disarray, everything where it was supposed to be. The framed pictures around the room tastefully serviced the room. Decor art. She came back with a glass of fruit juice, placed it on a coaster, aligning its edge with that of the table.

Carla Martell had long, slim fingers, with nails as well manicured as the room, and played with the pendant, as if she were signaling someone with flashes of gold and silver on a chain that matched her hair color.

It was quiet enough in the living room to hear the pendant tinking as she handled it, the ticking of a clock in the kitchen, the kids skateboarding across the street.

"You might have called first," she said.

"If I had, you may not have answered the door."

"Shall we do first names, Paul? It seems . . . justified."

"If you'd like."

"So you would have come anyway, if I'd said I didn't want to talk to the son of Russel Strickland?"

"I would have tried again."

She smiled at that. "There's a word for a certain kind of persistence, and it's against the law. Did you think I'd slam the door in your face?"

"That crossed my mind."

"Well, it seems your instinct was correct. Sometimes it's better not to have time to think beforehand and let that get the better of curiosity. I also never learn. I always let them in first and ask questions later. A bad habit that's occasionally gotten me into trouble. Are you going to be trouble, Paul?"

"I'd like to know what happened that day."

"You know that, don't you? I mean, you tracked me down to tell you what you already know?"

"I don't know why your father changed his mind about Russel Strickland being alive."

She sipped her drink. "How did you find me?"

I told her. Not about Sam; mostly about my conversation with William Martell.

"Chilly Billy. Calling him the black sheep of the family would be doing him a compliment. My mother moved away because of him."

"Phoenix."

"You must have gotten him when he wasn't drunk. That's right. Phoenix. Like the weather we're having."

"He told me your father wasn't there when it happened."

"That's true, and that's about the only thing he told you that probably is. Bill Martell's a bastard, and the only thing wrong with his boozing is that he hasn't done enough of it yet to kill him."

"What happened?"

"The truth of what happened was that Trudy had a fight with Mom. She was getting to be that age. The argument had been festering over the week, about an older boy Trudy wanted to date. He seemed nice enough to me, though he had this greaser reputation and Mom didn't think he was appropriate for a fifteen-year-old girl. The boat ride to Chelan was supposed to smooth things over, but it didn't work out that way. The confines of the boat only made them get on each other's nerves."

"So there was a fight?"

"A real screaming match. In front of the lodge. I remember thinking, 'Why doesn't the policeman do something.' Not realizing the 'policeman' was a ranger. They stalked off in different directions. I had to choose between them, and I went after Trudy because she went toward the woods and Mom took off toward the water. I chose Trudy in part because I had gotten a pretty bad sunburn the day before at the beach, and more on the boat even though Mom told me to stay inside. The woods were cool and the sun wouldn't get me. That and the fact that Trudy didn't seem to be as angry as Mom was."

Carla heard something outside, drew back the curtains, her glass in her hand. The ice tinkled: faraway bells. How many people had she ever talked to about this? Where was the evidence of her family? Not in this room.

"Are you expecting someone?"

"As a matter of fact, I am. He's a stockbroker who takes bread home in a doggie bag from restaurants, but he's good in bed."

"Is that why you let me in, because he's arriving soon?"

"I let you in because I wanted to. It's true what they say about telling strangers things you wouldn't tell anyone else. But you're not a stranger, not really."

She kept looking out the window. "They're setting up for the Tivoli fair in the parking lot across the street. It's late this year for some reason." She let the curtain fall back.

"It was a long time ago, Paul. You blank out a lot. You have to. I would know him if I saw him again, even now, but I can't sit here and give you a good description of him, or my sister, for that matter. She was beautiful and her hair was a lot lighter than mine, and I always wished I had hair like that. She had longer legs than I did, and that was why I couldn't keep up. I kept calling for her to stop, after I couldn't see her on the path anymore.

"I don't see how he got her so quietly, without me hearing. I couldn't have been more than thirty yards behind them on the path. He had to have been waiting, but he couldn't have known we would do what we did going into the woods."

"Maybe he was on the boat."

"Funny you should say that. That's the first thing I thought of when I turned around on the path to see if I could still see the water. That's when I saw him. I thought, 'That's the man on the boat,' who should have been smoking a cigarette because that's what you did when you were all by yourself and looking away at something. My father was always doing that, and my uncles.

"He just appeared, stepping out into the path, between me and the water. He had my sister in front of him, and a knife to her neck, one hand around her mouth so she couldn't scream. Her hands were tied in front of her. I always thought her eyes should have been big, big as silver dollars, but they were closed, like she was expecting to die any second.

"She was shaking so badly it made the knife twitch against her neck. He'd already pricked her with it because there was already blood, a single trail of it, down her neck, into her blouse. He was big, bigger than my father and had black hair that was slick like an animal's when it's just come out of the water, and he was smiling over the top of my sister's head.

"I tried to scream but nothing came out. It was like I'd gotten the wind knocked out of me. For weeks afterward, I couldn't talk. It was like I left every word I knew in those woods.

"I ran. He laughed because he was blocking the path toward help and the only place I could run was deeper into the woods, where he was going. I ran and ran. I kept looking back and so I didn't see the root across the path. My foot caught in it and I twisted as I fell and did something to my left knee. I got up. It was no good. I could hobble but the knee hurt badly. I was crying so much I couldn't see the path and he had no trouble catching up to me. Trudy's eyes were open now because she was crying, too.

"I remember his voice as deep and he talked quickly. He said he was going to have to kill his 'little red Indian' for trying to escape. He put his lips to Trudy's ear. 'Any last words for your sister? If you scream, I'll cut your throat.' His hand slipped from her mouth. Trudy pleaded with him to let me go. 'You don't want her,' she said. 'She's hurt. She won't be able to keep up.'

"He stared at her. He was staring at the blood trickling down her neck. He didn't look back down the trail to see if anyone was coming. He didn't seem worried about that at all. He just kept looking at Trudy, who was standing by me. I could feel her shaking next to me.

"He reached over and smeared his fingers with the blood on her neck, then licked the fingers.

"He said . . . he said to Trudy, 'Okay, we'll start right, you and I.' He pushed her ahead, up the trail a little, then said to me, pointing a finger, 'Don't think you're anything special. You're not the first I let live. A boy was first.' "

"He said that? He said, 'A boy was first'?"

"His exact words. They're not something you forget. He said it like it was me who had done something wrong. Like I was spoiled or something. He was talking about you, wasn't he?"

"He must have meant my brother, Steven."

I want to see him . . . he's my son.

Not anymore he isn't.

"Did he say anything else?"

"Yes. He took a harmonica from his back pocket and tossed it at my feet. He asked me if I knew how to play it. I couldn't speak, I couldn't even nod my head or shake it. He took that for a no. 'I'll teach you sometime,' he said, and laughed. He ripped the bead necklace from Trudy's neck and tossed that to me, too. 'Something to remember your sister,' he said.

"I watched them go. He kept pushing her to go faster, and I remember thinking, hoping Trudy would fall, too, because then he might let her go, too, and then I thought, no, he'd kill her if she did. I began crying even more because I didn't know what to think or what to hope for. Trudy was gone and I knew I'd never see her again, and all that was left of her was that bead necklace that looked like one of those poisonous snakes with the venom that paralyzes you, kills you in minutes, that you see in books about the jungle but not here.

"I was holding the necklace when they found me and I still have it. I left everything back there when I moved to Seattle, but I took Trudy's necklace. I've never been back there, but then sometimes I feel I never left. You try. You try to move on, tell yourself it was a long time ago, and not to feel sorry for yourself. After all, I'm the one who lived."

"Do you think sometimes that your sister might still be alive, Carla?" I said it softly.

"Thinking and hoping are different things."

"What did your father . . . think?"

"Did my uncle tell you what happened in 1981?"

"No. We didn't talk for long."

"He has that wonderful ability with people, my uncle. He could have told you my father received a knife, a beautifully made knife that had the initials JPS on it. A letter came with it, with a Redding, California, postmark. The letter was from . . . him, from Russel Strickland."

"It couldn't have been him. He was found dead in a cabin by that lake in Ferry County."

"So they say. I'm telling you what name was on that letter. That's what the letter said. Russel Strickland, your father."

"My father was Charles Sinclair, the man who raised my brother and—"

"What do you care then? Why are you here rolling in this shit?"

"What did the letter say?"

"Do you want the exact words? I mean, I have them, every single last one of them. I threw away the letter, I burned it, but you can't burn away what you remember, can you, even if you want to.

"He said, '*I just want you to know that your daughter is still alive. She is my wife now and she's safe now. We have a home and we have a child. A boy. My first two were taken away but I have another now. I've actually gone back to school. I give music lessons to help out with the money. Note to Carla: Have you learned how to play the harmonica yet? Trudy wanted me to tell you that she's all right. It's her birthday and I've written this because she asked me to. See, I'm not such a bad guy after all. Birthdays are very important to us, so I said yes. I told her she's my queen for a day, just like the old TV show when things were still black-and-white, which is so much better I think. I said yes because I can't let her out, which is what she really wants every year. I know you won't believe me, so I've sent you the knife I took from John Stivers. I killed him with his own knife. You know what happened to the others. It was messy but I took a swim in the river afterwards. I'm doing this for my wife. If I find out you've been to the police with this, Trudy is dead. I don't want to kill her. If I had to kill her, I don't know what I'd do. I might pick up where I left off, the angel looking homeward again, to butcher a Wolfe, and we don't want that, do we?' "*

Carla Martell got up and closed the front door. As if to compensate for that, she opened the drapes. It was getting dark, and across the street, workers were finishing up work on the temporary booths and stalls of the Tivoli fair. Headlights swept across the house.

She didn't sit down but stood by her chair, looking out the window. One hand brushed the top of the side table, back and forth. The other was playing with her pendant.

"You look like you want to go, Paul."

"No, I don't. There's—"

"Because I wouldn't have closed the door if I wanted you to go. Two people who have so much in common should have some privacy, don't you think?"

"Until Mr. Doggie Bag gets here."

"That's good. I'll have to remember to call him that when I see him. It won't be tonight, though. That was a little lie. I'm glad I fibbed, aren't you?"

"What did your father do about the letter?"

"What would you have done? It was preposterous. What was he supposed to believe now, with this letter? I mean, even if we'd had doubts about that body they found in that cabin, it was crazy to believe Trudy was still alive with him after so many years. That she'd married him? Come on. Why didn't he send a picture of Trudy?

"My father went to the police. They said it sounded like some sicko, someone that we knew, who'd had fantasies about Trudy. My sister was very pretty. I mean, I'm okay, but I have to work out six times a week to stay there. Trudy was something else again. That's why my mother was always so worried. The police said the letter sounded like the work of a copycat, a wanna-be, who knew the details of what happened and put the initials on the knife. They said if anything else was sent to Dad, et cetera, et cetera, they'd check into it as a matter of harassment. But nothing else came.

"My father believed Trudy was still alive and that Strickland had her. Why would a neighbor or someone we knew wait twenty years? That wasn't any more likely than Strickland. Why would some sicko copycat go to the trouble and expense of putting the Stivers initials on a hundred-dollar German knife, for a one-shot prank? Dad believed Strickland sent the knife, instead of a photo, for proof because he wanted to back up his warning in a more threatening way.

"But in the end he believed it because he wanted to believe Trudy was still alive. He couldn't do anything about it, of course, except hire a private investigator he couldn't afford, who took a month and most of Dad's savings and came up with nothing. My parents divorced. Dad died two years later of a heart attack, so there was no foul play, but it was just as if your father had killed him."

She was still standing in front of her chair and her hand ceased its movement over the table. She glanced out the bay window. Beyond my truck, the street, some kids were hanging out, sitting on the logs that separated the parking lot from the fence.

"They like to use the lot at the end where the big hedge is and the freight container," Carla said. "Sometimes they just fuck in their cars or drink beer and throw the bottles on the pavement. I call the cops, but they never come. It's bad for the weeks around the Fourth of July. The parking lot is like a war zone with kids setting off their firecrackers. I had a dog once but she took off the day before one Fourth and I never found her. I named her Ketchup when she was a puppy because she liked to lick the ketchup off my plate when I cooked hamburgers for us."

She closed the drapes with three pulls of the string. "I can see the parking lot from my bedroom window. Tom—Mr. Doggie

Bag—and I were just getting going last night, waiting for wood as the porn studs say, when I saw the truck out there. It was someone new, because nothing was going on around it, no kids, no drinking, and you can't make out in a pickup, can you, Paul? It made me notice, and so did Tom, in spite of what was going on, or about to go in, I should say. Tom actually suggested we invite the guy in—you—for a two-for-one. It wouldn't have been the first time, but I declined like a good little girl. Not him, Tom, I said, not *him*. And Tom said, 'What do you mean *him*?' And I said the man who's watching the house."

"Carla . . ."

"That all it was, Paul, just looking for my address? The missing link? Well, you've found it. I feel I know you better than even Tom, and he knows my tastes, and I work with him. But he knows nothing about what I told you."

"You think he's still alive, don't you?"

She didn't answer. She opened the table drawer and took out a semiautomatic pistol that looked huge in her pale hands.

The kickback of the saw happened quicker, but I felt the same way.

I got up to leave. She swung the gun around, pointed it at my chest.

"Sit down, just for a while longer. *Then* you can go. Don't worry. I mean, it *is* loaded, but I'm not going to shoot you. I mean, I *could*. I doubt whether anyone knows you're here. A visit like this, or last night even, it's not something you'd tell the wifey. She wouldn't understand, would she, Paul? Or maybe you're lying to her. Maybe you're lying about this whole thing. Maybe you're like that wannabe who maybe wrote the letter. I mean, I don't really know, do I? Maybe you're not even his son. *Say you are, Paul.* If you don't, then you're lying." She wiggled the gun.

"Why don't you put that away?"

"You're sweating. You want that drink now? Then say you are. *Say it.*"

"The gun isn't helping anything, Carla."

"Sure it is. You got what you came for. Now I'm getting mine. I've always wanted to take this out and kill him when he came to teach me how to fucking play. You're the next best thing, aren't you?"

When she came over to me, she was holding the gun at her side and her finger wasn't on the trigger. She came close, so close I could smell her fruity perfume, the lemon on her breath. Her eyes were so dark. They weren't blinking. When she reached out to feel my heart, the pendants tinkled.

She grinned. "You're like a freight train. Are you a fast freight, Paul?" She glanced down. "You're not wetting your pants. Good boy."

The pendant hung inches away from my face, a silver apple and a gold apple, each the size of a fingernail, on a single chain.

"He was about this close, you see. He stank like sweat and the woods, like mushrooms. I can't stand them to this day. I didn't tell you he touched me. Not where you'd think. On the eyes. His hands were big, the fingers, but not thick like a carpenter's. He pulled my eyelids down, shutting out everything. So I was nothing then, only darkness, but I heard everything. His breathing, the sounds of the woods, my sister's sobbing, and his laugh at the end, when he told me to open my eyes again."

She reached out. "Don't move, you *son of a bitch*. What did you expect? *Don't move, I said.* You won't say it so we have to do this."

She touched my eyes, the left, then the right. Her fingertips were cold. When her fingers left, I opened my eyes to the silver and gold apples.

You're the apple of my eye.

Can the ripest apple be plucked too soon?

She turned away, lowering the gun.

"That will have to do. You can go now. If you want." She put the gun back in the drawer. No wonder she hadn't wanted me to sit there. No wonder she let me in. She'd been waiting for . . . *him* her whole life.

I got up. I walked over to her, not the door. She didn't back away when I drew out the apple pendant. The silver and gold apples were tiny and glistened like the sweat in my palm.

"I can see it," she said softly, staring at my chest. "Fast freight. What does it feel like inside, Paul? Like it's going to burst? That's how it is for me sometimes. You're a fast freight now, all right."

"*Who gave you this, Carla?*"

"My, such vehemence!"

"Who?"

"A friend."

"When?"

"A while ago."

"Why?"

"Why? We were lovers. What do you give your lovers, give the wifey? It didn't last long; none of them do. I wear it every now and then. It's from an Irish poem, he said. I forget which one. You want the thing, take it. Rip it off my neck." She was whispering now, insistent. "It's a start. Maybe Froggie will come a-courting after all. For a stockbroker he's unpredictable. Go ahead. Rip it off. It's what you want to do."

"No, it isn't."

"Most men would. Your father did. Don't *you* want to touch me, Fast Freight?"

"Did he tell you the words?"

"The words?"

"The poem."

"I don't remember them."

"You remembered the letter."

"That was different."

"What's his name?"

"Why do you want his name?"

"Just tell me."

"Why should I do that?"

"Lovers' afterglow. In case you didn't know it, we've just fucked each other."

"They usually don't leave as fast as you. It's Peter Masskey."

The name sounded familiar, but I couldn't place it. "Where does he live?"

"I don't know. He always came over here. He teaches at Cascade Pacific. English. What's this about?"

"Maybe you've been keeping that gun for the wrong man."

I walked to the door to put on my shoes, and she followed as if I were late for the night shift and she had my lunch pail.

"You mean Peter? Peter Masskey's the one who took his shoes off the first night I brought him home. I thought, 'Here's a well-trained man; do I want a well-trained man?'"

I stood. She was so close. The metallic moon and sun clinked-clinked as she turned them in her hand.

"Did he say anything about his past?" I took the pendant from her, stretched the chain taut, closer, but not Carla Martell. "Did he give you anything else?"

"You're nuts."

"Possibly. Russel Strickland said you weren't the first. He said there was the boy. I'm thinking now the boy wasn't my brother. Take care of yourself, Carla," I said, "and be careful who you let in next time."

I walked to the pickup.

She stayed on the porch, watching me leave. Not something she probably did with Peter Masskey. Then again, she hadn't pulled out the gun with any of them, either.

Driving home, I thought of Mrs. Clarke's owls and the apple she had given me when I left for Chelan to see a man named Sam Jameson, and the one that had been on the table by my father's chair the night he died. Had he eaten that, watching the blood seep from my father? How long does it take to eat an apple. Five minutes. He had plenty of time.

You're the apple of my eye! Happy 7th, Michael. A sick birthday greeting to the grandson of the man who had terrorized a seven-year-old Peter Masskey? Whoever Peter Masskey was.

Carla Martell had her gun; I had mine, waiting for me, if I was right, and not completely nuts to think that Russel Strickland might have meant someone else besides his eldest son when he told Carla Martell she wasn't the first one he'd let live.

A boy was first.

Maybe Sam Jameson was wrong, too, waiting for the wrong man.

Was Peter Masskey the boy? Where had I seen that name before?

Can the ripest apple be plucked too soon?

Carla Martell couldn't recall the words to the poem he had recited, but I remembered one. I knew the words to it even before I went to Ireland. Yeats was a favorite of mine, Ellie's, too, and I could remember just when and where we had found that out about each other, when I'd recited the words:

> I will find out where she has gone,
> And kiss her lips and take her hands;
> And walk among long dappled grass,
> And pluck till time and times are done
> The silver apples of the moon,
> The golden apples of the sun.

Chapter 25

STORM CHASER

I left the house shortly after sunrise, well before Ellie and Michael would be getting up. Fifteen minutes after, I was through the I-90 tunnel heading east on the bridge over Lake Washington, heading for the mountains.

I got to Sam's house by noon. He was still in Stehekin.

The Chelan skies were still gray, but the smoke in the air wasn't as bad as before. The fires in the hills around the town had been contained. But there were others.

I put the gun and box of ammo in a cigar box I'd brought.

Hours later, on a deserted logging road off the reopened Route 2, a few miles east of Stevens Pass, I shot off six rounds into an alder the width of my hand from a distance of twenty feet. I hit the tree three times.

Back in the truck, I put the gun back in the cigar box and slid it under my seat.

It was chilly up in the mountains at four thousand feet. As I drove down a long, steep grade, I passed a succession of signs for a runaway-truck ramp, a graveled road that broke off from the highway and cut through the forest, rising almost to the top of a ridge. There were swerving tire ruts in the gravel, evidence the ramp had been used by some truck that had lost its brakes, was barreling out of control, the driver scared shitless. I could feel his fear because it had me, too.

You're right, Sam. There is someone out there. It's not the Pied

Piper. He's dead. But maybe someone has taken his place. So I'm going home with a box of ammo and a .38 he took from someone else long ago . . .

. . . to find out where she has gone . . . and pluck till time and times are done.

Going home. For whom?

For Peter Masskey.

I tried the brakes, the mental brakes, again. Wasn't it possible that Carla Martell had a lover who just happened to like Yeats and gave her a gift, a harmless signature of apples? Was that enough to send me . . . ten hours over the mountains and back . . . *he'll be coming 'round the mountain when he comes* . . . to get a gun because I was under the . . . the what?

The delusion, the you're-fucking-nuts idea that someone who . . . who, just whom are you talking about, my man?

Who?

A victim of Russel Strickland's?

A victim who was exacting revenge on people who had known the Pied Piper? So what if there had been the core of an apple in my father's living room or that both the Jamesons and the Stiverses had lived surrounded by apple orchards? And a little girl's father *could* have written a note to go along with his daughter's crayon apple.

Carla Martell's letter? Like the police said, a cruel prank.

That's it. Before you start orbiting out there with Sam Jameson and Carla Martell. Because if you keep accelerating, you're going to leave Ellie behind. Keep going like this, and one of these days she leaves and takes Michael and they won't be back.

My son, I want to see him.

Think your old man's going Looney Toons?

Hey, tell me now if it runs in the family.

The wallet? Someone simply returned it to the address on the driver's license. . . . No one killed Dad. The letters? He weighted the box, shuffled twenty yards—he could do that—and dumped them in the Sound.

Sara? Sara Bowers and Steven had simply run into predators. At the same time? It happens. Odds? What were the odds of a daughter losing her balance and falling to her death as she was emptying her mother's ashes from an urn? That happened a while ago in California. What were the odds of witnessing the abduction of a girl in Ballard?

Sam? An old man obsessed with something he felt he should have done, that would have kept seven people alive, and his sister.

Carla said Peter Masskey . . . not Stivers. Masskey. Every one of the Stivers family was killed. It was highly unlikely that the other victims of the Pied Piper—the mountain trappers and hermits, the grandparents and their granddaughter murdered on the bluff over-looking the newly built Rocky Reach dam—would have avengers.

There was no one else.

Who else? If Peter Massky was nothing more than a lover of Carla Martell's who liked to read Yeats and take his shoes off en-tering a house . . . who?

There was only Russel Strickland's other mercy.

A boy was first.

Steven. He had to have meant Steven. His firstborn.

Steven.

Steven?

I swerved over, stopped the pickup. A logging truck blared its horn, roared past me. I hadn't realized he'd been following so closely. I killed the engine. I couldn't drive.

Steven?

I sat there, numbed, and the volume was cranked waaaayyyyy up.

Is it you, Steven?

Why else would I have turned around, gone back on that trail below the falls, if something inside wasn't telling me my brother *was* still alive? Not just missing him, wanting him to still be with me, sittin' high, but *knowing* deep down he wasn't dead?

Steven . . . to Peter Masskey.

A college English teacher? Is that what you chose, finally, to do, Steven? You, the big pain in the ass to your high school teachers be-cause you always had that precision of mind that drove them nuts, catching them with their intellectual pants down? They weren't in your league, and you and they all knew it. I knew it; I came after you, I had to deal with their first looks when they read the name: Sinclair. Not another one. Maybe this one will be easier. Math was too easy, so you chose literature, a subjective field where you could turn the hues of gray into your favorite colors of black and white, the ones so necessary to fix the blame.

Is it you, Steven? Is it really you, the kid who always hated to get dirty, even though Dad would tell you not to worry about it because that's what we had washing machines and soap for? I should tell you, when I see you, that Carla Martell kept one fastidious habit of yours that you developed later. Did you start that after you murdered your own mother, who always kept her Mustang so cherry, who was obsessive about cleaning her hands after working on the car?

It's all coming back now. Even that night of your biggest triumph on the field. You and Charlotte Bender, the prettiest, most popular girl in the class, and you left her, went back, by yourself, to the field where you scored three touchdowns against Shorecrest, caught eight passes for 236 yards from J. R. Jenkins, who had the talent but not the height for the Pac 10? You were in the zone that day, sittin' high, way high. Charlotte was furious at being dumped so. I thought then that anyone who could do that, could do anything. Anyone who could walk away and leave something that others desired so much, were so envious about, was someone who was capable of anything.

I couldn't have done that. At the very least I would have taken her with me. You didn't. You had to walk that field once more, alone. You knew that what would be remembered was that day on the field, not some girl who would probably later marry a stockbroker like Mr. Doggie Bag or a lawyer and become a buyer for Nordstrom's after a brief fling at modeling. Even then you could walk away from the world because you saw where it was going, that sooner or later the monkeys would rule Oz and the pipes would stop skirling in Brigadoon. You knew it wouldn't get any better than a rare cloudless day in late October, in front of a thousand people who knew you by name.

Charlotte and I did it instead, in the caboose, and I still wonder why she didn't tell you.

What did happen back East that caused you to leave college so suddenly? You never told me in the caboose. Nothing lasts forever, sure, but that's what it was for. Then again, I never told you what Charlotte and I did there. But if we were in the caboose now, what would you say? That you found Dad's letters from Sara and read them all, not just one? I wish you'd told me. Did you go away to Alaska and stay away, to brood, slowly manufacturing your ver-

sion of an accelerant that hastens fires? Of course you took the box of letters. Who else would want them if not the Piper's son?

Do you know I thought you were after Ellie?

I did, so help me, I did. Crazy, huh?

There was a time, after I met her, when I was scared that all I'd done is pimped for you, not that you ever needed help with women, who always seemed at that age to be attracted by the ones most capable of spurning them. I actually thought for a while you'd take her from me. I worked with my hands; you worked with your mind. Did you ever notice how uncomfortable I was when you were around Ellie and me? She liked you so much. Was it me, or was it the idea of marrying into such a literary and artistic family that appealed to her, the brother who was capable of anything, including the solitude necessary for writing a novel, what she wanted to do? You were all over her, but you had to leave, the Legionnaire, and so you told me not to let this one go. Do you know that I had one explanation for your disappearance—while it still seemed temporary? That you'd gone off in secret mourning because she'd married me and not you, like in that Scottish song "I Once Loved a Lass," which you played so well on your guitar those times in the caboose.

What happened, Steven? When? When did you snap? When did the fire go out of control? When you realized what you really were, where you really came from and how big the lies were? It was like an equation where all the assumptions were wrong and you always seemed to have the answers up till then. Someone who is always so precise with equations, so logical and forceful with his opinions, has to fix blame, assign betrayal.

I don't believe—Jesus, I can't believe, Steven—that you deliberately set out to kill Sara Bowers, even if you damned her twice, for abandoning you, and for pushing Mom to suicide. Maybe Sam was right and it wasn't like that.

But you had to have read all the letters so you assigned the worst. Is that why Dad made such a point of hiding the box of letters from me? Because he suspected you might have come across them? Didn't want a replay. What did he protect me from? You'd know. His terrible suspicion that you may have had something to do with Sara Bowers's disappearance?

In all things, even in this, you came before me. Did the rage come by degrees, one thing leading to another, until the thought of killing her didn't seem so extraordinary? You were a predator; you just didn't know it until it happened.

You've been wearing the cougar skin all along ever since Russel Strickland draped it over your shoulders at his trapper's cabin beyond Stehekin. Russel Strickland, the hideous laughing shaman.

And once it happened, you had to disappear. Forever. Surfacing a very safe number of years later to kill Dad for his part in the betrayal, the lie, or maybe because he always suspected.

The letter to James Martell? You did your homework all right. Creative writing for the budding novelist. A cover. To make people think Russel Strickland—first your obsession, then mine—was still alive.

It's you, Steven. My God, it really is.

Did you wait so long to kill Dad because you needed the distance? And even then, well, he wasn't really our father. He must have been shocked. Were you hoping for a heart attack?

But he didn't have to kill himself. Maybe it was enough, with you standing over him, over the cast with the name he'd written himself, your name, Steven, for Dad to put the gun himself into his mouth and pull the trigger after you'd told him what you'd done. And you took the letters, which no other killer, no other mere killer, Steven, would bother to steal.

You're so close. You always have been, haven't you? At some time we probably passed each other, somewhere. I might not recognize you. It's been so long.

Do you follow us, like Sara did, coming to see us, staying in the background, the shadows? Maybe you were even there at Shilshole.

Did you finish the job for me, the reflexive instinct of the older brother? No. You wouldn't have been such an animal, done what was done to Thomas Van Horn. Or would you? You killed before. Did you rip him apart like a cougar? Then return the wallet? Remember what Dad told us when we were younger? If one of us came home beaten up, the other better have some bruises, too? Was that you, Steven? For old times' sake? Or just to keep in practice? How many miles have you put on our old van, anyway? Jesus, how close do you want to stay to us?

But I have to know whether it was to help me or hurt me. You know, some kind of insurance in case I recognized you.

I have to think it's over, unless you're going to kill me, and then
surface with a story only Ellie the novelist could appreciate. She's
still beautiful, but then you know that. I'm sure you've kept tabs
on that. Is that it? The return of the prodigal who will take charge
and pluck the apples after my tragic death? Predators abound these
days. Things have gone to the dogs; the fields are full of ticks.
Maybe you've been setting me up all along, feeding my paranoia
like you would a pigeon. I always come back for more, don't I? If
not, you must know how far I've come, how far I've traveled, whom
I've talked to. You must know I'll be coming to see you, with truck-
loads of questions. And when I do, something has to give, doesn't
it? The concentric orbits are decaying and have to merge. I can't
live a life knowing you're out there, knowing what you've done. I
can't go to the police. They'd laugh me out of the station. I have
nothing. And I have everything. Everything I need.

Peter and Paul. Peter Masskey. I remember now where I saw
that name, Steven.

I came down out of the mountains in the last light of day. Lake
Sammamish, near where Ted Bundy picked up his first victim, was
black glass. There was an accident on I-5—a semi had jackknifed
just north of the downtown Seattle lids. It took almost an hour to
worm under the concrete nether-stone of the Convention Center and
Freeway Park. The flashing lights of two police cars, a Medic One
van, and a tow truck spun against the walls, keeping almost perfect
time to the rap music coming from the Trans Am ahead of me.

I had two pints of Guinness at the Dubliner and got back home
near midnight. I didn't go in. I parked the truck down the block,
far enough so Ellie couldn't see it if she looked out her study window, but close enough so I could tell when her light went out. She
wouldn't have heard the distinctive rattle of my pickup, the muffler
that had loosened on the first trip to Chelan. Her study was her co-
coon, and she never needed white noise like other writers did when
they worked—classical or rock music or even the hum of a fan.
Her white noise was silence, or something close to it.

I always woke first, during the night, when Emma or Michael
was teething or had a nightmare. I was always the first to hear
them, crying or suffering through a sickness. Sometimes I'd nudge

her and she'd go down, to soothe them in the rocking chair. Sometimes I'd go down myself and let her sleep. But always I heard them first.

"You're my ears," she would say.

That's right, I am, Ellie. And only I can hear the Piper's music. It's being played by someone else now. That would be you, Steven. Do you remember how bad Ellie's hearing is, the left ear?

One of the first things I had to accept about Ellie McKenna was how loud she had to keep the volume on the radio and the stereo. I wondered how many times over the years, when we made love, she had actually heard me when I whispered to her that I loved her.

I said it again, now, in the car, feeling like a sentry, someone with the watch, though it could have been something else, such as watching Carla Martell's house, something Steven would also do. Had done.

How many times have you driven by this house, Steven? How long did you wait for me to leave our father's house on Bainbridge?

Our orbits are decaying. They're merging. Only one of us can continue.

I waited an hour before Ellie was finished writing and the light went out, then longer still, to give her time to get to sleep. Then I drove the pickup into the driveway. I left the cigar box under the seat. Whatever Steven had in mind, he wouldn't be breaking into the house to do it. Not there.

I checked on Michael before going upstairs, paused to hear Ellie's soft breathing. Then I continued down the hallway to her study, shut the door, and turned on the light.

To my left was her desk, the shelves over the computer filled with reference books, supplies, the small bear sculpture Dad had given her, all the notes to remind her of this and that, a picture of Michael and me taken last winter when we were sledding up in the mountains. On an adjacent, smaller desk she had more notes, a book on construction of a replica of the *Susan Constant*, a Jamestown-era ship; books on early frontier living—and the manuscript in progress, already the thickness of a seventeenth-century gravestone.

To my right, her books filled floor-to-ceiling shelves. I'd lugged all those boxes of books up here, helped her put them on the shelves. Fiction toward the window, nonfiction toward the door, and all of it alphabetized. That, too, was Ellie: logical, ordered, rational. It wouldn't take me long to find it.

Maybe even less time than it took Dad to tell you where he'd hidden the box of letters, Steven.

The title had something to do with a storm. I remembered because the day we moved in, the front page of the *P-I* had disaster coverage of a tornado that had plowed through the town of Clement, Kansas, on a Saturday afternoon, killing twenty-six people, and Ellie had said, shaking her head, "They should rename the town *Inclement* now." The newspaper picture, an aerial, struck me because the path of the tornado had crossed the main street almost at right angles, making a giant cross of destruction.

I found it, pulled it out: *Storm-Chasers: Velocities of self-destruction in modern American literature. By Peter Masskey.* I hesitated, my heart pounding at the prospect of seeing my brother's picture on the back cover, the final proof of what he had done.

But there wasn't a picture of him on the back, only reviews by university presses. Nor was there a picture at the end of the cover blurb, only the simple "Peter Masskey lives in Seattle and teaches at Cascade Pacific University."

But there was a note, on the title page. *Ellie: It was pleasant chatting with you over the phone the other day. Please accept this personal copy of my book. I certainly hope you sell the other two you said you have in stock. I liked your title better,* The Art of Darkness, *though I'm sure Conrad's ghost, not to mention my publisher, wouldn't have since it's already been used, for a book about Stephen King, I believe. Good luck with your novel. Writers are sometimes plagued with coming up with better titles after publication. I hope you evade that fate.*

The note and signature were written in a precise but assertive hand. I made a mental note to compare it with some of Steven's letters and writing stored in the caboose. And the condolence note for Emma and Michael's birthday card.

I didn't need a photograph. I was foolish to think there'd be one. Even after years of thinning hair, added pounds, eyeglasses, and a beard perhaps, she would have recognized him.

I put the book back, left the room, and went to bed. Ellie was on her side, her back to me. She moved away. It wasn't just the heat upstairs.

"A woman called asking for you," she said.

Ellie still had her back to me; we weren't touching. If we had been, she would have felt me stiffen as if I'd been shot through with a bolt of electricity.

"Who was it?"

"She wouldn't give her name. She laughed when I said you weren't home, though."

"What did she want?"

"She said just to tell you she remembered the name of the poem: 'The Song of Wandering Aengus.' Then she hung up."

Three hours? Three hours right now, just like with Sam, straight through it all? Instead I told her about a customer named Mary Clarke, who'd called me at the shop the night before about ordering a wagon for her son for Christmas, and we got on the subject of Ireland and poetry.

Ellie sighed her disbelief. Then again, she wouldn't have believed the other either, not until I paid a visit to my brother.

"You're a lousy liar," she said. "You sure her initials aren't KDC?"

"KDC?"

"I found a bracelet with the initials KDC on the front steps."

"Ellie, I don't know anyone with the initials KDC."

"It wasn't the kind of thing our postman or paperboy would wear, you know. Or maybe we have people hanging out on our porch and we don't know it."

She got up and headed for the stairs.

"It's time we talked, I think," I said, even though she'd never believe me, not until I had some proof about Steven.

"Why, so you can just tell me it's something else, someone else?"

"It is, Ellie. It's a whole lot of something else."

But she was already down the stairs when I said it. "Whoever this KDC is, Paul," she shouted up, "the woman has lousy taste in jewelry."

THE CAGE: 7

His smell is strong this time, the strongest it's ever been.

Maybe it's because I'm sitting close to the cage for once, close enough to reach out in the darkness and run my free hand along the four-by-fours, feeling the bolts, the shallow dents and abrasions where I used to throw the books, pound on the wood with the spines of his books or my fists, until the books fell apart and my hands were too bruised and bloodied. My hands used to be so sore I couldn't pick up my food to eat, but they've healed now, so I can hold the gun.

It seems so stupid—that huddling in a far corner, the attempt to keep as far away from him as I could, as if that would make a difference. So useless.

I'm as close to him now as I can get, right next to his cage, this thing that both separates and joins us. He's sitting with his back against the door. He's only been inside the cage. He's delivered my food, taken away my pan of shit and piss. The air purifier hums the one note in the darkness. He can't see me when I raise my right arm and point the gun at his breathing.

I could do it so easily. End it now. He's given me the power to do that. For both of us. I could do it—BOOM. One shot. But if I did, I wouldn't be able to take the stuffed animal home from the fair.

I lower the gun. "You stink, Franklin," I tell him.

"That's the tenth time you've said that name since I gave you the gun."

"You're keeping score?"

"The name isn't even close. Where did you come up with it?"

"What does it matter? It's my name for you, since you won't tell me your real one. I know you don't like it and I don't care. I don't like BobBee either, but you keep using it."

"Okay. Fair's fair. I shall be Franklin for the duration."

"You still stink. Didn't you take a shower?"

He pauses. "I haven't taken a shower in years."

"You smell like it."

"I take baths. You can't hear anything outside when you take a shower."

"Psycho psych you out?"

"You couldn't hear what I was doing downstairs. That's how perfectly I've sealed you in here. You couldn't hear the thumping and clanging of the weights when I was working out."

"Gotta be strong so you can kill them all, is that it?"

"You never know when physical strength will matter."

I lift the gun, point it at his voice. "I have all the strength I need in my finger, Franklin."

"You like your gift, don't you? You never thanked me."

"I will when the time comes."

"That should be soon."

He flicks the flashlight in the corner, where I used to be when we talked in the darkness, signals an SOS and laughs. "Don't underestimate yourself, your physical strength. If we were to compare ourselves, you might be surprised how much you stack up to me."

"How do you know that?"

"You forget. I brought you into the world. This is your delivery room. I brought you here, stripped you naked as a newborn, and diapered you with my own clothes. I feed you and talk to you and give you gifts. Like any infant, you've squalled and raged against your helplessness, but you're growing up. Fast. You're learning the language I speak. So I know you're muscled. I didn't expect to find that. You must have worked out."

"I used to go to a health club five times a week."

"Getting that hard body you thought Kerrie Caldwell would enjoy, or other mannequins like her?"

"Maybe. So what?"

"I'll bet she never saw it. Few women did, or men. You're not a

gym rat, one for shirtless, pickup basketball games with the broth-
ers. So there are few, if any, who've seen you as I have, who will
know what you look like underneath your work blazer and rep tie
and those silly little fish pins you wore on your lapel, or that crossed-
fork-and-knife tie clasp. My God, no wonder they all laughed be-
hind your back!"

"Management was required to wear those things. They were
called PRAs—public relations accoutrements. Standard issue,
corporate—"

"STOP IT, JUST SHUT UP, WILL YOU?"

His explosion startles me. I have the feeling it's Franklin who's
in the cage, who can't get out, and not me. His anger subsides as
quickly as it erupted.

"I'm sorry," he says. "It's my fault. I shouldn't have brought up
the past."

To hear him say that astounds me as much as his giving me
the gun.

"Do you understand?" he says softly.

He said it first so I tell him I'm sorry, too. "Understand what?"

"The pair we are, you and I—please, don't back away."

I didn't realize I had. How does he know, in the dark?

"Come closer," he says. "Put your hand through the cage."

As I do, I hear him moving closer, too. When his fingers touch
mine, I feel almost an electric shock, an involuntary shuddering,
like a testing of reflexes. The fingers aren't enough. He clasps my
hand tightly, so tightly I imagine I can see the whitening flesh even
in this blackness. Our hands seem equally large, a match, like
brothers. Our grips are so strong it's as if one of us has saved the
other from being swept away. What would happen if the cage were
not there to separate us?

"It's just that I can't stand to hear you defend a life that no
longer exists," *he says, letting go first. I still have the gun in my*
other hand. I'm so close to him, the muzzle could reach his flesh.

"At first," *he whispers,* "you were just a physical match, unique
only in the uncanny closeness of that match, the luck of finding
you. I could have dressed as you for a busy Saturday night and
from the back no one would have known the difference. Your
meaningless, pitiful life mattered only to me in terms of how much
it annoyed me.

"*But you've come so far! So quickly! You've become me, in more than the sum of physical parts. That's why it angered me when you reverted back to what you once were. You were so brilliant with Ellie on the phone. I couldn't have done it better myself.*"

"*What does it matter if you're going to kill me?*"

"*Because you've become so much more. I won't be killing another. I will be killing myself. Do you see now? We are the same. Do you understand now?*"

"*I'm going to take your place, aren't I?*"

"*Yes. The gift of your life will be the rest of mine. I have my pride so I can't become someone who was once like you, BobBee, so please forgive me the outburst. Your gift, please believe me, is as magnificent an offering as any soldier who dies saving the life of a comrade.*"

"*Who wants the medal if you can't wear it.*"

"*I'll be wearing it for you always.*"

"*We're creating someone new, aren't we?*"

"*Yes.*"

"*Tell me how it will go.*"

"*Paul and Ellie have to die at a special time. We know that. And that time is almost here. When I've killed them, finally it will be our turn. We won't feel a thing, I promise you. The wet work, as they say, will happen after. The police will find a headless corpse and they will think it is me, killed by someone from a long time ago. No one will connect your earlier disappearance from Fisherman's Terminal to the headless body. This room will be gone, without a trace of what's gone on here, and that is a sadness. Perhaps I will step into your life and name, cash and carry—I've had years to plan and save—with an explanation for the long absence. Perhaps I will adopt a new name. It's occurred to me you've given me half of one.*"

"*Franklin is as good as any, isn't it?*"

"*It surely is. I will surface later, as you, a man who just couldn't continue his previous, pathetic life any longer and had to start over, somewhere else, who's long dreamed of writing books and finally has made good on that dream.*"

"*I don't want to die, Franklin.*"

"*I know. I know.*" He speaks so soothingly. "*Neither do I. But for both of us it's necessary, don't you see, so that one of us may* live. But in one sense, I will be 'dying,' too. I have to die because there have been too many times when I feel a man named Strickland is looking for me, looking to kill me for what I did to Paul's mother. He may be dead; he probably is, but this feeling is so strong, so often, I cannot wholly dismiss it, even though all my efforts to find him, and kill him first, have been unsuccessful. Sometimes I feel he's watching me, but that can't be because he would have killed me by now, kept a promise he made to me long ago by the banks of a river.

"So you must be me in death, and I must be you in life. First, the nature of your death will, I hope, leave a trail that will lead to Strickland, if he's alive. Or if it doesn't he will, at least, believe I'm dead. And lastly I have to die so another trail will not lead to me after Paul and Ellie are found dead.

"With any of the three, freedom lies at the end."

"And for me?"

"Purpose, it's co-equal."

"Then I want to know everything. I want to know what it will be like after. Will you tell me your name now?"

"Yes, I surely will. You've earned it."

He begins with his name. And as he speaks, I hear a jingling and he tells me it's a new gift he'll leave me, to replace KDC's bracelet; a rosary, he says, with a small laugh, or worry stones that relax you, make you feel better.

This one, he says, is in the shape of suns and moons, a gift he had to take back from a woman who never did like the poetry of Yeats, a woman named Carla Martell, who, he says, had always been waiting for someone like him to take back the gift.

Then, he goes on. He does not have to speak loudly, because I am right here, curled up by the cage in the darkness and warmth of this small room, holding the gun so close I lick the barrel, before putting it into my mouth.

Over the hum of the air purifier, his voice seems to come from afar, from outside, and I try hard to think of that voice as mine. It's dark as a womb but that's not right because I've already been born. So it's more like a bedtime story, what I imagine it would have been like, if anyone had done that for me. I know it's a bedtime story because he's talking about someone called the Pied Piper. I know that one because it's about a man who takes away all but one of the *children through the mountains to another place and they never come back. It's not really what he's talking about. He's talking about Russel Strickland, the Pied Piper's real name. But it's close enough. It's okay, because the way he's telling the story, it seems as if it's all mine, the most wonderful thing I've ever had, something worth living for, finally, and thus dying for.*

Let others raft the Amazon or sail past Cape Horn, I have this; so I take the hard, suckled thumb of the gun barrel from my mouth, my finger away from the trigger.

PART THREE

THE PIED PIPER

Chapter 26

CROSSING OVER

I sat in the pickup parked in front of my shop, wondering when Ellie had taken the gun from underneath the seat.

Down the street a tree service crew was trimming branches of trees lining the canal. A worker wearing a headset was feeding lopped branches into a wood chipper with the unlikely name of Vermeer. The machine devoured the branches with a searing, intermittent violence, and for a moment I imagined a machine from which a man could withdraw, with quiet magic, living branches for grafting upon the dying.

Ellie had found the last straw, in the morning. I'd slept late and she and Michael were already gone.

I looked for it this morning, in a panic, but all I found were a couple of Michael's X-Men figures, a P. G. Wodehouse paperback with a curled-up cover, scraps of Michael's schoolwork, a crumpled-up Starbucks coffee cup. No gun.

The phone number for "Peter Masskey" was unlisted. So no home address. Of course Steven wouldn't have listed the number. If you're playing hide-and-seek, you don't want to get tagged.

When I left the truck, I felt as if I'd been months away at sea, the solidity of land and concrete something to get used to again.

It was noon. I hadn't eaten anything yet. If I had, I would have thrown it up.

I could have driven, parked somewhere on the campus. But I wanted to walk. You don't bridge the years so suddenly—do you?—

by pulling up with your truck, as if you and your brother are going to the ball game. Or do you walk because you're simply scared, fearful enough of what he'd become, and whatever it was that had to be said and had to be done?

I passed by the *Waiting for the Interurban* sculpture, just north of the bridge. The stone commuters were festively draped. Balloons rose from strings and bounced in the wind. I looked because the sign said HAPPY 40TH MIKE!

My son's birthday was tomorrow.

I waited for the blue and orange Fremont bridge to rise and let a green and white Foss tug through. At the barrier, a covey of bicyclists in harlequin spandex hemmed me in, sucking on their water bottles while they waited. One of the bicyclists pointed his spout at the neon Rapunzel in the bridge tower.

The bridge rumbled down and I crossed over the canal.

The wind was brisk enough to scatter litter on the bridge and to whitecap Lake Union to the east and made the heat unbearable. Where had the days gone in Seattle when sunlight seemed like something poured between the clouds every hour? It was a day like Emma's last one, the day of her sixth birthday. We drove across the Lake Washington bridge, heading east toward Snoqualmie Falls . . .

I want to see where the Indians were, Daddy.

That ancient meeting place.

Sure, honey. Just you and me.

And she said the water looked like birthday cake frosting she'd never want to eat. When you're that age you can pretend the wind knows you're about to have a birthday. I remember thinking that I'd have to tell Ellie when we got back, that Emma had her mother's imagination.

Are you going to tell me you were there, Steven? It was such a powerful feeling and I had to look back, go back along the trail because I still loved you more than I was ever jealous or angry or bewildered with you. I missed the sittin' high, and because of that, that brief negligence, my Emma died.

You were at Shilshole, too. What one brother starts, the other finishes. Did you finish it? What are brothers for, huh, Steven? Maybe you were even at the car wash, too. Shadowing again, like mother like son. And took care of the asshole's dog later since Daddy/Paul didn't do it.

Who caused Emma's death? You, the proof now of my sanity, the proof that someone was there all along, following, watching, as Sara Bowers had done, the mother who had to abandon us, to give us a second birth.

No. Emma's death will always be mine. I know that.

But there are the others, Steven. You have Sara and Dad, and they weren't accidental or deserved. Is it going to end there? I don't think so. It can't because I know now, and I think you want me to know. But you won't do anything today, not at noon on a day so much like the day Emma died. Neither can I. But you can't get away with what you did. You killed Dad, you killed Sara, and if you killed them, you will have to kill me, won't you? I don't have the gun Sam gave me, so it can't be today, thanks to Ellie. Sam's looking in the wrong place, for the wrong guy. I found you first, isn't that a kick, and he's been looking for so much longer.

Who the hell is KDC, Steven? Isn't it a kick Ellie thought I was fooling around, only to believe something worse now. That I'm the one who's the danger, the one on the cliff over Snoqualmie, the Tuned Looney, and can you really blame her, finding a loaded pistol in the truck that takes our only surviving child to play? Did you know she's freaky about guns? Her best friend in sixth grade shot herself through the throat with a gun her father kept at home in a drawer he didn't bother to lock.

I walked quickly, for a half mile past a commercial area that doesn't quite end as you go through the campus. Cascade Pacific University is a modest Christian college of four thousand students, tucked in at the bottom of Queen Anne Hill, bordered by the Ship Canal.

From there, Steven could have seen me entering or leaving my shop across the canal, or making the passage out to the Sound on the *Constellation*. He could have been one of many strolling the embankment, watching the big schooner pass by. He knew we were gone somewhere, anyway, because he returned the wallet I'd lost at Shilshole, while we were gone giving Dad's ashes to the sea. Saving my ass, or keeping it all in the family for another reason? A final act?

As I walked through the campus quadrangle, a scruffy dog with a red kerchief around his neck raced past me to snag a Frisbee from the air. Then the dog veered away from me, leery of the stranger who might take the prize from him.

At a kiosk near Peterson Hall, a Victorian-era building of colored brickwork, I found a campus map and the location of the Humanities offices.

Tiffany Hall was less old than Peterson, built of wood, brick, and stucco and quiet as a funeral parlor when I went in. I heard voices off to my right in the secretary's office. As I passed, a woman laughed and half turned, touching the sleeve of the man's T-shirt that said 10 K BEAT THE BRIDGE RUN. She saw me but didn't come out.

Ahead there was a display case full of debate trophies and on the opposite wall, above a steam radiator, a framed listing of the teachers and their offices.

Peter Masskey's—Steven's—was 311.

The carpeted stairs creaked. Prints of ancient cities—the kind you read about in required reading—lined the walls. The second-floor landing seemed like a cage, enclosed in wired glass. There were three fire extinguishers around, a fire escape behind me. The place was a firetrap.

Narrower stairs led up to the tighter confines of the third and last floor. The boards creaked and cracked under the green, musty-smelling rug. The third-floor landing was smaller than the second, the corridor narrower.

I startled a slim, red-faced woman coming out of 301. She put down her briefcase, fumbled with her keys, as she locked her office.

"Can't start too soon if you're in English these days," she said, smiling thinly. I nodded. I assumed she meant preparations for the coming semester until I whiffed her coffee/whisky breath as I maneuvered around her. I caught her glancing back from the stairs, and wondered which made her more nervous: the daytime office boozing or a close brush with a stranger who hadn't shaved in three days and obviously wasn't a student.

The second-floor-landing door wheezed open and shut below, and she was gone with her secret. It was quiet again. I followed the numbers. The panel doors had oval brass handles and the kind of keyholes you can look through. Most of the glass transoms above the doors were open. Next to each door, holders were stuffed with papers and exams. A Doonesbury cartoon was tacked to one door. Behind another, a phone message recording kicked in.

The corridor ended with 307 and another fire escape. The last two rooms were around the corner, and 311 was just past slanting sunlight from the fire escape window: PETER MASSKEY—ENGLISH.

A dead end abandoned for the summer. Would Steven be in his office? Probably not, but it was my only option given the unlisted number and address. But he wasn't on vacation. He was around.

Because you've been a busy boy, Steven.

I could hear nothing from within 311, no rustling of papers or phone conversation. Then something fell within, behind the closed door. A clatter. Then silence again. Then a faint rustling.

He's in there. My brother's in there.

My heart was hammering.

Time to come out of the woods, Steven.

I took a few deep breaths and knocked, hard, punishing my trembling, sweaty hand.

Long time, no see.

No response. I knocked again.

Where do you want to start? With Sara, or Dad?

After the third time, I tried the loose oval doorknob.

The door gave. I stood there, pushed it all the way open.

The room had the smell of heat trapped in old places—and cat litter. From a corner where the litter box was hidden, a tabby darted past me and out the door, further scattering the pencils and pens and holder she'd knocked from the desk.

So you like cats now, Steven. Things change; you never did before.

The office was small enough to be dominated by the desk, with a brown wooden captain's chair behind and a smaller one in front. Within a visitor's reach was a small bowl of apples, stacked like a pyramid with the apex missing. A briefcase lay flat on the desk, perfectly aligned with the near edge. The filing cabinet partially blocked a narrow window. Behind the visitor's chair a high, narrow display case boasted a dozen trophies, with a dusting rag folded on top. Books overflowed from the shelves behind the desk, to neat stacks on the floor. Between the window and the books was the framed cover of *Stormchasers*, Masskey's book.

I walked to his desk, no more than a few steps. The briefcase was locked, but an address was on the tag below the handle:

Peter Masskey
29 West Comstock
Seattle, WA

I don't know why the trophies drew me back. Maybe it was because Steven had never, for all his athletic skill, much cared for the water. I was always the one for boats. Maybe because it seemed so strange for someone to put trophies in so small a place, an office no less.

The trophies told me, and one in particular: the smallest, with the cheap bronzed swimmer poised for entry.

Steven, I can't tell you . . . I can't say to you how sorry I am.

I missed him so much, for so many years, the only way I could bring him back was as a killer. The trophy read:

Tri-County Invitational
1966
1st Place Freestyle
15–16

Steven was eleven years old in 1966, the year we both learned to swim at Camp Parsons on the Hood Canal.

He wasn't Peter Masskey.

I'm sorry, Steven. My God, I'm so sorry.

I left the office quickly, didn't close the door. Let him . . . let Peter Masskey find it open and wonder. What's to steal besides the teacher's address? His apples? Books? Who steals books anymore? Someone else's trophies? Not even those from the YMCA meets in Chelan and Wenatchee.

Downstairs the secretary saw me this time. "Can I help . . ."

I was already out the door. *Help me?*

No, but Peter Masskey can. He named his book after what I'm doing. He's all I have left. He can tell me how a guy from apple country comes across the mountains, from where a fellow I know is still looking in the wrong place, to find Yeats and Carla Martell and tell my wife that sometimes the name surfaces after you thought you were all finished. A thoughtful guy, this Peter Masskey, who sends a handmade birthday card to a boy he's never met.

Chapter 27

GONE

I went back home to get the radio and found the hastily written note in the kitchen, on the cutting board.

Ellie had come back—to pick up what? Presents for the birthday Michael would have without me?

As I read the note, the siamang monkeys began whooping at the nearby zoo. The derisive, laughing chorus seemed as if it were next door.

Paul,

Michael and I have gone off for a few days, maybe longer, I don't know. However long it will take you to get over the anger—if that's what you're feeling now that you know I took the gun I found in the truck. Anger was only part of what I felt when I found that loaded gun and the box of ammunition. All the rest we'll have to talk about when I get back. But the gun won't be anywhere close. I have it now. I couldn't give it to the police and I couldn't throw it away. You have to know I kept it under the cushion when I slept downstairs last night.

Perhaps I should be saying this to you face-to-face. I don't think so. We need a little distance before we sit down to talk, and not with a Colt revolver around.

What's going on? A loaded gun, a gun you never told me about, in the truck that Michael's in all the time? What were you thinking? What? God, to think he could have found that before I did.

For a while I thought we were back on track, after your dad's death, with plans for Ireland. But it seems like one thing after another. It's been a tough time I know, with your father and what happened at Shilshole. But something's going on. If only it were another woman. At the zoo it was like watching a stranger. You aren't working, I know that. Where have you been—taking off early, coming back late? And this obsession with your father's letters . . . It's the dog and one thing after another and what would have been the next, after the gun? I don't know what I would do if we lost Michael, too, if he had an accident with that gun. I'm afraid of what I might do.

I was scared, Paul. I still am. I'm also not one of those women who wait and wait, and hope and then realize it's too late. I'll be coming back without Michael—he'll be elsewhere—and it will be just you and me talking, and hopefully we can figure out what we can do about what is happening.

Michael's asking what's going on and I can't tell him because I don't know.

I love you. Michael loves you, too, so much. I'm sorry about his birthday but it can't be helped.

Ellie

She was wrong. I wasn't angry she had gone. No, that wasn't what she had done. She'd fled, fled as surely as Sara Bowers had fled from Russel Strickland, taking her young son with her. Fled because she was scared of me and didn't throw the gun away because she wanted it still, because she didn't know, didn't know what I might do.

One thing after another . . .

They had names: Emma and Dad and Thomas Van Horn. Take those names one by one and you could mourn them, explain them, justify them. Take them together and she thinks, *He was around all of them and they died. And now he's gotten a gun he never told me about.*

There was no anger boiling within me, no rage at being abandoned, none of what consumed Russel Strickland. I felt relief that she and Michael were gone. Because at least for the time being they were safe, not from me, but from the one who had always been so close behind.

Peter Masskey.

Even if Ellie had stayed, and we'd talked, she still wouldn't have believed me, and she would have been just as scared as she was now. She wouldn't have believed me because she couldn't, because she hadn't been with the others when they died. She hadn't felt the presence of someone else, someone I alone knew existed.

Proof has to exist outside of someone's mind, even for someone you love. That's what I needed now, almost as much as knowing my wife and son were safe.

I found matches in the utility drawer and burned Ellie's note in the kitchen sink. There was no reason to keep it. I knew all the words, just as Carla Martell knew the words to the letter sent to her father long ago by . . . whom? Russel Strickland, the Pied Piper— my . . . father? Or Peter Masskey? Whoever he was.

He's the only one left, that's who he is.

I figured I had a better chance of getting Ellie's folks in Bellevue across the lake than her brother when I called, but Ben was the one I got. He didn't sound at all uncomfortable about being caught in the middle, but then when you're an ex–Navy SEAL and also divorced, you've pretty much seen it all.

"Yes, they're here," he said carefully, warily.

"I'd like to talk to her, Ben."

He's my son, too.

"She took Michael to a movie. Look, Paul, Ellie told me she just wants to lie low for a few days. I don't know what's going on, and it really isn't my business unless she came over here busted up. Everything else is pretty much a failure to communicate like that guy said in the movie, and I could write a book about that. You want to tell me what's going on?"

"Didn't Ellie tell you?"

"Well, I didn't ask, and she hasn't said much other than it wouldn't be for the best if you came over."

"I wasn't planning that. I just wanted to call."

"I'll let her know, Paul. Michael, too."

"His birthday's tomorrow."

There was a pause. "We'll do it up for him."

"It's his seventh. Tell him I love him. Ellie, too."

"You doing okay?" It came a little more softly than the rest.

"I'll let you know after I eat the eggs."

"What? Oh, the movie."

"We'll work it out, Ben." *We did before . . .*

"Don't eat too many eggs." He hung up.

I left the house and took off so quickly I almost backed into a car coming down the street, a '65 Mustang, but this one was blue, not red, like Sara Bowers's, and it was missing the pony on the grille. I also forgot the radio I'd come back for, a minor-league boom box we had bought to take to the beach, and I went back to get it. I might not have to use it, but you never know when one might come in handy, and radios seemed to run in the family, too. If Sam Jameson could take one into the woods, I could take one to Queen Anne Hill, where Peter Masskey lived.

Chapter 28

SHRINE

Queen Anne Hill used to have a sibling, Denny Hill, to the south, but that glacial mound was devoured in a fit of Victorian civic cannibalism and regurgitated to fill in parts of the harbor. Along Highland Avenue on Queen Anne, you can look across to the Space Needle at Seattle Center, the site of the 1962 World's Fair.

The houses on West Comstock stepped down to the north, though they faced the east, and the grade was so steep the sidewalks had cleats in them. Number 29 was one in from the corner and, like many of the other houses on the tree-lined street, had the garage underneath, with doors that swung open, sagging with age.

It was a large house, probably built in the twenties, in Seattle bungalow fashion: heavy-browed, with exposed, decorative joists and a long, deep porch. There was no front yard, only terraces, through which the walkway switchbacked up to the porch.

Masskey had chosen gray with red and white trim. Near the top of the side chimney, alternating bricks were painted red and white. From the large dormer facing the front of the house, he had a stunning view of Lake Union and the Capitol Hill ridge beyond.

No car was parked in the short driveway, or nearby in the street, nor could I see any activity in the house. I drove around the block twice, the second time taking the alley behind. A fence blocked off the backyard. The shades were drawn in the second-story windows closest to the northeast corner, and curious, I slowed the truck down.

It seemed odd that Masskey would keep the shades drawn in a room that offered one of the best views.

I backed out of the alley into the street and parked in the shade of an oak on Division Street, letting the engine idle before turning it off. Masskey wouldn't see the truck if he returned from his office at the college. He'd be coming from below, up the hill. He was probably still there, come back from lunch, but there was only one way of finding out for sure that he wasn't in that room taking a nap, with the shades drawn, his car in the garage.

I took the Sony with me and walked around the corner of the block to his house. The porch was bare except for a swing that looked as if it hadn't been used in years. There were no toys or bikes, nothing to indicate the guy had kids or was even married. The place had the feel of someone who lived alone.

I rang the bell three times, giving him plenty of time between, scanned the neighborhood. A car came up the hill, and my heart took off because I didn't know what kind of car he drove. But two people were in the car, which continued up the hill.

I left the porch and went around the side of the house opposite the garage where a high fence and a row of cherry trees shielded Masskey's house from the one on the corner.

The backyard was large and private, surrounded by more trees and a six-foot-high plank fence, and dominated by four square beds of roses, each one edged and banked perfectly. Some roses were in bloom; the others had been carefully pruned. A pair of gardening gloves lay on a single white chair, more evidence that Peter Masskey lived alone. A narrow path led through the roses, to the back gate and the alley.

Two racks, each with a narrow, sloping roof, were screwed into the house, flanking the door to the basement. From their pegs Peter Masskey's gardening implements were arranged precisely as a surgeon's implements on a tray, from large to small: spades to pruners, electric edger to trowels. Hoses and an orange extension cord were coiled in perfect circles.

Such order from a homebody, a man who'd subtitled his book *Velocities of Self-destruction*?

Next to the back steps Masskey had piled a low stack of four-by-fours, and on top was a half-empty hundred-pound bag of sand,

and neatly folded canvas spotted with mold. Whatever project he was working on wasn't visible outside.

I tried the basement door and the back-porch door. Both were locked. I knocked on the porch door and waited, to give myself final assurance the guy wasn't home.

I needed a window.

There were six, of varying sizes, at various heights on the back of the house. One cellar window was barred on the inside. The only one I could possibly reach without a ladder was about eight feet off the ground, to the right of the cellar door.

I angled two of the eight-foot lengths of four-by-fours against the house, blocking the ground ends with a shovel and spade sunk deep into the perfect lawn. The angle was still steep, but it could work. It had to. I didn't want to have to punch through a window in the front of the house.

I turned on the radio. Neil Young and Pearl Jam would be loud enough to help mask the sound of breaking glass but not attract a neighbor's complaint. I rubbed my hands in the bag of sand to dry the sweat, stuffed a trowel in my back pocket. Then I started up the makeshift ramp, thankful I was wearing running shoes. I crept up the incline, inches at a time, sliding my hands upward, and almost fell off when I caught a splinter in my palm, but after five minutes I reached the windowsill. The roof of the tool rack, maybe eight inches wide, offered some support, but I didn't give all my weight to it. I scrunched up a little higher.

One foot on the top of the tool rack, an elbow on the windowsill, I leaned as far forward as I could and lifted the spade from my back pocket.

Three strikes of the handle did it. The sound of shattering glass interrupted Neil Young's whiny vocals. I waited a minute, to make sure no one had heard, then used the trowel to pare off the jagged shards of glass along the edges of the window.

I hauled myself in, with elbows, then knees, hopped down onto the floor of the first-floor bathroom, crunching glass underfoot.

I gave myself twenty minutes to find the proof.

Of what? That you're not loco like Sam? Some kind of vindication about Emma? That someone was back there on the trail? You're closing fast. You've broken into a house, in broad daylight, and what happens if he suddenly arrives? You don't even know

250   Bruce Chandler Fergusson

what you're looking for. The letters? Think he took the letters? Dad never mentioned a guy named Peter Masskey, so why would a stranger take a box of letters? You think Mr. Chips ate one of his office apples in your father's living room after killing him?

And if you find the proof, what then? Ask Ellie for the gun so you can kill him?

The radio music was faint outside as I walked through the kitchen.

You're inside out, Paul, outside in. Sam said Strickland broke into his house, torched it. But it wasn't Strickland. It was someone else. And you found him first.

He was one of those bachelors who disliked washing dishes because on the counter near the refrigerator were plastic bags full of paper plates and plastic utensils. He didn't trust the tap water: underneath the counter were a half dozen plastic jugs of purified water.

The living room was dim, heavily paneled with darkly stained wood. He'd turned the living room into a workout area, with exercise mats and a full complement of free weights. A bench and no other chairs or couches. There was no television, only a stereo system that rivaled Carla Martell's. Music to pump iron by. No wonder he hadn't brought her here. He obviously wasn't the entertaining type. This place was all for him. Something was missing.

Books.

You'd expect the living room of an English professor to be crammed with books, but not a one was in sight. Were they all in his office at the college, like the trophies? He had to have some here. He had to have a study here in this house, someplace where he wrote, took work home.

A place where he might keep other things. More trophies?

And why *did* he keep a trophy case in that small office? So people could see them there, if not at home, the usual place.

Why not at home? Because he didn't like people coming here? Now, why was that?

Did he have something to hide?

The last room I checked on the first floor was just off the entry hall and the stairs. The door was locked.

Why would Masskey, living alone, keep a room locked?

I hurried back to the living room, lifted the barbells off the metal rest above the weight bench. He'd been working with two hundred pounds, my weight. I took off two light blue, fifty-pound disks, tightened the outside collars again. On each weight, the initials PM were written in black permanent ink.

What, did he think someone was going to steal his weights? He was like a little boy, putting his name on everything, his trophies where everyone could see . . . a little boy . . .

You're not the first. There was a boy.

But they're all dead. So whose boy are you, Masskey?

In front of the locked door again, I began swinging the barbell, slowly at first, then faster, aiming for the metal plate extending below the doorknob. The end of the barbell cracked against the plate, a hundred pounds slamming into the metal, the *chunk-chunk* reverberating in the hallway. The blows shivered my hands and arms, torqued my back.

Careful . . .

The grunts came louder, almost shouts, as I swung the weight hard, harder still, each time the door snapping against the frame. The plate loosened, the screws popped out, and now I was missing the metal, hitting, smashing, punching holes into the door.

A collar came loose, the weights slid along the bar, almost falling off. I yanked them off all the way, picked up a fifty-pound disk with both hands and hammered at the doorknob, pounding it as if it were a spike until sweat dripped from my face and my arms were numb with fatigue . . . as they had been at Shilshole, when I'd had a man's head in my hand, pounding his skull into the concrete steps.

I dropped the weight. It clattered around on its edge, then was still.

The door had to be close to breaking. I was panting, had to rest for a minute. Then I pushed on the door. It was loose, the lock almost ready to pop. I took a deep breath five feet away and launched myself at the door, hitting it with my side.

The door burst inward, the guts of the lock spilling out in splinters and metal, with such force it banged against the wall inside and smacked my leg on the rebound as my momentum shoved me stumbling forward.

It was a small room, not much larger than Masskey's office. There were no books, only a standing lamp, and a desk and a chair to my right near the single window that, with its shade pulled down, allowed only dim light to filter into Peter Masskey's secret place.

I flicked on the overhead light.

Maps covered half a wall: one of Washington State, smaller ones of Bellingham, Bainbridge Island, and greater Seattle, all marked in a neon orange marker, a crazy spider's web of routes with tight clusters of colored pins, like an insect's compound eye, marking the destinations.

A lunatic's war room. The underneath of a big rock just flipped over. I'd gotten what I came for, but the magnitude of the violation stunned me.

There were so many of them, pinned to the other half of the wall, there was scarcely any space between them, a collage of photos of every person who had ever been in my life, taken in places I remembered, and places and times I had forgotten about, until now. Most of them shot from afar, with a telephoto lens, all of them dated, identified, annotated in type clear and concise as newspaper cutlines:

Ellie and Paul coming out of St. James, 1980 (*oh, the happy couple . . . did they hear the earth move that morning in each other's arms before the big day . . . Big for me, too, even if I had to borrow Sara's invitation! . . . Is that worry behind Chucky's smile: where is she???!!*); *Chucky at Discovery Park sculpture unveiling, 1976* (*I don't care what they say—his work is primitive*); *Sara waxing Mustang in front of Bellingham house, 1979* (*she's not bad for a grease monkey . . . should daughter L. go, too?? Naah, let her be orphaned, too*); *Steven and Paul on Zodiac, Lake Union berth, 1978* (*which one's the marrying kind, the world wants to know!*); *Hannah, gardening, Bainbridge house, 1967* (*serves her right— God took care of that business for me*); *Sam, leaving boat at Stehekin landing, 1980* (*gave him matches for his pipe. Your turn, after Paul and Ellie*); *Chucky and Sara coming out of restaurant in Edmonds, 1988* (*so tempting to tell Joe and Frank, the <u>Hardly</u> Boys but no*); *Paul and Michael playing catch, front yard Fremont house, 1994* (*Can I play, too?!*); *Ellie at the bookstore, 1992* (*she wears a lot of black and brights—the hair . . . she is beautiful . . . what a waste on Paul . . . hmmmmm!*); *Paul delivering wagon to customer in Madison Park, 1993*; *Paul leaving shop with Emma, 1986* (*awww . . . lookit Daddy's li'l helper*); *Ellie and Paul selling*

the van, 1992 (do you guys know how much I paid for that, and to
fix it up???); Paul, Ellie, and Michael, flying kite, Gasworks Park,
1993 (the family that flies, dies); Paul with woman on catboat,
Lake Union, 1989 (marital intermission . . . followed them to her
apartment near Alaskan Way Viaduct . . . a Fuck by the Duck? . . .
it won't help, bucko, I got Sweet-E popcorn!); Paul and Ellie, 1991
at Folklife Festival (pregnant with Michael . . . let's try it again,
honey??? . . . the clock ticks louder now); Paul and Ellie, playing
softball together, Holman Playfield, 1995 (they shall die together,
too) . . .

There were two more boxes of photos, but I didn't bother going
through them. I felt as if I were going to be sick. I wanted to escape
my skin. The names were doing it, the first names he used for us all,
as if we were family.

On another wall black albums, scrapbooks, filled two shelves.
Each of the scrapbooks had a date, one per year, beginning in 1964
and ending in the present.

I don't know why I went over to look at them—I knew what
would be in those albums. I picked them out at random, then just
dropped them on the floor. Everything was there. Newspaper articles about the crimes of Russel Strickland, the Pied Piper, mostly
from the *Wenatchee World*; articles about Dad's work; a whimsical
piece from the *Seattle Times* about the delivery of the caboose to
Bainbridge; articles about the suicide of my mother, the disappear-
ances of Sara Bowers and Steven; a flyer for work I had at the Gallery
of Fine Woodworking; a bookmark from Ellie's bookstore; our wedding invitation. He must have gotten that after he killed Sara. It was
hers. He took the invitation Dad sent her.

And Michael's birth notice and the article about Emma's death.

A drowning accident yesterday below Snoqualmie Falls claimed
the life of a six-year-old Seattle girl.

King County police spokesman Sgt. Larry Wohlers said the acci-
dent occurred shortly before noon Monday, when Emma Sinclair
and her father, Paul Sinclair, were . . .

And an article, from the *Seattle Times*, about the rape and murder
of a thirty-two-year-old waitress named Kerrie Caldwell in her Lake
City apartment.

KDC? The bracelet . . .

I wished I'd stopped then. But I went on, in a frenzy, as if I hadn't yet found the proof, as if this hideous shrine were not proof itself. I didn't see any box of letters. *Where were the letters?*

I wished I'd stopped then because the last album I took down had Ellie in it.

She'd written a note to him.

I swept the remaining scrapbooks from the shelves, burying the one I'd dropped, the weight suddenly too heavy to hold. Two swipes and they were gone, tumbling to the oak floor, with a popping of rings, a scattering of sheets and paper. I clawed at the other wall, scraping off the photographs, in a spray of pushpins. I swiped at the standing lamp, smashing it against the desk, the lightbulb popping. There was a mug on the desk with coffee still in it. I threw the mug against the wall, cracking the plaster. Coffee sprayed against the wall, staining it, trickling down.

He sat here, sipping his Starbucks, gazing at his hoard.

I ripped away the camera and binoculars hanging by straps on the wall behind his chair and flung them through the window. The explosion of glass woke me, as if what I was doing were no more than unconscious violence, the predations of a nightmare. The sound of the radio I'd left outside, once faint, came louder to me now, as if someone were outside who had suddenly turned up the volume.

I left the ruins of Peter Masskey's shrine, the wreckage, feeling the current of something as powerful and destructive as surging waters. He had Emma up there, and Steven. He had us all. He had Ellie. . . . He had killed my father and Sara Bowers and he had . . .

God . . . Ellie, oh, Ellie . . .

From the hallway, I stared at the front door, expecting to see Masskey walk in, hoping he would, trying to conjure his arrival so I could do what I wanted to do and prop his dead body in that chair, point him at the wall and scream at him, *Look now, look all you want.*

The sense of presence wouldn't go away. I kept listening for his arrival, heard no steps on the front porch, nothing except the radio, playing "Hotel California." But there was someone here.

Someone close. Just as there had been all along.

Your heart's like a freight train, Paul.

Someone was in the house, even without the sound, someone not listening, or watching, but . . . there . . . here.

Someone upstairs, in the room whose shades had been drawn?

Was that the room he took you to, Ellie? You wouldn't have brought him home. That would have been too much. You wouldn't have done that. I hadn't, not to the Bainbridge house, even when Dad had been in Portland for a week, though it was probably Bellingham.

Knowledge is a presence. Was that what I sensed now, the steps my wife had taken past the locked shrine of Peter Masskey, up the stairs to the room where it would happen? I could see him smiling beside her, a smile she had mistaken for something else because she didn't know.

You didn't know, Ellie, you didn't.

Each step up the stairs sickened me but I had to go, and the feeling of presence in this house swelled, a monstrous tick engorging itself on the host's blood. Nothing else fed the feeling; no sound. The house was still quiet, except for the radio outside. But at the top of the stairs something else was in the air, a fetid, organic smell this Peter Masskey would not have tolerated, a stink of something left behind, abandoned.

Across the landing was the door to another room, and this one, too, was locked, with a thick padlock and two bolts. The door and the framing around it had been strengthened with wood stripping.

Someone was inside. The smell was strongest here.

I could hear nothing except a clock ticking in another room, and the radio, much fainter now. If someone was inside, surely I would hear.

I banged a fist on the door, wanting to punch it through.

There was no reply. And I hit the door again. Nothing.

Was someone within? Who?

Who's he keeping in here?

Someone I knew, someone close. That's what the room downstairs was all about.

I pounded the door with my fists—to get out as much as in— smashed at it with my fists until they were too bruised and hurt to go on. The cuts on my palm and thumb opened more, and blood smeared on the white paint of the door.

No one was answering, pounding back, shouting back from within.

The padlock was fixed so the bolt couldn't be shoved back. I needed something more than the weights downstairs to open this. I needed a gun.

Where would he most likely keep one? The . . . shrine? I raced down, went through his desk, found nothing. I hurried back upstairs to his bedroom, across the hallway from the locked room.

The double bed filled most of the dormer area.

Don't think about it. Don't think about what they may have done here, together, watching the lights starring Lake Union at night.

I yanked out the two drawers of the bedside table, spilling out everything—tissues, medications, notepaper, pencil—everything except a gun. He'd made the bed. A red and gold spread, military neat. I tore into it. Nothing under the pillows. I heaved up the mattress, got the same, flung it down.

That's when I saw the blue van pulling into the driveway. The same I'd seen before.

He saw me before I ducked back from the window. I heard the van's sudden acceleration, then the squeaking of brakes.

Even if I had a gun to blow off that lock, there was no time to get into that room now. And Masskey might, at this very instant, be taking a gun from the glove compartment of that van.

I sprinted for the stairs, took them two at a time, ran for the back door. The lock wasn't working right. Or my fingers. I thought I heard him on the front porch now. But he'd be slowing down now, not knowing whether I was waiting for him inside, with a weapon.

I had one but you took it, Ellie. You've saved his life, for now, because if I had the gun you took, I'd do it here. He was planning on killing us. He said we'd die together.

The lock finally gave, but for one long second I hesitated still, with the fear that Masskey had gone around the house instead, that I hadn't really heard him on the front porch, that I'd swing open this door to see him there, smiling, pointing the gun at my chest.

I opened the door.

The backyard was empty. I wanted to sprint for the fence gate and alley. It was one of the hardest things I've ever done, simply shutting that door quietly, so he wouldn't hear, so he would wonder as I had, so he might still think I had chosen this time and not another.

Jimmy Buffett was singing "Margaritaville" on the radio. I walked quickly to the fence gate, lifted the catch, slipped through. I looked back, tempted to wait until I saw him slowly open the door, to see the face of the man I was going to kill.

I didn't wait. He'd be upstairs, checking to see if that room remained intact, just as I would have, if I were Peter Masskey.

I jogged back to the truck and wound my way down the hill through the lower Queen Anne neighborhoods to get on Aurora Avenue north. I went to Green Lake, parked in the lot next to the boathouse, and watched the tiny sailboats tacking across the lake, the roller skaters and bicyclists weaving in and out of the joggers and walkers, watching but not seeing.

I took the crumpled note out of my pocket. It was Ellie's handwriting, precise and flowing but not cramped. She once said her handwriting was too good to be a writer's.

She'd taken few words to tell Masskey it was over:

Peter,

You probably knew this was coming after the other night. But I just wanted to tell you that this really has more to do with me, and what's going on in my life, than you. It's a difficult time for me now, certainly not the right time for us to continue.

Ellie

How did it happen? As easily as it had for me, with an artist named Laney Andrews, during the long months of our separation. He had set it up with the phone call, the inscribed book he sent Ellie, and followed it up with a visit to the bookstore and left with a phone number and Ellie thinking, why not?

Why not?

I'd said the same thing. But for me there'd been no notes. And this one was a useless thing. Out of all that I could have taken from his house, there was only her note. If I showed it to Ellie, she could only think the wrong thing, that I was obsessed with what she'd done and never mind I'd done the same thing, that I'd found out about it and stolen the note and had gotten the gun to do something about it.

She and Michael were safe. They were safe; that's all that mattered for the moment. If I tried to tell her now, she wouldn't believe me. She would ask questions I couldn't answer. Whatever Peter Masskey had told her about himself, it wasn't the truth. I couldn't tell her who he was, *why* he was doing this, his connection to Russel Strickland, the Pied Piper.

Why? Why?

All I knew was that he'd killed before, taking revenge on all those who were linked with Russel Strickland. One by one. He was going to kill again. And whoever was in that room in his house would be the last.

He was coming after. He had to now. He'd known Ellie and I were separated. He knew everything. That was part of it. He had watched us, his surrogate family, followed us, waited, played with us, biding his time, playing with us like Strickland played his music, like Sam said. Drawing out the notes. For what? Why did he wait? For a family to evolve . . . *which one's the marrying kind?* . . . for the right time to snuff it out?

Now the time had come.

For both of us.

A floating lawn-mower barge was churning up milfoil on the lake.

And we both know the best place for that, don't we? I'd surely pick it if I were you. You know I can't go to the police. You were at Shilshole. Couldn't have anything happen to me and upset your applecart. You know. You'll get rid of everything in the rooms. Maybe you're doing that right now. You know everything about who we are and where we go, and that's what I'm counting on. You know I can't just take off because, if you don't come after, you'll still be here, waiting, as you always have. So we have to finish it, whoever you are, and we have to finish it now, don't we? And all I have to do is get there before you. You know everything else about us, so you'll know where the birthday celebration will be. I don't have a gun, but that's the one thing you will never know, before it's too late.

I got out of the pickup. The asphalt lakeside path was busy. As I crossed, a young couple bore down on me, holding hands and going fast on their in-line skates. Between the two of them they wore two pairs of cutoffs and a halter top. They let go at the last minute, then reconnected, and I could still hear them laughing about their trick when I threw Ellie's Dear John note in the trash bin.

THE CAGE: 8

The bolt slides back. I aim the gun where the door will open. The lights flick out. I keep the gun ready, holding it with two hands, a cradle for the precious single bullet. The darkness reassures me that it's Peter. Still, you can never tell. Habits, such as shutting off the light, can be duplicated. If it is Paul, he could have thought he was turning on the light instead of off.

But I know it's Peter, even before he speaks. I know his shape, how he enters the room, softly, always without shoes, like the cats he keeps and sometimes strangles when the females come into their first heat. He can't stand the abandoned-baby noise they make. I probably wouldn't either. I can't remember the name of the cat I once had, just that I adopted her as a stray and never had her long enough to hear that noise.

I lower the gun to my lap, the weight as insignificant as a kitten's.

He leaves the door open about a foot, enough for me to see his kneeling silhouette. Usually he sits. This won't be a long visit.

"It's a mess downstairs," he says. "Paul was here."

"I know."

"You could hear?"

"Not much, but the sounds were there, different enough so I knew it wasn't you. What did he do?"

"What didn't he do? An animal was loose down there. You should see what he did, so you know how dangerous he is."

"*I don't have to see to know that. If I could hear what he did, through all this, I know it must be bad out there.*"

"*If I hadn't arrived when I did, he would have broken in here and killed you.*"

"*That's why I was silent.*"

"*I'm proud of you.*"

"*How did he find this place?*"

"*I'm sure he came to my office at the college. Someone had been in there. The cat was out. He must have gotten my address from my briefcase. The phone here and address are unlisted. But how he found out where I worked—I don't know, but I have an idea.*"

"*Did he break into your office, too?*"

"*I left it unlocked when I went to lunch.*"

"*You did that?*"

"*I do it all the time. It's an evangelical Christian college.*"

"*He's been a busy boy.*"

"*So have I,*" Peter says.

This will be our last time together so that's why the silence goes on. Silence has movement and can carry much, I've learned that here, too. Is that where the expression train of thought *comes from? I should ask Peter, he would know. But it's not the time.*

The air purifier hums. I hear the sound of a radio, faint, not the kind of music Peter plays. When he first brought me here, I couldn't have heard such faint sounds, but I can now. My hearing has gotten so much better. I wonder if that would happen to Paul's wife, if she had been truly here, and not just on the phone. Ellie, who is so beautiful and athletic in my mind, who has the bad ear, whom Peter took such a delight in telling me about, telling me how he likes to fuck someone he knows he's going to kill later, like Kerrie and Carla and, of course, Sara Bowers.

I know about them all. I know a lot more than Paul does, even now. I know as much as Peter. I know everything he knows now.

I ask him, "If you had caught him here, would you have killed him?"

"*I might have had to.*"

"*I'm glad it didn't happen.*"

"*Why?*" *I hear the wariness in his voice and it saddens me. I thought he would have trusted me by now.*

"*Why? Because it would have had no meaning. It would have*

been like slashing the canvas of a painting the artist has worked on for so long. It would have been like something Russel Strickland would have done, just to kill when he had the chance. That's the difference between you and me and the Pied Piper, the crucial difference. We have a purpose, a lifework, you for longer than me, but in the end it amounts to the same thing. And there's another reason."

He can't see me raise the gun and point it at his chest, pretending it's someone else. Then an awful thought occurs to me.

"Yes?" he says.

"If you'd killed him today, I couldn't imagine killing him myself."

My finger tightens on the trigger, gently, because he really could be anyone in this darkness. I could have been wrong. He could be Paul in here and I would lose my last chance forever.

He speaks carefully, slowly, as if he knows the gun is on him. *"I think that's the most important of the reasons you have given me."*

It isn't enough. *"What was the nickname you gave me?"* Peter would have told Paul my real name.

"I used to call you BobBee."

"Okay. I'm sorry, Peter. I had to know for sure."

"I understand. It's all right. Better safe than sorry."

Better safe than sorry he says.

I drop the gun, so hard and quickly there's a flash of fear that it might go off, wasting the precious bullet, though that's almost impossible to happen. But there's an explosion anyway, the flaring of light within me that hurts my eyes from within, and I rush the cage so quickly he backs away, into the door, slamming it shut so our darkness is complete.

The words come out like vomit, gushing, involuntary. *"Because Paul is the one who put me in here. He and his brother should have borne the consequences, but they didn't. They were hustled to safety out of the burning building. They escaped sentencing and I haven't. They might just have paid someone else to take their place. I read about that in one of your books, about the men in the Civil War who paid others to take their place."*

"Steven paid long ago."

"So you say."

"Go on."

"Shut up! You don't have to tell me to go on. Paul doesn't know what it's been like in here, having no one to talk to but you. I could

have killed you a moment ago, but if I had, there would have been no one to kill Paul and his family. It sickens me to think of him and his brother growing up, protected so wonderfully from the truth about who they were. I wish I could have killed Sara and Chucky, the two most responsible for the conspiracy of injustice. If Paul didn't exist, if he'd known all along, none of this would have happened, and I wouldn't be here. He deserves to die. I just wish it was going to be me who does the killing."

"But you're so much a part of it! We agree about the boy. He has to stay alive, he has to be spared. I've waited too long for him to come of age so he will be capable of remembering what he will see and hear, just as I have, and now you."

"I know. I know that. If I left right now, to go kill them, instead of you, I wouldn't kill Michael. It wouldn't be right. It wouldn't be part of it; I know that, you don't have to tell me, Peter. Do you think I haven't been listening *to you? Do you think I haven't* learned *anything? You've told* me *everything.* I know it by heart now. *Do you think I'm* stupid?*"*

"I've never thought you were stupid," he says, as if I wanted him to answer the question. His weakness suddenly appears to me, like someone rounding a corner. He's the one who's rigid, the bean counter, the unimaginative one, for all his games. He's been in control for so long he thinks he always will be.

"I thought your life was pathetic, I thought you were useless except for your one remarkable attribute," he says softly, "but I don't think that anymore. I couldn't have hoped for anything better. You should be proud of yourself; I know it wasn't easy. You've done wonderfully since I brought you here."

"Of course I have. What did you expect?"

"Nothing so good as what you've become. I mean that. I'm going to miss you."

"You'd better go now. It's time you go."

"Yes, it is."

He gets to his feet. I hear his hand on the doorknob.

I stand, too. "I know where you're going, where you're going to do it."

He opens the door a little. "You surely do," he says. I flinch from the light and not his gentle laugh of amazement, the acknowledgment of how far I've gone and so quickly, without traveling;

*how much I've learned and remembered breathing the same air
here as him.*

"What if they're not there, Peter?"

*"They will be. I know them, I know where they've retreated
to in the past. They need a place they think is safe, to decide what
to do."*

"But if they're not there?"

"Paul will be," he says, "and where he is the others will come."

"Will you keep the light off, please."

"Why?"

"It will make it easier to be with you, to be there."

"You will be."

*He leaves with this last gift. The door closes, the bolt slides home.
And the light doesn't go on as it always has in the past. I don't need
it anymore. It's better this way.*

*The image of a ship comes to me, as I crawl back to a corner of
my room, to await the time, hours hence, when I will know Paul
and Ellie will be dead. I believe I will recognize the moment of
their deaths. It seems to me that all my time here has come down to
that, that if there is any justice at all in the universe, I will be compensated with that small gift: knowing when Peter has finally killed
them. When we have. Together.*

*The ship is a puzzle though. I don't know where it came from.
No, I do. Peter once told me he always felt himself to be like a survivor of a great ship that sank, leaving him all alone in a warm sea,
clinging to a scrap of debris. But he's not alone. A lifeboat materi-
alizes out of the dark, full of other survivors who have no more
right to live than he, who refuse to bring him aboard even though
they have room. But they don't die, none of them do, and with the
dawn comes rescue and the realization that his life now has a purpose far exceeding what he had before.*

*When he returns, he won't pull me aboard. We are the same
now, with that. So why then did he give me the single bullet, if not
to rescue me?*

Chapter 29

TRITON

I drove north on I-5 and after an hour passed the farms of the Skagit River floodplain. West of the interstate the land was flat as Kansas; to the east rose the foothills of the Cascades. At exit 230 I headed west on Route 20, which cut through dairy farms, fields of tulips, turf and berries.

Route 20 lifted to a bridge over the Swinomish slough, the fertile delta supporting a new cash crop: The Swinomish tribe's huge casino and bingo halls, easily visible from the bridge.

It was five o'clock when I arrived at the holding area for the San Juan ferries at the northern edge of Fidalgo Island, just west of the town of Anacortes. The ticket cashier said there'd be no problem making the six-thirty ferry to Triton, the smallest and most southerly of the archipelago's islands to have ferry service.

Five vehicles were ahead of me in the lane designated for Triton. Masskey's van was not among them. Twice over the next hour and a half, I checked the dozen vehicles in back of me. Still no van.

So he'd be taking the last ferry from Anacortes, at nine, arriving at Triton with the descending darkness.

I would have done the same thing. I'd have three hours to get ready for him.

He'd be coming. The feeling was as strong as it had ever been for me, as strong as it had been in the woods, on the steps leading down to the beach at Shilshole, and at Snoqualmie Falls.

After what I did at his house, he'd be coming, all right.

The ferry rounded the point, heading into the landing. People were returning to the cars. The ferry's horn blared. At almost four hundred feet, capable of carrying 160 vehicles and 2,500 passengers, the *Chelan* took a while after docking to purge its load and take on another.

I stayed in the truck for the rest of the boarding—the braking cars, the shouts, the slamming of doors and kids getting out, the bass sounding of departure. As the *Chelan* headed out, I went up to the passenger deck. The weather was coming out of the west, funneling through the passage between Blakeley and Decatur Islands, making a tough go for the sailboats beating upwind. We soon left them behind and overtook others. This run for the *Chelan* would take her, without stopping, past Lopez, Shaw, and Orcas, then on to Friday Harbor on San Juan Island, and lastly, Triton.

I tried to get some sleep, but it was no good. I kept imagining what Peter Masskey would look like and where I would be when I finally found out, how close he would have to come for me to kill him. I knew where I'd bury him after I killed him with the ax I'd left by the woodpile the last time Ellie and Michael and I had been to the cabin, in June, a fickle month when a fire at night can be a necessity.

The Sisters of Our Lady of the Island monastery began working the Triton landing shortly after regular ferry service began in the sixties. Sister Catherine was waiting for us when we docked. I knew it was Sister Catherine because she was the only one who always rolled up the sleeves of her brown habit and wore amber-tinted sunglasses. She had one hand on the control button, ready to lower the ferry transfer span; the other held a walkie-talkie over her heart. When she was done, she walked away, neither slowly nor quickly, as if she were going to pray in the chapel.

Half the walk-ons and cars that left the ferry stopped at the general store next to the landing that included a laundromat, post office, and the chapel with its small bell tower. The Sisters ran the place, Triton's only store. They had decorated one wall with the logos of old grape and fruit crates and kept the books with a laptop computer.

From the ferry landing, Jenkins Road makes a semicircle, past Dory Bay, where the remains of reef netters with their spidery bow towers can be seen, stacked on the shore above rails leading down to the water.

The road, lined with zigzagging split-rail fences, continues past the monastery's fifty acres inland, to Ebey's Cove, a prime hidey-hole for rumrunners during Prohibition.

Thompson Inlet almost cuts the island in two, east and west. The northern half comprises over two-thirds of the island, with most of the tillable land.

The southern portion of Triton is much more rugged and wooded and useless from a practical standpoint. But it's an area where eagles abound and orcas surface in Bailey Passage.

Triton is a private place and the people are friendly, will always wave in passing. But apart from a desire to keep Triton undeveloped, there's little sense of community, and many private-access gravel lanes off the main roads.

By the time I reached the junction of Jenkins and Lime Kiln Roads, I was all alone, except for one car and a couple of bicycles parked next to the old one-room schoolhouse that faces the tiny library and log cabin museum across the road.

Ten more minutes would get me to our cabin on the southern edge of Bones Bluff overlooking the head of Thompson Inlet. Not many bones were left to be found on that high ground, but there used to be. It was the site of a massacre. Before white men arrived, northern tribes from what is now British Columbia would come down to raid in their huge cedar dugout canoes, to kill, to take slaves and young women from the more peaceful tribes.

Aeneas MacLynn arrived with his family in Seattle in 1898, almost penniless after his passage from Glasgow, but within twenty years he owned most of Triton, having made his fortune shipping Puget Sound timber from Port Blakely, on Bainbridge, to San Francisco. He had two sons—Lindsay and Donald. His bequest of his property on Triton reflected his judgments of the two. Lindsay was given the northern tracts, and Donald, the ne'er-do-well who refused to go into the family business, the southern. Lindsay died first and his brother inherited everything. Some say he sold off Lindsay's portion because he needed the money. He probably did, but I preferred the other, "screw you" theory, since Donald also gave away a lot of the acreage to the Catholic sisters: Aeneas MacLynn had been found dead in a Pioneer Square brothel in Seattle.

Why Donald MacLynn kept the wreck of an old Liberty freighter on the beach of Thompson Inlet was another guess.

Coming back from the Aleutians in 1943, with the coast blacked out—and most important the Point Cummings and Jensen Island lights—the *William R. Chace* mistook the inlet for Bailey Passage. The freighter steamed over manacles of rocks—Jeremiah Reef— that rise midpoint in the inlet and grounded on the beach, her bow shuddering still within a stone's throw of a tenacious madrona that hangs over the gravelly strand and its own partially exposed roots.

The navy had salvage jurisdiction but did nothing about it. The islanders' explanation supposes that the navy didn't think the freighter—a total loss—was worth the effort, not when Liberties were being built all around the country at a rate of one a day. Salvage would have been dangerous as well. Japanese submarines prowled offshore; one had shelled the Estevan Lighthouse north of Barkley Sound. A salvage operation would attract attention and more ships, and lives might be lost.

Whatever the reason, the *Chace* stayed where it was. Donald MacLynn might have sold it for scrap, but again the theories diverge. Did he keep it there as a bizarre memorial to his only son, who died when his destroyer sank off Guadalcanal? Was he thumbing his nose at his father, or lamenting the wreck of his own life? He wound up a twice-divorced alcoholic.

Ellie's uncle was a Bellevue lawyer when Donald MacLynn came to him for a messy second divorce. In lieu of payment, MacLynn gave him ten acres on the low bluff at the southern end of the beach. Ellie's father bought it from him when he moved to the Southwest and much later gave the acreage to us as a wedding gift, a kind of family Homestead Act, since the lien on the gift—in spirit, if not words—challenged us to do something with the "crappy kind of land people used to emigrate from."

The good thing about people like Ellie's parents is that you can tell them to go to hell and they won't be mortally offended. John McKenna gave us the ten acres anyway. Working weekends, we finished the two-bedroom cabin six months before Emma was conceived there in 1983. All the wood, stone, and rock we used came from the ten acres.

From the cabin one can see the wreck of the *Chace* in the distance, listing away from us and the scaling bark of the madrona whose color matches that of Ellie's hair. We used to think that her father may have had the wreck in mind in 1980 when he gave his youngest, dreamiest, and most rebellious daughter away to a man who wanted most of all to work with his hands. My hands were all I would have now, waiting for the one who murdered my father.

I turned off Lime Kiln onto the rough gravel road that leads to our cabin, a lane of twin ruts scabbed with rock that winds through dense, dripping firs, madrona, hemlock, and chinaberry. Fifty yards from the cabin the lane turns at an outcropping of rock that Emma was climbing when she was only three. After the turn it's a straight shot to the cabin. The blackberries, salal, and wild rosebushes swept the sides of the truck.

I saw the car.

For a second I refused to believe she was here, believed it was someone else's car I saw through the roiling dust of the lane.

It was hers. She was here with Michael.

Jesus, Ellie, no . . . not here.

She'd parked in front, where the lane circles around below the gentle grade of steps leading up to the cabin.

Give Ben a 9.9 for lying.

Just tell him we're there if he calls. He'll call; he won't go there, Ben.

I had to force a calm on myself because what I wanted to do was gun the truck ahead and get my wife and son the hell out of here before the dust settled. But that would only add a wallop of fear to her surprise when she heard me. She would think I was angry. I wasn't. There wasn't time for that.

She had to go, to grab Michael and get the hell out of here.

It took a conscious effort to ease the truck slowly in, and there was a price to be paid because I felt a sickening kinship with Peter Masskey, as if I were his point man, knowing what he would do when he came: park the truck at Emma's Rock and take the last fifty yards on foot, so no one in the darkened cabin would hear me approach, so I would wake no one until l wanted them to awaken, until I was inside the cabin.

He's coming, Ellie. He's on his way. You cannot be here when he arrives.

They didn't hear my approach, not even when I parked the truck next to Ellie's car, and that wasn't right. It wasn't right that I could get this close. Was I too late? Had Masskey gotten here already? No, that wasn't possible.

Why hadn't they heard me coming?

I honked the horn and only then did the curtains part briefly and the window fill so modestly with Michael's face, reminding me, as if I'd forgotten, how young my son was, and when the curtain fell back after his smile, how much I loved him.

I honked again, as if we were late for an outing, to eviscerate the thought that Ellie might have for the gun, for protection against someone—her own husband—who was not supposed to be here either.

I was halfway up the steps when I heard Ellie call out Michael's name, and a second later he was hugging me around the waist. I tousled his hair. *Just like you always do. Keep it calm.*

"We're playing Monopoly," he said.

"Who's winning?"

"Me. Mom isn't letting me either."

She was standing in the doorway, her hands dug in her jeans. Her madrona hair tied back but still wild somehow, as if she'd been out on the water, too, in the wind. She wasn't smiling.

"Michael, go out in the back, please."

"Can I go down to the beach then?"

"No, just the back. You know the rules about the wreck, Michael."

He looked at me, his last hope, trying divide-and-conquer. I shook my head. He didn't know how that rule began, with the sister he knew nothing about, how she went off by herself once to the freighter, undaunted by that colossal, leaning thing.

"Could you go with me after dinner, Dad?"

"Not this time, Michael. Go on now."

"You're not going to stay, are you?" Before I could answer, he shouted, "I don't want to hear you two fighting anyway." He ran past, bumping her.

Ellie shook her head. "It hasn't been good."

I followed her inside, feeling like a stranger, an unwanted guest in a place we'd built together.

She stood by the trestle table, where they'd been playing the game, her arms folded now, looking out the back window at Michael. I watched him, too. He headed for the path down to the beach, then turned back. He had the wooden sword he'd made, to play pirates down by the wreck. He began whacking it against a Japanese maple Emma and I had planted together when she was two. We watched him longer than we might have. It was like taking oxygen. We'd done it before, those times after a fight when we didn't know what to say to each other, how to come back.

It was hot in the living room. My hands were sweating, the salt stinging the cuts on my hands: useless evidence. Anything I could say to my wife would be useless, too; the only thing that would make a difference was her seeing that room at Peter Masskey's house, but that didn't matter. They had to get out of here.

"So Ben told you we were coming here."

"No, he told me what you wanted him to say."

"Just a good guess, then?"

"I didn't come looking for you and Michael."

"Then why are you here? You must have read the note?"

"Yes . . . Ellie, I came for another reason. I had no idea you were here and I wish to God you and Michael *were* at Ben's and not here. What it boils down to is that you and Michael have to leave here now. Take Michael, take what you need for the night, and hole up somewhere on the island. I'll meet you in the morning, at the—"

"What in *hell* are you saying?"

"Let me finish."

"This isn't talking. We're not *talking*."

"It would take hours to explain why it's necessary and there isn't time for that. Tomorrow, when we're back in Seattle, I'll take you to the place I was at today, and you will understand why you had to leave now and why I have to stay."

"Paul . . . this is crazy. You—my God—you come here, say we have to leave, but you're not saying why. *How deep is this shit?*"

"We're in trouble."

"Oh, you're right about that."

"Ellie . . . listen. Please. I didn't think you'd be here, I told you that. But you are and you've got to leave, you have to believe me."

"*Believe you?* You come here like a madman, telling us we have to *go-go-go*, and you won't even tell me what the trouble is . . . why you had that gun."

The wind gusted through the room, pushing the door more open, lifting a few pink and blue pieces of game money off the table. I looked behind me. I didn't see Michael, but at least the back door was closed in case he was listening.

"What about that gun, Paul?"

You have to tell her. You have to. She thinks you've gone off the deep end anyway.

I took a deep breath for words I should have said before, if ever there had been a time for them.

"There's a man coming here, on the next ferry, who's going to kill us if he finds us here. I didn't know for sure, about him, before. But after I saw that room in his house today, I was."

"Kill us? A room? God, do you know how this sounds to me?"

"Yes, I do. But there's no other way, now that you're here."

"Do you *hear* yourself? Do you want to know what I believe? You still think someone killed your father and he's coming after us. When is this going to end, Paul, when?"

I took a deep breath. "Ellie, here's what I'm going to do now. I'm going to get Michael and take him to a safe place on the island, if that's what it's going to take to get you out of here."

She left the side of the table and went to the front window. "That gun is behind the curtains, on the window ledge. *If you try to take Michael away . . .*"

I spoke softly. "You'll what . . . kill me? Ellie . . . the gun isn't even there."

"It is."

I shook my head. "You weren't expecting me. Michael would have seen it there when he saw me outside."

"Paul, you're the one who has to go."

"No, I can't. He's coming."

"*Who?* Who is this . . . man you think is coming?"

"If I told you, you would think this is all about something else, something that happened after Emma died."

"*Who is he?*" Her eyes were wet, glistening.

"You'll know tomorrow."

"No, I won't. It's over. It's over." She was crying now. "Because I'm *looking* at the trouble. There isn't anyone coming. He's here. Oh, God, they . . ."

Stay calm. One of us has to. He's coming.

"They what, Ellie?"

"Emma, your father . . . what happened at Shilshole."

"The other man killed him, after I left. I told you."

"Of *course* you did. That's right. It's *always* what you tell me. It's always something or someone else. It's *always* an accident. And I've believed that, haven't I? But I can't any longer. There's been too many. Don't you see how I can't believe you anymore? *They all die around you, Paul.*"

Do it. Do it now. Go get him. Go get Michael.

"Yes, they do, Ellie. That's why I have to take Michael now. We'll be at the ferry waiting for you. I'll leave the car at the landing, where he won't see it in the dark, coming off the ferry. He'll drive off, and then you and Michael will walk on board and take the ferry back to Anacortes and stay the night there and rent a car. I have to stay here."

I turned to go get our son.

"*Paul!*" Ellie called out, a rasping scream through her tears. Even though I knew the gun wasn't there, I couldn't be sure she hadn't put it some other place close. For a second I wondered if everything that had gone before was a premonition of this moment, when my wife would shoot me from behind.

Someone always, always behind . . .

"*PAUL!*"

I looked back. She didn't have a gun pointed at me. She wasn't even facing me. She was looking out the window that still had the Sylvester the Cat sticker Michael had put in the lower right-hand corner. She was blocking the window, her left hand at her face, so I couldn't see. I didn't have to.

Peter Masskey was here.

Chapter 30

RADIO ROOM

Ellie backed away from the window, whispered, "He's . . . he's just watching."

I locked the front door, rushed to Ellie at the side of the window, parting the light blue drapes just enough to see.

He was under the shadow of a mountain ash, whose branches hung over the lane forty yards from the house. He stood off the shoulder, his face obscured by heavy, sagging vines of a blackberry bush. If it hadn't been for the white of his running shoes, he would have been almost invisible with the khaki vest and dark pants. I don't know how Ellie had seen him, or how I'd missed him in the van. He had to have been on the same ferry I took. His sunglasses were the same amber tint as Sister Catherine's.

"Who is he?" she asked.

"Peter Masskey."

"Peter Masskey?"

"It's not what you think, Ellie. That doesn't matter."

"Paul, I . . ."

I grabbed her hand. "We've got to move."

On the way to the back door she knocked into the table, scattering game pieces on the board to the floor.

In the back, Michael was still hacking at the blackberry bushes with the wooden sword. He'd been eating a few; his mouth was stained red.

Ellie's hands were trembling. So were mine.

We quickly decided: the freighter wreck. Emma's hiding place.

"But you're coming with us?"

"I have to get behind him. It's the only way. He's going to be armed."

"You can't . . ."

"Have to. Where's the gun?"

"In the car, glove compartment. The clip's in the trunk."

"Okay. Get down there fast." I touched her face, a brush. Her eyes were still wet and red. She squeezed my hand and was gone.

I followed her outside, watching her sprint for Michael. She knelt for a few seconds, then rose, taking him by the hand. He looked back at me, the sword still in his hand. I waved, a push. *Go . . . Go . . .*

I walked quickly around the side of the cabin closest to an outcropping of rock, higher than the chimney and thick with scrubby firs flanking the shake-sided water tank. The space between the outcropping and the cabin was narrow, shadowed, congested with piping, shovels, a wheelbarrow, and lengths of lumber and stone never needed for the small deck out back.

My chances weren't good if he came around this way. But the other side of the house had to look better for him. The trees were thick there, too, but cleared between, with the woodpile angling off waist high from the path around the cabin.

Was he still watching the house or coming ahead now? By the cars? If he had gotten that far, he had to be thinking he was okay, that we didn't have a gun, otherwise I would have fired at him. He would be confident now, assured that if I had a weapon, I would have used it at his house. There would have been no time since then to get one. And we wouldn't be the type of parents to keep a gun around a kid at the family cabin. He knew us, knew I didn't hunt, knew I spent my time on boats and playing ball.

I bumped the wheelbarrow but grabbed the handles before it tipped fully over, making noise he was sure to hear.

The corner of the cabin was only a few yards away, and I crept on lower, in a crouch, gripping a shovel by the shank. If in the next few moments he appeared, there was only one thing to do: bolt ahead, smashing his gun hand with the shovel. For a split second he would be startled. It's all I had.

I got to the corner and slowly . . . slowly peered around.

He was walking from the cars now, looking around. Family come to call, a salesman with our radio in his left hand. Even if he assumed we'd seen him, had fled, he had to check the house first, to make sure no one got behind him.

He was smiling, his teeth as white as the surgical gloves he wore, a big man, maybe six foot three and over two hundred pounds, shoulders and upper body of a swimmer. He wore a dark green T-shirt underneath the khaki fishing vest. One of the pockets of the vest sagged unmistakably. His blond hair was just long enough to be styled, but it was probably dyed because his eyes were dark.

A crooked nose leaned away from faint red crescents on his left cheek: half-moon scars, perfectly concentric except where his jaw-line broke the lower curve that curled from ear to mouth.

He put the radio down slowly.

That's it. Take your time.

He tried the door and shook his head. His grin broadened, dis-tending the strange facial scars. He reached into the sagging vest pocket.

Coming straight ahead. No more fucking around. The camera's put away after all the years of watching, waiting.

I leaned back just before he fired.

I hoped that when they heard the echoing shot, Ellie and Mi-chael would be on the wreck, far away but not far enough, in the place where we'd found her.

I was just looking for treasure, Daddy.

I heard him chunking around, slamming doors. It wouldn't take him long to check the house, see we'd gone.

I waited until I heard him at the back door, then I moved—and moved fast—glancing at the opened front door, the radio he'd left on the porch. The same radio I'd left at his house. I'd needed it to mask a break-in. Why did he need it?

I slipped over a low facing stone wall I'd made the summer Emma wandered off to the wreck, when we thought she'd been taking a nap.

I sprinted for Ellie's car, reached in through the open window for the glove compartment.

The pistol wasn't there.

Had he taken it, tossed it into the woods?

Even if I knew for sure he'd done that, I couldn't take the time to look.

The keys weren't in the ignition, either, and I prayed that Ellie had them. I checked the pickup for mine.

Gone.

I looked down the lane. A Chevy Blazer was parked thirty yards back. No wonder I hadn't noticed him on the ferry. I didn't bother to check the Blazer. He'd have taken those keys.

Even if I had wanted to risk the time, there was no way to drive for help. The nearest house was a half mile away and back in the woods off Lime Kiln Road, and even if I found someone, it would be too long before the police could get here. There weren't any on Triton.

The splitting maul leaning against the nearby stack of firewood? Too heavy, too awkward; I needed close and quick. I ran for the cabin, bursting through the door, which rebounded with a clatter. In the kitchen I scattered a half dozen utensils from the drawer before I found the chef's knife: pitiful compared to a gun, but better than nothing. I hurried from the cabin, hopped off the deck, and stopped where the path begins with the blueberry bushes on the low bluff and winds down to the beach.

At first I didn't see Masskey anywhere on the scimitar strand, or near the freighter hulk careened on the rocks that had shackled it for fifty years. The rocks were smooth, angled shelves to seaward, visible now at low tide. But they roughened toward land, and the *Chace* had caught on them, barbed, held fast even at high tide, unsalvageable.

They look like a giant's face, Daddy! He's sleeping under the sand, but if he sneezes because of all that sand, he could blow the Ace *back out to sea just like a cartoon. It wouldn't be stuck anymore.*

The old Liberty freighter was about the length of a football field, including the end zones, but given the narrowness of the sheltering inlet, the wreck of the *Chace* was a huge thing, something cast off from the gods, impossible to ignore or pass by.

I saw him then, coming down from the cabin Donald MacLynn had built on the highest point of the bluff northeast of our own, to gaze upon the wreck. Masskey couldn't have known the cabin had been abandoned for years. From our place the A-frame still seems intact. The path from our cabin to MacLynn's cabin is tough going.

He was going down the stairs stitched into the scrubby, eroding face of the bluff. Sections of the steps had given way, and Masskey twice had to jump to continue his descent to the beach.

He walked toward the freighter wreck, and I almost shouted his name, so he'd see me and divert his hunt to me and away from Ellie and Michael. He could only think that we'd fled together, were together, and the next place he was going to hunt was the wreck. He was being systematic. He couldn't overlook the wreck, even if he thought it more likely that we were huddling in the dark woods that curved above and around the end of the beach. Because if he bypassed the freighter—and we were there—we might have a chance to get back to Ellie's car, if she'd taken her keys, as she always did.

I didn't call out. The only advantage we had was his not knowing I was behind him, hunting him. I couldn't lose that until I was close, until, for once, I was the one behind. There were plenty of places to get close to him on that wreck.

As soon as he disappeared behind the bow of the freighter, I took off at a run.

The starboard side of the Liberty ship loomed higher than the walls of any prison, her hull blistered, flaking, leprotic. The Plimsoll line was still visible, but only as a darker rust. Streaks of bleaching white and gray—fifty years of gull droppings—stained the corroded iron plates. Emma always called the wreck the *Ace*, because those were the only letters still discernible on the starboard bow.

The *Chace* had kept on long enough after grinding onto the shelving rocks to tilt forward—on the fulcrum of the face of Emma's sleeping giant. The decline wasn't enough to sever the freighter amidships, but it was enough to keep most of the prop and rudder out of the water at low tide, settling the ship to port, at an angle of perhaps fifteen degrees.

Just past the bow I slowed. The starboard anchor high above was a rusted lesion against the hull. The port anchor had snapped its chain and lay on the rocks, staining them red.

There was no sign of Masskey on the deck. But he was up there, somewhere, and I kept as close to the ship as possible—which wasn't as close as I wanted.

Much of the deckside matériel that had ripped loose, smashing through or over the port bulwark to slide into the chilly black waters that night, had long since been looted or swept away. But enough remained to make a junkyard in the freighter's lee, and I had to move away from the wreck as I headed toward the stern into the muck and stranded pools of the low tide.

Tiny crabs scuttled through the half-sunken remains of jeeps and trucks vandalized and rotted down to the water. Closer to the ship, next to the splotched arch of a 20mm gun tub, the ship's funnel rested in the shallows, split lengthwise, like the curving halves of a huge baking pan. Parts of collapsed ventilators, their metal skin thin as parchment now, were scattered nearby.

Only one of the three masts was still intact. The other two had toppled at some point, broken in two. The mast booms, the freighter's "sticks," which had once hoisted cargo into the five holds, had all given way and lay crisscrossed over the port rail and the busted, scarecrow limbs of the davits. The port life rafts had long since been taken from their skeletal support structures, which hung over the bulwark in a tangle of rusting iron.

The only access to the wreck was amidships—with the lean of the freighter, about twenty feet off the muck. That access was a ziggurat of junk—stacked driftwood and timber, crates, logs, booms, anything that a few people could heave into place over the core of the incline: two trucks that had broken free of their chains and slid off the hatch covering of the No. 4 hold.

You needed feet and hands to get to the sloping deck of the *Chace.* The climb was difficult, depending on what the tide washed in or took away. When Emma did it, there had been a crude ramp of graying, splintered two-by-twos, which did little to diminish our astonishment that a five-year-old could climb up. Ellie and I had talked about it afterward—where she'd gotten her fearlessness, her recklessness, and whether it would later be a gift or a curse.

The two-by-twos were gone now, replaced by other detritus for the ramp, but something else was stuck in the clutter, something that made it no easier to climb, but made me do it as fast as I could.

Michael had taken his sword. Maybe Ellie had thought that would get him moving quicker, make him run faster from the back, down to the wreck. But he'd dropped it climbing up the incline of debris, and there was no time for a dangerous retrieval.

If I'd seen it, Peter Masskey must have, too; the boyhood sword, painted silver and gold, like the apples of the moon, nicked and scarred but newer and resplendent compared to the surrounding junk.

That's why I hadn't seen him. He was already searching the warren of cabins amidships in the main superstructure where my wife and son lay, hidden treasure, in the radio room where we'd finally found Emma.

Chapter 31

Wreck of the *Ace*

I pulled myself over the midships rail, took the knife from my mouth. There was no way Masskey could see me from above, from the looming decks of the main superstructure. The aft stairs to the overhanging boat deck were closer, so I turned left, walking as quickly as I could, given the listing wreck, needing the twisted, distended rail. I gripped the knife in my right hand.

The wind rattled a beer can along the narrow passageway. Little more than two hours of daylight was left, and already the *Chace*, tucked in the forested inlet, was deep in twilight.

I stopped at the end of the passageway, not wanting to go out onto the open deck, giving him a clear shot at me. For all I knew he could be right above me, waiting.

I listened for a moment, hearing nothing except the wind, the beer can . . . and a faint knocking sound somewhere behind me.

I spun—low, balanced, ready . . .

Nothing. Not this time.

I was about to go on, take the stairway up to the boat deck, when I heard the rasping: steps on metal. I looked around the corner of the midships housing, just enough to see.

He was across the fifty-foot width of the ship, halfway up the starboard stairs to the boat deck. He'd finished searching the midships housing below, the crew and gunners' mess, the galley with the coal-burning stove.

Get him away from them, get him aft.

If he took fifteen minutes to hunt in the boat deck, he'd find Ellie and Michael within five more. The bridge deck was smaller, con-
taining only the radio and chart rooms, the captain's quarters, and
the wheelhouse—the inside bridge.

I scuttled over to the corner of the No. 4 hold. The hatch rose
three feet off the deck, still covered with a few scraps of the thick
layers of canvas and rubber sheeting, but in most places the hatch
cover had rotted down to the wooden base, the three-inch-thick
plank sections weathered down to a thin trap that probably couldn't
bear a man's weight.

I took a deep breath, exhaled silently—then rapped the hilt of
the knife against the base of the hatch cover. At the top of the
stairs, thirty feet away, Masskey whirled. I ducked a second before
he fired. The shot spit up a rusty chunk of deck two feet away.

I took off, scrambling low. He didn't fire again; there was too
much between us—bulky winches sandwiching the looming aft mast
house, the tangle of crates and ventilators, rotted-out fifty-foot sticks
littering the 4 and 5 holds.

Nearing the stern, I glanced back to make sure he was following.
Yes: a hundred feet away, passing No. 4 hold, leaning with the
list of the ship. I had a minute, no more, to get to the place where I
could take him, where his gun would be useless—the farthest place
I could think to lead him away from Ellie and Michael. I ducked
into the passageway underneath the platform for the aft gun tubs,
the five-inch and the two 20mm antiaircraft machine guns.

The rotten, blackened oak doors to the tiny cabins in the aft-
house—where the Armed Guard had berthed—were either open or
smashed in, crammed with litter, toppled metal bunks, lockers.

Masskey was seconds away. I heard a thumping and scraping on
the other side of the aft-house: he was searching the steering engine
room, with the adjacent magazines for the guns.

On the starboard side of the aft-house, just forward of the hospital, was a hatch I'd peered in a few times, though I'd never gone
down, for good reason: it led straight down to the propeller-shaft
tunnel forty feet below.

The hatch was rusted halfway shut, but I managed to squeeze
through.

Gripping the knife in my teeth again, I reached out for the ladder, to the only place where the narrow wedge of light reached—and swung across the narrow, black void.

As I slowly climbed down, flakes of rust from rungs slipped off in my hands. The coolness rising from below chilled my skin. The stench was so great I had to fight off the urge to gag—or lose the knife. I needed both hands to climb down. So would Masskey.

I didn't stop till I was twenty feet down, enough of a lead so he wouldn't have the angle to shoot from the hatch. Soon as he began his climb down after me and settled himself, I'd extend the lead. Though the vertical shaft was narrow, he couldn't see me. If he did fire one-handed, there was a good chance—not a great one—that he'd miss.

I looked up, seizing on the splinter of light, waiting for the eclipse of Peter Masskey.

He has to be done with the aft-house. There's no other place to look.

I shivered with the upwelling cold. My jaw was aching from clamping the knife.

Come on! Come on!

Somewhere down there the shaft ended and the tunnel began, and that's where I'd take him.

Come on . . . where are you?

The eclipse came with chaos.

The ladder broke in a sudden lurch, shearing free of the shaft wall. It happened too quickly to scream, but I lost the knife anyway, felt it hit my knee, as my legs swung away. I bicycled wildly in the black air. The ladder ground to a halt, with a screeching of metal on metal, buckling against the opposite wall of the shaft.

Somehow I held onto the rungs. My legs dangled over the abyss.

I had to get farther down, where the ladder was still bolted to the wall, before my weight snapped the rungs.

Above, Peter Masskey was laughing.

I flailed my legs, unable to gain purchase, until I kicked out, away from the ladder. My feet clanged against the metal wall. I pushed off, a pendulum.

Don't break . . . not now, not now.

My feet found rungs. I climbed down, fighting the pressure of the angle, holding on until the ladder straightened and bore my weight again.

I draped my arms over the rungs, exhausted.

"Hello, Paul." Masskey spoke slowly, his high-pitched whisper magnified by the chamber of the shaft. "You're breathing like an engine, fella."

I went down another ten feet, to get away from the weakened section of the ladder, but I could still hear him, as if he were right next to me.

"Did you think I'd be that stupid? Did you think I'd follow you down there where I couldn't see, when I know Ellie and Michael aren't there?"

My breathing filled the narrow sound chamber of the shaft.

"You couldn't get a boy down there, Paul. They're somewhere else, and while you're down there, I'll find them. You had an invitation to the party, but I'll just have to enjoy it without you. You know what Bobbie Burns said about the best-laid plans? I'd say you're fucked, but let's make sure you stay fucked."

He tried to ram the hatch shut, again and again, kept at it for a minute, his grunts echoing the rage that he'd kept from his words. I didn't wait to see if he succeeded in busting the weld of rust. I started down again. Even if he didn't, there was no way I could climb up using the ruined ladder. But there was another way that he couldn't know about.

Or maybe he did. Maybe he knew, too, that the tunnel housing the 125-foot length of the propeller shaft could well be flooded. And at the other end, the decking leading up past the three-story-high engine could be a tangled mass of twisted metal, and the hatches through the engine housing could be shut, sealed with rust.

There was no place else to go.

I climbed down, down, fighting surges of panic, the certainty that I was trapped, as surely as Peter Masskey thought I was, trapped and crawling into a tomb. Even if I got through, could I do it in time to get to him before he found Ellie and Michael?

I went down, hurrying because of that greater fear, down in the total blackness, racing the fuse of panic. There was this at least: if I slipped, I wouldn't have far to fall now. My breathing came as echoes now. Other echoes, too: the moaning, the eerie grinding and gnashing of a ship long dead; the rising tide, bringing flotsam and junk to knock against the decaying hull.

Or was it Masskey above, taking his time now, thinking he'd won, hitting this, smacking that, knowing the echoes would find me? Thinking he had me trapped just like the one in that other room small enough to kill its echoes before they were born.

Get out . . . get out . . . have to get out of here.

The pounding grew louder, then ended abruptly.

Nothing under my feet, no more ladder.

Go on, GO ON, keep going!

My feet splashed the water, colder than anything before, colder than Chelan's glacial water, and thicker, a soup of rust and algae, cold enough to make me gasp.

I sank in that water up to my knees, then waist, gripping the last rung of the ladder with one hand, and wheeling the other, trying to find direction in this blackness. I reached as far as I dared and found nothing, no grab. An air pocket was above me, but the water was too deep under.

And the tide was coming in, a tide that rose notoriously fast in this scabbard cove, that might fill the tunnel before I could get out.

Get out, get out.

I almost lost it then. It was too far to go. I felt as if I were slowly being crushed, suffocated in the darkness of a sealed tomb.

No! Keep going! You can't stay here! Stay here you die, Ellie and Michael will die.

The way out is the way through.

Through the image of Masskey, getting closer to my wife and son. He wasn't going to get them, they weren't going to be swept away.

Not this time, not again.

I reached out . . . and left the ladder . . . reached out . . .

My fingertips brushed something hard, curved, and I rose, higher like a man come back from drowning, and my hands curled over, slipping over the *Chace*'s horizontal propeller shaft, a lifeline thick as a telephone pole.

It was slimy, coated with inches of muck, sunken to a hemisphere in the water. From the surface of the water to the top of the tunnel there was only a foot and a half of airspace. My hands were numbed. I was shivering violently, my arms knocking the propeller shaft, but I managed to crook my left arm over.

I began paddling with my right—until something hit me in the forehead. I felt for it—piping or an electrical conduit sagging from the tunnel ceiling. Two inches closer, I lose an eye.

I turned around, worked an improvised backstroke. If I was going to run into something, better to bruise the back of my head than spear an eye.

I made quicker progress each time my arm slid into a bearing housing—which was the purpose for the propeller-shaft tunnel. I'd gotten a book on the Libertys. The ship's engineer had to check the housings that supported the long propeller length. There were eight of them. I pushed off each housing as hard as I could, counting each one.

Three.

The distances between each decreased until I was able to use the push from one to get to the next.

Four.

I was getting tired. And so cold. The numbness was spreading, the shivering slowing me down.

Five.

Twice more I ran into the ceiling piping, and once in the back. I wasn't going fast—not nearly as fast as I wanted, had to, so the collision didn't do any damage. But it was a reminder that things were falling, that I was under virtually all of the wreck, except for the keel, under the aft holds. At some point the ship would collapse. It was all I could do to keep my mind off thousands of tons of iron above me, pressing, *pressing* down.

Six.

The pocket of air was decreasing. My arm was sliding through water by now, and I had to tilt my face up.

So tired . . . so tired.

Seven.

I felt for the top of the tunnel, and I used the sagging piping to pull myself along, instead of paddling now.

Eight.

The air seemed different: a greater void. And then my arm slid into a greater mass, something rising, and I maneuvered around it until—finally, my feet hit something solid as well. A step.

Grating. The engine room.

I rose, leaving the water at my waist, then knees, running a hand along a handrail, ploughing slime. Water poured off my clothes.

I had to hurry, but how can a blind man hurry when a misstep off the edge of the grating would be the end? I followed the rail to a corner, turned with it, impatient to feel it end—the opening for the stairs up.

Too impatient.

The railing gave way—and I almost went with it, but stumbled back just in time and almost fell again, recoiling back into a fallen section of pipe. I lost a precious minute finding the railing again. Even when the railing ended and veered vertically, I had to consciously brake myself. The higher up I went, the more deadly the consequences of a misstep. I tested each step before giving my weight to it, but up I went, slowly.

Too slowly. He'd be there. He must have found them by now.

It seemed as if I'd been down here forever.

Twice I had to duck under, then over, more fallen pipes that had bent and twisted the railings, my lifeline through this midnight junkyard of corroded, scaling, slippery metal. I kept on, finding the steps up, stepping high so I didn't trip.

The air . . .

Was the air getting better?

Yes!

And the interior echoing of the ship had become fainter. I had to be above the main deck now, getting close to the boat deck, where access hatches led through the engine housing.

Somewhere above, Ellie and Michael huddled, or had he . . .

Too much time.

But I hadn't heard any shots.

Then I saw it: the angle of orange-red light, where one of the six lids of the engine casing still remained open—just a crack; and the round hole left by a ventilator ripped from the sloping roof of the casing. Twin beacons that led me up the last tier of stairs at a run, to even greater light.

The starboard hatch was wide open, and even as I raced up toward it, the exhilaration of being free—free from entombment below—was quickly consumed by the certainty that Masskey had had more than enough time to find Ellie and Michael.

I stepped quickly through the hatch, squinting even in the low light of dusk. The starboard ladder up to the bridge deck was gone. I ran around the engine casing, slowing only to hurdle the fallen ventilator. The stairs were wobbly, shook perilously with my weight, but they held as I took the steps two at a time. Crossing the aft promenade of the bridge deck, I stopped at the entrance where more stairs led up to the top of the superstructure, the flying bridge, and down again to the interior of the boat deck.

I heard nothing except the keening of seagulls, the distant buzzing of a light plane—but no sound from within. I looked around for a weapon. Nothing I could carry, use. I yanked on the stair railing, which gave a little.

He thought I was still down there, too far gone for screams. It would have to be enough.

I walked ahead slowly, listening, my heart pounding, terrified to approach the reason for the silence within. The passageway was dark, but nothing compared to where I'd been. Dim light filtered in through portholes, just enough light to make my way in the narrow corridor.

I turned a corner, slid along the wall, edging closer to the radio room, and stopped at the doorway. The door was open, the room dark, silent.

I called out softly to them, and again, telling Ellie something only I would know, in case she was there, unsure if it was *him* or me.

Silence.

It took only a few seconds in there to know the room was empty. Either they'd hidden somewhere else or Masskey had taken them to . . .

Where?

Where? Where he could see them?

The chart room was empty, as was the captain's office, with its flaking, graffiti-smeared walls. The last place on this deck was the wheelhouse, where the light was the best. At the door I paused, hearing nothing, no muffled breathing, the rasping of a hand sliding on skin. I bolted in low, anyway.

Empty. Nothing except the sores in the warped, ruptured deck, where all the fittings had been. Wires and cable hung from the scaling roof. I pushed the tentacles aside, going to the three square windows facing forward.

Where were they?

If Masskey had them, he wouldn't have exchanged the dimness of one deck for another. The main deck? I didn't see them out there, though the thick storm glass of the windows was cracked and dirty.

Which meant Ellie and Michael were hiding elsewhere, somewhere among the debris and hatchways of two hundred feet of deck ahead. The holds? Just below, No. 3 was still covered, but the other two were black rectangles, still gridded by beams that had once supported the caved-in hatch covers.

Or above. The flying bridge, the closest, with all the light left in the world.

I left on the starboard side of the bridge deck, went up the outside ladder. If he was there, waiting for me . . .

No gopher shot.

If he'd killed my wife and son up there and was waiting for me now, he didn't have a gun big enough to stop me from taking him with me over the side.

I came hard and fast, a burst, ready to roll.

Seagulls scattered, shrieking.

And nothing. Again.

The corners of the top deck were flanked by the tubs for the antiaircraft guns, frosted with decades of rust and gull shit. Cable stays snaked into the gaping hole in the center, where the funnel had once been. The ventilators were gone.

However much time I was in that tunnel, Masskey wouldn't have had enough to take them off the ship.

Where were they?

Where was Masskey?

I went down the aft ladder to the boat deck, took another down to the main deck, and cautiously took the portside passageway forward and stopped in the shadows, leaning away from the ship's list.

He was ahead, somewhere among all the two hundred feet of rusting junk, stumps of masts and cargo booms, amputated ventilators, tangled cable.

Somewhere.

But not on deck. I caught no movement, nothing shifting.

Below? Or inside? Inside one of the two mast housings. The hatch to the near one, between holds 2 and 3, was shut; he wouldn't have closed it on himself. The other?

Turn the tables. Seal him below as he was looking for Ellie and Michael. He didn't have them. He wouldn't have taken them forward. *Let Ellie have crept out, seen him from the wheelhouse going forward and hurried aft and off the ship. Let it be just me and him now.*

I detoured around a pitted spare anchor, ducking under a length of cargo boom, moving quickly but carefully.

From a corner of the No. 3 hatch, I snapped off a thick, protruding band of iron, used to bundle the wooden hatch covers together. Hefted the three, four pounds. It would do.

Just as I passed the mast housing between the No. 3 and 2 holds, I heard the faint crying from within the housing, a crying cut off sharply at the same moment Peter Masskey stepped out of the hatch in the foremast house, the half-circle scars on his cheek visible sixty feet away.

I tossed the iron by the mast housing, said loudly as I dared, "Ellie! Five minutes, then leave!"

No time to wait for her reply. I scrambled low toward the open hatch of No. 2 hold.

Masskey was forty feet away when he stopped, fired. The first shot twanged off a broken boom spanning the hatch beams. The second bit the rim of the hatch two feet away. I leaned over, spun on the rim, swinging over as Masskey fired again. Too close this time. Shards grazed my hands.

I held on until my feet had my weight on the second rung of the hatch ladder.

Hold . . . hold . . . don't fall.

I had my back to him, heard him running as I scrambled down, into the cool darkness.

The tween deck was over ten feet below, and I reached the end of the straight ladder just as Masskey appeared above. I lunged for the edge of the gray rectangle of light, the only light that broke the utter darkness of the hold.

Water sloshed in a fetid ditch where the tilting deck met the side of the ship. The *Chace* had been a troop carrier. Metal bunks creaked and gnawed against one another as the wreck rocked gently with the tide. The tiers of bunks nearest to me lay in a jumble against the port side, but others had survived the wrecking and the vandalism, their dimly illuminated surfaces like those of the ledges of catacombs. Beyond these few I could see nothing of the vastness of the hold. The blackness closed in quickly. The tween deck was big as a ballroom. In the center was another hatch, down to the lower hold.

The hatch to the mast housing where Ellie and Michael were hidden faced No. 3 hold—away from Masskey. He'd have his back to them.

Do it, Ellie! Go! When he comes down.

If she heard me . . . her bad ear, hushing Michael.

Then he was . . . there. Above. Panting.

"I know . . . what's . . . down there, Paul. I know . . . about the wreck. I did a little sight-seeing once . . . when I came up here to have a look at your place one last time. You were going on the *Constellation* that weekend."

He isn't showing himself, isn't sure I have a gun.

"I watched you board at the south end of Lake Union. I was close enough to hear you ask Ellie to run back to the car and get your working gloves. Michael said he'd go, but you and Ellie overruled him because to get back to the car from the dock you have to go through the pergola and sometimes bums are there, drinking out of paper bags. You've always been very careful with Michael, after what happened to Emma, haven't you, Paul?"

That's it . . . keep talking . . . keep going.

He leaned over the rim of the hatch, a silhouette, not much of one, but . . . closer. *Can I get him down here?*

"So I went up here. When I came back, I looked up Liberty ships. They were called 'the expendables.' We built thousands of them. Couldn't have won the war without them. Some of them carried troops, especially in the Pacific. No *Queen Mary*s out here, soldier. The *Chace* made the Aleutian run, during the 1942 buildup way up there. Terrible weather, Paul. The winter of '43 was one of the worst on record."

More of a silhouette. Elbows on the edge. Silence drawing him closer.

"I personally think the ship in *Mister Roberts* was a converted Liberty, but one could argue otherwise. Remember Henry Fonda in the movie? Mr. Roberts thought he had finally gotten what he wanted, getting off his loser ship, and he winds up getting killed by a kamikaze that smashed into the destroyer he'd been assigned to.

The ole be-careful-what-you-wish-for-you-may-get-it. You ever wonder how often hope leads to self-destruction? You ever think about that? Paul?"

Go, Ellie. GO NOW.

"Do you know what's bothering me, Paul? I know you're down there, but the thing is, I don't hear the boy. He should be crying. I don't hear him crying. That's not good. It's unnatural. Or maybe Ellie has his mouth stuffed with her hand."

His screaming filled the hold: "Did you tell him what we did, Ellie?"

Did you hear me, Ellie? Do it now . . . GO!

"People will *fuck* anywhere, Paul. Sometimes they fuck even when they know a boy is watching and listening. It's too bad Michael has to listen to this, but take my word for it, sometimes a boy doesn't have any choice, even with his hands over his ears and a dirty sock in his mouth so he can't scream.

"I can't hear him. I can't hear Michael. Ellie can keep her mouth shut. But that's tough to do when you're a seven-year-old boy, pissing in your pants. I don't suppose it would help to tell him that the last thing I want to do is kill him; only you first, Paul, and then a sweet reprise with your wife before she goes, too.

"There's no way I could get you to believe I won't harm the boy. But just tell him anyway, will you do that? I'll be listening. Tell him that I was a boy, too, once, so I understand what he's going through right now. Paul? *Paul!* If I don't hear him answer you, I'll have to pry the tops of the hatch ladders loose—it shouldn't be too hard to do. I don't know how you got out the last time, but it won't happen again. Then I'll have another peek hereabouts. It's a beautiful day in the neighborhood, so I'm thinking Ellie and Michael aren't down there with you after all. I'll find them. Once you're hidden, it's very hard to come out. That's something I learned very early."

I walked toward the ladder, closer to him so he could hear me, but stayed in the darkness. He was hanging far over the lip of the hatch, his arm and gun like the snout of an animal.

"They're gone, Masskey. They left the ship even before you began ranting. She's getting help now, so you may as well come down here."

"Nice try, bucko."

"I'm waiting for you. What's the matter? You've got the gun. Scared of the dark?"

"I said no!"

Masskey backed quickly away, almost as if he was fearful of falling in now. The silhouette of the gun receded last.

"You don't have the balls to come down here."

He heard me. He hesitated above, or turned. It was enough.

Because both of us were right about Ellie.

He must have seen her soon enough, coming up behind him. There was a shriek with the loud pop, a sharp grunt, then the shrieking formed into my name, Ellie screaming my name. By the time that scream ended, I was scrambling up the ladder.

Masskey stumbled back against the rim of the hatch, blotting out the light. I thought he was going to fall, and I was closer now, close enough to reach up, pull him down. The gun he dropped hit my arm, bounced off a rung of the ladder, and into the black. Closer now, I saw Ellie swing the length of iron again, saw just her quick arm. Her grunts burst shrilly, wildly.

I tore up through the hatch, in time to see Masskey punching Ellie, sending her sprawling backward.

He whirled to face me, the brands on his face grotesque smiles. He backpedaled toward the bow, clawing at a vest pocket.

Another pistol. The listing wreck made him move drunkenly; he backed into the winch at the corner of the hatch, had just freed the gun when I was on him. I tackled him, driving my shoulder into his chest, my hands going for his right arm before he could level the gun. It went off around my ear, a deafening roar, obliterating Ellie's groans and Masskey's snarling, to silence.

He drove a knee into my thigh, missing my groin. We slid off the winch, hit the mast house. He was too smart to punch my head, ruin his hand, but he caught me in the stomach, a blow I only partially blocked. I dropped, spinning him around, both hands still gripping his right wrist, trying to break the hold on the gun. He fired again. The bullet whined off the curve of a ventilator behind him.

I didn't let go. We spun together, dervishes, angling down, the way the wreck wanted us to go. Everything was tilted, askew, pulling, dogging my balance. Masskey was no better off. I smashed into the corner of the No. 1 hatch first. Masskey twisted over me. We fell back and I fought to get out from under him, because there was nothing under my back. He was panting wildly, trying to lift, push me over, spitting, working the muzzle of the gun around to me, the blood from his split forehead pooling into his twitching right eye, spraying my face. He fired two more shots. My ears were roaring, ringing, my arms leaden. I was almost horizontal now . . . *He's breaking my back . . .*

I let go my left hand, punched the gash as hard as I could, digging knuckles into the gash.

He screamed, loosened his grip on the gun, enough so I could punch it from his hand. I shoved him off, gained my balance, and before he could recover, jabbed hard at his face, the gash, jabbed twice, snapping his head back. He staggered away. I spun for the gun, kicking it up toward the bow, where it hit the angled spray shield, ricocheted back.

He pushed me aside, going for the gun. As I fell, off balance, I swatted his ankle, and he fell, too, his outstretched arm only a few feet from the gun.

He got up, kicked at me, but I snared one of his feet and pulled him back. He twisted free, got to his knees, his chest heaving, his face dripping blood. Ellie was groggy, still hurt, blood streaming from a broken nose. She wouldn't be able to reach the gun.

The hatch was behind me, a chasm thirty-five feet long. There was no place I could sidestep him, not with that much emptiness behind me. He had the advantage of the sloping deck. There was no way I could stop him. I got up to face him, feigning defeat, to let him think he was going to ram me right over the three-foot-high rim of the hatch.

I dropped to a crouch at the last moment but kept my head up. Reached for his legs. His knee slammed into my jaw, stunning me, but not enough. Then he was over me, unable to stop the momentum, which was his last weapon, which should have done it for him if I hadn't ducked. Jarred by his knee, I lost one of his legs, but lifted the other. I heaved up, rising, pushing off with the last strength I had in my legs, twisting and falling at the same time, flinging Masskey over me—and let him go when my hip slammed into the rim of the hatch.

I was halfway over the rim. I almost fell into the maw of the hold. Masskey screamed, stretched out, spitted above a cold, cold fire. His shoes snagged over a section of a broken boom that slanted across the hatch. His arms were crooked around one of the hatch support beams that spanned the open hold.

I pulled hard on the boom, yanking a huge tiller. With little left in my arms, I had to give it my shoulder to move it. Still that wasn't enough, until Ellie came over. Together we did it.

Masskey screamed again as we shoved the boom away from his feet. His legs swung like a pendulum into the blackness. He was still holding onto the beam. He tried to move sideways, his hands bloody and punctured by shards of rusting iron.

I knelt by the hatch, too exhausted to do anything but watch Peter Masskey's last moments. Ellie had come back with the gun now. I reached out for her and she thought I meant the gun and she put it in my hand, but that weight of the gun seemed too much to hold and I shook my head and dropped my hand and turned back just in time to see Peter Masskey's hands slip from the beam. His arms flailed. His legs pedaled furiously. The echoing scream outlasted the thud of his landing on the deck below and the unmistakable cracking of bone.

He'd rolled to port, and all I could see was his left hand. He wasn't moving, or groaning. It must have been twenty-five feet down to the bottom of the hold above the deep tanks, but Masskey had fallen only ten, to the tween deck.

Ellie's hands were smeared with blood from her face. "Michael," she said, and left to get him.

It was almost dark now. I stood facing aft, the gun in my hand, listening to Masskey's groaning below, and then I left, too.

Keeping the gun at my side, where Michael couldn't see it, I knelt to hold him and Ellie so hard. He was crying uncontrollably, but trying to say something, about trying hard not to cry, to be quiet because of the bad man, and I kept telling him through my own cries that it was okay now . . . it's okay now . . . *it's okay now.*

Ellie took him then and I followed. In the passageway she stopped and turned into me, and I stroked her hair with one hand because I had the gun in the other and whispered again the only words I had, before I told her I had something to do. "Wait for me."

She nodded, holding Michael, rocking him.

I went to the aft-house and left the gun in one of the cabins. Because he wasn't dead, yet. Even with a broken leg or arm, he might still be able to get out somehow. I was going to have to come back to make sure he couldn't.

It took us ten minutes to get down. As we passed the bow, splashing through the water, I heard something and turned, the sense of presence flaring.

No one was behind us, and then I realized what it had to be: the faint shuffling and moaning of Peter Masskey trapped within the wreckage of his tomb. The sounds faded but the sense of presence did not. I kept looking back all the way up from the beach, because I couldn't shake the feeling that someone was watching us, someone who, even now, was still behind me.

Chapter 32

PROMISES

We didn't stay in the cabin that night.

There were no other accommodations on the island, and there were no more eastbound ferries until seven-thirty in the morning, so Ellie and I decided on Becket Cove. While she stayed with Michael in her car, I gathered up everything we'd need: blankets, flashlights, a liter of bottled water, towels, washcloths, clothes, the first aid kit. I made two quick trips.

Becket Cove, a secluded place on Triton's north shore, had one of the few sandy beaches in the San Juans. NO TRESPASSING signs were everywhere. We didn't give a damn the area was off-limits, part of a University of Washington Biological Preserve. It wasn't that or the forty-foot ketch moored out in the cove or the warm night that was the reason why I didn't build a fire, nor Ellie or Michael ask for one.

Michael and I took off our clothes and waded into the chilly water, which held just enough of the summer's heat to be bearable. After we put on our change of clothes, Ellie took her turn. Then we huddled together on the thick layering of blankets.

It took a long time for Michael to fall asleep on Ellie's lap. Soon after he did, I told Ellie I had to go back. She didn't want me to.

"You'll be okay here. No one knows we're here. No one followed us."

"I'm not worried about us here."

"We have to make sure, Ell."

"All right. But be careful, Paul," she whispered, squeezing my hand. "Please . . . be careful."

She tasted like the sea when I kissed her, and I left, a flashlight in each hand.

He hadn't gotten out.

Or at least the Blazer was still there. The lights were still on in the cabin. I'd forgotten to turn them off in the haste to get away. I left them on anyway, as a beacon, even though they reminded me—though not as much as the radio on the porch—of just how close Masskey had always been.

I put the spare flashlight in my back pocket, so I could carry the radio. It took me fifteen minutes to walk back down to the wreck, to begin hearing what Peter Masskey was hearing even now: the discordant music of the wreck, the creaking and shifting of his cavernous tomb, which had almost been Ellie's and mine. The strange and awful thing: I almost believed what he had said about letting my son live.

The tide had come in. I slogged through, getting wet up to my knees. In the dark, with only the flashlight to guide me, another twenty minutes had passed after I'd retrieved the gun from the aft-house and cautiously made my way forward along the port passageway, to where Peter Masskey was going to die.

I shone the light down into the hold.

He wasn't where he'd fallen. I flicked the light around the tween deck, the perimeter surrounding the empty hatch to the lower hold. He'd moved. He was still alive; he'd moved. . . .

"Masskey!"

I swerved the light back and forth, waiting for him to show, his voice to rise from below. He was down there. He had to be.

"*Masskey!*"

I made another careful circuit of the hatch with the flashlight. There was no evidence of an escape, nothing he might have piled up from below, but I shone the light all around me on the deck, turning slowly. I sensed someone here. It had to be Masskey. He wasn't dead. Not yet.

I called out, listening for him shuffling below.

Nothing.

I kept the flashlight on the radio, hoping it had survived the bangs and jostling of the climb up to the main deck. I switched it on, moved through static to the first clear station. Country music.

The radio did it, pulling up weak laughter from below. The gun was steady in my right hand, pointing down, waiting for him to show. I moved the flashlight around and stopped when his head appeared, then the pockets of his vest. His face was smeared with blood and rust that obscured the circles of the smiling brands. His bloodshot eyes squinted in the beam of light. He was crawling up the tween deck, toward the hatch, using his elbows, his left leg trailing at a gruesome angle.

Then he stopped, resting on his side, grinning.

I turned the radio off.

"You came back," he said. "Didn't think I'd learn how to swim, but I did. I learned very well. Got the trophies. I keep my promises."

"Who's in the room, Masskey?"

"You know who's in the room. Long time no see. You should see this—it's like a prehistoric cave down here. Faux Lascaux. Wet walls, all these graffiti-banditti." He cackled. "People will go anywhere. I'm not the first down here. Then it got dark and I couldn't see anymore. No rats yet for scabby tabbies."

"Who's in the room?"

"So you came back to kill me but you can't, you know, because I learned how to swim. You have to keep your promises, too."

Was he talking about me or . . . Russel Strickland? I asked him the same question again but didn't expect an answer. He was delirious.

"Someone who knows all about you."

"Who?"

"Who do you want it to be?"

He collapsed to his elbow, his laughing weaker, a hacking. He rested his head on his arm in a way that reminded me of a child. "It's not over, you know," he said in a singsong way. "I'll die here, whether you finish me off or not, but it won't end with me, just as it didn't end with you. You've been dead for a long time, but you wouldn't know it, what with so many people thinking you were still alive."

Russel Strickland . . .

I was a foot from the rim, close as Masskey was, when I was down there, when Ellie came up from behind and hit him.

I couldn't help it then. The instinct, or fear, whatever it was took over, and I had to step back from the edge and shine the light on the deck around me.

"Where are you? Where'd you go?" he said, then laughed. "Don't leave me in the dark."

I didn't. Closer again, I kept the light square in his face. "You were at Snoqualmie Falls, following me, weren't you?"

"I've followed you many places."

"You killed my father and that man at Shilshole. You put the wallet I lost there in my mailbox. You sent the birthday card. You dropped the bracelet of the woman you raped and killed. You've been toying with us. Why? Because Strickland hurt you?"

"Could you turn on the radio, please? Way up. It helps when it's loud, so no one will hear."

The beam of the flashlight lifted, spotlighting the forward gun tub as I rose to leave. I wouldn't be getting any more answers from him.

"Don't you want to talk anymore?" he said. "I still have my voice. I haven't lost it like before, when I was a boy. We'll talk until the light comes on. I like to talk in the dark. Tell me what it's like, coming back from the dead. Tell me what you've found out."

I picked up the radio and dropped it into the hold. It missed the tween deck and smashed at the bottom of the hold. I shone the flashlight one last time on him. He'd crawled to the edge of the tween-deck hatch, his face fractured with rage.

"*You shouldn't have done that! The radio is all I had.* So here's something I'll always have and you won't. I found Sara before you could. You want me to describe her dress for you, and how beautiful and happy she was on the way to your wedding? She never got there. It was a yellow and white dress, and I can tell you just how far her hair fell to her shoulders. I didn't just kill her. I took my time before I killed her—"

If I hadn't walked away, I would have shot him, and he couldn't be found with a bullet in him. But it was more than that, more than wanting the police to make as much of a mistake with his death as they had with my father's, for people to wonder what had happened to him, just as so many had wondered what happened to Sara Bowers.

A bullet would have been a mercy. I didn't have that in me.

I left him still screaming that it wasn't over. He was right. It wasn't over yet. I kept the gun with me when I left the wreck, slowly, carefully, my passage through the dark wreck accompanied by his echoing screams; carefully, as I'd promised Ellie. Masskey had his delirium. I had mine, a walking delirium.

Tell me now if it runs in the family.

There was no one else on that ship, of course, except the one I'd left. Even so, I drove miles out of my way to make sure no one was following me back to my family, the one Peter Masskey claimed for his own but never finished killing.

When I returned to Becket Cove, Ellie was still awake. Michael, a restless sleeper, had left her lap, but he was close by, eyes closed to the constellations of the bears, all three of them, his breathing scarcely louder than the lapping water. Ellie still held one of his hands, and perhaps that was helping him with his dreams.

A party was going on the yacht out there in the middle of the cove. "I can hear almost every word," Ellie said. "Just like in the place with Michael, when you came. There's the two of them leaning over the transom. They've gone from the stock market to the Seahawks' chances this fall, back to the market, if you can believe it, on a night like this. Is he dead, Paul?"

She whispered this as I stood at the water's edge, ten feet from her.

"He will be soon," I said, and tossed the gun far into the water. The splash wasn't loud. The two on the ketch didn't move. "It's over now, Ell."

She gave me half her blanket. Her hands were warm underneath.

We watched the running lights of the few boats making their way through Hornet Passage beyond the cove, below the half-moon hanging over the dark outline of Lopez.

"He would have found us there," she said. "We left the radio room because I thought he'd find us there. If we found Emma there, he could find us. I kept thinking, 'Get out, get out, not here.' "

"We made it because you did. It gave . . . us time." *And maybe, Ell, you wanted it to be somewhere else, if it happened, not where we found Emma that time. Because she was there and you didn't want him to find her, too.*

"I have to tell you now," she said. "I was on my way to the door, to go get the gun, when I saw him. That's how I saw him, Paul, that's how . . ."

I held her tightly, telling her we'd both live long enough together to hear her sound like she sounded now, breathing through her busted nose; she said she'd look like it, too, then asked why one or the other of us hadn't called for the damn ball in the outfield and asked if anyone—least of all the doctor tomorrow—would believe that. Then she began to cry, which made it worse for her, and I whispered to her that it was over, that we were safe, all of us, that he was gone now.

And, for a while, he was.

Chapter 33

THE CAGE

I parked Ellie's car where I had the truck the day before. It was eleven p.m. Queen Anne Hill had not yet fallen quiet, was not yet listening.

Down the street, someone was taking out the garbage, scraping the plastic bin on the concrete instead of picking it up. The head-lights of a car swerved into a driveway, and bounced up and down, like at Carla Martell's place. The blue-gray glow of television sets ghosted shades and windows.

I waited by the car, making sure no one was about, keeping the crowbar tight against my jeans. I wore a dark, long-sleeve shirt. The air was cooler than it had been at night for weeks; forecasters were predicting the end of the abnormal heat by week's end. A gen-tle breeze stirred the oaks cloistering the street.

I waited another minute, then walked down the alley in back of Masskey's house, looked around again, and went through the fence gate into his backyard.

Even if the adjacent houses hadn't been dark, even if there'd been a party going on next door, I would still have gone ahead.

Was there anything to match the gift of this summer night's breeze to someone who had forgotten what one felt like?

Who do you want it to be?

I believed either my brother or Sara was in that room.

Ellie was waiting, prepared for . . . whomever I'd be bringing home, though we both realized that Steven or Sara would require more help than was possible for us to give.

Ellie knew everything now, but there had been no question of her coming with me, not to this house, not . . . to the upstairs hallway she had passed before. Someone had to be with Michael after what had happened. Even if she had wanted to come with me, we couldn't have left Michael with anyone else, not even Ben or her parents. One of us had to stay behind, in case something happened.

On Masskey's back porch, I flicked on the flashlight briefly, and close to the door, allowing myself just enough illumination to mark the place for the crowbar.

The wood splintered, but the sound wasn't as loud as I'd expected. The lock popped on the eighth gouging pull. I pushed open the door, and the smell of Peter Masskey's house greeted me, the sickly sweet stench of rotting fruit, apples, and wood paneling and the heat of trapped, stale air.

Something skittered, rustling over paper, to my left. Masskey's kitchen had mice. I kept the flashlight pointed down and stopped, right there in the middle of the kitchen, as if there were a precipice in the darkness, just beyond the light, into which I would fall, joining the one who would be laughing even as he was dying, urging me on. I felt I was back at the wreck, spearing that other volume of blackness with light, where Masskey might still be alive.

Who do you want it to be?

Sara or Steven was in that upstairs room. Why else would it be locked so securely? Had he faked his delirium? Probably not. But whether he really believed I was Russel Strickland, he'd admitted there was someone up there.

Who do you want it to be?

Who else could it be except Steven or Sara? Who else but one of them would he take to his lair, to keep alive and locked away, as a constant reminder of his purpose? A living totem.

He wanted me to go to the room, so I could see that, as he said, it wasn't over. Steven . . . Sara . . . either would remain damaged long after Peter Masskey was dead. He knew I'd go, because whoever was in that room had the answers Masskey wouldn't—or couldn't—give me.

Which one did you save for me in case you were the one to die?

I bolted through the darkness, through the dining room, the living room, careening with the light ahead of me. The crowbar banged against furniture, the edges of this claustrophobic interior, then the railing post of the stairwell. I ran up the steps and, at the top, played the light over the hallway, the door to the room, the dead bolts, the two of them.

Two.

It's Steven.

Steven's in there. Two bolts to imprison a man of his size and strength. Before that seeped away as the days of solitude turned to years.

Not Sara.

I was going to buy you a red Mustang so we could take that ride, with the top down. It was a convertible, wasn't it? Because you kept your hair long. Dad remembered your long hair, and I saw it in the picture Sam gave me.

One of them had to be dead, and that filled me with a sudden rage at a choice I couldn't, didn't want to make.

I found the hall light, bruised it on, squinting with the sudden brightness. I dropped the flashlight and rammed the point of the crowbar into the door, again and again, gouging a space to hook the other end, and wishing it were Masskey I was doing this to because there were two dead bolts and that meant he'd killed her and I would never hear her voice.

I levered the crowbar, thrust it up into the gouged wood, and yanked down, again and again, shouting out my brother's name.

"Steven! It's me! It's Paul!"

I ripped off the top dead bolt and it fell to the floor, the screws scattering wildly.

Then the other one. Another five minutes and I ripped that one, too, off the wood, tore off the thick metal scab—and pushed the ruined door open, giving the darkened room a wedge of light. The insides made me cough, a stench worse than Peter Masskey's tomb.

"Steven!" I shouted again.

No echoes here.

I flicked on the light, but it went out, the briefest of flares. So it was the light from the hallway that revealed a palisade of four-by-fours and my brother huddling in the corner's shadow. He shifted

on his side, turning toward me, his hands splayed, shielding, pro-
tecting his face, as if frightened by what I had done.

He groaned through the pale, quivering bars of his crooked fingers, "Oh, God, Paul, it's you."

THE CAGE: 9

I scream the name Peter gave me, the brother's name. Paul's shouting it, too. The cage light went out—a tink—*when he flicked it on, but I had my hands over my face and he didn't see me when the light flashed and vanished. There's only the light from the hall and he's blocking most of it; that and his flashlight, whose beam seems to be weakening. So much the better. He can't see the gun, which is behind me. He still hasn't recognized me; who could with my long hair and long beard? He keeps sweeping the flashlight back and forth. Peter said he hasn't seen Steven since 1980. I'm not worried. I've got the beard. And you see what you want to see, you hear what you want to hear. Especially when you're frantic, and Paul is loco. Crazy. The door is a splintered mess. No wonder Peter wanted this animal dead. He's here so that means Peter could be dead. Even if he isn't, it's up to me now. Peter covered for that. Gave me the gun. So brilliant! Plan B, that's me.*

"Paul! Get a saw! Cut me out of here!"

He doesn't answer. He doesn't go for a saw. Maybe he doesn't hear me through his fury. He's snarling, grunting, and the hall light glistens wetly on the side of his face. He's smashing with the crowbar, driving the end into the wood around the lock plates on the cage door. There are two of them—I've felt them—two set three feet apart, each with a padlock. The cage shudders every time he spears or rips or levers with the thick crowbar. What a mess he must have made of the room downstairs, the family room Peter told me about. But that couldn't be any worse than this. Paul is berserk.

I keep saying his name, over and over, telling him to hurry, like it's necessary. He bellows every time he strikes with the crowbar. He's this wild horse and doesn't know he's being ridden. The light from the hall doesn't reach me in the corner. He's stood the flashlight on end to see what he's doing. The light shimmies with aftershocks. He can't see me smiling. I've got him.

The first lock—plate, padlock, everything, falls with a thump to the floor, knocking the flashlight down. The beam veers wildly, catches me in the corner and then rolls.

Then, he rips loose the second. The screws plink against the humming air purifier. He's panting now, exhausted. He picks up the flashlight and shines it on my hands and arms covering my face. He backs away to stand in the doorway, his silhouette heaving.

He just stays there.

Why doesn't he come in, closer? He has to be closer.

"Now," he says. "Come on . . . out of there . . . and tell me who the hell you are."

The question stuns me. I turn away from the light. Why would he let me out if he knows I'm not his brother?

He's still holding the crowbar. Quickly now. He knows. But he can't know; he hasn't seen my face.

DO IT!

NOW!

I reach behind me slowly and bring the gun up. The flashlight crosses the barrel. I need a half second to steady the gun, to aim, to make sure with the single bullet . . .

Too long.

He's quick. Flicks the hall light out, a hair trigger. The gun flashes yellow. The shock of the gun's blast snaps at my eardrums. Yellow balls float in front of my eyes. I breathe deeply, taking in the acrid smoke. It's all mine. It's over. I can't see him but I must have hit him. I've aimed at the door too many times to have missed.

"Paul?"

He has to be dead, or dying. But there's no sound of him dying.

"Paul!"

The air purifier is humming louder or maybe it's the ringing in my ears. My ears are so sensitive. The refrigerator compressor kicks in downstairs. It's all coming back. I must have killed him instantly because I can't hear any moaning or breathing and he's close, as close now to me as Peter always was and I could hear his *breathing.*

The cage door creaks and wobbles when I go through.

What if he's alive? What if I missed and he's waiting for me to come ahead?

I can feel the currents of air outside. It's like a pool out there, and something tells me to be cautious because you're most vulnerable when you dip your head to drink. No matter how thirsty you are, you have to be careful. Any animal in the woods knows that. Peter would be proud of my caution, that I didn't just abandon our cage pell-mell.

My hand is on the edge of the door. I fired at this side so that's where he turned off the hall light. I snake my arm around. The switch will be somewhere, it . . .

. . . erupts/from the pool/strikes over my eyes/but it can't/it's dead/I'm drowning/how can you still be so thirsty and drown . . .

The light comes back on. My head feels as if it's going to burst. I see him through pressing weights. He's sitting on the floor, his legs crossed, Indian fashion. He has the gun. The crowbar straddles his knees. He's shaking. He tosses the wet, folded washcloth, which plops into my chest, falls to my lap. I sit up, lean back against a wall. That helps. So does the cool washcloth against my forehead. The washcloth comes away blotted with blood.

"How long do I have?" I ask him.

"That's up to you."

"You wouldn't have stayed if you're not going to kill me."

He ignored that, so I know it's true. "Tell me your name."

Is this a dream? It must be because I can't remember, not right away. Peter is the only name I can think of now. My head hurts so bad. Maybe that's it.

It hurts to talk, to tell him he can't do it with the gun. "Peter gave me only one bullet."

He nods. "I've checked."

"It's all your fault. It all started with you. If it hadn't been for you, Peter wouldn't have brought me here to take his place."

He shakes his head at this, but not in disagreement. No, some-

thing closer to disbelief that fills me with pride, because I've endured so much more than he.

"Do you know why he only gave you one bullet for this?" He's holding it as if there were still bullets in it.

"He didn't want me to blow off the locks and escape."

"That's one reason. The other is that he thought one bullet would be enough. That after one bullet it would be over."

"Where is he?"

"Where he won't hurt anyone else."

"So he's dead."

"If he isn't, he's very close."

"I know where you killed him, I know the place."

"It's over."

"Not yet. You won't let me go."

"You tried to kill me. What do you think I should do with you?"

I don't answer. It hurts to talk. I lean my head back against the wall. My head hurts terribly but I have to ask him, "How did you know I wasn't Steven?"

"Your hands. My brother's hands were much bigger than yours. They were big enough to palm a basketball."

"I know. Like your father's."

"No, Russel Strickland's."

"Peter told me everything. He had to because I had to die for him, so they would think your father came back and killed him and you and Ellie. But not the boy."

He's silent for a long time, a silence that reminds me of those with Peter, with only the air purifier going. He asks me my name again and I can't remember. He waits but I can't remember.

"Are you the one who called my home, asking for Steven, or was it Masskey?"

"We both did. We couldn't have done it without the other."

"The person who called said his name was Bobby Cage. Is that your name?"

"No, but it's close enough. Your name isn't the one you were born with either. By the way, Steven is dead. He was in here and Peter killed him."

"Do you have proof of that? Something of his Masskey kept?"

"No, but Peter told me he killed him."

"*He must have told you a lot. Tell me everything else, then.*"
"*Yes, he did tell me everything.*" I shove the pride in his face.
"*Then you can tell me everything.*"
"*You tell me. How did you find this house? Carla Martell?*"
"*Masskey knew her. Start with her then.*"
"*I sought her out,*" I tell him. "*I was curious how she had turned out. Like you did.*"
"*You're talking like you're Masskey.*"
I laugh. "*So I am. He was going to take my place, wasn't he? Who else is there to be now?*"

It does seem easier that way. Peter would approve, I bet. It feels good to talk, to get it out, to tell someone else what I know. It doesn't hurt to talk anymore. The pain in my head is going away now. I'm clear as a bell now.

"*Okay,*" he says slowly, as if he's dealing with a lunatic.

" '*Okay,' he says. Fuck you. I'm not the lunatic. I'm not the one who just bashed in here thinking my brother is still alive after eighteen years. Talk about lunatics.*"

He's calm, I'll give him that. Peter was calm, too. "*What did you tell Carla about yourself?*"

"*Very little. You think it was an affair of victims, where each caresses the other's wounds? Show me yours and I'll show you mine? I might have but I didn't. For one thing, I felt I might ruin a perfectly good sexual liaison by telling her.*"

He's looking at me as if I'm nuts, not even blinking his blues. But I'm not the one who just killed Peter. He's holding the crowbar so tightly his big knuckles are white, his muscles bunched, as if he's going to use it but he won't, not as long as I keep talking. Then he'll have to. He'll have no other choice. I wonder if he realizes his back is to the stairwell. Does he really think I'll give up so easily, after all he's done?

"*Go on,*" he says slowly.

"*The other reason was pride. Carla rolled in the shit of her victimhood. She was only asking for what she got. Her victimhood was her sole definition, much as she's strived for appearances otherwise. I haven't. I've refused to let the past completely define my life, though you may think otherwise. I've done quite well, despite everything, despite knowing the names they call me behind my back, because of my scars, names like Mr. Smiles.*

"*I turned that to my advantage, weeding out those who couldn't or wouldn't see beyond that. Life is short; why waste it on those who see only the surface. Now, Ellie certainly wasn't one of those.*"

He doesn't take the bait, give me an opportunity. He's a cool one, all right. But then, so am I. My chance will come. Peter would say I've made the varsity.

"*You've been to my office, I know you have, so don't let its size fool you. Tenure lurks in the unlikeliest of places, and I would have gotten it, if I chose.*"

He's looking past me. "*You're not listening, Paul,*" I tell him, as if he's one of my dreamier students.

"*You're the boy,*" he says. "*She said . . . Carla Martell said Russel Strickland told her she wasn't the first one he let go. There was a boy.*"

"*Yes, there was a boy.*"

"*Tell me what happened to . . . you.*"

"*And if I don't?*"

"*Then no one will ever know what you've been through. Do you want that?*"

He says this soothingly, reasonably. I hate him for it, but I have to match his calmness.

"*Do you?*" he says.

"*No, I suppose I don't.*"

"*I'd like to hear it, then.*"

"*It . . . it was my birthday . . . but it wasn't going to be a big deal. Where we were living back then—you've seen how the land is there, how spread apart the farms are along the river where the orchards are. You've been there?*"

"*Yes.*"

"*Well, back then there were fewer farms, with less migrants to help with the crop. Even kids had to help pick the fruit. So when you had a birthday, as I did that day, a week before I was to start in a new school, it wasn't like you could collect a neighborhood full of pals for your party.*

"*So for my birthday, I had only one friend. His name was Peter Masskey.*"

"*Yours is . . . Stivers,*" he whispers.

"*That's right. Karl Stivers.*"

"But there weren't any survivors."

"I'm getting to that, Paul. You'll see. Like I was saying, it was my birthday. My first birthday in our new home. We were new to the area. We came from a place in eastern Montana, one of those places where the water tower was the highest thing around except for the mountains, where the women grin when men say things like 'ride 'em hard and bring 'em home wet.' Dickens, Montana. I've been back twice, you know. At the Friday-night football games, the visiting side still screams out, 'Dick Dickens.' Some things never change; others are going fast. It's a place that people are fleeing to now, mostly from California, but back then it was a place to get away from.

"The farm near Entiat was a repossession, butchered into parcels. We got sixty acres, but that was fifty more than the Masskeys had. They lived a mile away and Mr. Masskey worked out of a '52 Ford pickup—and a Bible he always kept on the passenger seat. He went around to farms, repairing machinery and equipment the farmers and orchardists couldn't fix themselves. The Masskeys had only arrived a year before.

"It was going to be a party for two, a pathetic thing but a celebration nonetheless. My sister was four years older than me, so she couldn't have cared less. She'd been strange ever since our older brother had the accident and died where we used to live, before we came to Washington state. She thought I could have done something to help my brother, go get help, no matter how many times our parents told her I couldn't have, that I was only five. I could have, but no way was I ever going to tell my parents that. The thing with them was always 'Keep Rina busy.' So she was out in the orchards, helping my father. Peter and I had just come inside, to see how the birthday cake was doing, and my mother said fifteen minutes. So instead of going outside again, we went into the room I shared with my sister, to sneak a look at things I knew she wouldn't want us to look at.

"I don't know what happened outside. We didn't hear anything except my dog barking. My mother must have heard that and taken a look out the back kitchen door. Whatever she saw she brought to the room where Peter and I were.

"At first I thought she was angry that I was going through Rina's things, but that wasn't it because she didn't yell like I thought

she would. Then I thought she was sick because she was all white and trembling and her eyes were big and it didn't seem like she was looking at us, but she was. It all came out like one big word: 'There's trouble both of you get in Daddy's and Mommy's room the closet and stay there no matter what don't say a word.'

"*I tried to ask her what was happening but she made me promise to do what she said. The last words I ever heard her say were* 'Promise me, promise me.'

"*Peter wouldn't go in. I was first in the closet but Peter wouldn't go in. He was more scared about the closet than trouble he couldn't see. He kept crying, saying he wanted to go home, and I kept telling him he couldn't, to shut up, be quiet, like my mother said. I suppose it made it worse when I hit him to shut him up because he left, still crying, saying he hated me and my stupid family.*

"*I waited and was almost about to go out myself when the noises began, the screams, in the kitchen. It's funny what you think of. I kept thinking the cake is burning in the oven so I won't have a birthday, and all the while there were screams: my mother's shrieks and a man's voice.*

"*Here's a word from our sponsor, Paul: Do you think it's right I should have heard that voice, and not you? That I keep hearing it, and you don't? It's on every station for me, you know.*"

I wait for Paul to say something but he just tells me, softly, to go on. He doesn't understand. *How can he?* He never heard that voice, did he? *He got away, scot-free.*

"*I heard the silverware drawer fall to the floor so I think my mother was going for a knife, and then the radio came on loudly. I heard that even though I'd covered my head with clothes from the closet, yanked them down, my mother's dresses, my father's pants. Probably your father turned that radio on, left it on like the other one, but it could have been my mother who turned on the radio. I'm sure you can imagine why.*

"*Then they were in the bedroom. I could hear, even with all those clothes over me, my mother crying, and that's when I began crying, too, and stuffed the dirty sock in my mouth so I'd keep quiet like I promised her. I pulled more clothes down to stop the shaking, so I wouldn't hear, but I could feel the sounds in the room anyway, the vibrations, the shudders.*

"*It seemed to go on, those trembles in that crappy frame house that creaked in a breeze that couldn't dry laundry on a line. Then it was over and everything was quiet. I should have heard or felt him leaving, but I didn't. I thought he was still there, in the room, so I stayed in the dark closet. For a long time, I stayed there, until I stopped crying and the shaking was only a trembling. Then I felt someone coming back into the room—the floorboards told me— and I knew it was someone else besides your father, Paul, because why would he come back?*

"I sloughed off all the clothes and was about to go out—and that's when the closet door opened, letting in the light.

"We saw each other. The radio was still on and your father was standing in front of me, naked, wet. For a moment it seemed so normal, like he was my father, just come out of the shower, getting ready to dress, while the radio was on, like everyone does. He looked annoyed, not angry at all. He even said the same thing my father would have said.

" 'All right, get out of there,' he said.

"He said he needed clothes to get dressed. I couldn't move, I couldn't speak. The only thing that seemed to be working were my eyes, seeing him there, filling up a world, replacing the one I knew didn't exist anymore. The first thing I saw, that made me realize that, was the lack of water around his feet. If things were normal, if he'd been in the shower, there would have been water around his feet.

" 'You don't want me to take your Daddy's clothes, is that it?'

"I couldn't speak.

" 'S'matter, cat got your tongue?' he said.

"I don't know why he just didn't yank me out of the closet. He began talking to me. 'I'm not going to kill you, if that's what you're scared about. If I was going to do that, I'd have done it already. Anyhow, you got nowhere to go now except to follow me. You're not hiding anymore, since we found each other. So you may as well come out of there so I can get dressed and show you where your mommy and daddy are and your sister and brother. They're down by the river.'

"I don't know why it was different for me. He'd killed Peter and Rina, and my parents; I knew that. But it was like he found me, so that made it different for him somehow.

"I came out. I suppose I could have run, followed the trail of my mother's blood out the door, out of the house. But I didn't. I

*knew he could catch me with his long legs if I ran. He looked fast.
I just stared at the messed-up bed where he'd killed her, staring at
all the blood that had soaked into the flowered sheets and that
made me look down at my pants to see how my trousers had
soaked up my pee. As he was dressing with my father's clothes, and
watching me looking at the bed, he was saying how lucky I was because he'd already swum in the river to wash and he didn't want to
bother with that again.*

*"My mother must have just finished icing the birthday cake. It
was sitting on the counter beside the stove, under a glass top so the
flies wouldn't get on it. The cake seemed like one of those miracles
Peter said he was learning about at church, to have the cake sitting
there, the icing perfectly swirled, my name and the* HAPPY BIRTH-
DAY *perfectly lettered, under the perfect glass.*

*"Everything else in the kitchen was all over the place. We scuffed
through the silverware scattered on the floor. The radio was still
on, and I could hear it for a long time after we left the house.*

*"Much later I learned what your father had done to them all.
You know, don't you? He hacked off their heads and stuffed the
bodies into apple crates. The heads were never found. He must
have thrown them into the river, and the Columbia, where we
were, is half a mile wide.*

*"But at the time I didn't see anything; for some reason he didn't
take me to where he'd butchered them. There must have been a
trail of my mother's from the house, but I didn't see it.*

*"If you don't see something, and you want it to be there, you
think that maybe it is there. You think that, don't you, even though
you know they're dead, that he killed them, and he's going to kill
you, too.*

*"At the river's edge, the air was full of the scent of apples. We'd
come to the end and I wanted to know where they were, before he
killed me. I asked him.*

*" 'So you can talk after all,' he said. 'Well, let's see, they were
here the last time I saw them.' He was grinning. 'They must have
gone down a ways,' he said, pointing at the river. 'Why don't you
go on in and look for them.'*

" 'I can't swim.'

*"Something came over him then. The grin vanished and I thought
he was going to kill me then. 'What're you talking about, big boy*

like you? What're you—seven, eight? Didn't your daddy teach you anything?'

" 'He was gonna,' I said. He had tried but I was too scared. The first time he tried was after my mother had drowned the kittens. Dumped them into a burlap bag and tossed it into the pond we had in Montana that always seemed to be dry, except for this time. She tossed the bag into the water, and instead of turning away with her, I watched the bag sink.

" 'He was gonna,' I said again.

" 'I'll teach you then,' he said.

" 'I don't want to.'

" 'So how're you going to get to your mommy and daddy and your brother and sister then?' Of course, he thought Peter was my brother. He waded into the river, wetting my father's pants up to the belt, holding out his arm, beckoning me with his big hands like he wanted to baptize me.

"I wouldn't go in.

" 'Come on,' he said.

" 'You're going to hurt me if I do.'

" 'I will if you don't,' he said.

" 'It's my birthday,' I said, as if that somehow would change his mind. I ran then, but I was so scared my legs were next to nothing and I didn't get far. He caught me and dragged me back to the house, into the kitchen, his arm around my neck. His shoes squelched with water.

" 'You got my pants soaked for nothing,' he said as he turned on one of the stove's front burners. 'A boy should learn how to swim. If he doesn't, things could happen. You could drown. Someone else could drown because you don't know how to save them. Consequences. You know what consquences are?'

"He forced my head down to the burner, turned my head to the right. I couldn't see it but I could feel the heat. I was crying and the drops sizzled on the burner, just like the way my mother would sprinkle water in the pan to see if it was hot enough for pancakes.

" 'If you don't learn, I'll be back and it will be even worse for you if I've found out you still can't swim. Do you hear? Do you promise me?'

"I tried to nod but I couldn't and he said, 'Just to make sure you do . . .'

"He shoved the side of my face to the burner, held it there for a second, then let go, and I fell back to the floor, screaming, wild with white pain. My face felt like it was on fire. I scuttled back into a corner, banged my head hard on a leg of the table, but I didn't feel that; the other was too awful. He flicked off the stove but not the radio, picked up a knife from the floor, flung off the glass over the cake. It crashed against the wall, where the phone had been ripped out, showering glass over me. He cut a piece of my cake and took it with him when he walked out. But it wasn't the last I saw of him.

"My face . . . the pain was unbearable. I had the idea that if I ran, it would be better, like the fan my mother always kept going in our room during the summer. I ran. I didn't know I was heading to the river again, but that's where I wound up. I ran right in, scream-ing, splashing in the cold water, plunged my head in, and swal-lowed, and came up, gasping and coughing. For a moment it was better, but then the pain came back. It was still there. And so was your father, watching me on the road leading to the highway, in our truck, with the dust billowing around. He was grinning like he was proud of me after all.

"I threw up. From the pain, the water, and when I was done, he was gone, the only thing left of him the settling, exhausted clouds of dust.

"I ran. I ran and kept on going to our road, then the highway. I didn't know where I was going, only that I had to find someone. I hadn't been on the highway long when a truck came along.

"It was Mr. Masskey, coming to pick up his son. I was crying, I couldn't talk but I didn't have to. He got me in the truck, told me to hold onto the Bible. 'It isn't ice, but it will do.'

"He sped back to our farm, told me to wait in the truck, and took an ax handle with him.

"Everything seemed like it was before, except no one was there. I could see, through the blur of my eyes, the tall ladder among the apple trees, where my father had been working. The laundry was still on the line, the white sheets snapping in the wind.

"Mr. Masskey came back out. He said nothing and I couldn't have given him any answers anyway. His lips were as tight as one of the pages from the Bible I couldn't hold either. He kept the Bible in his lap like a puppy from the pound, the whole way back to his house.

"*He called the police, while Mrs. Masskey stayed with me on the living-room sofa, praying out loud, while she pressed ice against my face until the water streamed through her fingers, her tears down her face.*

"*They must have decided, in the few hours before the sheriff came to talk to them. They'd put me in Peter's room, and through the thin walls I could hear them praying for a long time after the police left. Whatever they told the police, no one came to take me away.*

"*The next morning they told me that I was their son now. They told me I was a second gift, given to them by God, to replace the son they'd lost. I was their son now, who would be better off with them rather than an orphanage, where God can be hard to come by.*

"*And for the third time, I was asked to keep a promise, this time to keep a secret, for my own good, to save me from a fallen terrible world, from a killer who'd taken their child, so he would never know where I was.*"

Paul has moved away from me, has his back against the stairwell balustrade, taking away what little opportunity I had. He's holding the crowbar on his shoulder as if he's waiting in the on-deck circle, Mr. All-American Boy, who knows nothing of consequences and everything about shelter. If I rush him, he will hammer my skull with the crowbar. Patience. The crowbar isn't like a gun. The crowbar will take longer. I could have one last chance.

I don't even try to hide the anger in my voice. It doesn't matter now. "You want to hear now how I killed George and Rachel Masskey, don't you, Paul?"

He shifts the crowbar to the other shoulder. "If that's what happened."

"I didn't. I had nothing to do with the fire. I was only fourteen when the farmhouse burned. I'm not saying we didn't have problems. They were very protective and older; they'd had Peter when they were in their early forties. They were strict and the household was stifling. Sometimes when they were angry with me, they'd tell me, 'Peter wouldn't have done this, Peter wouldn't have done that.' Peter this, Peter that. I'd scream at them and tell them they'd go to jail for what they did. Once they even told me that if I didn't 'hew to God,' they would turn me out, and the Pied Piper would return for me. Even they couldn't pass up the temptation to summon the devil. But I forgave them that, and I even forgave them burning the *scrapbook I'd secretly begun when I was twelve, because they saved my life. I was their life. They were good people; they saved me.*

"So I know you don't believe me, but I didn't kill them. It didn't matter that they'd burned the scrapbook. I'd looked at it so often I had everything in my head about what the papers had written about Russel Strickland, and Sam Jameson, the brother of the pregnant woman whose escape with her young son ignited the Pied Piper's rampage."

"How did it begin with Sara Bowers?" he asks.

"As the years went by, the idea of revenge centered on her, that she would eventually lead me to Russel Strickland. I didn't believe he was dead, not for a minute. I figured I would eventually find out where Sara Bowers and her children lived, believing she would be glad to meet the person who would finally kill him for her. Or if she didn't want to have anything to do with me, I would wait and watch, wait for Russel Strickland to find her first.

"I broke into Sam Jameson's house and got her address from a letter. I kept a vigil, off and on, while I worked my way through college and began my ascent into the world. The vigil was confusing: not seeing her sons, but a daughter whose age didn't fit with the child she'd been carrying when she fled down that trail to Stehekin.

"I kept it up, watching her comings and goings, and saw the pattern and realized what she had done. I was outraged, felt betrayed. The family I'd once seen almost as kin were now the opposite. That was when I added another dimension to my purpose, and toward that end I had to concede the possibility that Russel Strickland might be dead. I still was hunting him, and I believe even now he may be hunting me for what I did to Sara Bowers. Sometimes I sense his presence so strongly—as you may have sensed mine—that I think he's watching me, biding his time for some chosen moment, as I have waited for mine.

"But back then I had to accommodate my fury at your escape from fate, you and your brother. So the plan broadened and eventually focused on you all. I would have to wait, to see which of her sons had a child first. He or she had to come of age. That was the whole thing, you see. Because of poor Emma's death, thanks to your negligence, I had to wait longer than I wanted. Sam Jameson went away so I couldn't get him. Sara couldn't wait, but I decided

to wait to get Charles Sinclair because I was worried that his death might somehow alter his stepsons' lives and put them out of my reach.

"But it isn't over yet, is it, Paul? You have to kill me now, don't you?"

He gets slowly up and walks over to me, stands there just out of my reach. He raises the crowbar, a thick, ugly thing, in his big, workman's hand. I wonder how many blows to the head it will take before I die, and I think of the ice that Rachel Masskey held against my face, as the water seeped between her fingers and ran down my neck.

The edge of the stairwell is not even ten feet away. I have to do it—DO IT—before he begins hitting me with the crowbar. Drive him back, shove him over the edge. He'll lose the crowbar and . . .

DO IT. NOW!

He reaches beyond me and flicks off the hall light with the end of the crowbar. "Masskey did this to you, didn't he? Kept the lights off."

I can't see him. I hear him moving away, away from the stairs, as if he knows.

"Didn't he?"

"When we were in the room together, yes."

"I'm going to go now. It's over. You're not Masskey. Masskey did this to you. But if I see you anywhere close to my home, anywhere close to my wife and son, I'll kill you. Do you understand?" He says this softly, and in the dark I feel him bring the crowbar against my right ear, pressing it hard. I shiver. The iron is cold.

"Do you understand what I said?" he says again.

"Yes," I tell him, but I'm thinking that surely he knows threats are useless, that he should kill me, smash my head in. Who does he think he is, to bestow mercy? All he's doing is giving me a second chance.

"I'd like the box of letters," he says. "Do you know where it is?"

"In there, the cage."

"Go get it."

"I can't see."

"Then get the flashlight. It's over there."

He steps back, asks me if I read the letters.

"No."

"Masskey?"

"No. He was waiting for me to read them first."

It takes a few minutes to find the flashlight, then the box of letters. He takes both from me. He has the gun now, stuffs it into the box, which he puts under one arm. He shines the light in my face, a few steps down the stairs, too far away.

"Do you remember your real name now?"

I shake my head. "It doesn't matter, now."

"Yes, it does, Bobby. I hope you do remember it," he says, and leaves, just as Peter always did, except now I'm not in the room. I hear him downstairs, moving around. The sounds are almost painful to my ears, like having skin not used to the sun. Soon, it's quiet in the house, but that holds pain. Now that he's gone, my head starts hurting me again.

When I get up, to turn the light back on, the dizziness is so bad I lose my balance and fall back into the cage, and the fear of being trapped there momentarily surpasses the pain and I crawl out the door and get up and this time it takes, and my hand brushes the light switch.

The washcloth is bloody from the gash on my forehead. I have to rinse the blood from the washcloth he gave me. I stumble into a bedroom to find the adjoining bathroom and a mirror.

The gash is ugly but not as bad as I thought it would be. A doctor would give me stitches, but I don't want a doctor. I have everything I need here.

I wash the gash, put on antibiotic and a bandage as best I can. I swallow four aspirin. I feel a little better now after splashes of cold water in my face. My beard soaks up the water and the water runs down my throat, cold as melting ice, and it occurs to me I might feel even better without the beard.

I use scissors from the medicine chest to cut off the beard, then carefully shave off what's left, carefully, just as if I had the scars. I wipe off the few bloody nicks until the bleeding stops.

My head still feels as if a knife is in it, but it's getting better now. I even cut my hair, so that it's off my neck. It shines with grease but washing will have to wait.

Back to the mirror.

Peter wouldn't have such crappy-looking hair. He'd have $40 haircuts and so will I, too, someday. But even so, even with the bandage on my forehead, I have to think I'm looking at him, except for the scars. Peter said that he and I looked very much alike; that was the reason why he chose me after searching for a long time. The only way to find out for sure what I have to know is to find a picture of him somewhere.

I search for half an hour upstairs but can't find one. It's strange there'd be none, but then again, didn't Peter once say that no one really knew what the Pied Piper looked like except for a few people? There were no pictures of him.

I lean on the railing when I go downstairs. Maybe there's a picture of Peter in the family room, the room that Paul trashed.

It's empty. The night air sifts through the broken window. There are shelves and a desk and chair but nothing else. The desk drawers are empty, and after I bend down to check them, the dizziness swells and I have to sit down.

He's cleaned it out. Taken the evidence, Paul did. But he wouldn't have had the time, because I remember now smelling the smoke from the gun when I regained consciousness upstairs. Did Peter do it instead?

Must have. Cleared the room out, so there would be nothing Paul could show the police. That's Peter. Careful, meticulous. That's me. That's us. The bean-counter boys. I have to know which side to do it on. That's so important.

Doing it will be more than finally seeing Peter, even though he'll be dead soon, seeing how much alike we are. It will be like what the Indians used to do, taking something from dead predators, a totem, the mantle of their spirit, to help you become what they had been.

I'm hungry. I go to the kitchen. There's nothing much handy except a bag of wrinkled Gala apples. Peter said they're planting more Galas and Fujis than Delicious now because they taste better. I munch on one as I walk to the front door and out onto the porch, thinking whether there will be enough light, where Paul left Peter to die, to see him finally and compare ourselves.

I know where he is, where Paul will go back, too. They do that, killers. Peter went back to all those places. Trappers do that, too. How can you see if the bait you've left has caught anything if you don't go back?

That's why Paul let me go, of course. He intends to kill me where he killed Peter, where no one will find us. Someone might *have seen him coming here. Someone might have seen him taking my body out. Paul's crazy but no fool. People don't understand there's a difference. Paul knows he isn't safe as long as I'm alive. He knows I'll go there. So it isn't over yet. He'll be waiting for me, and watching for me. He does that, too. Runs in the family, you might say. It takes one to know one.*

There's more to do. Such as find where Peter kept the money he'd hoarded for his new life somewhere. And tell the university that . . . I . . . had suddenly decided I didn't want to teach anymore. There's no one else to tell. I was all Peter had. We had each other. We had so much in common, after all. We still do.

He made a nice start in the study, but the house could use a cleanup, upstairs and down. There's a lot of work that needs to be done around here, and no one to do it except me.

But first things first.

It bothers me that there is no picture of Peter to make sure I get it right. Yet the more I think about those minutes in the Stivers kitchen, the more I see it, where everything was, where they were. It's as if I were there. So it's not like a choice at all. I feel certain now about my decision. I have Peter to thank. He didn't spare the details.

I go into the kitchen and turn on the left front burner of the stove and lower the left side of my face, not the right. I may not remember my name, but I'm free, just as Peter would have been if Paul hadn't killed him.

As the burner begins to glow, I think of something Peter might have said about freedom, about what it means to be free—nothing more, really, than the capability of inflicting pain on yourself with no one else to help.

Chapter 34

RETURN

We had to return to the island to get the keys from Masskey's body: the ones he had taken from my pickup and the Blazer's. We couldn't let the Blazer stay where it was for too long. Sooner or later he'd be discovered, and the police would find out he hadn't owned a pickup truck, but one man did, who used to own the cabin overlooking the beach where the *Chace* still lay bitten by the teeth of Emma's sleeping giant, defying the years in that sheltered inlet, living on after death.

It took me four tries but I finally managed to reach Sam at his Chelan home a few days before we left for Triton. I talked to him for a half hour, telling him about what had happened. He wanted to see me again in Stehekin, but it would be a hit-or-miss thing catching him at the cabin since he'd be in the woods. So he told me to wait for him if I had the time and sooner or later he'd be back.

"Bring Ellie and Michael. I'd like to meet them."

Meet the man who may have started a forest fire around there? All I said was, "Sam, you don't have to go out there anymore."

"Where else am I going to go? Hell, Paul, it's a habit by now, and some are hard to break."

The night before we left, Ellie came downstairs, found me on the couch by the living room window.

"I can't sleep either," she said. She took my hand and nestled between my legs, the silk of her robe sleek against my chest and belly. I gathered my arms around her and we lay there together on the couch, staring out the window at the street lamp, its light made superfluous by the full moon.

It had been four days now. We hadn't seen him yet, Masskey's captive, Bobby Cage. He may have circled a date on a calendar, when he would come and try to finish what Peter Masskey had begun. Or we could have been the last thing on his mind.

We didn't dare believe that. While Michael was in school, I put in an alarm system for the windows, installed extra locks on the doors. I slept downstairs. The gun I took from Masskey's house was behind books in the floor-to-ceiling bookcase in the living room, where Michael couldn't reach. I'd bought ammunition, so it was loaded. I timed myself: it took me on average four seconds to get it, couch to bookshelf. Ellie woke me up twice for the test, tapping on a window from the outside. We told Michael he had to sleep upstairs for the time being because we wanted to paint his room. I hadn't begun that yet.

If Bobby Cage was going to come, he would do it soon. He wouldn't wait a long time, like Masskey. So Ellie and I told each other.

It helped with Michael back in school. Whenever I left the house, I did so after Ellie and Michael, and I made sure I was always back by three before Michael came home on the bus, so I could check the house thoroughly.

It had to be this way. Ellie felt so, too. It was better than knowing for the rest of my life that I smashed his head in with a crowbar as he knelt before me, a man who, despite a dangerous delusion, was innocent when he was taken by Peter Masskey, who hadn't killed anyone even if he thought he had.

I felt no anger toward him, even though he had tried to kill me. I didn't think this then, with him, but I have since: that I might not have fared much better in that room, the closet that Peter Masskey had re-created from his boyhood nightmare.

I didn't think Bobby Cage had yet remembered who he had been when Masskey took him. If he had, he might have gone to the police. One thing was certain: if he came, I'd keep the promise I made to him.

It must have been close to two, but Ellie still didn't go upstairs for sleep. Maybe we both knew this was more important than sleep now, and not just the vigil.

We heard the siren of a fire truck and listened to the engines coming our way from the station near B. F. Day Elementary, heading north on Fremont Avenue, past us.

For the past four days the front page of both papers had been filled with more news of the latest fire north of Stehekin that still hadn't been fully contained. Four firefighters had now died since the eastern-Washington fires began in mid-August, though none in the area of Stehekin.

After a brief respite, the weather continued hot—in the eighties in Seattle, which meant it was even hotter and drier east of the mountains.

We never did hear the fire engines coming back along Fremont Avenue. We fell asleep, finally, and Michael woke us up shortly after seven, shaking first Ellie, then me. "It's time to go to Grandma and Grandpa's," he said. It was Saturday morning and he was already dressed. He wore his Mariners cap and had his baseball mitt. Ben was going to pick him up at Ellie's parents and take him to the ball game in the evening. They thought Ellie and I were taking a much needed getaway for the day.

When we set it up with Ben, he asked me about the eggs.

If Michael told them, or Ben, about the bad man, we had a story about a prowler at the cabin. But they might never mention anything to us later. After all, their grandson had an active imagination and had stormed around their home once when he was almost four, shouting dialogue he'd picked up from a Robin Hood video.

The wait for the ferry at the Anacortes terminal wasn't as long as we expected; only two hours, and we slept most of it, woken by the blast of the *Chelan*'s horn as the ferry approached the dock. We got to the island by mid-afternoon. Sister Catherine was at the landing again, and her only concession to the heat was a blue bottle of mineral water she sipped as the cars rumbled past her, disgorged from the ferry.

We got to the cabin and waited at the edge of the bluff for a couple to finish strolling on the beach and gawking at the freighter wreck. Ellie had the flashlights; I carried a twenty-foot length of rope.

The couple disappeared around the bow, but I knew they wouldn't go farther than the water's edge.

When it happened it would probably be a group, one of whom

would go down into the hold on a dare or to see if anything was left to take. Or someone would have an accident and fall in or drop something into the hold, something too valuable to forget about.

The couple didn't reappear, and given the list of the freighter, we couldn't tell if they were on the wreck, exploring, or not.

Half an hour passed before we saw them again. The woman was combing her shoulder-length blond hair and the man was tucking his shirt into his jeans. They took their time, laughing about something.

"You think McGahern saw us that time?" Ellie said.

Ireland. Our honeymoon. "The walls were too high," I said.

"But his cottage was on the hill. And he had those binoculars, in case someone got in trouble on the water, he said."

I thought of Mrs. Clarke. "No, he didn't see us. He was alive when we got back. If he'd seen us, it would have shocked his never-married Gaelic heart to a full stop."

"It's stopped by now."

"If only to get away from those formidable sisters of his and the dog that kept nipping at his heels, 'tha dairty t'ing.' "

"Well, even if they aren't, the fort will be."

"It'll be there, Ell."

On our honeymoon we had rented a boat from an old man named Gaff McGahern and rowed out on a small lake in County Clare and laughed about becoming Veterans of Foreign Oars. Peat stained the water black as Guinness. A ring fort filled most of a rocky island in the middle of the lake. We explored a souterrain and found passages in the walls. We joked about being McAdam and Eve because this bleak garden was as elemental as you could get. All we had was ourselves, the rain that fell more as a mist, and a lot of stone, grass, and water beyond. It wouldn't get any simpler. I spread my newly bought Irish sweater on the grass. In the middle of the ring fort, surrounded by curving ramparts a thousand years old, we made love on the dark Irish sweater that had the scent of lanolin in the wool. It still does.

The couple took another ten minutes to leave the beach, disappearing at the far end, where the beach meets the thicker woods. There's a trail that leads to the road beyond and a turnout for parking a car. Above the bluff, a red-tailed hawk was beating hard in the light air, a snake dangling and twisting in its claws.

We walked down to the beach. The heat rose from the gravelly sand, and the glare of the sun off the freighter made me squint. As we neared the bow of the wreck, I stopped and looked back at our cabin, then scanned the ridge leading from the cabin to Donald MacLynn's old A-frame.

We were alone now.

The tide was out and the muck, in this heat, smelled like a sewer. The water in the cove was smooth as glass. The stillness of the afternoon was broken only by the keening of gulls. Nearby a gimpy-legged gull pecked at small crab caught scuttling between tidal pools.

We climbed up the ramp of debris, made our way slowly forward along the port rail. Everything was warm, heated to the touch. No wind stirred the carcass of the wreck, moving what little could still be moved.

I stopped to shrug the rope back on my shoulder. Halfway into the shadows of the passageway, a gull flared off from the boat deck, with something white and flaccid drooping from the downward curl of its beak.

Behind me, Ellie said, "Did he have what I think he had?"

"He did."

We passed the mast house where Ellie and Michael had hidden. We approached the dark rectangle of the No. 1 hold, rousting five or six gulls from the edges of the hatch. Four more flew out of the hold, joining others occupying the bow gun tub.

I dropped the rope, waiting a moment before handing her the end since she was looking at the gulls, probably thinking the same thing I was: *He's had visitors.* Most of the gulls remained, to wait us out.

Ellie secured the rope through a hawsehole, flaking off chunks of iron, and tied it off. We pulled on it. I could feel her strength.

"That will work," I said.

"I hope so. You taught me the knot."

I tumbled the rest of the rope into the hold, heard it thump on the tween deck. I had about two feet to spare. Ellie kneeled beside me but didn't look down.

He was down there. He was dead. He had to be after four days, with this heat and no water or food, after that fall that shattered his leg.

I felt the sun baking my back, but peering over the edge of that hatch was worse. It was like sticking your head into an oven . . .

. . . or opening a closet door in a house where the heat built up during the day, over the long days of summer, swelling, bloating the insides so that it was hard to breathe . . .

The heat welled up from the maw of the ship with a stench of decay that couldn't all be from Peter Masskey, not if he'd only been dead for two or three days. But the gulls had been down there. Someone was down there.

The thing was, I didn't see his body.

"He's crawled somewhere," I said. "There's a lot of room down there."

"But he broke his leg."

"He didn't go far. He's down there. Let's get this over with."

Ellie bit her lip. "I'll say it one last time. I don't want you to do this."

"Neither do I. But we need the keys, Ell."

I clipped the butt ring of the flashlight onto my belt. I took a deep breath, blew it out, and slid over the lip of the hatch, wrapping the rope around my hands, fisting it until I was sure of the ladder, giving it a fraction of my weight.

I began going down, the rope slowly sliding through my hands, past where the sunlight ended and the darkness began, feeling the heat squeezing the sweat from my body.

The darkness enveloped me. My foot touched the tween deck. I let the rope go, unclipped the flashlight, coughing, breathing through my mouth, wondering how much the gulls had feasted.

Ellie's voice echoed: "Paul?"

"So far so good." I swung the flashlight up toward her, then down, around, looking for him.

"Keep talking to me, all right?"

"I am."

"You see him?"

"Not yet."

As soon as I said it, the flashlight beam crossed his ankles. I slowly traced it up his body.

He'd crawled away from the port side, where rainwater had pooled, submerging the lower third of a vast archipelago of debris—the jutting, tangled remains of hundreds of soldiers' bunks. He was fifteen feet away, slumped in a starboard alley between a row of six-high bunks that had not yet collapsed. His head lolled in an odd way, but maybe it was just the incline of the deck that made the angle seem acute. His hands splayed out to his sides, palms up, in a parody of crucifixion, the fingers curled, darkened, smeared with rust. His lower left leg was bent sharply outward. But something was different. Something was wrong about him.

"Paul?"

Ellie's voice came low, so close it startled me, because I was looking at Masskey and for a moment thought he was the one who spoke.

"I see him, Ellie. He's dead."

I walked on, dowsing the flashlight directly ahead to make sure I wouldn't stumble, lose my balance, fall into him, or back. The hatch opening in the tween deck was less than five feet away and another twenty-five down to the bottom of the hold.

There was no light except for the flashlight. I looked back seeing my own approach through Peter Masskey's dead eyes. Faint sunlight framed the black mirror of the hatch.

I stopped a yard from his twisted leg. The bone sticking out was white as a gull. My throat thickened, clotted.

They'd feasted all right. His eyes were empty, pecked sockets, his face ripped up, the flesh hanging in tattered strips and chunks, the scars at his jawline mutilated but still visible. The gulls had worked at the soft flesh of his neck to the point of decapitation.

His vest was gone. Why would he have taken it off?

I flicked the flashlight around but didn't see the vest close by. I brought the light back.

Okay, okay, get the keys, get out of here.

I kept the light on the pocket, then saw the problem. Masskey's corpse had bloated, pressing against the jeans. A bulge was there. The keys. It would be difficult to get my hand inside the pocket, and the thought of it filled me with revulsion, though not as much as did the time it would take hacking and cutting away the tough cloth—and slicing into his corpse—with the knife I'd brought.

Do it . . . reach in, pull the pocket inside out, and the keys with it.

I listened to the raggedness of my breathing, wiped the sweat from my face, swallowing hard.

Come on . . . do it, get it over with.

I knelt down at his right side, wiped my face again with the back of my arm. I kept the flashlight on the pocket area. I didn't want to see his face again. I needed two hands to work the pocket. I propped the flashlight by my feet, aiming it at the pocket.

I dug my fingers into his pocket, pulling on the inside, drawing it out inch by inch, trying not to feel the . . . deadness of Peter Masskey, but it was impossible. He was no longer stiff with rigor. My throat was constricting, the bile rising. I kept fighting the urge to throw up.

I worked the pocket until it was free.

A pocketknife popped out. No keys.

I had to do it again, the other pocket. There was no bulge but maybe it was the Blazer key, flat, with no accessory.

I shifted to his other side, reached into the pocket and pulled, pulled . . .

Nothing.

He should have the keys. Where are the keys?

I must have shouted or cursed or said something because Ellie yelled down, *"Paul, what's the matter?"*

"They aren't here. The keys aren't here . . . the vest . . ."

"The vest? Paul get out of there."

"They *have* to be here."

"Forget the fucking keys!"

Someone had to have taken them. They're in the vest. Why would he take off the vest? Maybe he didn't. Maybe . . .

Sweat dripped down my sides. I wiped it from my eyes. My belly was in the jaws of a closing vise.

Someone else?

Someone here . . . someone still here . . .

"Paul . . . please come up!"

. . . waiting for me here, waiting to finish what Masskey had begun.

The presence of another was overwhelming now, stronger than at Shilshole bluff, the path below Snoqualmie Falls.

Was it . . . Bobby Cage, who knew if we came back here, we'd do so without the . . . boy . . . Michael? Was he alive down here in this place big enough to cram in hundreds of men, alive down here, keeping quiet, hidden in the dark, as "his" mother had told him to do?

Promise me, promise me . . .

Only this time he wasn't going to be helpless. This time he was waiting not for someone to go away, but for someone to *come*.

I knew you'd return. Sooner or later you'd return. You can't see me but I'm here, and as soon as you move toward the ladder . . . Try to get out, go ahead.

GET OUT . . . GET OUT . . .

I wanted to but I couldn't move. The darkness was a darkness of acid, soaking me, stinging all over, sizzling and frothing, the whispers of acid telling me now that he was going to wait until I was almost free, halfway up the ladder.

"Paul, I'm coming down."

"No!"

She was coming down anyway. Her feet swung over the side of the hatch, her hands were on the rope.

I darted toward the ladder, was under her, screaming, *"Get back, get back!"*

She stopped. I whirled, expecting to see a shadow colliding with the light, bursting free, coming toward me . . .

But nothing broke free of the perimeter of light. I went up the ladder, forgetting about the rope. Ellie was out now, reaching down for me with her hand, fierceness in her eyes.

I shined the flashlight into the recesses of the hold, swaying on the ladder like an acrobat waiting for a partner to scribe her arc far above a crowd waiting for the connection to be made, or for one of us to fall.

Then I saw him, at the edge of the pool, on the other side of the tilting deck, hidden in a space under the wreckage of bunks, as if he'd crawled to get away. Just the soles of his shoes were showing.

I squeezed Ellie's rust-stained hands and let go and started back down again.

"Paul, no . . ."

"It's okay, Ellie. It's okay now."

"What? What are you doing?"

It would really be so stupid if I fell now, so I was careful going down again, and making my way over to the body.

I pulled him out slowly from the place he had crawled into. Turned him over. Why had he gone in there, a cage within a cage? To die? Why?

The body was past rigor but not as bloated as Masskey's. A later death. He hadn't broken his leg. He hadn't broken anything. He'd climbed down. Some of his blood was still pooled, decanted by the list of the wreck, but it trailed away. There was a single bullet hole in his chest, the blood blossoming darkly on the soiled shirt.

Somehow the bandage he'd put on his forehead still remained stuck to his skin, where I'd hit him with the crowbar, still white against the greenish red flesh that almost, but not quite, hid the circular blistering on his cheek, burn marks that weren't there four days ago. They were above the jawline where Masskey's scars were, but on the same side. Bobby Cage had guessed right when he did it.

"Do you promise me?" the Pied Pier said. "Just to make sure you do . . ."

He was wearing the vest, and I found the keys in one of the bloodstained pockets. Three sets: mine, the Blazer's, and another, the one to the van I'd seen in the driveway of the house when I left him. He'd hidden it somewhere on the island. He was going to kill us. And when we didn't show up soon enough he . . .

So Bobby Cage put Masskey's vest on, in a bizarre final communion, and committed suicide?

But in the chest? Why didn't he put the gun barrel in his mouth, to his temple like they usually do? Yet, in the dark anything can happen. You think you're aiming for your face and you hit your chest. Or maybe he tripped as he fired. One thing was certain: Masskey didn't pull the trigger.

For a moment I held the keys, far above the fetid water in the bottom of the hold. *A sack of kittens about to go into the pond . . .*

I shined the light all around, looking for the gun he would have dropped. I didn't see it. Then again, he could have shot himself by the hatch to the lower hold, dropped it down there, gone forever, and crawled away to die.

Ellie was calling frantically, her voice hoarse.

This time, I went back up the ladder to her. Her hands, then her arms, were a wondrous thing.

I didn't look back down.

Chapter 35

Blowup

Ellie saw it first, two days later.

She was waiting on the front porch when I came back from walking Michael to the school bus stop. She had her hands in her back pockets and her hair was still morning wild. I hadn't had a chance to read the paper, have breakfast or coffee. I'd left her sleepy twenty minutes ago. She wasn't now.

"It's in the paper," she said.

That stopped me, halfway up the front steps. "They found them."

"No. I think they found Sam."

She had a cup of coffee waiting for me there, next to the morning *P-I* on the dining room table. She cradled hers as if her hands were cold.

It took me ten minutes to read it all, about the big fire, called the Rainbow Complex because it had started north of Rainbow Falls, that territory where Russel Strickland had taken Sara and Steven long ago.

Sam's death had been relegated to the last two paragraphs of a current summary of the destructiveness of the Rainbow Complex, his death less significant than those of the firefighters who had died around Leavenworth and west of Chelan, because he had been foolish enough to be where he shouldn't have been.

He was found four miles away from the center of the wildfire, caught on the side of a ridge, in a "blowup," the thing feared most by those who battle forest fires. When the prevailing winds hit an area superheated by smoke and gases, the woods can explode into flame. Sixteen firefighters had died in a blowup in Colorado the year before.

Blowups run uphill.

R. L. Larson, a spokesman for the Chelan County Sheriff's Department, said the man shouldn't have been in that area, that it had been sealed off for a week. "He had no reason to be in those woods."

His body, charred beyond recognition, was found on the lower slope of Catspaw Ridge, with a shapeless, melted mass of plastic welded to his hand.

I put the paper down.

"It's him, isn't it?" Ellie said.

I nodded. "That was the radio, what melted in his hand. The last time I saw him he was carrying a radio."

"I'm sorry, honey."

"Well, I knew him for all of three hours, Ell. He was on the fringe and he scared me because I felt I was heading there myself. But he had it right, didn't he? He was obsessed about the wrong man for pretty much the right reasons."

"Do you really think he set one of those fires?"

"I got that impression, all right. Jesus, it's an awful way to go, Ellie, but if Sam did do the fire around Stehekin, it's hard to feel too sorry if he was caught in it."

It was quiet in the house. The clock ticked on the kitchen wall above the telephone. A school bus rumbled by.

I reached over the table, brushing aside Cheerios left from Michael's breakfast.

Ellie's hand was warm from the coffee cup. She put her other over mine. If I had closed my eyes, I could have been back at the freighter, reaching out, coming up from below. But I didn't because I couldn't remember having ever held her hand over this table, not even the day after Emma died.

For the rest of the day I tried to get my mind off Sam's death, his incineration in that fire. I tried to get some work done at my shop but didn't accomplish anything worth a damn. That night, I couldn't get to sleep. It was hot and the fan didn't help much, and neither Ellie nor I felt like making love, so we talked about Ireland, and how we'd make it a second honeymoon. It worked better for Ellie than me, and finally I left so at least she could get some sleep.

I went downstairs and sat in the dark. It wasn't just the what-ifs. Or the fact that I wanted to feel sorrow about Sam's death but couldn't because he probably was responsible for the fire that killed him and could have killed others in that area.

Something else was bothering me about Sam. It took a neighbor, coming home late, to remind me what it was.

They had the car windows open and so I heard—for a moment before they turned it off—Lyle Lovett on their radio.

Sam Jameson was a lonely man, as Ellie said, but even so, why did he take a radio into the wilderness?

A radio.

Peter Masskey had brought a radio to our cabin.

And Bobby Cage had, as Peter Masskey, told me about the radio in the Stivers kitchen that terrible day.

And then the radio came on loudly.

Probably your father turned that radio on.

I'm sure you can imagine why.

Not all the letters in the box I'd taken from Bobby Cage were from Sara Bowers to Charles Sinclair. At three-thirty in the morning, I found the one that would stay with me for the rest of my life, the letter I would read once and, like Carla Martell, ever remember, word for word.

March 7, 1986

Dear Charley,

Thanks for writing back, and so quickly.

I wasn't going to tell you about Sam's death because it might bring up things about Mom. It has for me. But I had to tell someone, share this terrible news. I was and still am shocked and upset by it.

I'm trying to stay calm, like you said, and keep in mind that his murder in the robbery at his house in Spokane has no bearing on my life here in Connecticut. Keep telling me that.

I just keep coming back to his obsession with Mom's disappearance. You never met him so you wouldn't know about his paranoia, his insistence that the guy who killed her was still out there, scot-free. He only mentioned it a few times—when he'd been drinking—but it was enough.

I feel guilty about this—but when he said he'd had enough of the East Coast and wanted to go back to Washington, I was relieved. His heart of gold came with a black cloud that was never far away. He said he had unfinished business back home, but the closest he could get with a decent job was Spokane.

The last time I phoned him—he insisted I always do the phoning—he said he was going to take an early retirement, spend his time in the Cascades, searching for "the guy." Part of it was the fallout from his whistle-blowing, something involving fake building-code inspections. It was in the papers there for a while. He said he also wanted to write a book, said he had enough material in his journals to write five. But he had to find the guy first. He sounded like he had something to make up to Mom, that he'd been running away or something. "Going home again to face the music," he said.

But you can't go home again, can you, and I wish he hadn't tried.

It saddens me that he was probably buried with so few at his funeral. He wasn't in Spokane long and wasn't the type to make friends easily anywhere. I only found out about his death weeks after it happened, when I got worried and called his work.

There was no next of kin for him. He told me once he always burned my letters as a precaution. Evidently there was no record of me anywhere in his effects. It was like I didn't exist on paper anywhere, only, I suppose, in his heart.

He'll remain in mine.

Lisa

EPILOGUE

It's December. The rains came, finally, in early October, and since then we've already had snow, unusual for Seattle, right after Thanksgiving, but there wasn't enough for Michael and me to make a proper snowman. "I hate dwarf snows," he said.

It's been a month since he began sleeping again in his own room, downstairs. For a while it was bad, when Ellie and I took turns down there with him, perhaps as much for us as him.

The Christmas lights are up on the Space Needle and the old high school at the top of Queen Anne Hill. I've been by Masskey's house once, in early November. That was a month after the newspaper article appeared concerning the disappearance of an English professor at Cascade Pacific University. There wasn't a For Sale sign out front yet. I wonder how long they're going to wait, just as I wonder what the police made of that room upstairs.

We've sold my father's house on Bainbridge.

It's Saturday and we're cleaning the house now, our "last ups" as Michael said on the way over on the ferry this morning.

Ellie's with me in Dad's workshop. I'm finishing up the jewelry box for the girl, Jessica. When it's done, I'll just put it on her yard, by the street, as if someone left it by accident. Perhaps she'll take it in, keep it until the owner returns for it. He never will. Perhaps she'll keep it.

A week ago we found out Ellie's pregnant. I promised Ellie I'd make another box, whether it's a girl or boy. It's strange how we can talk about Emma now, and before we couldn't.

Ellie keeps her eyes on my hands as I work. I wonder if she can hear Michael nearby, playing in the caboose. Michael loves that thing, always has. A lawyer-lawyer couple fleeing Los Angeles bought the house. They're bringing three kids and an honest-to-goodness Irish nanny. The couple offered us $5,000 for the caboose, even though the real estate agent and I told them it wasn't for sale at any price. He went to seven before giving up.

The caboose will go to Ben's house until we get one of our own next year, since he doesn't give a damn what his neighbors think. Ellie's father thinks we're nuts—both of us crazy—to have sold the cabin on Triton and kept a railroad caboose.

When our little one is three or so, we plan to live in Ireland for six months. Michael keeps reminding me of my promise to show him the castles there, and in Scotland, where the Sinclairs once sheltered the last of the Knights Templar, or so my father told me.

We're serious about trying to locate Lisa. She is out there somewhere. I don't think she was ever in danger from Masskey or Strickland. All we have to go on is P.O. boxes and information in the letters themselves. If it takes a private investigator, that's what we'll do. We want her back in the family and I think she'd want that, too.

Ellie predicts she'll finish *Crossing Alone* sometime after she stops getting sick in the mornings. She's eager to begin her next one, about the three daughters, their single dad, and the minor league player who comes to live with them for the summer season. She's tentatively titled it *Rounding Third*.

It's another baseball book, sure, but you can't have too many of them, I tell her, especially if the latest one is written by a woman who loves to slide, who never saw a softball single she couldn't stretch for more, who catches everything that comes her way and believes, as I do, that there'll be a woman playing second or short in The Show before you know it. Twenty years, max. We're hoping it's a girl.

Ellie and I wonder if this winter's storms will finally break up the freighter. The bodies haven't been found yet—Masskey and Bobby Cage. I try not to talk about it, now that Ellie is pregnant.

But sometimes I wake up at night, sweating and dizzy to the

point of nausea. Ellie wants me to go to the doctor, but there's nothing a doctor could do.

I wake up at night realizing the man I talked to in the cabin was Russel Strickland. The Pied Piper. He'll never be my father. Charles Sinclair will always be my father.

But Strickland will always be the man who, by chance, saw Sam Jameson's name in a Spokane paper, killed him, and took not only Sam's place but also the obsession Sam detailed so thoroughly in his journals.

What Strickland read, he owned.

He knew someone *out there* had killed Sara, maybe even assumed his mantle, someone from the past. Sam thought it was Strickland, but Strickland knew it was someone else. And when I called him, he knew where it would all end, and it ended with a bullet in Bobby Cage's chest.

He was one of the Piper's sons too, just like Steven and I, and yes, Peter Masskey. Bobby Cage. Can you feel a deep sadness for someone like him, for what Masskey did to him, and at the same time realize you would have killed him if he came after your family? That territory stretches far, but, yes, it's mine.

Maybe Strickland thought that territory was only his. So he killed one last time to protect his only surviving son?

I wake up, too, with that.

I thought, briefly, that maybe I was wrong, that Masskey was the one who robbed and murdered Sam in 1986.

He couldn't have. The one who killed Sam took his journals. I saw them in the cabin.

There was, after all, a picture of the Pied Piper. I saw that, too—in Masskey's shrine and Peter Masskey snapped the photo in 1988.

He never knew.

He thought it was Sam Jameson . . . *Your turn, after Paul and Ellie* . . . But Sam had been dead for two years.

They were on that boat together, Masskey and Strickland. Neither had seen the other for almost forty years. Face to face with the man who had branded him, mutilated his life, close enough to offer him matches for his pipe and Peter Masskey never knew the man was the Pied Piper. Nor did I. I no longer wonder how Strickland could have become Sam Jameson. Neither man had been in the Chelan area for a long time when Strickland arrived as Sam Jameson. He was a creature of the rural fringe and wilderness. He was a criminal who had survived for a long time by knowing how to get what he needed. In the end, the Pied Piper chose not to survive. Ellie thinks he was caught in that fire. I believe he chose that way to kill himself. *Where else am I going to go?* Either way he's gone.

Yet the questions, the wondering, will always be with Ellie and me, a shared secret that will, long after Ireland, long after our children grow up, break up only with our own deaths, just as that freighter cannot last forever.

Ellie's leaving now to go see how Michael's doing in the caboose.

After a while I hear them in there laughing over dorky class photos of Dad, or whatever. There are silences, too. The caboose is full of them also.

Keeping the caboose is as much for me as it is for Michael, as it will be for our daughter—or son-to-be. I may be in it someday, when Michael is away at college—whenever—just rummaging around, looking over the same things they are now, and I'll hear someone coming in.

And there he'll be.

My brother.

Steven.

I know that's as likely as a legendary white dragon rising from the depths of Lake Chelan. I know that Bobby Cage said Masskey killed him. But there's no proof of that, is there? The ones who discovered Sam Jameson's body at his home found no evidence of next of kin. Maybe you can go home again. Maybe my brother is alive, and not just in my heart.

And then . . . he'll come into the caboose, you see? And we'll talk and I hope he'll tell me, after I'm done, why he disappeared, and where he's been all these years, how far away—or how close he's been all along.

We'll be sittin' high again, Steven and I, old goats on the rock. Maybe we'll read the box of letters I've put in there, if he wants to read them, that is.

Before he leaves again, as I'm sure he will, I think we will also have talked about Sara Bowers and all those things we would rather forget but can't forget, and never will.

You can do that in the caboose. You can say things you might not otherwise say, imagine laughter you've never heard or don't ever want to forget because there was so much of it in so short a time. If there's a better reason for keeping the caboose, I don't know what it might be.

· A NOTE ON THE TYPE ·

The typeface used in this book is a version of Sabon, originally designed in the 1960s by Jan Tschichold (1902–1974) at the behest of a consortium of manufacturers of metal type. As one who began as an outspoken design revolutionary—calling for the elimination of serifs, scorning revivals of historic typefaces—Tschichold seemed an odd choice, but he met the challenge brilliantly: The typeface was to be based on the fonts of the sixteenth-century French typefounder Claude Garamond but five percent narrower; it had to be identical for three different processes, working around the quirks of each, such as linotype's inability to "kern" (allow one character into the space of another, the way the top of a lowercase f overhangs other letters). Aside from Sabon, named for a sixteenth-century French punchcutter to avoid problems of attribution to Garamond, Tschichold is best remembered as the designer of the Penguin paperbacks of the late 1940s.